LIBERATION

JESSICA LAUREN

ISBN 978-1-7770151-1-4

Editing by Christy Distler
Cover design by Cherie Chapman

To contact author, email authorjlauren@gmail.com

For more information about author and upcoming books visit: https://authorjlauren.com

For the One who knows my every flaw
and still calls me Daughter

Chapter 1

A jagged shard of wood punctures my palm. I wince, dropping the battered board to the hardwood floor. Its clatter echoes through the house's empty dining room.

After raising my hand to my mouth, I clench the shard's tip between my teeth and pull. The tang of metallic blood and old pine meld on my tongue.

It never gets easier. My tweezers rusted over last month, and I haven't been able to remove the slivers thoroughly since. Splinters are a common occurrence for me. Though I should be accustomed to their pain by now, I'm never prepared for their sudden sting—and with the larger ones such as this, the stubborn ache they leave behind.

Still, I suppose that's what I deserve for letting my mind wander off. Again.

I drop to my knees and rifle through my tool satchel for a cloth, then tear a strip of its tattered material and lay it over my palm. My brother, Renan, would nearly faint at the sight if he were here. Now eight years old, he's been begging me for weeks to bring him along on one of my installation jobs. He no longer tolerates my "No, it would bore you" answer the way he used to.

I'd like to say my refusal is for his protection. That is true, after all. But not entirely. Of course, I couldn't forgive myself if something were to happen to him. But my other reason is simple: on average days—unlike today—the hour I take for myself after school is the only time I get to be alone, to unwind and ignore my chronic worries. Does that make me selfish? Perhaps. But if I couldn't steal time to forget the risks my parents are taking every day, I wouldn't be able to bear the burden of my existence.

I tie the cloth at the back of my hand and pull the knot tight with my teeth.

The fear took root the day Mom married Dad. She was my promising rainbow after a lifelong storm, instilling peace amid my misery. But along with her comfort came a dangerous secret. One that, if discovered, would result in her being ripped from our family as seamlessly as she arrived. She would be locked away for years. In fact, we'd likely never see her again.

I suppress the all-too-familiar terror brought by that train of thought and fist my fingers to test the makeshift bandage's endurance. It'll have to do for now.

"What happened?" a queasy voice blurts from behind me.

Still on my knees, I swivel toward the doorway. "It's nothing."

Foster Peterson, a boy from my class and the son of Dad's ex-friend, grips the doorframe, staring at my wrapped wrist. His mouth lingers open, then relief floods his face when the front door sweeps open and gives him an excuse to look away.

"Foster?" The rich, rumbling tone stirs up unpleasant old memories. Squealing footsteps approach the dining hall. "Are you...?" Foster's father stops as he turns the corner.

My throat tightens and I lurch to my feet, the broken cupboard shelf in hand.

His dark-rimmed eyes sear into mine. "What is this?"

"She's here to fix our cabinet." Foster steps forward, creating a human barrier between Mr. Peterson and me. "You asked me to find someone to—"

"I told you to hire a qualified carpenter." Mr. Peterson paces around Foster toward me. "Not some teenaged lower-class lumberjack!"

I let my mind numb his words from upsetting me.

"She's not just some lumberjack." Foster plants himself in front of his father again. "Her work's better than any qualified carpenter I've seen. And besides, you know her father, Evan—"

"That arrogant snake," Mr. Peterson says through his teeth. His narrowed eyes send chills up my spine.

For once, I almost want to defend my father. Because as much as I loathe him, I hate this man more. If Mr. Peterson had ended his friendship with Dad merely because of the fistfight, I might even side with him. But I know the truth, the real reason he shut us out and relocated his family to the inner region. It was more than an argument. Mr. Peterson held affections for Mom even after she married Dad, and their vows did nothing to prevent him from acting on his desires.

"Do not bring up that man's name in my house again. Or his disgraceful mistress, for that matter."

Every part of me wants to shout back, "How dare you insult her?" but I can't risk enraging the reason for my prior fear, the trigger of my palm's injury. It was *him* racking my mind. Distant memories of him, at least. Because he *knows.* I'm sure he does. He was friends with my parents long enough to discover their secret.

So I ignore his remark and gather my tools. The giant

bronze wall clock above the dining table reads 4:42. My heart skips a beat as I recall what day it is. The fourth and last mandatory Gathering at the Phalanx Centre begins at five o'clock. From here, it'll take me at least ten minutes to walk, and we must assemble early for sign-in. I knew I should've refused Foster's insistence that I come by after school today.

"I've got to go," I say, brushing sawdust from my pants.

"I suppose that is to be expected from a commoner. Poor work ethic. Unable to finish what she begins." Mr. Peterson shakes his head as he probes the emptied cabinet's missing shelf. "A future freeloader. Like father like daughter, I suppose."

I have no desire or time to debate my worth with a man who detests my very existence. "I'll come back tomorrow to replace the shelf." While I can force a meek tone, my tools get shoved into their satchel with unnecessary strength.

"Don't bother. I'll find someone else to finish the job. This, of course, means I cannot pay you in full." His expression remains sombre, but his tone bounces in a way that hints at a hidden pleasure in saying this aloud. "Such a shame—your father's work dismissal. Leaving your step-wench he calls a wife sole provider for the family." He sneers. "That'll last long."

I grit my teeth. "Say whatever you want about my father or me. But leave my mom out of it." I collect my bags and vacate the dining hall.

"*Mom?*" He follows me to the front door. "So that's what it's come to? Not *Miriam* or *stepmom?* She's sure got you fooled, doesn't she?"

My cheeks heat. This is just another thing for him to use against me. I've become so accustomed to calling her *Mom* since she married Dad when I was seven. My birth mother left me to my father's poor care shortly after I was born and never returned. But it doesn't feel like Miriam's unrelated. To be honest, my stepmother is more of a real mother than my real *father* is a real father.

I tug my warped zipper until it jams midway up my coat, then squeeze my tool satchel inside my schoolbag and heave the strap over my shoulder. Before slugging out of the house, I give Mr. Peterson one last bitter glare.

"Gooday, Miss Rutherford." He slams and locks the door behind me.

Foster appears in the spotless front window of their two-tiered mansion, then scurries away.

I always wondered how Mr. Peterson could treat us that way. Like we're inferior to him. As if he's forgotten he once was one of us. But after exploring his hardwood-floored house and feeling the steady heat circulate through the vents like he's got money to burn…

Of course, he's come to take it for granted. If my family somehow moved up in the ranks, not a day would pass I wouldn't ponder how such fortune could find us, only hoping it wouldn't be snatched away.

"Rielle!" Foster bursts through the front door and down the porch steps.

I cross my arms and hasten down the boulevard.

"Wait up." He chases after me.

I stop and turn around. "I told you what a stupid idea it was."

"I'm sorry. I thought maybe it would clear things up…to show my dad you helped him. I was wrong." He huffs, muddling a hand inside his jeans pocket. "For your work." His stubby fingers unfold to reveal seven faded coins.

I stare in shock, then collect myself. "No need for that.

It's more than I get for a completed installation job, much less a repair job I'm fired from halfway through."

The coins clink in his hand. "It's to compensate for my father's behaviour."

"I don't need your pity money." Well, I do. But I don't want to take it.

"Then it's an early birthday gift."

"My sixteenth was two months ago—"

"A late gift." He exhales impatiently.

I falter as the dread inside me spirals. "This is about the Gathering…isn't it?"

If I'm right, the Gatherings would've been attended yesterday by the northern and eastern parts of Kinborough, both outer and inner regions. But since Foster's family lives in the southern inner region, he would've attended before lunchtime today.

"I've heard whispers that Ulric is back." Saying the king's name aloud feels strange. He hasn't hosted a Gathering or appeared at a public event since his wife, Queen Narah, died three years ago. After her passing, our regional leader, Head Damien, took over the speeches and has hosted ever since.

"You know we're not supposed to talk about them until they're all over," Foster says.

"Is it true? Is he back?" The king wouldn't decide to host unannounced for anything trivial. If he's back, it's got to mean something huge.

He avoids my gaze. "Just take the money, Rielle. You've earned it."

"Forget it." I walk away. "I don't have time for this."

"Sure. Better not be late." The thumping sound of coins makes me turn to see him dropping them all to the dirt. One brow raised, he glares at me and shrugs before plodding home.

I groan, then wait until he's back inside before crouching to collect all seven coins. The last thing I want is to accept Foster's money, giving his father additional motive to hate me. But seeing as the coins will likely become some stranger's wealth, I pocket them. Perhaps I'll slip them in his bag at school tomorrow when he's not looking.

A sullen old woman scowls down at me from her window as I trek down the shadowy avenue. I drop my gaze to the colour-drained clay, coddling my injured hand.

On second thought, I'm not sure I'd want to move here even if given the opportunity. Though our house is old, increasingly crammed, and consumes half our income to heat during winter, it is home. It's lively and comfortable, with tiny bouquets of Mom's favourite blue flowers on the windowsills and a permanent cinnamon scent from Renan's candle-making in the kitchen. It may not be structurally sound, I may have to repair the creaky floorboards frequently, and buckets may need to be arranged beneath holes in the roof to collect April's abundant rainwater, but I can't complain. That has been our way of life forever. It is a good home.

I grip my knitted hat as a cold gust nearly lifts it off my head. I can't afford to lose this hat, as it's the one item I have left from my birth mother. As I hold it in place until the wind dies down, the bandage on my hand snags in my mess of auburn curls. I swat them away.

During the early days of autumn, the air cools off gradually. But by mid-December, a flurry to the face will steal your breath and freeze the saliva on your tongue the instant you open your mouth. As November approaches, frost tramples the dusty roads and creeps up the towering manors by night, only to thaw the next day. Winter grime already accumulates on the undersides of idle vehicles that belong to the wealthier residents who can afford them.

Unlike them, my family, residing in the outer region of Kinborough, cannot. We travel everywhere on foot. It's not so bad though, since most anyplace we need to go is near enough to walk.

Luckily, my winter pants from last year still fit well enough to use against the cold another season. Everyone's got the same type—thin and flexible yet insulated with layers of fleece and finished with a tight, wind-breaking exterior. That is, if they can afford them.

We weren't always a poor nation. But the civil war left Ulcadia, formerly called Canada, in ruins. The rest of the world is apparently in just as bad or worse shape than us, but our region of Kinborough was established in the country's southeastern area, which was least damaged by the war. I suppose I should be grateful for the decision to rename and unite our country in the Final Election fifty-seven years ago. It resulted in the anointing of the late Asena, Ulcadia's first queen, along with heads to lead each of Ulcadia's fifteen divided regions. This act ceased the country's inner conflicts and destruction to fortify our future.

And I wouldn't mind any of it, if not for that one law.

I pace down winding back streets that I'd all too quickly become lost on if I gave my thoughts room to play, passing brick storefronts and dingy apartments. My stomach groans. All I want is to go home, eat dinner, and carve the concerns of this awful day away.

At least there are only two mandatory Gatherings per year. The head prepares months in advance, addressing the most important or controversial topics or law changes that need explaining.

I fidget with Foster's coins in my pocket.

Something's going to be different this time. I've sensed it all day. People have been oddly agitated. Maybe not everyone, but the ones I know—like Foster, who rarely pays me a scrap of attention even though he sits beside me in last-period History. Today he nagged me relentlessly to repair that cabinet shelf after school, convinced his dad would discipline him if he hadn't hired a carpenter by tonight. And his blatant disregard of my questions about the king's return tells me the rumour is likely true. He knows something.

I sprint the final stretch of street to arrive at the front lot of the Phalanx Centre. The knot of dread in my stomach thickens.

Almost everyone has filed inside the spherical sculpted-marble building. Mom's sandy-blonde hair catches my eye among the crowd. Looking relieved, she waves me over and roots her feet as the remaining citizens funnel around her.

I hurry to her and grasp her hand.

Her stillness radiates through me, relaxing my stomach's ache some, though nothing ever relieves it entirely. If she'd just disregard her beliefs, we'd have nothing to fear. However, that's a dead-end desire. For Mom, her faith exceeds all else.

Yet how can she remain so confident in a belief our nation forbids? That's the question I've struggled to solve since the day I learned of her secret.

Two guards clad in the standard black uniform hurry us through the building's entrance and latch the doors shut behind us. At a side counter, I hand over my citizen ID card to be scanned and returned. Another guard grips my shoulder and seizes my schoolbag. "No bags beyond this point."

Turning to a wall of lockers, he stuffs it into an empty cubby and hands me a metal chip with the locker number and combination for retrieval later.

Though dome-shaped from the outside, the Phalanx Centre's ceiling is flat across within, because King Ulric's office and living quarters are on the level above us. Five massive crystal chandeliers hang from the ceiling, and the inside crème-and-grey marble walls match the outside pattern. No structure in all of Ulcadia compares to the Phalanx Centre. Kinborough, being the largest and most prosperous region of Ulcadia, is King Ulric's permanent home.

Mom leads me to where Dad and Renan wait near the back of the crowd. Side by side, Renan looks like a much shorter, slimmer version of Dad, though I imagine the muscle he's bound to put on when he's grown will make them virtually identical. Ren hurries over and wraps his small arms around my waist. I hold him close and pat his dark, dishevelled hair, inhaling the cinnamon waft that clings to him wherever he goes.

"What happened to your hand?" His jade eyes gleam in the chandelier light. He traces my knotted bandage with nimble fingers. "Is it bad?"

I shake my head. "It's just a scratch."

Dad's jaw clenches in that disapproving look reserved especially for me. His thick brows sink, webbed with years of worry lines. I've never seen my biological mother, but I know I must look like her because all I inherited from Dad are his bland eyes that match our neighbourhood's dusty trails.

"Where were you?" he asks in a low growl. "What were you doing?"

I give him a daring glance as if to say, "You know what I

was doing."

I don't hate my father. At least I think I don't. He stopped abusing me years ago, around the time he met Mom. She introduced him to her secret faith in a forbidden God, and he took to it. He's since changed into a decent, possibly pleasant man. However, just because he's changed doesn't mean he's ever apologized. He doesn't talk about or even seem to acknowledge the past. Perhaps he was too drunk to remember it. If that were the case, I might even pardon his years of unrepentant ignorance. But he always seems to carry an air of guilt around me, and usually over-looks my presence entirely unless he is displeased with me. I know he remembers.

I glance around, jumbling the coins in my pocket.

He sighs. "We talked about house jobs, Rielle. They can't interfere with…"

I gather the coins and pour them in his hand.

He glares at them suspiciously. "Whose house was it? No one around our neighbourhood can afford half this much." Though he waits for an answer, I say nothing. "Just tell me." His tone is now impatient.

I lower my gaze. "Foster's house."

"Who is Foster?" He frowns, hesitating. "You mean—"

"Mr. Peterson's son." There's no point in lying now. Though I wish I could, I can't change the past. And as much as he'd argue the fact, neither can Dad.

"You worked for Connell Peterson? You took his mon-ey?" He grimaces as our regional leader, Head Damien, ambles out from the left back-stage curtain and the crowd applauds. Dad grabs my hand and dumps the coins back into it. "We'll talk about this at home."

I flinch as he thrusts my arm away.

With over three thousand citizens—a quarter of our region's population—crammed into one room with no seating, naturally people are ill-mannered and irritable. For those of us too short to see over the crowd, Head Damien appears on two television screens mounted to either stage side wall. Clutching a crème folder to his chest, he approaches the charcoal podium at the front of the dark, polished stage. The camera pans in on his face to show sweat seeping above his clean-shaven lip and his forehead glinting against the spotlight.

He dabs his brow with a handkerchief and sets his folder on the podium. Licking a finger, he fumbles through the folder's sheets. His eyes dart around, as dark as the thinning hair on his head. A golden tie gleams beneath his stark black suit, disguising the sagging skin of his neck.

He scans the audience, pursing his lips. Everyone hushes. He clears his throat and leans into the microphone. "Greetings, citizens of western Kinborough. And welcome to our final Phalanx Gathering of the year." He actually stutters to get the words out. "I want to thank you all for assembling here today…" He swallows hard, flipping a page.

He's already spoken once today and twice yesterday. Why is he so unrehearsed and nervous?

"Now, without further delay…I'd like to introduce His Majesty, Rule—Ruler of the nation…King Ulric." He motions to the curtain, then withdraws as if allergic to the spotlight.

So it is true. He's back.

Clad in a navy-blue suit pleated with golden crests, King Ulric strides to centre stage. An embellished crown moulds into his lush hair. He humbly assumes the stage and elevates the microphone to his stubbly jaw. "Thank you, Damien, for that delightful introduction." His crisp voice resounds like a dagger plunging into crusty earth. Other than the fact that his hair has turned greyer, he seems to have only grown stronger and more striking over the past three years.

Head Damien bows courteously, then shrinks backward.

The crowd applauds, but I stand motionless. Though Ulric has been our beloved king for more than a decade longer than I've been alive, I've never been able to trust him fully. Perhaps it's due to his rigidly perfect posture—too perfect— as if overcompensating for years spent hunched behind closed doors. Or because he left his people in the dark about the details of his wife's death. Or that if he *were* trustworthy, he'd have changed that disturbing law by now.

Ulric gives a charming smile. "Now, before we reach the main matter of today's Gathering, I would like to discuss some historical facts, prior to the rise of Ulcadia and even our former nation of Canada. Yes, we will examine a summary of the past several thousand years of global civilization."

So Ulric deserts his people for three years, and when he returns, he doesn't so much as give an explanation or an apology before diving right into his proposition? And we're expected to pardon him and go along with it, despite knowing nothing of his three-year absence?

Timeline images replace his face on the screens. I don't bother deciphering them.

"From the start of civilization, there have been confusions, conflicts, and wars. Peoples and nations that thrived, sometimes for thousands of years, were either ravaged by other countries or destroyed due to rivalries among their own people. Civil war nearly abolished our country over half a century ago. However, what shrivelled many others to desolate dust, we endured and conquered."

He continues about ancient civilizations, some of the strongest being ancient Egypt and Mesopotamia, and how, after such cultures withstood thousands of years longer than our own, they all ended up collapsing. "Of course, many of these civilizations were struck by others and forced to surrender. But their declines were already underway before any external attacks. They virtually always started within and of themselves. And our research determines that the leading contributor to the instigation of civil war, even in our own nation's standpoint, is opposing beliefs."

He studies the audience, sighing. "I assure you, I have postponed this for as long as possible. But the effects are inevitably too real to ignore. And I cannot stand by while this nation dwindles due to exactly what impaired it before. It is my obligation as your king to do right on behalf of my people. And the facts disguised in countless societal plummets in history, including Canada's, declare that Christianity is the leading religious belief to cause such downfalls."

I stiffen as the crowd rumbles in confusion.

Dad clasps Mom's hand.

"Christianity is a cruel, hateful cult whose followers violate regulations, force their fear-based beliefs onto the innocent minds of their children, and will stop at nothing to eliminate those who oppose or fall short of their strict standards. We mustn't let them get away with these horrid crimes." He puffs air through his cheeks and clears his throat. "The civil war cleansed the land of most, but their numbers are once again on the rise. Christians were the masterminds behind the collapse of Canada. I will not permit them to do the same to Ulcadia. They have taken enough from us."

He can't be serious.

"Starting tomorrow, there will be searches and rewards for those who remain loyal to their country in disclosing their knowledge of likely believers. Since the founding of Ulcadia, the law was introduced that Christians, upon discovery, would serve jail time. However, to ensure the safety of our nation's future, I have no choice but to alter this law…" He looks down. "Whoever will not submit to our way of life and adapt to our Christian-free society will surely be arrested and tried. If deemed guilty, they will receive the chance to renounce their faith. And if they refuse to renounce, we will then carry out the proper protocol for…lawful execution."

Chapter 2

Execution?

My pulse throbs in my ears as they tune in and out, unable to distinguish the audience's murmurs and applause from the jumbled voices in my head.

I clutch Renan's hand through the conclusion of Ulric's speech, tight enough that he should complain. But he doesn't. He lets me cling to him in my meagre attempt to find some sense of stability. Or perhaps he's simply as numb as I am and therefore can't feel my grip.

Minutes blur by. Eventually, Mom rubs my shoulder and forces a half smile to disguise the twitch of her lip. Then she plods toward the back doors that drain the crowd into the streets.

The Gathering is over. The crowd shuffles out. A plump woman steps on my foot, then grumbles at *me* for the interference. I retrieve my bag from the locker on our way out. It's all a haze. My legs slog along without my urging them to do so. I rejoin my family outside in the biting air and grasp Renan's hand again. Only when we arrive home do I loosen my grip.

Stale air greets us as we step inside our front hall.

Dad reaches around the corner and twists the thermostat's valve above the kitchen counter. The heater rattles on, diffusing warm air that stinks of melting plastic. "Rielle,"—he snags my attention—"please take Renan to your room." After kicking off his boots, he steps into our sitting room on the right.

"Get something to eat first," Mom adds as she trails Dad into the snug room.

RENAN SLUMPS ON the edge of his bed, glaring down at his feet. He doesn't seem confused. Just sad and tired, suppressing the fear—a skill we've all mastered over the years. Then curling up on his side facing away from me, he crunches into his apple. He doesn't bother removing his coat.

After the last bite of my own apple, I toss the core into the trash tin by the door. "Hey, Ren, want to come watch me carve?" The words scrape my throat.

He doesn't move, so I drag myself over and sit on the edge of his mattress.

Gripping the wooden dove I carved for him when he was four, he mumbles, "You don't have to do that."

"Do what?"

"Pretend everything's fine. You know I heard what the king said."

I swallow. "I'm not pretending anything. I heard it too…and all it means is we'll have to be extra careful." My voice wobbles on the last two words.

He rotates the dove between his fingers. It's his only possession he won't take with him anywhere for fear of losing it. Whenever he leaves, he tucks it beneath his pillow for protection.

The grimy lightbulb in the corner flickers out as the power shuts off, just as it does each evening throughout the outer region. This daily event terrified Renan for years, especially in the winter months when the sun set earlier and the house turned pitch black when it shut off.

Even now, his breath snags.

I rummage through my dresser drawer for a lighter and illuminate the room with Ren's homemade candles. The melting wax emits a faint cinnamon scent that eases my nerves.

The flickering glow draws him. He shuffles over to face me. The candlelight casts shadows through his wavy hair and over his cheekbones in a way that makes him keenly mirror Dad. His glossy eyes gaze through me, unfocused.

I long to comfort him by assuring everything will be all right, but how can I promise that? I can't guarantee anything at this point.

So I tousle his hair and muster enough strength to stand. Then I rummage through my tool satchel, eager to uncover my chisel. Its smooth wooden grip eases the spasm in my fingers. I crawl across my lumpy mattress to where its far side supports my work desk. Wedged between the bed and the wall, the desk's position effectively saves space, considering there are two single beds in a room designed for one. My mattress doubling as a bench, I dangle my legs beneath the desk and get to work.

The four-inch-tall carving I've whittled whenever possible over the past few weeks sits on my desktop. It depicts a woman from the neck up, a hand covering her mouth and her eyes ridden with despair. Using my mallet, I tap the chisel into the crevices between the hand's fingers. Then my sander grates down the sharp edges of the face's cheekbones and jawline until they are soft and elegant yet reveal a fierce quality. I focus on every minuscule detail, ignoring the fact that after it's finished I'll move on to the next carving for relief this one no longer offers me, and the distraught, silenced girl will just be another for the bin collecting dust on my closet's top shelf.

Or will it even come to that? Will they catch us before I get a chance to begin a new piece?

I thump the carving to my desk.

The house has warmed, so I remove my coat and toss it to the foot of my bed. Foster's coins rattle within the pocket, and my stomach flutters. He *knew*. That's why he was acting strange all day, why he gave me the money. He knows our secret and he pities us. Why didn't he just tell me then? Or at least give me a heads up?

I rise from my bed, the flame of rage growing.

Renan breathes rhythmically on his mattress, eyes closed.

I drape his cotton blanket over him and blow out all but one candle on his nightstand. In hopes he will remain resting, I sneak out the door and close it behind me. As I creep toward the sitting room, each tender step rouses groans within the floorboards that I'd intended to fix tonight.

Flickering candles and the hanging gas-lit lantern glow through the doorway of our silent sitting room. I peer around the corner just as Dad speaks.

"We knew it was getting bad again." He paces the room, rubbing the back of his neck. "But I didn't expect such drastic measures to be decided so quickly."

Mom hunches on the battered sofa, eyes damp. She weaves blonde locks through her fingers and stares at the burning candles on the coffee table. "We've been threatened and silenced for decades. Still, it's not enough for him."

"How can he manipulate them so easily?" Dad's voice raises.

Mom's gaze simmers in the candlelight. "Evan, we have neighbours," she whispers, eyeing the wall behind her. Then her stern expression wilts. "We'll hide as long as possible. But if it comes to lying about it all, I don't know if…" She trails off as she spots me.

Dad eyes me, then returns his focus to Mom. "If it comes to lying,"—he sits down beside her—"we will do what's necessary to keep our family safe." He rests a hand on hers.

Mom swallows and resumes watching the candles.

Their conversation withers to unbearable silence.

I lean against the doorframe. "Ulric said something about searches starting tomorrow. What if they…find it? Nothing else'll matter then. We have to get rid of it."

"No." Mom rises. "I won't throw it away."

So she would discard this family instead? That *book* means more to her than our safety?

Her faith was always a concern for me, but it was never life-threatening before. I hoped if the time came, she'd surrender her beliefs. But even now she'd risk us all for her God?

"We will not throw it away." Dad secures her hand in his, and she leans into him. "It may come to that eventually…but we will do our best to hide it now."

Unbelievable. But seeing that they're serious, I'll take what I can get. Quietly I return to my bedroom and grab my tool satchel, then join Mom and Dad in their bedroom.

Mom closes the curtains, and Dad shifts their dresser out from the wall, revealing a secret shelf built into the back. She sets a candle tray on the dresser as he extracts the book. His hand strokes the dull leather cover with the faded gold words *Holy Bible* inscribed on front and across the spine.

How could it be worth risking our family for what's within that book's ragged pages? Mom occasionally read its stories to me when I was curious as a kid, but I could never pinpoint their value.

Dad starts to drag the dresser back.

"I'll pull the boards up beneath it," I say.

He passes the Bible to Mom, who eagerly flips through its gold-edged sheets.

On hands and knees, I rap my knuckles against the floorboards until a hollow sound resonates. Then I pry the nails out with my hammer and detach the board. An empty cavity nestles between two horizontal shafts below the floor.

Mom shuts the frail book, hesitates, and hands it to me.

I slide it between the two beams, then hammer the board back over it.

Dad drives the dresser back to the wall, and the tension in the room diminishes. Mom folds an arm around me and pulls me close.

I inhale the lavender-scented perfume I bought her last summer. She's worn it most days since, as it subdues the stench of metal and processed meat from the factory she works at—the same factory Dad was fired from recently. But this is the first embrace from her I long to escape. Because as much as I love her, I can't condone the risks she's taking. I never imagined there'd come a day when she'd disregard our family for her faith.

I withdraw from her.

"Goodnight," she sighs.

The door creaks as I enter my room.

Renan jolts awake, forcing himself up on his elbows. One hand grips his dove in the candlelight. Spotting me, he settles.

I scowl at the door. "Sorry. Didn't mean to wake you. Go

back to sleep." My tone lulls him. After his eyes again close, I smother the candle on his nightstand.

Curled up in my bed, I'm comforted knowing the one item that could expose us is safely hidden. But our situation has become grave. It gambles much more than jail time. Now both my parents will die if that book is discovered.

I pull my blanket up, forcing my eyes shut to avoid observing the night's shadows through the window's thin drape.

My mind contorts today's experiences. Mr. Peterson's condescending criticisms loop continually, only making me furious I couldn't retaliate. Well, not that I couldn't… I was lying to myself, thinking I endured his comments solely to protect my family. The real reason was that I knew he would ultimately win the battle. I can't fight his criticisms when, deep down, I know every insult is accurate. Painful to hear, yes, but valid nonetheless. I *am* everything Mr. Peterson said.

Dreams come and go. One lingers in memory—that of a masked soldier shoving my parents into a truck, hands tied behind their backs. The scene shifts to Renan lying in his bed. He startles awake and glances around. Where our house once crouched, only his bed remains. Frightened, he searches the barren land, calling for Mom and Dad. He cries my name, then returns to his bed and upheaves his pillow and blankets. As he struggles to haul his mattress off its frame, I realize what it is he's hunting for. His dove. A masked soldier then emerges from the charred dirt, clutching the dove in hand. Renan lunges for it, but the soldier throws it to the dirt and it engulfs in flames. He covers Renan's head in a mesh bag and slogs him down the street, crunching the scorched dove underfoot.

I gasp awake. My fists seize lumps of the bedsheet.

Across the room, Renan sleeps on his stomach, one arm slung over the side of his mattress. He is safe.

Regaining a grasp of reality, I detect the outline of a folded paper at the foot of my bed. I retrieve it and smooth out its centre crease. My name is at the top, scrolled in Mom's handwriting that resembles her countless other letters to me over the years. Since before I ever spoke a word to her, we conversed through writing.

My fingers still, and a faint smile tugs at my lips. I strike a match and light a candle on my desk. Dangling my bare feet over the bedside, I study the page's crisp words.

Rielle,

I know this is frightening for you, as it is for us all. I brought my faith into this family, and I am sorry for how hard it has been on you. But I want you to know that this isn't some choice I am making. I am not choosing my faith over this family, though it may seem so. My faith saved my life. It is the truth that gives me peace in knowing this world is not our real home. I know if it weren't for my faith in God, I would not have found my family in you. He has blessed me beyond measure.

I love you more than you'll ever know. Though we are not related by blood, and I will never replace your birth mother, I hope I am filling the role you need me to fill as best I can. I am sorry, and honestly, terrified for how things are happening beyond my control. It is taking a toll on all of us. Just rest assured that I will do whatever I can to protect you. To protect us all.

Also, know that I don't expect you to believe what I believe. It is natural to be wary and unable to understand why I choose to keep my faith though the law forbids it. I thought the same of my father when I was young. I used to ask him how he could risk so much, just as I am sure you must be wondering now about me. So I will end with precisely what he used to tell me: You will understand someday; you just have to seek.

Miriam

I close my eyes, pondering her words that bring comfort but also further my confusion. What she seemed to think would clarify questions in her last remarks only generate new ones. But at least now I know she won't abandon our family when trials arise, as my birth mother did.

She is afraid. She understands our future is beyond her control, but she will not submit to the fear. She will do what is required to protect us, without betraying her beliefs. This is the confidence she has always breathed. Even now, staring death in the face, she will not surrender.

The carving on my desk assumes a whole new persona. The eyes slant in the same manner as Mom's did tonight. Weary and fearful, as if striving to communicate through expression alone. Like she must connect without words as the hand of Ulric prevents her from speaking or defending herself. Even this letter, I assume, Mom will have me hand over to burn at breakfast.

I blow out my candle. The murky moonlight prowls through the window. Though my desk clock reads four a.m., there's no chance I'll reclaim sleep now.

I shawl my blanket around my shoulders and slide my feet into the worn slippers by my bedside. Mom's letter in hand, I sneak out the door and blindly find my way to the sitting room. The floorboards creak under my feet as I undrape the small front window to observe our still street. On the windowsill sits a vase of blue flowers, their petals sealed shut as if cocooned for warmth.

Moonlight spreads through the room, and I spot Mom sprawled on the couch behind me. She couldn't sleep either,

I suppose.

She stretches, sits up, and scoots over, patting the cushion beside her. She notices her letter in my hand but doesn't ask for it back. She lets me keep it. For now, at least.

I curl up beside her, lay my head against her shoulder and spread my blanket over us. Her quiet presence calms me.

As I clutch her letter, we doze until dawn's creamy blush expels the darkness.

I JAR AWAKE at the sudden strikes that resound through the front hallway.

Mom tenses beside me. She waits motionless as if needing proof the knock wasn't her imagination.

But the fist pounds again.

She unwraps the blanket from her legs and gets up, then peers out the side window and hurries to the front door.

I wrap my blanket around my shoulders and follow her.

As she cracks the door open, a booming voice sends her stepping backward.

"My apologies for the disruption of your morning, ma'am." A broad-shouldered soldier enters, towering over her. "But I've received orders from Head Damien, on behalf of King Ulric, to inspect the premises of your house for reasons specified at last night's Gathering." He lifts a sheet of paper to her face—a warrant.

Beneath my blanket, I burrow Mom's letter in the pocket of my pants.

Chapter 3

Dad staggers from his bedroom down the hall, fastening the belt of his housecoat around his waist. He scowls at the commotion but straightens when he spots the soldier looming in our doorway.

Mom smooths the wrinkles in her blouse. "Are you here just for our house? Or is this a neighbourhood search?"

Dad rushes to her side.

"Region-wide precaution sweep. Starting with the outer-west and working our way eastward." The soldier steps inside. "It'll only take a few minutes." He glares at me, then moves his attention to Dad. "But I must ask that all members of the household evacuate the premises for the duration of the search."

I hug my blanket around me and hurry down the hall to my bedroom. "Ren, wake up." I lift his limp arm and let it drop back on the mattress.

Eyes shut, he rolls over. "What time is it?" Red sleep lines from his pillow mark his cheek.

I glance at my desk clock. "Six thirty."

He squishes his face back into his pillow.

I yank the blanket off his body, and he moans. "Come on, Ren. We have to go outside for a few minutes." I set his boots by the bedside.

He stiffens and sits up. "What's happening?"

"Someone just has to check our house." I force a casual tone.

His eyes widen, and he shoves his dove inside his pillowcase, then slinks his bare feet into his boots and throws a sweater on over his pyjamas.

I wrap my housecoat around me and step into my untied boots.

In the front hall, the soldier ushers us to the door.

I avoid eye contact while fitting my knitted hat to my head. But isn't that something a guilty person would do? I panic and decide to hold his stare for several seconds.

His brows furrow. He hesitates, then thumps the door closed between us.

My face flushes. I feel violated. As if by holding his stare I let him read my thoughts. Infiltrate my soul. Extract my secret. My parents say I'm a terrible liar—that my eyes betray me. Could he have sensed the guilt in my gaze?

I shake the question from mind, knowing from practice that I'll pointlessly dissect my every action if I submit to the fear. The Bible is hidden. He won't find it.

Mom and Dad idle in the front yard, and Renan stands alongside me at the road's edge. Sharp stones nearly push through the thinning soles of my boots.

From our hillside neighbourhood in the outer region, a peaceful view of sun-kissed clouds drifting over the inner region's valley contradicts our current circumstance.

Several other families along our street slouch on their porch steps while soldiers raid their houses. A few doors down, two grubby-faced toddlers sit side by side on the road, tracing twigs in the dirt.

To be a child again, if only for a day... No fear. No sorrow. No responsibility.

I draw Renan into me as he watches the children play.

He seems puzzled by their oblivious nature, as if he's forgotten he once thrived with a similar carefree state of mind. Though still young, he's been robbed of his childhood much too soon. Toppled by the burden of fear never meant for his shoulders to carry. For years I struggled to guard him from the very thing that stole my childhood. But relying on my own anxiety to extinguish the fear rooting in Renan seems to be precisely what made it flourish.

I suppose Mom's right in one of her common sayings—fear cannot cast out fear.

More soldiers approach houses farther up the street, some with harnessed dogs by their sides. At least our soldier didn't bring a search dog to sniff out our Bible.

The crisp wind makes my eyes water. I tighten my housecoat around me, eyeing our front door. The only differences between our home and every other rundown house in the neighbourhood are the new porch railings I installed last summer and the number 4 nailed above our mailbox.

Clanking and crashing sounds drift in the wind. The soldier must be searching our kitchen now.

I clutch Mom's letter in my pocket. If he pats us down, we're goners.

Why didn't she burn the letter?

I fidget with the strip of fabric wrapped around my hand as the soldier charges from our house. My hand jolts, tearing the bandage, and it unravels in the breeze.

He's found it.

The soldier rushes past us, then halts as if just now reminded of our existence. "Urgent commands from the headsman." He taps a metal band on his wrist—a communicator. "I got through most of the house. I'll have to return later this evening to finish. But so far, you're clear." He gives a reassuring nod before sprinting down the street.

My shoulders loosen, and I drag in my first full breath since he arrived.

MY FINGERS START to thaw once we're inside. Though I'm grateful the soldier left early, my stomach grows queasy, dreading his return this evening.

Mom slumps into the nearest chair at the kitchen table and presses her face into her palms. "Thank you," she murmurs. "Please save us tonight too."

I adapted to the one-way conversations she calls *prayer* years ago. But for now, I give her space.

In the bathroom, I stoop over the sink. The questions resurface like they often do. Is Mom right about her beliefs? Might there really be some unseen God who creates life from nothing and hears her every prayer? I unravel the last of the fabric around my palm and wince as I pluck stubborn fragments of wood from the cut.

I can't say I've ever felt God or heard him speak to me, but on days like this, I can't help wondering if she's right about his existence. Because that soldier could've brought a search dog, could've discovered the book. But he didn't.

The wound seems to be healing nicely. To be safe, however, I invade the medical cabinet above the toilet and locate a packaged square of transparent tape.

Foreboding thoughts counteract the previous hopeful ones. Since the soldier will only be returning to check *our* house tonight, he'll probably take his time, probing every inch of the bedrooms. What if he brings a search dog this time? What if he recalls my guilty glare and questions us further? Mom didn't exactly agree with Dad's verdict last night of lying to protect us.

I force the thoughts aside and rinse my hand under icy water. Then I snip a patch of gauze, squeeze a glob of healing ointment on it, and mask it to my hand with the tape.

In an effort to settle my stomach, I slow my breathing. The last thing I want to do is eat, but all I had for dinner last night was an apple. So I go into the kitchen, fire up the old stovetop, and crack our last two eggs in a pan. Only four potatoes, three apples, and a lettuce head remain in the fridge now.

As Mom acquires discounts at the factory, we stock up on bread and soup, sometimes meat, for winter. Fruits and vegetables are harder to come by in the colder months. Fortunately, Dad's old friend Spencer Elscott is a farmer who tends a greenhouse. We buy from him exclusively through the winter.

When the eggs are scrambled, I plop them onto a plate and share half with Renan. I offer Mom a bite of mine, which she politely declines. Renan pokes at his eggs in silence.

These are the moments I long to be on my ledge, up in the hillside by the lumber yard. I stumbled upon the abandoned foresting site years ago, and it quickly became my secret place for chopping, preparing, and stocking provisions. Dangling my legs over the rocky lookout and gazing across the region, I wouldn't be able to feel the chaos drowning Mom and Renan inside.

If only I could risk hiking up there once more.

The first time the lumber yard was scorched down, along with my stockpile of wood and carvings, I mistook it for a coincidence—perhaps lightning struck it or one of the war's undetonated bombs went off—but now that it's occurred twice, I can't risk the charges for trespassing and exposing my family. Thankfully, before the last fire I stashed enough wood here to continue my work a while longer from home, because I must help support my family until Dad finds a job.

As much as it pains me, I can't go up there again.

But I do need to go *somewhere*. Away from Mom and Renan. I love them, but their thoughts are deafening at the moment. As if my own aren't loud enough. Since my ledge is out of the question, I'll visit Mr. Elscott and restock our food supply. Plus, he's not bad company at times like these, when it feels like the world's ending and all—which is annoyingly more often than not. The farm is just a ten-minute trek from here, and school won't start for over an hour.

That is, if I even attend school today.

Somehow, I persuade Dad to fill my role of walking Renan to school. Whether he was fully paying attention, I doubt, but he *did* agree to it.

I tie my laces and zip Mom's letter inside my tool satchel's secret compartment—safer than my jacket pocket. On the off chance Mr. Elscott will accept my help around his barn, my tool satchel is also shoved into my schoolbag. I wriggle my hands into the fingerless gloves that match the pale pink of my hat, then sneak a glance at the nearly finished carving on my desk and head out.

Mr. Elscott's farm lies on the northern border of Kinborough, housing a giant greenhouse year round, and wheat or corn fields through the summer and fall. He also manages the chicken coop where we get our eggs, and stables where he breeds and trains horses for the king's soldiers.

Outside our neighbourhood, the sparse forests begin. The

rising sun casts shadows of bare branches to the leafy floor, and winter birds huddle in their nests to ward off the cold. Last week my trek to the farm was peaceful. Today I contemplate the odds of this trip ever occurring again.

As I trudge up the farm's gravel pathway, the stones wage war on my heels as the worn soles of my boots barely separate my feet from the ground. I worked for Mr. Elscott around the farm a couple summers ago and bought these boots with my earnings. I just can't bring myself to buy a new pair. As strange as it sounds, I need something in life to remain constant. Familiar. Even if that something happens to be a miserable pair of boots.

Headed toward the coop, Mr. Elscott carries two metal buckets of seed.

"Well, look who's finally off to feed those poor chickens." I feign a disappointed tone. "Late another morning."

He sets the buckets to the dirt. "Yes, shame on me." His weathered face crinkles as he smirks. "How 'bout *you* try getting out here in the cold at the crack of dawn to tend the farm. Haven't seen you here this early in years."

"I've been up for a while. Thought I'd see if I could buy our food a bit early this week."

He squints at me in that mind-reading way I've learned to endure, and his expression softens. "They checked your house."

I kick at the gravel and nod. Mr. Elscott's known and kept our secret for years, but it's still a tough subject. For me, anyway.

"Man, they're early risers." His eyes search mine. "How you holding up?"

"Fine, for now. The soldier got called away before finishing the search. Said he'd be back tonight." I bite my cheek, mustering the nerve to ask him what I've wanted to know for years. "Mr. Elscott—"

Two of his employees pass us on their way to the greenhouse.

He eyes them and lifts the buckets. "Come with me." He plods to the coop.

Smart. With the sound of chicken chatter, no one will overhear us.

I help him scatter seed on the ground, my stomach roiling. "Do you…think it's worth it? What my parents are risking?"

His hand goes limp, and the seed within falls to the ground. He puffs air through his cheeks and pauses a while. "I've known your father for some time, and he's a smart man. He's changed greatly since he met Miriam, and he's stubborn—I'm sure it took a lot to convince him of her beliefs." He ruffles a calloused hand through his hair. "Truthfully…I can't say if they're right about their beliefs, or if it's worth risking your family. But I do know that what Ulric's doing…" His mouth pinches. "He shouldn't have the power to do anything of the sort. He tries to justify it, but can't." With a slow shake of his head, he locks my gaze. "I might not believe what your family believes, but I want you to know…if I had to pick sides, I'm on yours. And I'll support your family in any way I can."

The tension in my body melts. "Thank you." My voice barely lifts above a whisper.

"Now, how about you swing by after school and I'll have a basket arranged for you."

"About that…" I clear my throat. "Do you need anything fixed around the farm?"

He arches a brow. "Skipping today is not the smartest

move on your part. They monitor that kind of thing after the Gatherings. It'll only rouse suspicions."

"Right." I knew convincing him to let me stay was a long-shot. "I'll stop by after school." I pull out all seven of Foster's coins. "Throw in however much food this will cover."

He doesn't even glance at them. "My promise to support your family means I will no longer take your money." He scatters the last of the chicken seed. "The food's yours."

"That's thoughtful but unnecessary." I know he's been struggling with money. His wife, Ginny, who used to tend the farm with him, passed away last year, and hiring extra help has stretched him thin. "Please take it." I extend my arm.

He collects the empty buckets and heads off toward the stables.

I follow him. "Really, I don't mind paying." I think of dropping the coins to the ground as Foster did with me, but then recall Mr. Elscott's had recent back problems and scrap the idea.

He chuckles to himself. "Stubborn like your father."

Warmth floods my face. I sigh, pocketing the coins. Then I remove my tool satchel from my schoolbag and slide it onto a high shelf in the wall. He gives me a curious look, and I say, "No tools—or as they call them, *weapons*—at school. I'll pick it up after."

On my way out, I stroke Sinta, the horse Mr. Elscott used to teach me to ride. "Maybe I'll take you out for a ride too." I rub behind her ear where she likes it and plant a kiss on her muzzle.

"Good idea. She needs the exercise." He waves and proceeds to unload bales of hay into the horses' troughs. "See you soon, dear."

I leave and pass two soldiers on the path heading up to the farm. Thankfully, they ignore me.

MRS. JENNINGS DRONES on in last-period History, answering endless questions about King Ulric's speech at the Gathering.

I shrivel in my seat, longing to disappear. To avoid imagining the soldier's return tonight, I spend my time wondering why Foster selected the seat in front of me even though the chair beside me was free. Is he mad at me for rejecting his money? Does he feel guilty for neglecting to warn me about the speech?

Well, he *should* feel guilty. And if anything, *I* should be mad at *him*.

Mrs. Jennings scribbles on the front board, taking another question.

I should've skipped. I could've been riding Sinta through the fields right now.

Suddenly I realize something I should have hours ago. *Stupid, stupid, stupid!* I left my satchel in the barn. Mom's letter is inside the secret pocket. If the soldiers found it during the search, they'd arrest Mr. Elscott.

If something happens to him because of me—

Foster scrapes his chair on the tiled floor, jolting me back to class. He peers over his shoulder, eyes baggy, face drained of colour. He mustn't have slept at all last night. When our eyes meet, his gaze jerks back to the chalkboard.

The second time he glances back at me, I lock my eyes on his and mouth, "What?"

He shifts to look out the window, rapping his pencil on

his binder.

Mrs. Jennings halts mid-sentence, eyeing the door at the back of the room. "Can I help you?"

Every student follows her stare. Except for Foster. He just freezes, posture stiff.

My pulse thumps in my ears as I turn in my chair.

A soldier stands in the doorway. "My apologies for the intrusion." His rich voice resonates through the room. "I am Headsman Malachi, sent with orders from King Ulric to... *escort* Miss Rielle Rutherford."

Chapter 4

Twenty-five pairs of eyes scrutinize me.

I focus on the floor, feet numb as I force myself to stand. Why is he here? Unless the soldier actually did find the book this morning or they broke into our home while we weren't there, they don't know about the Bible.

I lift my schoolbag and inch toward the headsman.

Maybe it's for my years of trespassing in the lumber yard. Yes. Please let this be for trespassing. I'll gladly pay that penalty if it means keeping my family alive.

The headsman ushers me out, and whispers among my classmates follow me into the hallway.

Another soldier waits there. Black hair frames her ashen face, and her ice-blue eyes assault me—the heavy eyeliner only emphasizing their menacing edge. "Drop the bag and face the wall, hands on your head."

The rasp in her voice makes my skin crawl. I do as she says.

My backpack sags to the ground, and the headsman lifts it as delicately as one would handle a stick of dynamite.

Arms raised, fingers linked behind my head, I turn slowly toward the wall of metal lockers.

She pats me down, collects all the coins from my pocket, then forces me against a locker. After joining my wrists behind my back, she cuffs them. "All right, let's go."

I root my feet as she pulls me away from the wall. "Not until you tell me what this is about."

She grips my upper arm, each finger inducing bone-bruising pain. "Don't play dumb with us, girl." She shunts me down the hall.

Headsman Malachi follows while rifling through my bag. "You know full well what this is for."

Actually, I don't. I have multiple theories by now—the highest being that they found Mom's letter in my tool satchel and traced the names written within it to my family. But that would mean Mr. Elscott's in trouble too. For failing to turn us in. Probably just for knowing us.

Quick footsteps across the floor make me look back, and Foster stumbles out the door. "I'm so sorry, Rielle. I-I tried to talk him out of it." His voice strains and his eyes wilt. "I didn't think he'd actually go through with it."

The headsman and soldier stop, both eyeing Foster.

What? He tried to talk *who* out of doing *what?*

"I tried to show him you could help us," Foster sputters. "That's why I asked you to fix the shelf yesterday. I'm sorry. I should've just told you then."

Mr. Peterson. It was him. He sold us out. That's why they're arresting me.

My knees weaken, and my arm tingles as the soldier's grip obstructs its circulation. "You *knew* about this?"

"My dad's drowning in debt and he…" His voice cracks. "That was no good reason for him to…but he did. And I…I'm sorry I didn't warn you."

He turned us in for the reward.

Foster eyes the headsman with disgust. "She's a good person. Never done anything wrong." He nearly spits in his face. "Don't take her. She's innocent!"

The headsman glares back, jaw braced. "What's your name, kid?"

Foster swallows. His cheeks flush and his breathing shallows.

"Your *name*," the woman says, clenching my arm tighter. "You may be a minor, but that doesn't grant you immunity from acts of treason." She blows side bangs back from her eye.

"Foster," he exhales. "Foster Peterson."

"ID, please." The headsman retrieves a device from his belt and scans Foster's ID chip once he hands it over. He glances behind Foster to the classroom as Mrs. Jennings peers out the doorway. "This is your *one* warning, kid. Get back to class." He returns Foster's chip.

I hold his puffy-eyed stare.

The nerve! First, he neglects to warn me about the king's speech and Mr. Peterson's plan. Now he comes apologizing, begging them to release me. Useless. And idiotic. Trying to help me now has only gotten him in trouble. He didn't help when it mattered most. What can he do now? Nothing. It's already done. Irreversible.

I grit my teeth. "Better get back to class, *kid*." The words burn my throat. I never exactly saw him as a friend. But I surely never thought my family would be destroyed on account of his cowardice.

"We're done here." The woman tows me down the hall.

I plant my feet and twist around to see him again. But he's gone.

She elbows me, and I yelp at the sudden strike to my spine. "Cooperating will make this phase a lot less painful for you," she hisses.

The headsman trails us outside. Toward a navy-blue box truck.

The cuffs grind into my wrists like rusted nails as the woman thrusts me into the vehicle's trunk. She follows me inside and fastens a dark mesh bag over my head.

"Take it easy, Taima." Headsman Malachi's voice echoes from outside. "All we got on her family is one accusation. No proof yet."

"You might need the traditional physical evidence or a confession to believe something's real, Mal, but I already have my proof. Those eyes of hers…they're a confession in themselves." She yanks the seam snug around my neck.

Gravel crunches under the headsman's boots. The trunk doors slam, stealing all daylight from the mesh's tight weave. Seconds later, the engine rumbles and the vehicle rolls ahead.

Cross-legged against the side wall, I fight the force of the heaving turns. I only wish my first vehicle ride was under better circumstances. The mesh scrapes my neck and muffles my breath.

How could I be so blind? I put so much effort into hiding that book that I neglected the part of Ulric's speech promising to reward those who share their knowledge on possible suspects.

I lower my head, sensing the soldier's cruel stare even through the mesh.

If they're detaining us solely for Mr. Peterson's accusation, that means the soldiers didn't find Mom's letter at Mr. Elscott's. If they don't find the letter or the Bible, they'll have no solid proof. To get our lives back, all we must do is deny the accusation.

My stomach reels with each twist in the road. The suffocating air of my head covering enhances the nausea.

After a moment of idling, the headsman drives down a slope onto a smooth, level road.

I know exactly where they're taking me. Though I've never seen it—or hoped I ever would—everyone knows Kinborough's prison lies underground, partially beneath the Phalanx Centre.

We creep along and roll back into a turn. The brakes squeal, then the engine cuts out.

The soldier grunts, and the floor wobbles as she stands. A harsh light pierces my head covering as the doors open. She fits her hand around my arm again and hauls me from the trunk.

I leap blindly to the ground. The echo of our footsteps suggests the room is large, made of concrete. It smells of mouldy drainpipes. Maybe an underground parking garage.

The headsman's heavy footsteps guide me. When they stop, I stop. Something buzzes, and a door whooshes open. A gust of frigid air greets us with its bitter, metallic stench.

The soldier tugs me inside.

I wrench my arm from her grip, the coldness infuriating me. "What is this even about?"

She re-attaches her hand, steering me down twists and turns in the long hallways.

"Sir!" an eager voice calls from down the hall.

The headsman clomps ahead. His rumbling tone murmurs exchanges with the other man. "All right. Thank you for informing me." He finishes his private conversation.

Down another warmer hallway, a door whooshes open and closes behind me. The soldier uncovers my head. A gleaming metal desk occupies the centre of the grey room, a metal chair on either side. To my surprise, the soldier unlocks my cuffs.

I dodge her and bolt for the door. The headsman sneers as I struggle to turn the knob. Locked. I kick the door and pound on the window.

The soldier smirks, then tows me back and tugs the coat from my arms. She makes me step out of my boots and winter pants, leaving me in my old slacks and long-sleeved tee. Finally, she swipes my gloves and hat.

I grasp for the hat, but she throws it on the pile with the rest of my clothes and restrains me to the nearest metal chair. She collects my belongings and leaves the room.

Shivers slink up my arms.

"All right, here's how this'll work." The headsman rounds the desk and straddles the chair across from me. "I will ask you two questions." He sets a small device on the desk. "If you respond to each with the right answer, you'll live. If not…" He dips his head. "Well, let's hope you respond correctly." He flips a switch on the device, and a light flashes green.

I curl my sock-covered toes on the concrete floor.

"First question." He rests his forearms on the desk, the fabric of his suit moulding to his bulging biceps. "Are your parents Christians, and/or do they own any Christian items—items including, but not limited to, a book called *The Bible*?"

I stare at my hands. If, like the soldier said, my eyes alone convict me, he may detect my guilt even if I lie.

"No comment?" He scratches his mouth with a thumb. "Doesn't matter. I've received word that your mother's already confessed. You can't save her. The only one your answers have the power to save is yourself."

She confessed.

I knew I couldn't count on her to lie. She will always hold

her faith closer than life. And that is exactly what it has cost her. Her life. And perhaps all of ours.

The recording device's light flashes every few seconds.

"Good thing Grace Taima didn't stay." The headsman shifts his weight, leaning in toward me. "Because, unlike her, I'm generous. You've got another chance." His lip curls. "Question number two is the one that counts. It can grant life. It can sentence death." Shadows deepen around his eyes. "All in how you answer." His black shoulder plates reflect light in my face.

I squeeze the chains restraining me to the desk and glare at him.

"The second question," he whispers in a guttural growl. "Do *you* believe in God?"

An uneasiness creeps through me. My stare falters.

Do I believe?

Mom wouldn't risk our lives for something unless she fully believed it was worth it. But how could a belief be more valuable than our family?

He waits. "Well?" His jaw clenches and his Adam's apple bobs.

There's got to be some reason for Mom's beliefs to be punishable by death. If Christianity were harmless, King Ulric wouldn't execute people for it. Does it threaten him in some way?

The headsman eyes the recording device. "Answer the question."

But if this belief happens to be powerful enough to intimidate the king, why don't more people stand up for it? And if God is real and loves us like Mom says, why have I never felt him?

I open my mouth, then snap it shut.

He groans. "Answer the question. I don't have all day!"

Apparently, I may not either.

He stands, pressing his palms to the desk. "Answer—"

"I don't know!" I hold his stare, knowing my eyes likely reveal my inner dispute. What does it matter if I live anyway if my parents die?

His eyes relax and he nods. "Okay." He stops the recording device. "Your uncertainty may have saved you."

His words oddly instill guilt. As if I've somehow betrayed my family in trying to protect it.

He covers my head, unlocks the chains, and cuffs my hands behind my back again.

"I've got it from here, Mal," Soldier Taima says from the doorway. "Head over to the boy's school. I'll catch up."

The boy…

I struggle to swallow a lump in my throat.

Renan.

How did I go through that whole interrogation, risking my life by stating my uncertainty about God, without once pondering the consequences my answer would have on Renan? If the headsman had sentenced me to death, Ren would have no one left.

"For being my second-in-command, you sure order me around a lot," the headsman says. "You do realize I'm your future *king*, right?"

I can almost see her roll her eyes from within the mesh bag. "And you, *Your Highness*, realize I won't stop, even after you become king."

The headsman sighs and plods away. "Don't be long."

Down a long hallway and through a creaky door, Taima fumbles with the mesh bag and snatches some of my hair away with it. She unlocks my cuffs. Then thrusts me to the floor of a jail cell.

Is she aware the headsman declared me innocent? Why is she locking me away?

"Where's my family?" I yell.

She swings the metal door closed, but I stick my leg out. She kicks my shin. "Watch it, girl. I could've cut a limb off."

"Tell me where they are!"

"Rielle?" a distant voice calls.

Taima's eyes widen, and she glances down the hall.

My heart skips. "Mom?" I jump up, throwing my weight against the half-closed door.

"Rielle! Are you all right?" Mom's cry echoes.

"Yes." I fight half my body through the door. "Where's Dad and"—Taima pushes me back in the cell—"and Ren? Are they all right?"

"Shut it." Taima sends me to the ground with a punch to the gut.

Curled up on the floor, I moan. But I have to help Mom escape. She's dead if she stays here. I kick my leg out the door again to buy me some time.

Taima locks her icy eyes on me.

I've gone too far this time.

Holding firm eye contact, she slams the door. Then jerks it open after a grating screech escapes my throat. The thick metal retracts from my shin.

I recoil into the shadows of the cell as blood seeps through my right pant leg. My lungs trap screams within themselves. I can't get a breath.

She glares at my leg. "Lucky I only wanted to shut you up. Next time you rebel, I'll do more than break it."

The door groans closed, shutting out the light—all but for a high barred window. She bolts it from the outside.

I gasp for air whenever my lungs release their lock. But my leg! The pressure. The throbbing, scorching, air-stealing agony. I curl it up, then stretch it at the knee. The pain intensifies.

A voice resonates beyond the door. I can't decipher the words, but judging by the tone, it's Mom.

I can't answer, let alone breathe. My hearing goes in and out. My body burns and tingles. The queasiness grows with every subtle move. I spot the base of a toilet across the cell but can't reach it. Instead, I shut my eyes.

The pain engulfs me. And the lack of oxygen sends me to sleep.

WHEN I WAKE, it takes a while to recall where I am and accept that this is not just a nightmare. A gnawing ache has replaced the burn in my leg. Considering the stiffness of my joints and the numbness throughout my body, I've been asleep on the cold floor at least an hour.

Metal chains glint in the dull light, securing a bed frame to the wall opposite the toilet.

I take deep, even breaths to reduce the dizziness and gain strength. Then I pull myself up and collapse on the thin mattress. My jacket, winter pants, boots, hat, and gloves are piled beside me. Someone must've brought them in while I was passed out. I pull my hat on.

Though sweat soaks my clothing, I shiver from the cold. I tug at the bloody fabric of my slacks, but it won't rip. So I slide them off and change into my winter pants. Tenderly rolling the right pant leg above my knee reveals the wound.

My shin twists slightly inward. Dried blood clots the gashes on either side. I look away as acid rises in my throat.

I can do this. Have to do this. I scan around the toilet. No toilet paper to wrap the wound. I peel off my shirt, leaving only my old tank top for warmth, and tear the sleeves at their seams with my teeth. To prevent further blood loss, one sleeve gets tightly tied above my knee, then the other binds the break and bandages the gashes.

Goosebumps form on my bare arms. I press the back of my hand to my forehead, and it's burning. I pull on my jacket, but the zipper is gone. Taima must've removed it. My boots will help warm me up, but their leather sags without laces to hold them together. She took those too.

When the pain becomes bearable, I regain enough energy to limp to the door. The window is too high to reach. But the light also breaches an inch-high gap beneath the door. I lie on my side, bringing my mouth close to the gap, and call, "Mom?"

I wait.

No response.

"Mom, are you there?" My tone quivers.

Minutes turn to hours. My voice turns to sand. And she doesn't answer.

I paw at the gap, trying to find something—a stone, a loose nail—anything to use against this chamber of isolation. My fingers come across nothing but smooth concrete.

I bash the door with my palm.

My leg throbs the more I let anger get the best of me. I resign my search and hunch over the edge of the suspended bed.

The hallway's lights shut off eventually, sheathing me in utter darkness.

I thrust my elbow into the wall behind me. Then stop.

Fighting won't do me any good. If anything, it will cause

more problems. They'll probably come and break my other leg.

But why didn't Mom answer? There's been no sign of her since Taima closed the door. And why have I heard only *her?* Not Dad? Or Ren?

My heart sinks.

Have they already been executed?

No. That's crazy. If Ulric decides to execute them, he'll make me watch. They're alive. For now. And what about Renan? Ulric wouldn't kill a child for his parents' crimes, would he?

I strike the wall again, tired of unanswered questions. They don't deserve this!

Curled up on the hard mattress, I shove my hat over my face to block the smell of blood. My head pounds, and I shiver from the cold. Pressure swells behind my eyes, yet no tears fall.

Is Renan alone in the dark too?

I think back, years ago, to when the power went out in our entire western region. Renan—four years old at the time—was terrified of staying inside the house. So I bought some wax from the market and took him into our backyard to watch it melt in a pot over the fire. Mom gave him cinnamon spice to stir in. Then I poured the liquid wax into glasses and let them cool. We made over twenty in total and lit them in every room of the house. There were extras, so we went door to door around the neighbourhood and sold them. The power turned on three days later, and Ren continued to light the candles in his room at night. That's how his candle-making hobby began.

Concocted from memory, I catch a sweet whiff of cinnamon.

He will be all right. He has to be.

My leg throbs.

How can Mom still believe there's a God while she's trapped in prison, awaiting execution? This morning I thought she might be right about her beliefs because the book wasn't discovered. But now we are here…

And where is God?

Fear tightens its grip on me, and I wipe my now-wet cheeks.

God…if you're as real as Mom believes you are, I can't think of a better time for you to intervene. Please, if you hear me, help us.

"Don't let Renan sleep alone in the dark," I whisper as sleep drags me under.

Chapter 5

I sleep through the fever half the night until the hall light flickers on.

My heart speeds.

Two sets of footsteps plod toward my cell. Shadows flood beneath the door as it unbolts and creaks open.

I squint up into the headsman's sunken eyes.

"Geez, Taima." Gazing at my leg, he scrunches his face in disgust. "What were you trying to do, kill her?"

Purple swelling creeps from the wrapped wound down to my ankle.

"Broken legs heal, Mal." Taima appears beside him. "Other slaves have worked with worse conditions. I had to show her we don't tolerate defiance."

Slaves?

"Well, once my father sees what little use she is to him with that injury,"—the headsman heaves me from the mattress—"she's as good as dead."

I pretend I didn't hear him utter those words. Straightening my injured leg, I test it under my weight. Pain bites within the bone, and I lift my foot.

He turns me around, cuffs my wrists, and tightens the mesh bag over my head. "Since I'm hoping to keep the boy in better shape than her, *I'll* go get him," he says. "You take her. It seems you've already done all the damage you can do."

"Trust me, there's more where this came from." She nudges my shin with her boot.

I gasp and hold my breath to avoid crying out in pain.

"For both her sake and yours, there better not be." The headsman plods away.

I force all my weight to my good leg.

Taima grips my arm and tugs me out of the cell.

I limp behind her, straining to keep up.

"Faster!" She jolts my arm. "That leg will be the least of your worries once the night's over."

Sweat beads on my forehead as I exploit my injury with each step. Pain surges and my knee gives out. Taima lets me fall. With my hands restrained, I wait helplessly on the floor until she hoists me up. I hobble beside her down the snaking hallways. She then opens a door and shoves me to a cold wall within.

"Rielle?" Mom's voice strains from the back of the room.

"Not her too." Dad's tone rumbles from the same direction.

They're both here? I freeze. Shivers prick the nape of my neck. This is it. This is where they die.

Thick metal shackles clench my wrists, replacing the flimsy cuffs. Heavy chains weigh my arms down. Taima releases her grip.

I blindly chase my parents' voices. The shackles jerk my wrists, and the chains draw me back. Then Taima removes my head covering.

Across the room, two guards stand beside a table of guns, whips, and other weapons. Dried spits of blood stain the back wall, where Mom and Dad are chained side by side.

Dad's left eye has swollen shut amid black bruising. Blood masks the side of his nose.

Mom's chains clatter as she backs against the wall, staring at my leg. "What have you done to my daughter?" Rage consumes her tone in a way I've never heard her express before.

Taima ignores her.

The headsman marches through the door with Renan in tow.

My throat tightens.

Cuffs restrain his small hands behind his back. The headsman lifts his head covering, and he appears to be uninjured. Well rested, even. He swallows numbly, studying the table of weapons.

Taima takes him and chains him beside me. The shackles slip off his wrists, so she extends the chains and fastens them around his ankles. She absorbs the view of my restrained family and eyes my broken leg with satisfaction. Then she tosses a set of keys to the headsman and leaves the room.

Dad fists his hands, eyeing the headsman. "My children have done nothing to deserve this!"

"They won't die. At least that much has been decided."

Dad's jaw tightens. "Then they don't need to be here."

"Yes, they do." A crisp voice blasts through the opening door, and King Ulric strides into the room. "This is their example of what happens to those who consciously contribute to the destruction of our nation." His stubby fingers adjust a crest on his suit.

Head Damien follows the king inside. He tugs on his golden tie and plants himself stiffly at the wall opposite my parents. Red veins course through the whites of his eyes.

A short, blond soldier rushes through the door, helmet clutched under one arm. He salutes Head Damien, then approaches King Ulric. "My king,"—he bows—"I'm afraid we've not found the item you requested."

"That's quite all right." Ulric smiles. "They've hidden it well, but we already have the evidence we need." He glares at Dad, then returns his attention to the soldier. "Burn it down."

The soldier hesitates, drawing his brows. "The house?"

"You heard correctly." Ulric lifts his chin. "We cannot lease property contaminated with a dead family's illegal possessions. If you cannot find the book…burn it, in its resting place, to the ground."

"Yes, of-of course, Your Majesty." The man bows again and hurries out the door.

Dad's swollen eye creases open. "You can't be serious. Burning my house? If you can't find the proof you're searching for, then clearly there's none to be found. And without proof, you have no legal excuse to kill us."

"Just because *you* deny your faith, Mr. Rutherford, doesn't mean everyone does."

Dad stiffens and looks at Mom. "You confessed?" He searches her eyes. "How could you? We discussed this. We agreed to do what we had to for our family's safety."

"I never agreed to deny my faith." Despite her hands shaking, her expression remains calm. "If I disown *him*, he will disown *me*."

A vein protrudes in Dad's forehead, and he averts his eyes.

Ulric joins his hands behind his back. "That is why my job is so simple. I catch the believers easily for one reason. True followers of God live by that phrase—and die by it. They would do anything but deny *him*." He observes Dad. "What does that say of you?"

Dad pulls against the chains, mere inches from Ulric.

The king doesn't budge.

"What about my children? What will happen to them once you've made them orphans?"

Ulric remains silent.

"Tell me!"

I recall the conversation between Taima and the headsman.

When Ulric refuses to answer, I limp forward. "We will become his slaves."

Dad and Ulric both glare at me. Dad, in revulsion. Ulric, enraged.

"No." Mom's voice grates.

Dad's jaw flexes. "Send them to live with my friend—"

"The law clearly states that if a parent is unable to raise their child, the child must be sent to live with a willing family member. I've already reviewed both of your family records." He eyes Mom, who drops her gaze, then looks behind himself, motioning for Head Damien to explain.

Damien ambles forward. "Miriam Rutherford—no siblings, mother died giving birth, father died of heart disease six years ago. And Evan Rutherford—orphaned at age two, relatives nonexistent."

"Therefore, the children automatically fall under my custody," Ulric says.

"My children…slaves." Dad studies Renan. "You can't do that to an eight-year-old."

"It wouldn't be the first time." Ulric shrugs. "They belong to me now. I will do with them what I please. The boy…" —he looks Dad over—"with your genes, will become a strong torturer. And the girl…" He ogles me up and down. "Too weak to be a torturer." He squints at my leg. "She'll become a servant. Tending to my personal needs."

Dad spits in Ulric's face. "You can't punish our children for our crimes."

"You should be grateful I'm letting them live. They'd both be executed alongside you if it weren't for our recent decline of slaves." He spots Headsman Malachi beside me. "Speaking of slaves, bring in your best, my son."

Malachi nods and exits the room.

Dad hangs his head, helplessness coursing through him. "Can I at least know the name of my betrayer? I know it wasn't from your search that we became suspects. Someone turned us in."

"Why do you think you deserve to know?"

"You're about to kill me. And my wife. Destroying my family. I deserve to know who—"

"Mr. Peterson," I say. "It was Mr. Peterson."

The chains rattle as Dad's shoulders tighten. "Of course."

Ulric's eyes narrow. He turns and towers over me. "I can make your training easy, or I can order Soldier Taima to give you a hard time. I do not tolerate defiance, and neither does she. So unless you want another broken leg, I suggest you keep your mouth shut, girl."

I lower my gaze.

The door opens, and Malachi shoves a young man—the slave—into the room.

Veins pulse in the slave's neck. Beads of sweat glint on his pale cheeks—or are they tears? Though muscles protrude beneath his black t-shirt, his face reveals his youth. He can't be older than eighteen.

The headsman elbows the slave forward, aiming a hand-gun at the back of his head.

The slave looks at me. Then Renan. He turns back to the

headsman and presses his forehead to the gun's barrel. The numbness in his expression pleads with the headsman to pull the trigger. His eyes shine with tears beneath messy chestnut hair.

The headsman snorts and lowers his gun. "You wish."

The slave eyes the back door bleakly.

The guards by the table move to either side of it as if daring him to try to escape.

Malachi grabs him and throws him to the middle of the room. "Remember what will happen to *her* if you disobey," he says through gritted teeth.

The slave's body slackens and his eyes glaze over.

Malachi points to the table of weapons, and the slave slogs toward it. He selects a handgun and loads it, but takes his sweet time doing so.

A camera emerges from a gap in the wall above the slave. Another extends over my head, and their lenses adjust to focus on Mom and Dad. Ulric takes ten steps back from my parents. On his command, Head Damien marches between him and my parents.

Damien clears his throat and assumes a new persona of confidence. "Mr. and Mrs. Rutherford. By sunrise, you will both be dead. Your home, burnt to a crisp. Your children made orphans." He glances into the camera's lens above the slave. "And this footage will be seen by the entire nation. Everyone will know of your treacherous crimes. Your Christian beliefs. Your illegal custody of a Bible. The fact that you attempted to hide said Bible from authorities. And—not to mention—forcing your beliefs on your children." He pauses. "However, there is a way around these dreadful consequences. King Ulric can grant you freedom. You'll be spared your lives, and everything will return to the way it was. As if your beliefs were never discovered. Never existed. Your king will fix everything."

I glare at Ulric, doubtful. Still, my stomach stirs with hope.

Damien swallows. "All you must do is renounce your faith. Dismiss your false god. Admit you were wrong to praise anyone but Ulric—your true king, protector, and provider. Submit to the only way of life that guarantees us a future."

Just do it, Mom, I plead internally.

Mom bites her lip, defiance steeling her gaze. "Never."

I shrivel back against the wall.

Damien peers at the camera above me and steps toward Dad. "Last chance."

"We know too much." Dad looks around Damien to Ulric. "You will kill us either way."

"I give you my word. You will suffer no further harm if you submit to our ways," Ulric says.

Dad's eyes meet Mom's. He then straightens and stares Ulric down. His silence his answer.

"So be it." Ulric hangs his head. "Damien, stay here to oversee their deaths." He turns to his son. "Malachi, you as well."

My leg turns numb. I watch Renan as he trips over his chains and slumps to the ground.

Head Damien takes his spot at the side wall, and the headsman plants himself beside me.

Ulric's eyes droop. Even while sentencing his own citizens to death, his eyes are infuriatingly calm. "You've made your choice. My job is finished here." He exits the room, followed by the two guards.

Renan rises, reaches for my hand, and pulls me toward

him as far as the chains will allow.

Malachi nods at the slave. "You're up."

The slave drags his feet to the middle of the room. He sniffs and raises the small black gun to his first target. Mom.

She stifles her quivering lip. Glances at Dad, Renan, and me. Then shuts her eyes. Her brows draw together, just as they do whenever she prays at the kitchen table.

The slave's finger caresses the trigger.

"No, wait!" I drop Ren's hand and wrench forward against the chains.

The slave turns to me but doesn't seem to see me. Like Renan often does, he stares through me, eyes foggy, so dark they blend with his pupils. His lips tighten, and I notice a discoloured scar across the side of his chin.

I scan my swollen leg, recalling Headsman Malachi's words. *With that injury…she's as good as dead.* I let the chains relax. "Shoot me instead."

"No!" Renan's cry is barely audible. He grasps for my hand and pulls me back.

"Rielle, this is not your fight," Dad says.

As if my words awaken him from his haze, the slave's eyes come into focus. He follows my gaze to my leg. His forehead creases, and he lowers the gun.

"Shut up." Malachi nudges my arm, then eyes the slave. "Ignore her."

"I promise my parents will never interfere with the law. Their faith doesn't change a thing. They don't force anyone to believe what they believe, including me and my brother. They only want peace." My vision blurs as I eye Renan. "My brother needs them. What kind of life will he have as an or-phaned slave? He's only eight. He's a child. And a child needs his parents."

The slave's eyes water as he observes Renan. His lips part, and he shifts his aim to my forehead.

My limbs quake. What have I done? Just because he kills me doesn't mean Mom and Dad will be spared. Now Renan will have no one.

He places his finger on the trigger.

I'm not ready. What happens to a person after death?

Ren scratches my hand, sinking to the floor. "Don't, Ree—" he chokes.

"Those weren't your orders!" Malachi wrestles the gun from his own belt.

The slave tilts his gun to my left and pulls the trigger. A deafening boom resounds.

And Malachi drops to the floor.

Head Damien darts to the table of weapons. He grabs a gun and loads it with shaking fingers.

But the slave aims at Damien's chest and fires again.

Chapter 6

Headsman Malachi claws his chest, blood seeping between his fingers. His face contorts as he breathes through gritted teeth.

The slave tucks his gun in the back of his pants and charges toward me. He drops to his knees, rips the set of keys from Malachi's belt, and sprints to my parents. Dad extends his chained wrists for the slave to unlock.

Head Damien scrapes his fingernails on the ground, sprawled beside the table of weapons. Dark blood drowns his golden tie.

Mom huffs for air, shaking. Her chewed lips part as she watches the men writhe in pain.

Amid raspy breaths, Head Damien croaks, "For-forgive me…" He shuts his eyes, and tears roll down his cheeks.

The slave flips through several keys on the ring before finding the right one. He frees my parents, and Dad enwraps Mom in his arms. The slave then stoops down beside me to unleash the shackles from Renan's ankles. The collar of his t-shirt lifts to expose the tips of faded scars at the nape of his neck—apparently a foretaste of what resides farther beneath his shirt.

I picture the slave chained. Back bare. The headsman's whip colliding with his flesh. Then the scene warps. Instead of the slave being tortured, it is Renan. I shake the image, realizing Renan has been saved from the exact fate the slave has suffered.

Once free, Renan folds his arms around me, and I hug him tightly. Then he bounds for Mom, and she squeezes him, wrapping herself around him like a shield.

The slave snags a second handgun from the table, loads it, and tosses it to Dad.

Dad's hands fold around the gun as if second nature to him. He also stuffs two extra packs of ammo in his pockets.

Mom hugs me as the slave frees my wrists.

Then he motions for us all to gather. "All right, listen. Get somewhere—anywhere safe where they won't think of looking." He coughs dryly, his voice raw. "Just find some-place secret, and make it quick."

"We can't escape this place," Dad says. "We won't make it past the guards."

"That's what the gun's for." The slave motions to the pis-tol in Dad's hand. "Not many guards have the early morning shift, but it won't be long before Ulric finds out what hap-pened. And when he does, he'll send search parties after you. They'll tear through every house in the region if they have to, so don't go home or hide anywhere around here." He eyes the recording cameras, then swipes a paper and pen from a folder on the door. He jots something down and hands the page to Dad, out of view of the cameras.

I crane my neck to make out the words.

Leaving the region is your safest bet.

Dad reads the paper, nods, and stuffs it in his pocket.

Headsman Malachi grows deathly pale, his blood pooling on the concrete.

"What about you?" Mom asks the slave. "When Ulric

finds out you shot them—"

The door swings open, and Taima wanders in, distracted by a sheet of paper in her hands. "Mal, we've got orders to…" Spotting Malachi and Damien on the floor, she blanches and sinks to Malachi's side. "Call an ambulance—" Her brittle voice chokes. She presses both palms to his chest and shrieks in the open door's direction, "We need a doctor!" Then into her communicator, "This is Soldier Taima, calling for—"

The slave raises his gun to her forehead, and she lifts her hands in surrender.

"Go! Get out!" The slave shoves us toward the door, keeping his aim on Taima. "Take two lefts, one right, pass a blue storage closet, and follow the strip of black paint on the wall to find the door to the parking garage."

If he knows the building's layout so well, why hasn't he successfully escaped before?

Dad pulls me toward the door.

"You're not coming?" Mom says to the slave.

"Don't worry about me. Just get your family to safety."

"You have no idea what this means to us. You've given us our lives back." Mom frowns. "What's your name?"

The slave hesitates, brushing his sweaty hair back from his brow. "Ezra."

"Ezra." Mom's lips tremble into a smile. "Thank you."

Dad grips the gun and lifts Renan onto his back. "We have to go. Now."

Mom throws my arm over her shoulder, and I lean on her as we trail Dad and Ren down the halls, following Ezra's directions.

An ignorant guard strolls into the hall up ahead.

We press against the side wall.

Dad raises his gun. But then he stops and shoves it in his pocket. He lowers Ren to the ground and charges for the guard, knocks him out cold with a blow to the temple. "Come on," he says, lifting Renan again.

We pass a blue storage closet and follow a black strip of paint on the wall to reach the parking garage. At least fifty trucks are parked row after row in the large underground space. The harsh ceiling lights cast shadows between the vehicles.

Security cameras must be scanning every inch of this place. Even if they're recording our escape, the few guards on duty will undoubtedly be pouring all their efforts into saving the two dying men in the execution room.

Dad hurries us around the corner from the garage's exit. An iron gate looms at the top of the sloped drive. We huddle in the shadows between a truck and the wall.

I sit down to rest my leg, back against the truck.

Dad peers around the corner. "We'll have to climb the gate."

Mom inspects my leg. "Rielle can't."

"We have to try. Lift her up over it or—"

"There'll be someone coming in or out eventually. For now, we should figure out a plan."

"Right. Once we're out, there's no time to chat." Dad debates several possibilities with Mom.

I'd suggest escaping through the forest beyond the lumber yard. I know those woods well enough. But it's too likely the authorities already know of my trespassing. That's the first place they'd look.

Renan slides down beside me and tucks his warm hand in mine.

Dad sighs. "I think our best bet is beyond the outskirts

like the slave said. I heard rumours years ago that the north-western land was up-and-coming."

"We can't go home, so we'll have no food, no supplies…"

A faint wailing echoes in the distance. An ambulance.

Dad shifts his weight. "We don't have a choice. We can't trust anyone to help or hide us."

But we *can* trust someone.

I weave my fingers through Renan's hair, reliving the relief I felt when Mr. Elscott said he was on our side. "Mr. Elscott's farm. It's on the northern outskirts. I went there yesterday morning, and he promised to help us with whatever we need. He told me to stop by after school and he'd have our food ready. We could get the food, then escape through the fields behind his farm. There's forest along the sides to conceal us—"

"Yes." Dad nods. "It's the fastest way out of the region."

Clashing sirens pierce the outside silence. They approach the gate, then abruptly shut off. A metallic clack echoes around the corner. Flashing blue lights dance among the shadows as two white ambulances barrel down the drive. Their tires screech to a halt in front of the prison door. Four paramedics exit the trunks and unload two gurneys.

"It's closing. Now's our only chance." Dad takes Renan's hand and sneaks up the slope.

Mom helps me to my feet and pulls me up the sloped drive. We slink through the last foot of space before the barred gate latches behind us.

I PANT AS Mom hauls me up the gravel pathway to the farmhouse.

Dad drops Renan's hand and pounds on the wooden front door.

It flies open mid-knock, and Mr. Elscott steps outside. His shoulders loosen, and he throws an arm around Dad. "You had me worried sick," he says, hugging me next. "I knew something was off when you didn't come for the food. I thought maybe you forgot, so I brought the basket to your house. But when I got there, soldiers had dragged all your things outside on the lawn and…"

Mom embraces him after me. "We're all right." Her words muffle in his flannel shirt.

Mr. Elscott nears Renan for a hug. Ren draws back, so Mr. Elscott gives him space.

"We were arrested," Dad says. "Sentenced to death. But we escaped the prison."

A shadow of horror fills Mr. Elscott's eyes. "Do you—do you want to come in?"

"No, we can't stay. We just came to get the food Rielle said you prepared." Dad raises a hand. "Add whatever will last us two weeks or more. We can pay extra."

Extra. That'll go over well.

"Two weeks?" Mr. Elscott pauses, then eyes each of us. "You're leaving the region."

"For your own safety, the less you know, the better." Dad glances around. "But yes."

"You won't get anywhere far on foot. They've got vehicles, and…" Mr. Elscott's eyes widen. "Take the horses."

"No, we can't. If they find them missing, they'll know you helped us."

"I insist." Mr. Elscott straightens. "Go on down to the barn, get them saddled. I'll be down with food and supplies in a few minutes."

Dad eyes Mr. Elscott's hardened jaw, then dips his head. "Thank you, Spencer." He pats him on the shoulder and heads to the barn with Renan.

Mom idles. "This is too much. You're risking everything."

He holds up a hand and gives a warm smile. "As I told Rielle earlier, I will help your family in any way I can. Now go on. We'll say our goodbyes in the barn."

She nods, eyes glistening, then helps me down the porch steps.

I sense Mr. Elscott's gaze on my injured leg and nearly trip over my laceless boots.

Once inside the barn, I let go of Mom and hobble toward Sinta's stall. Mom leads her out, and Dad heaves a saddle on her back. I pet her golden coat, willing my hand to quit shaking.

"Ren will ride with me." Dad saddles up the dark-maned stallion named Bandit in the next stall. "Mir, are you able to take Rielle?"

Dad is a skilled rider. But the last time Mom rode a horse was before Renan was born.

"I'm rusty." Mom wrings her hands. "But I'm sure I'll be fine."

"No, I can ride," I say. "Mom hasn't ridden in years. She can sit behind me."

Dad scoffs. "This is no time for jokes."

"I'm serious. I can do it."

Mom shakes her head. "Your leg—"

"It's fine. It doesn't hurt." I'm not lying, and I hold Mom's gaze to prove it. The chronic breeze has actually numbed the pain some.

Mom hesitates. "All right. But if it gets bad, let me know. We'll switch."

Mr. Elscott shuffles into the barn, carrying four blankets over one arm and two large mesh sacks over his shoulder. He sets the sacks on the ground, and Mom helps unload the blankets.

Beneath the blankets is a heavy black coat. Mr. Elscott gives it to Dad. I hadn't even noticed that Mom's and Dad's zippers were stolen too.

He holds another coat out for Mom, much larger than she is. "This one was mine when I was"—he looks down at his belly—"a lot smaller. Probably still too big for you though."

Mom slides into it and buttons it up. The sleeves hang past her hands. "It'll do." She grins.

Lastly, he holds out a leather coat and a pair of matching boots to me.

Bittersweet memories of Ginny, his wife, come rushing back. She wore them every day in the colder months. They complemented her caramel skin and warm brown eyes.

I stare at him. "I can't take those. They're *hers*."

He looks down and swallows. "She don't need 'em anymore."

I throw my own coat aside and slip into Ginny's fleece-filled one. It still smells of her—sugar and vanilla, from all the baking she used to do. The zipper glides smoothly to my chin. Since she was nearly as small as I am, it fits nicely. The boots fit a size bigger than I'm used to, but with my foot swelling from the injury, I'm glad for the extra toe room.

Dad zips up his jacket and clears his throat. "How much do you want for all this?"

As Mr. Elscott states that he will take nothing and Dad argues, I remember my tool satchel. I retrieve it from the shelf and unzip the secret pocket. Mom's letter is still inside.

"You may be stubborn, but you aren't winning this one, Evan," Mr. Elscott says.

If only Taima hadn't taken my coins, I'd have hidden them here for Mr. Elscott to find later.

Dad eventually backs down, and Mr. Elscott passes him the mesh sacks. "Save your thanks for when you find safety."

Dad smiles weakly and fastens the sacks to the saddles. He then hugs Mr. Elscott.

Unease rattles through me with the dread of leaving this refuge. I limp forward and wrap my arms around him. "We'll take care of Sinta and Bandit."

He nods and whispers, "I put a kit in the bag that might help that leg of yours."

I squeeze him tighter. "Thank you."

Mom hugs him one last time. "I'll be praying for your protection."

His eyes gleam, and he tousles Renan's hair.

With his help, I lodge my left foot in Sinta's stirrup and ease my right into the other.

The wind carries echoes of screeching tires, and Mr. Elscott shuts the barn's light off.

Dad mounts Bandit, and Mr. Elscott lifts Renan up behind him. Ren buries his cheek into Dad's coat.

Mom mounts behind me, links her arms around my waist.

Mr. Elscott shoves the back doors of the barn open. They lead into his field, where we'll travel the northwestern outskirts of Kinborough until we reach the neighbouring region.

Dad and Renan leave first, racing into the dark of early morning.

I look back at Mr. Elscott. At my limp leather boots by the empty stall.

Then slap the reins.

Chapter 7

I force myself through an hour of riding. But when my foot jolts out of the stirrup, I give in to the bounce of Sinta's gallop and nearly fall off.

Mom tightens her hold, steadying me until I can slow Sinta to a trot. "That's enough, Rielle. You're in pain. Let me ride for a bit."

I shove my foot back into the stirrup and grimace.

"Evan!" Mom yells ahead. "Slow down."

Dad doesn't seem to hear. He and Renan race through the grassy field along the forest line.

"I can wait till we catch up." I bite back a groan and slap the reins. The wind stings my eyes and whips my hair into Mom's face. If I hadn't stored my hat in my tool satchel before we took off, it would already be a victim of the wind.

Dad finally looks back at us and slows. "We can't stop long," he says once we catch up to him. "We're still in the outskirts." He eyes my leg, then glares at me. "Rielle, let Miriam ride."

I pull the reins. But Sinta's ears flick back and forth, and she speeds up instead.

The wind hisses, and she snorts.

"Come on, girl." I pull the reins.

Mom twists in the saddle to look behind us.

Then a bang rings through the field.

I jolt as Mom gasps, clenching her fingers into my abdomen.

"Mom?"

Another blast.

Sinta squeals and bucks.

Mom loses her grip and hits the ground. Hard.

"No!" I jump down after her.

Dad leaps off Bandit, and Ren falls from the saddle.

A metallic scent overwhelms me as I near her.

I shove my gloves in my pockets. My fingers rush to the seeping blood, and I force the words from my throat. "Don't move. It's just your shoulder." I slide my hand beneath the collar of her coat, pressing against the flow of warm liquid.

She has a chance. Don't overthink. Just stop the bleeding.

Dad stumbles beside her and rips her oversized coat open. He spots my hand covering the wound below her collarbone and scans her chest and stomach. No other bullet wounds.

My palms hinder the bleeding, but her face pales too rapidly in the muted moonlight. She grips my hand and wheezes. "Don't," she sputters. "It's not—"

More shots spook the horses.

Dad strokes Mom's cheek with the back of his hand. "We have to get you out of here." He lifts her, careful not to touch her shoulder.

She digs her fingernails into my palm and cries out in pain.

"What is it, Mir?" Dad sets her down. He gapes at his palms, freshly coated in blood. It pools on the ground beneath her coat.

She was shot in the back too.

Her body stiffens, shakes, and she coughs up frothy liquid.

I withdraw my hand from her shoulder wound. This can't be happening.

Her breathing rasps, and she loosens her grip on my fingers.

I drop her hand and stumble back. My head throbs with grief and confusion and helplessness, visions of blood glinting in the moonlight and conjured gunshot echoes. I can't keep up. I can't comprehend what I'm witnessing.

All I know is I need her and can't do anything to save her.

Renan drops beside me, taking my place in holding her hand. He squeezes his eyes shut, and I recall how he never could stand the sight of blood. His body trembles, but he doesn't faint or retreat. He stays with her.

In the distance behind us, a shadowy figure on horseback fires at us again. The bullet whizzes by.

I watch Mom's chest rise and fall rapidly as Renan lifts her hand to his cheek. My jumbled emotions form a raging hatred for the one who caused this. I swipe the gun from Dad's coat and mount Sinta. My body pulses with numbing electricity. If my leg hurts, I can't feel it. I pursue the figure.

I've never fired a gun before. But I pull back the sliding piece on top like the slave did in the execution room. Holding the reins in my left hand, I aim and fire with my right.

The soldier on horseback retreats, racing back in the direction he came.

I continue shooting but miss every time. The blasts reverberate up my arm, and I lose sight of the figure among the distant shadows.

Mom's killer is gone.

I slow down and pound my fists into my thighs. Screams

shred my throat until they grow hoarse and soundless. My body weakens and tears obscure my vision. The electric energy coursing through my veins turns to molten lead that weighs me down.

Sinta waits through my outburst, then turns and brings me back to my family.

I dismount her and find Mom cradled in Dad's arms, her face held to his chest as he sits in the grass. Her breathing is shallow and rigid.

Renan lies beside Mom, face buried in her sleeve. He shivers and inhales sharply.

I suppress the swelling in my chest and untie one of Mr. Elscott's blankets from Sinta's saddle. She doesn't have much time left.

Dad repositions her to rest his chin in her tangled hair. But she doesn't moan or give any indication of being in pain like she did earlier.

I catch a glimpse of her face as I drape the blanket over her body. Blood streaks her pasty lips, and her skin has become tight. Lifeless.

I wait for her chest to rise, but realize it's only Dad stealing shallow, rigid breaths. Not her.

She's already gone.

The gun slips from my hand. My leg flares with pain, and I drop to my knees. The sight of blood-soaked grass in front of me quenches the last of my strength.

I turn away, retching. My stomach empties itself of what little remains inside. The tears come viciously, and I succumb to them, weeping into the frozen grass.

Don't leave us. I need you! I can't do this alone. Not again—

I drag in a breath and wipe my eyes.

How can I be so selfish? Mom is the one who experienced unimaginable pain and died an undeserving death, and all I can think about is how much I need her?

I shudder as my elbows keep me from collapsing under the weight of this sorrow. Dad holds Mom's head in his hand, and I avert my eyes, unable to bear another moment watching him weep over her body.

The lashing wind convinces me to steal a blanket and flee the open field. I wrap the fleece material around my shoulders and sink to the base of a large pine in the forest. My chest aches as the sobs wrench through me.

The one person I want to console me in my grief is the very person I am grieving for. That awareness physically hurts.

I squish the blanket over my wet face and rest my forehead on my drawn knees.

Firing the gun at the killer did nothing of value except maybe scare him off. I should've stayed with Mom. I didn't know she'd be gone so quickly. I thought I had time. Why didn't I stay with her?

I yield to my exhaustion and shut my eyes as the tears continue through the hours.

I WAKE TO the congested rumbling of Renan's snore. He only ever snores when he's sick or after he has spent the night crying.

He slumps against my shoulder, puffy eyes closed.

Thick clouds cast a grey haze over the land, but what little daylight endures manages to make my swollen eyes sting.

My head pounds with the nightmare of last night's events. The images loop, but I still can't grasp them, can't accept them. She's not dead. She is simply asleep.

I cloak my blanket over Renan and unearth a long, sturdy stick to help me hobble out from the forest. But as I approach Dad, my thoughts surrender to my fears.

He slouches over her body, having cocooned her in the blanket. Her head lolls over the crook of his arm, and blonde waves caress her colour-drained face.

The morning light exposes crimson stains on Dad's coat. On my palms. Stuck under my nails.

She is not asleep.

I swallow a lump that sinks like a boulder to the pit of my stomach. Loneliness unlike I've ever felt wedges its way inside my heart, filling the hole left by her leaving. My chest aches. But this time, I couldn't cry if I wanted to. The acidic taste on my dry tongue tells me I'm awfully dehydrated.

I limp toward the grazing horses and sprawl another blanket on the ground beside Sinta. I should be worried about how exposed we are in this field, but that's the last thing on my mind at the moment.

Renan staggers out from the sparse forest line, hugging the blanket around him. He absently settles onto the right side of my blanket.

Sinta flicks her tail as I rummage through one of the mesh sacks to find a canteen. I twist its metal cap and bring the rim to my lips. Cool water floods my tongue, and I down a quarter of the canteen. I then lower it to Renan, but he shakes his head, glaring into the forest.

I sit beside him. The grief brimming in his eyes makes me look away. I've played the scenario over in my head a thousand times throughout the years—about how it would feel to lose her. Doing so in no way prepared me for the real thing. It's unbearable, dealing with the shock, let alone watching Renan try to cope. Knowing I can't comfort him. Knowing the only one who could possibly comfort him is *her*.

He looks back at Mom and after minutes of silence, says, "Are the stories true?"

I rub my nose. "What stories?"

"The ones she used to read to us," he says softly. "About when people died and then…came back?"

My thoughts swarm, and a fresh wave of emotion raids me. He thinks he can bring her back.

"The stories where, when people prayed, the dead ones came back to life? Are they true? Because if we try—"

"Enough, Renan." My throat burns and clenches. "They're just stories."

The tip of his nose reddens, and his pitch heightens in desperation. "But what if we—"

"No. Just…don't." My voice grates. "It's pointless."

He pauses, then lowers his chin to rest on his drawn knees. His eyes glaze over again.

Then the realization sinks in. I just robbed him of his last shred of hope. I want to apologize, tell him he can try praying if he wants. But if he does pray and nothing happens— which will no doubt be the outcome—it will leave him more hopeless than ever.

Mom's death confirms her beliefs were false. A god whom she devoted, risked, and ultimately lost her life for wouldn't let this happen if he were real. But Renan is clinging to any hope he can find. And if he were to learn the god Mom said loves us won't save her…it might very well break him. The sooner he deals with reality, the sooner he will heal. Better to extinguish the spark before it spreads.

So I don't apologize or tell him he can pray. I know it's for his own good, but watching him suppress his grief is killing me—as is grasping the fact Mom died for a lie.

I need a distraction.

Promptly, the pain in my leg flares. I rummage through the mesh sacks on both horses until I find the medical kit Mr. Elscott said he included. It contains various-sized bandages, a thick roll of gauze, tiny scissors, nail clippers, a thermometer, and a two-ounce bottle of antiseptic alcohol.

I roll my pant leg above my knee and slide off my boot and sock, then untie the torn sleeves of my shirt wrapped above my knee and around the wound.

The horizontal gashes on either side of my shin are deep, each a few inches long and an inch wide. Purple bruising has spread through the distended flesh. If my ability to process emotions hadn't run dry within the last few hours, I'd be scared the injury might be infected. Common sense tells me riding Sinta aggravated the break, but the chilly air numbs most of the pain, so I don't pay it much attention.

I look away as I rinse the blood from my hands using water from the canteen. I give up trying to scrub my cracked fingernails clean, but do what I can to sanitize my hands. Then with my leg stretched over the grass, I open the bottle of antiseptic. Bite my lip, hold my breath, and pour the alcohol over the left gash. It burns and itches. My toes curl, and I force myself to pour the liquid over the other side of my shin. After I've nearly used the whole bottle, I grip the edges of the blanket and wait for the sting to fade.

Ren jerks away as I bring my leg back onto the blanket.

"It's"—I wince—"it's not as bad as it looks."

He doesn't seem convinced.

When the alcohol dries, I unroll the gauze and wrap the end above my ankle, coiling it upward over the wounds. Though soft and flexible, it clings to itself and stiffens as it overlaps. I wrap it firmly, twice over, and snip the remainder of the roll free.

Dad appears in front of us, riding Bandit—our signal to leave. He holds Mom's blanketed body to his chest with one arm and controls the reins with the other hand. Despite the bruise bloating his eye, he focuses on her with care. Nurturing her as if she were still alive.

I tug my sock and boot back on, shove my pant leg down over the gauze cast, and pack everything back into the mesh bag. Renan hands me one blanket to tie down but clings to the other one, so I let him keep it.

I pull on my knitted gloves and hoist myself onto the saddle. Then I heave Renan up behind me. He hugs the blanket and wraps his arms around my waist.

We resume travelling along the forest line.

This time, Dad drifts behind us.

A TOWERING GATE comes into view over the rolling hills, enclosing everything along the horizon. Its black metal rods pierce the sky. Two trucks squat beside a large bungalow, and a small square room is built into the gate, joined to the left side of the house.

A door opens as we approach, and two masked guards exit the square room.

Dad takes the lead, holding Mom close, then halts within thirty feet of the guards. The reins fall from his hand, and he pulls the pistol from his coat. Without a trace of hesitation, he aims the gun and fires rapidly.

My gut spasms with every blast.

One guard collapses, and the other scrambles to fire his weapon roughly in our direction while dragging his injured partner toward the door.

I broaden my shoulders to shield Renan from any stray bullets.

Sinta stamps her hoofs and backs us up into the trees.

I rub her neck and coerce her forward.

Within the next five shots, Dad has hit the second guard more than once. He slips the gun back in his coat and trots up to the gate.

Renan lifts his face from my coat. "Is it over?"

I slacken. "Yeah."

We trail Dad as he inspects the dark windows from the saddle. "Take this." He hands me the gun, careful not to shift Mom. "Go inside. Find a way to open the gate."

I take the gun, barely processing the task's potential dangers before I dismount Sinta and hobble past the dead guards.

One-way windows cover three of the four walls in the square room, giving a broad spectrum of the land on either side of the gate. A half-open door in the only wall without a window connects the room to the house. Two long desks cower under the right window, one abundant with files and paper folders, and the other bearing two blank computer screens and a control panel of switches.

I sit down on a wobbly chair to study each of the switches. I flip a lever labelled *Gate*, and a grating screech comes from outside.

On the other side of the window, Renan covers his ears as the gate opens into the land beyond.

I step around the dead guards on my way out and blink back the tears before Dad sees them fall. I should be happy the guards are dead. After all, it was one of their kind who killed Mom.

Still, death is death.

I give the gun back to Dad, eyeing Mom's boots dangling out from the blanket.

We leave our home region behind. The gate remains open, even as it fades into the fog behind us. I suppose it will stay open until the switch is flipped back.

I fidget with the reins, moving cautiously along the jagged tree line. This new land only differs from Kinborough in how the soil is more upturned and barren. I look back at Dad every few seconds. He trails behind us, a constant twitch pulling at the corner of his mouth. He sets his gaze ahead, but can't seem to keep from glancing down at Mom's face.

A gust of wind carries shrivelled leaves from the ground into the sky. I bury my nose in the collar of my coat and squint through the breeze. Renan squeezes me as we lurch side to side at the mercy of Sinta's gait.

Reeling clouds cloak the sky. They grow darker ahead, thicker. But not impending-storm-like. Just duller, more depressing. Like they're forewarning us that the land beyond is more miserable than the one we came from.

If that's even possible.

SHALLOW CRATERS MARK the ground, patched over unevenly with dirt. Crumbling bricks lie sporadically among the grass. Over the next hill, several abnormal structures appear as distant silhouettes, and as we draw near, they become the skeletons of houses blown to bits.

We maneuver around heaps of scorched bricks in the street. Some buildings are merely missing roofs and windows, but most have been demolished entirely. Other than a few broad trails cleared through the piled debris, the place seems to have been abandoned years ago.

Disintegrating roof shingles lay among splintered shafts, and vines shred through the cracked concrete, their thorns choking the trunks of fallen trees.

We slow our horses as their clattering hoofs echo.

The nape of my neck tingles at the stillness of the deceased region. What is this place?

Renan peers around, drawing his blanket to his chin.

Dad clutches Mom's body closer, surveying the mounds of rubble. He points at a wooden foundation to the right with its walls and roof blasted out from it. In the past, it might've been a garden shed. "Rielle," he says, his low tone barely audible. "Go search through that debris. See if you can find a shovel."

I follow his command without hesitation.

If only I had bothered to ask what he needed the shovel for.

THE SOIL, BRITTLE and hard, is a challenging opponent for the rusted spade. Dad digs for hours at the edge of the field. During that time, Renan is to find flowers, leaves—anything pretty to bury Mom with.

Though I plead for a different task, Dad puts me in charge of preparing her body. "I can't do it," I choke out.

Dad's brows sink. "You think you're the only one unable to cope?" His eyes redden. "She was my *wife*. Renan's *mother*. You weren't even related to her. You weren't her real daughter. She wasn't your real mother."

Each word sears my soul. I try to shout back, "Yes, she is!" but can't form the words.

He immediately looks remorseful but nonetheless clamps

his jaw and turns away.

I know nothing I say will change his mind. If only I could run away. Bring Ren with me. I want to. But I can't leave Mom that way—in anger.

So I stay. I kneel beside her body and unwrap the blanket. Though Dad does all the physically demanding work of digging the grave, my job is the hardest. And he knows it.

This will be the last time I'll ever see her, and yet she's barely recognizable. Her blonde waves don't bounce as they did when she'd throw her head back in laughter. Her skin no longer maintains a warm glow. Instead, it's pasty, and so are her lips after I wipe the blood from them. The sweet smell of lavender no longer coats her nimble fingers made for gardening. They are now stiff, their tips turning blue. Her loving presence that had always calmed me in a crisis is gone, never to return. Nothing about her is the same. Nothing is right.

I grab Dad's attention and touch Mom's wedding ring. A small, square diamond coiled within a thin silver band.

He stares at it blankly, then shakes his head. He wants her to keep it.

We make her look somewhat herself again, somewhat elegant. The only flowers Renan finds to have weathered the cold are fingernail-sized, in beautiful shades of blue and freckled with yellow centres. Though Mom surely told me the name of that type of flower at some point over the years, I can't remember it.

I know I won't be able to speak. But I can't let her leave without a word. I remember her last note to me zipped in my tool satchel and realize I never wrote her back like I used to do with each of her letters. From my tool satchel I pull the notebook and pencil used for taking measurements at installation jobs. And I write back.

I am sorry, Mom. I wish I could've saved you. You got a taste of freedom while escaping the region, but were cheated of it too soon. I'd give anything to have you back.

I should've stayed with you in your final moments. You were the only one I've ever trusted to hold my heart, and now you're gone. But I just want to say thank you. Thank you for being my mother. You filled the role I needed you to fill perfectly. You were my rainbow of peace after a lifelong storm. And you didn't deserve this.

When my hand begins shaking and tears stain the page, I fold it and tuck it in her coat pocket.

The funeral is short.

Renan sprinkles the first handful of dirt over the blanket encasing her in the shallow grave. After Dad does the same, Renan leans into him with dreadful detachment in his gaze. I watch as Dad folds his arms around Renan and draws him closer.

He really does love Renan. As I hunch over the grave with a fist full of dirt, I wonder, *Since God and heaven aren't real, what has become of you, Mom? Did you simply cease to exist the moment your heart stopped?*

I have no energy to ponder the questions. And though I know she can't hear me, I look at Renan and make her a promise. *I will protect him, Mom. I won't let him become another of Ulric's innocent victims, like you.*

The loneliness slams me like a tsunami the instant I sprinkle the dirt over her body.

While Dad shovels the soil over her, I nail two wooden sticks into a rickety cross, then carve the name *Miriam Rutherford* along the horizontal board to mark the gravesite.

With the last shovelful of soil spread over Mom's patch

Chapter 8

Travelling east from the field of the desolate region, we take refuge in cleared-out basements at night. My dreams haunt me when I try to sleep, so I busy myself guarding the fires built on brick-laden floors for warmth.

By midafternoon of our third day, we reach a forest overrun with pines and cedars and sprinkled with the occasional oak, birch, or walnut tree. A small river snakes between rocky peaks that conceal us from the region's sight. We follow alongside the river and eventually stumble upon a tiny secluded cabin. Its walls splinter and its roof rots with moss and mildew.

Dad pries the front door open, and festering air welcomes us with its stale piney stench.

The brittle floorboards seem ready to snap in half under my weight as I step inside and scan the room. Straight ahead, a rusty bed frame supports a mattress with yellowed sheets. A wood-burning stove catches my eye in the kitchen to the right, along with a sink full of eroding cutlery, a tabletop counter and stool, and a cupboard full of dishes.

I should be happy at finding shelter, but I just feel empty.

Down a staircase to the left, I strike a match and light a lantern dangling from the low ceiling. The cobweb-laced basement holds a small cot and a wooden desk scattered of earth, an old feeling returns. So subtle, I almost don't notice it. But even so, it sets my world off course. It's been nine years since I last felt it, and now that it's returned, it seems as though it never left. The haunting unease of knowing my father is my sole caretaker.

I want to flee.

But I made Mom that promise. To protect Renan. As much as I know Dad's presence will summon menacing old memories, and as much as his prior words stung, I can't take Ren and run from him. Renan loves Dad. He couldn't handle losing another parent.

I have to stay. For him.

So I let the numbness smother me.

And the tears stop falling.

with papers. A musty roll-out mattress has been tucked inside a closet under the staircase, and I unroll it on the ground beside the cot.

Thankfully, this place seems to be more of an abandoned hunting lodge than a home. I was growing sick of discovering singed socks and children's stuffed toys among the wreckage of our shelters.

A silent understanding takes place among us—Dad gets the bed on the main level, Renan will use the cot downstairs, and I'll sleep on the roll-out mattress beside him.

Dad slumps face first into his bed without so much as changing the sheets.

BEFORE GETTING SETTLED inside, I locate a thick rope coiled in the basement closet and tether the horses to a tree by the riverbank. As they drink eagerly, I unload our supplies from their saddles. They've got all the water they'll need and enough grass in this cleared patch of land to sustain them several days. When the time comes, they can be moved to another pasture. For now, keeping my family fed and warm is most important.

I find an axe inside a tool bench by the front door.

My injured leg doubles the amount of time it takes to get around, even with the aid of a walking stick. But considering these tasks are the only distractions keeping my memories and emotions at bay, I'd rather not rush them. The drop in temperature throughout the evening dulls the pain in my leg, and I plan to take advantage of the numbness for as long as it lasts.

Beside a decaying birch that's been downed roughly six months, I twist my hair into a bun atop my head and get to work. With the axe I strip the tree's bark and chop the lower trunk into lengthwise quarters.

The strips of bark pop and sizzle when added to the fire I built in the sooty kitchen stove. I then throw in small logs to fuel the flame long enough for me to carry the remaining timber inside. I stack it all near the stove as Dad snores behind me.

Warmth soon floods the main level, thawing the chill in my bones. Smoke swells up the chimney, and I can only hope the steep hills and soaring pines around the cabin will disperse and disguise it from view. To be safe, we'll probably leave the area in a few days.

I head downstairs after adding more logs to the fire. At this rate, the icy basement will take much longer than the main level to heat up.

Renan stirs on the stripped cot, sleeping on his stomach. He rubs his cheek into the rough mattress and whimpers.

I wish I could let him sleep because he needs it. But a nightmare isn't worth waiting out. I lay my hand on his back.

He jolts and slaps my arm away.

I withdraw, then rub his shoulder as he comes to.

He squints up at me.

I force a calm smile, pretending not to suspect what he was dreaming about. "I've got a fire going. Want to come up?"

He wipes his forehead and sweeps his legs over the edge of the cot.

I follow him up with my walking stick, ignoring the jolt of pain with each step.

While Dad dozes and Renan slumps cross-legged in front of the stove, I spread our belongings out across the floor. Excluding the food we've already eaten, Mr. Elscott gave us two bricks of butter, four loaves of bread, twenty-three cans of vegetable soup, fifty potatoes, and fifty-seven apples. The rest of the supplies consists of four water canteens, a full box of matches, a roll of tinfoil, the medical kit, four folded bed-sheets, our three remaining blankets, a can opener, and a serrated hunting knife.

I assign each of us a bedsheet and blanket, then store the water canteens in the cabinet. Now that we've got a river flowing through our backyard, fresh water won't be hard to come by.

I mentally ration the food according to how much we should consume per day—four slices of bread, one can of soup, two and a half potatoes, and three or so apples. This way we might have enough for three weeks. By then, we'll need to have found an active region to stock up on food. Or if not, hunt our own.

I scrub a pot clean in the river and fill it with water to dilute the soup. I also rinse four porcelain bowls, then fight back the tears when I realize we only need three.

Keep yourself busy. Take care of Renan.

I can't let my emotions consume me. If I fall prey to them, I'll surely not get up again.

When steam rises from the pot, I open one large can of soup and mix its contents into the water with the cleanest spoon available. My hands shake—whether from nerves, hunger, or the cold, I can't tell. Some of the steaming liquid spills over as I set a bowl on the floor beside Dad's bed.

Having slept since our arrival, Dad groggily turns toward the salty aroma. He eyes the bowl skeptically. Then his mouth curls, not so much in a smile as in bewildered recognition that I did something nice. He rubs his bristly face and takes the bowl.

If only I had the words to tell him I'm keeping him fed and healthy for Renan. Not me.

Ren pulls the lopsided stool to the counter, rests his chin on his crossed arms, and glares at his bowl.

This can't be happening.

My eight-year-old brother doesn't care enough to feed himself.

He hasn't told me how he feels. Not that he needs to. The grief is there, in his eyes, paralyzing him from the inside out. It is a longing that begs for comfort, growing deeper each day since the burial. And it hurts to watch him yearn for comfort from the one person who cannot comfort him.

Ulric did this to him. To us. I was right to have mistrusted him all those years. He's caused such unbearable pain to our family, all to abolish a false belief that threatens him somehow. No one should hold power to do that to another person, to cause them so much sorrow over something so insignificant. How can Ulric get away with this? And not just get away with it but have the support of his entire nation behind him to do so?

I break away from my thoughts and look up to see Renan nearly asleep.

"Come on, Ren. You've barely eaten in days."

He sighs, then sits up and lifts the bowl. His lips mould lazily to its rim as he tips it up and swallows. The liquid drips down his chin, and he wipes it on his sleeve. When his bowl is half empty and he shows no sign of sipping the rest, I hold out my hand. He takes it, slips off the stool, and follows me downstairs.

I fold one of Mr. Elscott's bedsheets over Renan's mattress and tuck him into his cot.

Clutching his blanket, he nods off within seconds.

With a spare lantern found in the closet, I return upstairs to finish my own dinner.

Dad has fallen back asleep, still wearing his coat and winter pants. His empty bowl sits on the floor, and I take it to the sink.

I force myself to swallow my soup, and the unidentifiable vegetable chunks slosh down my throat. I sip until my stomach grows queasy, then wash it down with some water. After tidying our belongings spread across the floor, I stock the food in the cabinet and the supplies back in the bags. Afterward, I drape a blanket over Dad.

He and Ren are both asleep, but it can't be later than eight o'clock. My body aches from restless nights, but I can't sleep now. I must hold off the nightmares.

My leg surges with pain the longer I remain in the cabin's thawing warmth. Out here, in the middle of a forest with a broken, possibly infected limb, I can't afford to lose my leg. I need to be able to walk to perform basic tasks. And my leg won't heal quickly or properly if I keep using it.

So I retrieve my tool satchel and the dull axe and cut down a large, low branch from a nearby oak. The cloudy lantern illuminates my workspace behind the cabin as I use the axe to chop it into pieces, then slice off the bark. Starting with a square wedge of wood for the base, I nail an upright beam to it, about a foot high, then attach thinner segments out from the sides of the beam.

Hours pass as I work, the icy air dulling my pain. I shape and shift the wood, acquiring a few minor splinters along the way. When the base, leg, and supporting beams are connected firmly, I tear a strip from our extra bedsheet and fasten its ends to either side of the brace. The double-layered fabric acts as a sling, suspending my knee between the supporting beams and elevating my shin at an angle behind me. Another strip of fabric safeguards my leg from slipping out as I walk. Once the final adjustments are finished, I spend another hour sanding the contraption.

The silver moon glints off the horses' smooth coats and the river's flowing water.

The numbness in my mind retreats as images of Mom in that field flood back. Her face, pale in the moonlight. Her blood, glinting like the river…

With no one awake to take care of, no task to keep my thoughts quiet, the grief latches on, its hard knuckles rapping against my skull. I failed to avenge Mom by killing her killer. I let her murderer escape unharmed through the rolling fields, back to—

The farm.

I drop my sander on the ground as the awareness settles in.

Her murderer came from the farm's direction and retreated there as well. They followed us. They knew we were at Mr. Elscott's. Which means they know Mr. Elscott helped us escape, let us take the king's horses.

They'll kill him—if they haven't already. It won't matter if he denies the existence of God. He committed treason, and he'll pay for it greatly.

I lean back against the oak tree with its missing lower branch. Nauseated already from the soup, thoughts of Mr. Elscott chained in that execution room turn my stomach. All those peaceful mornings at the barn, all the light-humoured conversations with him weaken in memory. He saved our lives, but he was already dead from the minute we knocked on his door. It's our fault—my fault. I was the one to suggest we go to him for help in the first place.

My lethargic body shivers, begging for warmth and rest, and I no longer have the energy to protest.

When I lay down on my flimsy mattress in the basement, the memories come, and I can't stop them. I toss and turn, ultimately pitching my blanket that smells of Mr. Elscott's barn across the room.

As if that would shake the nightmares.

A TATTOO COVERS the exterior of Dad's left bicep. An anchor in black. Its chain curves from the top ring down behind the pointed flukes. Over the years, the ink has faded slightly, blending into his tan skin tone. And the lighter the anchor's edges fade, the sharper a thin cross symbol emerges along its midsection.

I stand over him, studying that anchor on his arm while he ignorantly snores the day away, and wonder if he meant for that cross to appear all along. Maybe he knew that the edges would fade to one day reveal a subtle symbol of his faith. He got it soon after he married Mom. After he stopped drinking, stopped hurting me. Though he never voiced what the symbol signified, he changed notably afterward. I think he got it as a reminder of his role as our family's leader. The tattoo summarizes his duties—or burdens—whatever he takes them as. Either way, he is our stability, our provider, and he does whatever it takes to protect us from the storm. He is our anchor.

Or…*was.*

For years, he successfully grounded us, provided for us, and kept us safe. But then he lost his job. And then his beliefs were exposed. And he has since reverted to the man he once was. Not in every way. But still…

In one sense, I pity him. For his inability to protect every member of his family when it mattered most. For losing the member that meant more to him than life itself. But part of me also blames him. For making enemies. Sure, it was bad— what Mr. Peterson did all those years ago—but Dad didn't have to beat him. He could've walked away, out of Mr. Peterson's life, and never have been troubled by him again. Nonetheless, he chose violence. And it cost him dearly.

Perhaps Dad blames himself too. Perhaps it's not only Mom's death that has kept him in that bed for three days straight, but also the knowledge that, had he acted differently, he could have prevented all of this.

I don't know. But until he figures out how to get up again, the crushing emotions will not win me over. Because if Dad can't be strong for Renan, I must be. Until Dad can pick himself up, I will assume his role as our anchor.

I have no choice but to do so. For Ren.

THE STOOL'S UNEVEN legs clunk the floor as Renan leans side to side, staring vacantly into the stove's flaming tendrils. The listless longing in his eyes for Mom's comfort deepens still. He only eats half of every meal I serve. Sometimes less.

Though he merely picks at his meals, our food supply shrinks faster than I had anticipated. Dad gorges himself, eating Renan's leftovers and raiding the cabinet through the night.

And the horses. I've moved them around the property, but they've grazed all the grass in sight. I will soon need to search for nearby pastures to keep them fed. Hopefully, I can convince Dad to move on from this place by tomorrow.

I've devoted all my time to my tasks. Chopping wood,

keeping the fire going, making meals. Washing clothes and sheets in the river, filling old buckets with river water for bathing, boiling water for drinking.

My handmade crutch has been an adjustment but a beneficial one. It keeps me off my leg yet still mobile while the injury heals. The pain worsens at night when I try to sleep, so I spend most of the pre-dawn hours outside, letting the cold numb the pain. I carve sticks into spears for future hunting and practice my knife-throwing skills of old to distract myself during those hours.

Today, when I try to sleep after making us all a breakfast of apple slices and buttered bread, my mind's shield of numbness washes away. The rickety cross over Mom's grave dances among the shadows of my closed eyelids. Then the image broadens to reveal another grave beside Mom's with an identical cross. However, the name is different. I look closer to read the engraved letters.

Renan Rutherford.

I lurch up from the mattress, panic gripping me. My hands shake as I stagger upstairs on my crutch.

Renan hugs his knees to his chest in front of the stove's dying fire.

He is safe. And safe he will stay.

I try to calm down, but this cabin is suffocating. I have to keep busy. Get out of my head.

I throw three more logs into the stove, then look back at Dad. Asleep, as always.

"Ren," I whisper. "I am going to be gone for a bit. An hour, maybe two."

"Why?" He stares at the fire.

"I've got to find grass for the horses." I think of Mr. Elscott, the pain he may be in for aiding our escape. Worse, he might already be dead. The least I can do is keep his beloved horses alive.

"Take me with you." Renan's wide jade eyes meet mine for the first time in days. I forgot just how much they resemble Mom's—they're the only part of him that proves he's her son.

Pressure swells behind my eyes, and I turn away.

"Please?" A hint of desperation enters his tone.

I clear a lump in my throat. "You know Dad would kill me if I let you come." I brush my fingers through his tangled curls. "I'll be back soon. Feed Dad if he wakes up before I'm back."

I fill one of the mesh sacks with a canteen of distilled river water, my blanket, the hunting knife, and one of my hand-carved spears. Then I dress in my winter apparel and head out. My knitted hat warms my ears as I hobble northwest through the forest, against the river's flow.

Leaves and needles smother every inch of the ground, and after hiking half an hour down a trail sparsely cleared of trees and branches, I've not found a single patch of grass. The ancient oaks trill, their branches thrashing in the sunshine.

The path narrows, and I trek deeper into the bushy terrain. The crutch snags on a hidden tree root, and I land on my hands and knees. My shin aches within the bone. I drag myself to the trunk of a pine tree, unfasten the crutch, and roll up my pant leg. This being the first time I've stopped to examine my leg in days, I halt mid-breath.

My boot bulges around the ankle. I press into the bloating leather, but there is no pain. I frown, then try wiggling my toes. They don't move. In fact, I can't even feel them. A tingling ache has persisted for days from the knee down, but I don't feel external pressure from the snug boot or the material of my sock. I untie my boot and poke at the cast, then wrap my hand around my swollen ankle and squeeze.

Nothing. It's completely numb.

When I get back I'll unwrap the cast to find out if it's cutting off my circulation. I didn't wrap it too tightly to begin with, but perhaps further inflammation has constricted blood flow. I take a swig of water from my canteen before standing up.

The midday sunlight casts an enchanting glow through the forest. Makes it seem as though these woods don't border a region of death. Nearby branches rustle as I bend to pick up my crutch. I squint toward a plump cedar tree with needles fluttering to the ground.

A twig snaps, and a masked soldier strides out from behind the tree.

My insides leap. I limp backward, reaching for the carved spear sticking from my bag.

Something hard strikes my spine.

I swipe my arm behind me, but a cold fist grips it.

Another soldier turns me around and thrusts me back against a tree. My throat constricts as he drives a blade to my neck. He presses himself against me, squeezing the breath from my lungs.

Both soldiers lift the tinted eyepieces of their helmets, towering over me.

"She's one of them," the man holding the knife to my neck says. "But not the one worth the reward."

Reward?

My vision blurs. Ulric has promised payment for our return. I should've expected as much.

"Tell us where your father is." The other soldier backs up,

flipping a dagger in his hand.

My chin shudders and my lungs quake. I shut my eyes, defenceless.

"How 'bout we make a deal." He throws the dagger, and it plunges into the tree's bark above my head. "You bring us to him, and we let you live."

I clench my fists. To betray my father is to betray my brother. And I cannot live knowing I sacrificed my brother's life to spare my own. I will not let Renan end up buried next to Mom.

"Let's get this over with, girl," he says. "We've already got one checked off the list."

"That's right, we saw the grave at the edge of the field," the other one jeers. "Pathetic."

Tears burn my eyes, and the blade slices my skin.

I'm sorry, Mom. I can't protect him. I'm sorry, Renan! I lied. I won't be back soon.

It stings, and warm liquid seeps down my neck. I thrust my chin upward, but the pain only intensifies. Black spots spread through my vision.

I can't fight. Can't breathe. Can't think.

Then the soldiers fall silent. And two shots explode, one after the other.

My hearing muffles as memories of Mom tumbling from the saddle resurface.

I hold my breath, waiting for the pain to register.

But the blade retracts from my skin instead, and the man's weight against my body regresses.

Both soldiers fall at my feet, hitting the ground hard.

Chapter 9

I limp away from the dying soldiers and shrivel to the base of another pine. Coughing for breath, I reach up to the blood seeping from the slanted incision in my neck. I didn't get away unscathed, but at least I got away.

My vision refocuses as I fill my lungs, and I half expect to see a gun pointed at my head.

Instead, a tall middle-aged woman with long grey dreadlocks stands calmly before me. A leather strap secures a rifle to her back, the tip of its barrel peeking over her shoulder.

My body trembles. I go to wipe my eyes, but turn my hands over to find blood staining my gloves. I jolt, struggling to pull them off and throw them away.

Images flash. Dad's stained jacket. My hands covered in Mom's blood.

The woman's eyes crease as she gives a sad smile. She must sense my panic because she kneels beside me and places a hand on my shoulder. Then opens her arms.

I'm taken aback. But such sincerity emanates from those deep, dark eyes. And her presence…it slowly expels my fear and sorrow, flowing with peaceful confidence unlike I've ever known. I let myself fall into her open arms.

This woman is a stranger. But somehow I feel I already know her. And that she cares for me deeply. She saved my life. I don't know why she did, but I know I can trust her for that.

I can't stop the tears as her embrace warms me, makes me feel safe. Loved, even. It's a soothing love that reminds me of Mom. But it's also a love unique to this woman.

When I finally loosen my grip around her, she examines the wound on my neck and gently touches my swollen leg. "Come with me, dear." Her voice is tender and silky. "I'll clean you up at my place."

I retrieve my bag and crutch, eager to be anywhere but here.

The blood-stained blade rests in the dead leaves beside the soldiers. My queasiness grows.

She tightens her arm around my back for support and leads me away from the soldiers. "My name's Susa."

"Rielle," I stammer.

She smiles, collects my gloves from the ground, and leads me through the brush. A thick-coated black horse waits for her on a hidden side trail. She ties my crutch and bag to the saddle, then mounts the horse and helps me up carefully behind her. I join my hands around her waist.

My heart rate slows, and I regain my strength during the hour-long ride. However, I'm still in desperate need of sleep. We trot around boulders, over hills, through rows of fir trees. Then a small wooden cottage comes into view within a secluded field.

Two bright-eyed children spot Susa from the front window. They squish their hands to the glass and push off. The front door bursts open, and the children, both maybe six years old, come bounding down the porch steps.

The little girl touches Susa's boot a split second before her brother. She then proceeds to bounce around and cheer like she just won a marathon, a front tooth missing from her gleeful grin. Her dark pixie-cut suits her petite yet outgoing manner.

The boy pouts for all of two seconds, then stands on his tiptoes, reaches up, and dangles from the horse's neck. He's got straight shoulder-length hair and the same brown eyes as his sister.

"Sue, Sue!" The girl taps Susa's leg. "Guess what Cree helped us make!"

"Well, I can smell peanut butter all the way out here. Hmm…cookies?" She arches a brow.

The girl giggles, nodding.

"They smell delicious!" Susa dismounts and helps me from the saddle before the children tackle her with hugs. Chuckling, she smacks a kiss on each of their foreheads. "These are my twins. Teagan"—she pats the girl's head—"and Talon." She slings an arm around the boy, pulling him closer. "And over there is their sister, Cree." She nods toward the cottage, where a girl around my age idles in the doorway.

Her children? Susa's complexion is fair, but their copper skin and high cheekbones suggest they're of Aboriginal descent. They may still be her biological children, but since they only call her *Sue* and not *Mom*, my guess is they're not blood related. Perhaps Susa adopted them.

Susa doesn't explain, and I don't ask. Instead, I focus on attaching the crutch to my leg.

"So what's your name?" the girl, Teagan, asks me. And after I tell her, she squats and runs her hand over my crutch as I adjust the fabric around my knee. "What's this for?"

"It helps me walk." Hopefully she won't ask me to elaborate.

"What happened to your leg—?"

"Kids," Susa cuts in, to my relief. "Please bring Rielle inside, help her get settled in the sitting room."

Her instructions distract the twins from my leg, and they each take one of my hands.

Susa winks at me. "I'll be right in. Just have to bring Selah to her stall." She leads the horse to the left of the field, where trees conceal a barn at the forest's edge.

I try to keep up as Talon and Teagan pull me up the porch steps and into the cottage. The older girl, Cree, holds the door open for me without meeting my eyes. She then zips toward the kitchen, her pleated skirt sweeping through the front foyer and around the corner.

My mouth waters at the smell of fresh peanut butter.

The twins tug me in the opposite direction, into a sunlit sitting room on the right. Large windows with tapered drapes frame the room, letting the sun illuminate it with a soothing glow. They set me down in a worn armchair, then bolt to the kitchen. Warm sunlight against my back, I detach my crutch and zip my coat over my neck so the children won't see the blood.

After minutes of hushed chatter, the little girl returns with both hands behind her back and a huge smile. She suppresses her giggling to ask, "You're not allergic to peanuts, right?"

I can't help but grin at her poor attempt to restrain her excitement. I shake my head.

From behind her back she pulls a plate piled with peanut butter cookies. The plate wobbles and one cookie falls to the carpeted floor.

I act amazed and take the plate gratefully. My stomach gurgles as I bite into a warm cookie. My taste buds dance. I didn't realize how hungry I was until now. "Mmm…" As the cookie melts in my mouth, I close my eyes and melt into the chair, emphasizing to Teagan how delicious her baking is. But I don't have to exaggerate much. After a week of eating the same plain food, this is bliss.

"I've already had three." A guilty grin on her face, she picks up the cookie that fell to the floor and takes a bite. "Don't tell Cree," she whispers, then stuffs the rest in her mouth.

I stifle a laugh and nod, swearing my oath to secrecy as Talon treads into the room with a full glass of orange juice. He hands it to me carefully, seemingly proud that he didn't spill. "We don't have much left, so we can only have one glass every week until Sue gets more on her trip. But you can have mine this week."

I smile, moved deeply by his generosity. "Thank you, Talon."

They both spew questions as I eat and drink. Where did I come from? Do I have a family? And why did Sue bring me here? I can't understand most of their babbling. Their voices grow louder with every question, each trying to overpower the other.

I open my mouth, assuming I'll have to yell above their voices to get a word in. But to my surprise, they silence themselves immediately, anticipating my response. "Well,"—I decide to answer their last question—"Susa brought me here because…she saved my life."

Their eyes widen. "Just like she did for us," Talon says to Teagan.

Their sister Cree appears in the doorway, clearing her throat. "Teagan, Talon, I think Sue might like some cookies when she comes in too."

The twins zip to the kitchen again.

Cree's long skirt flows as she leans against the doorway. She studies me with a hint of resentment. She looks like an older Teagan, but with longer hair and sharper eyes.

"I'm Rielle." I break the tense silence. "It's nice to meet you and the twins." I force a smile, though my neck stings with each word. "What did Talon mean when he said Susa saved—"

"Look," she interrupts. "I'm happy for you. I'm glad Sue was able to save you." She glances behind her as if to ensure the twins aren't eavesdropping. "But we don't need this."

"What do you mean?"

"I *mean*"—her almond-shaped eyes narrow—"that Sue is selfless. Sometimes too selfless for her own good. And if she saved your life, that means she put herself in danger to do it." She crosses her arms.

I shift awkwardly in the chair. "But she's fine."

"I know. But if you're out here, that means you're running from the law. And if you're running from the law, there will be soldiers searching for you—as I assume you realized today." She motions to the now-exposed slit on my neck. "And while searching for you, they might come across Sue instead. If she goes out hunting one day and doesn't come back..."—she eyes the floor solemnly—"we will have no one left."

"She's hiding from them too," I realize aloud. "What did she do?"

"We need Sue," Cree talks over me. "We haven't dealt with soldiers in years, but now that *you're* here... Just don't expect Sue to come to your rescue the next time you need saving."

I can understand what she means about losing the one who provides for her. But I can also read between the lines—she wishes Susa would've let me die today.

"I'm sorry that my survival is such a burden to you, but I didn't ask Susa to save me." I hold her stare. "She just did."

Cree's jaw hardens, her obvious spite growing. But then the front door opens, and she disappears down the hall.

I blink back tears of rage while the twins follow Susa into the sitting room. They surround her as she sits in the chair across from me. After presenting her a plate of cookies, they ask her if they can play outside, and Susa grants their request.

She watches them through the window as they race through the field, then studies my stiff expression. "Sorry if they overwhelmed you. I should've warned you they've been stuck inside since breakfast."

"Oh, no. It's not that." I wipe the agitation from my face. "The kids were great."

Cree drifts toward the front door, and Susa calls her over. "One thing before you go out, Cree. Could you bring my supplies, please?"

Cree nods, averting my gaze as she rushes away.

"Supplies?" I frown.

"Medical supplies," she clarifies. "There's another region just over a day's journey from here. I go once a month, trade summer crops for food I can't grow here, and sometimes barter for medical supplies. With those two munchkins, keeping stock is a must."

Oh, right. I shuffle in the chair. The whole reason she brought me here was to stitch my wound.

"Don't worry. I was a surgeon back in Kinborough." She stoops before me. "May I?" Before I can answer, she carefully unzips my coat to examine my neck.

"You lived in Kinborough?"

"Yes." She lifts my chin and turns my jaw side to side.

"Years ago."

"Why did you leave?" I ask to distract from the sting.

"Why did *you*?" She meets my gaze. "There's only one reason a person flees the region to hide out here. And it is for their faith."

"But the execution law was just decreed last week. Before then, it was only jail time."

"That might be true to the public's knowledge. But Ulric tried to sort and snuff us out under the radar for years. Until he realized we were greater in number than he'd predicted."

Cree's return ends our discussion. She dumps a large black bag and a wet cloth on the ground beside Susa. Before leaving, she glares at me.

"Thanks, dear." Susa looks between us as Cree marches out the cottage's front door. She unzips the medical bag, nodding to herself. "Whatever she said that upset you…don't take it personally. Cree means well. She's just protective. And afraid." She digs through the supplies and sets aside a gauze bandage. "She's got good reason for it though."

"What do you mean?" A hint of regret for my prior brashness forms.

"The kids aren't mine by blood. I just took them in when they had nowhere else to go." She dabs the cold, wet cloth over my neck to wipe the blood.

I wince.

"I used to be a doctor in the inner region. I was wealthy, had a family. But when my beliefs were discovered…it was all taken from me." Her lips thin as she dabs the wound with a numbing ointment. "I escaped before they could kill me." She threads a needle and begins stitching up the wound. "I came to blend in with the people here as I dealt with my grief. This region was thriving. But two years later, the bombs came. Many people got word beforehand and fled." She clears her throat. "I didn't, but still got to the woods in time. Found this secluded cottage for shelter. The following week, I rode out to check the damage. Along the way, I found a little girl carrying two squirming babies in her arms."

Cree and the twins.

"They were all skin and bones. Cree didn't speak for a year." Susa sighs. "The twins were only months old—they don't remember any of it. But Cree was ten. She lost her parents, her home…her life."

I swallow hard as she pulls the needle through. "So your real family…?"

"I lost them before I fled Kinborough." Her eyes glisten with tears, a deep well of grief momentarily exposed below their surface.

I let the silence draw on, fighting my own unsteady sea of emotion.

She ties off the suture and tapes a patch of gauze over the wound. "All done. The stitches should dissolve within a couple weeks. Now let's take a look at that leg of yours."

Thankful for the subject change, I roll my pant leg above my knee and slide off my boot.

Susa gives no indication of her thoughts as she lowers my foot in her lap. She observes the swelling and the gauze wrap. "When and how did it happen?"

I pause, not wanting to think back to that night. I decide to keep it brief. "About a week ago, a soldier slammed it in the door of a jail cell."

She nods with a fixated, professional expression. "Has it been this swollen for a while?"

"More so within the past few days. I realized today that I

can't move my toes anymore. And it's numb to the touch from the knee down."

She presses into my ankle. When I don't react, she says, "Mind if I unwrap it? If it's bound too tightly, it may be slowing the circulation, damaging the healing process."

She might as well. "I was going to remove it anyway for that same reason. It's numb to the touch, but it still hurts within the bone, and my ankle and foot usually tingle and burn."

She unwraps it and presses lightly into the bruises, careful not to touch the exposed gashes. "Does it keep you from sleeping?"

I nod. "The pain worsens at night."

"And the nightmares?"

I sense she's talking about more than just dreams from the physical trauma now. She means memories conjured from the stress of our escape—and she doesn't even know about Mom. "I haven't slept more than ten minutes at a time in days."

"I may have something to help you sleep. All-natural pills. They seem to work for Cree. I'll get them for you after." She turns my shin, observing the gashes on either side. "These don't look infected, but they're already scabbing over, which means it's too late to stitch them." She takes a needle and lightly pokes the skin. Then harder. "You don't feel that?"

I shake my head, relieved that I can't, but knowing by her forced calm expression that it isn't a good thing.

She gently bends my foot at the ankle. "Try moving your foot."

I try with all my might, but it only twitches inward slightly. "Did the break cause this? Or was it the swelling?" I try to block the tremble in my voice.

"I can't make a proper diagnosis without nerve tests. My hope is that when the bone heals properly and the swelling decreases, you'll slowly regain sensation and movement."

"But in your professional opinion?" I need the truth, no matter how bad.

"Only time can tell if the numbness will be a lasting effect. Without surgery, electrical tests, and monitoring by a team of medical experts, it is hard to imagine a complete recovery. The lack of sensation is either caused by the direct trauma, the compression of the swelling, or both. My guess is the tibial nerve has become obstructed."

"So you're saying the numbness—it might never leave?"

"It's a tricky situation. I can't say for sure until everything heals. But…yes, that is a possibility."

"And the pain? The tingling, the throbbing that keeps me awake all night?"

"The pain will likely decrease as the swelling does, and as the bone heals. But tingling, numbness, and burning sensations are all characteristics of tibial nerve dysfunction, and may be lasting effects." She takes my clammy hand. "Some people do recover fully though."

"And some don't." I choke back the emotion, unintentionally holding my breath until I feel lightheaded. All because of my useless leg. And because of Mom. Because of Dad's inability to function. Because of Renan's growing need for a comfort he can't have. And because I can't hold us all together.

Susa wraps my leg with new gauze, pressuring the break to straighten over time. "Focus on resting. Use your crutch like you've been doing. I do believe it's possible for you to have a full recovery."

I bring the back of my hand to my mouth, feeling my

mental shield deteriorate. Not here. Not in front of this kind woman I barely know. She shouldn't have to deal with my burdens. But as much as I try to keep strong, the words come spewing out.

"I can't do it! I can't win. Nothing I do matters. Now that they've killed my mother, my brother is the only reason I'm fighting to stay alive. But it seems the more I try to help him, the worse he gets. And now this leg…" Tears blur my vision, and I wish I could feel the sting of the stitches. Because feeling anything—even pain—would be better than this numbness.

"Oh, honey." Susa brushes my hair back from my face. "I'm so sorry. I can't imagine what it's been like for you." She hugs me as I sit frozen in her armchair. "But if the only thing sustaining you is your brother, you're going to fall short, no matter how much you love him. I've learned that the hard way." Her voice is wet. "The fulfilment you seek can only be found when you seek the same love that your mother found rest in. It's not easy, but it's possible. Just don't give up."

Though I'm not Susa's daughter, I feel like she loves me as one of her own children. I soak in the peace and sincerity of her comfort until my emotions are under control again. I don't want her to withdraw from the hug, but when the twins stumble through the front door, she hands me a tissue and retreats to the kitchen to get them some water.

They drink eagerly, panting for breath between gulps.

A sudden alarm overwhelms me, and I remember what I told Renan before I left. He must be terrified. "I have to go! I told my brother I'd be gone two hours at most." I jump to my feet and attach my crutch. My own panic, combined with my state of fatigue, makes me woozy when I walk.

Susa steadies me. "Relax. I'll bring you back. Just wait here a few minutes." I sit back down, and she leaves the room.

Minutes later, she returns with a large carton of eggs. "I've got hens out back and can bring your family more eggs every other week if you'd like. A bag of sleeping pills is inside. Take one or two half an hour before you sleep. They should help with the pain as well." She then hands me my gloves that had been soaked with blood earlier. They are now damp, cleansed of every stain.

I wish I didn't have to leave her haven of refuge. I long to bask in its peace, joy, and security for a while longer. But I must return to Renan. So I take the egg carton and cushion it with the blanket inside my bag. "Thank you, Susa." There is more depth to this thank-you than just appreciation for the eggs or the medical aid, and she knows it. It is a thank-you for saving my life.

Teagan and Talon hug me goodbye, oblivious to my distress.

Susa leaves the children with Cree, whom I wish to apologize to. But nothing I say can make the pain of her past more bearable. Instead, I simply offer an empathetic smile.

She doesn't smile back, but I assume that's because of her fear about Susa leaving again.

After she kisses her children, Susa and I begin our hour journey back to Renan.

Chapter 10

Susa seems to know every foot of this forest. When I mention the little old cabin, she knows exactly where it is. She finds the rushing river, and we follow it until I recognize the area where the soldiers attacked me.

And then I remember the whole reason why the soldiers found me in the first place. "Susa, would you happen to know of any nearby pastures?"

She ponders the question. "I believe there's a small meadow about a mile northeast from your cabin." She points through the trees beside us.

Figures. I travelled west…

I suppress a sigh and thank her for the information.

I'm too drowsy to stop myself from daydreaming along the journey. Thankfully, the thoughts are peaceful. I keep the events at Susa's cottage fresh in mind. But curiosity gnaws inside as I wonder why Susa has been so kind to me—a stranger who will never be able to repay her.

RENAN SPRINTS THROUGH the cabin's front door and traps me in a hug as soon as my feet hit the ground. "Where were you?" He trembles against me.

I squeeze him tighter. "I'm so sorry, Ren." Pulling away

for a moment, I turn my attention to Susa. "Thank you…for everything."

She shakes her head as if it were nothing.

Dad eyes Susa warily from the doorway before approaching.

Susa dismounts and introduces herself, then takes Dad aside to, I assume, explain all that happened.

Great. I'm never gonna live this down.

Dad then returns to the cabin, rubbing the back of his neck, and I tell Renan to go wait inside a minute.

Susa mounts her horse but studies me and loosens her hold on the reins. "What's wrong, dear?"

"Nothing. I-I'm just trying to understand." I pause to gather my words. "Why would you risk your life for a stranger? You didn't owe me anything. And I have nothing to repay you."

"Doesn't that make it all the more meaningful?" She arches a brow. "Helping someone just because you know them, or because you owe them or want something in return, that's not what I'm about. I know no one is perfect, and no one deserves a second chance. Nonetheless, love made a way." She throws her messy dreads over her shoulder. "I saved you because I've been in your position before, and I'm only alive today because a stranger saved me when I didn't think I deserved to be saved. It's because *he* showed me love and mercy that I can do the same for others."

I mull over her words.

No one deserves a second chance. Nonetheless, love made a way…

When she fades from view, my smile falters and I retreat to the cabin. Though shuddering from the cold, I don't stop by the fire-lit stove. In the basement, I throw my jacket to the floor, toss my crutch aside, and curl up on my mattress.

Closing my eyes, I try to reflect on Susa's words, the twins' bright faces, and the bliss of the time spent at her cottage. But I can only envision that soldier pinning me to the tree, slicing my neck with his knife.

The floorboards groan as Dad clomps down the stairs and towers over me. "From now on, you will stay within the borders of this property, and you will tell me before you go out each time." He is furious. "We searched for hours, Rielle. Renan was worried sick." The hanging lantern casts his broad-shouldered shadow over me. "You nearly gave us away today."

I scoff because he doesn't know me at all. He doesn't know that I was prepared to die to keep this location a secret. "I need to get the horses to a pasture."

"It's not worth risking our safety."

My head throbs, and I sit up. "Mr. Elscott is probably suffering because of us. He might already be dead. He didn't have to help us, but he did. I have to take care of his horses."

"No, you don't."

"So you want me to let them starve?"

"I will bring them to the pasture when the time is right," he says, trudging back upstairs.

I don't believe a word.

On my side again with my aching leg stretched out, I pull the blanket over my head.

Like an anchor, the weight of the day casts me deeper into darkness. It feels as if I'm drowning to keep my family afloat. Unable to avoid sleep any longer, I doze off before sundown, wondering how soon before I hit rock bottom.

THE SOLDIER PINS me to the pine tree and thrusts the knife to my neck. He lifts his eyepiece as I fight for breath. But instead of the soldier's face, it is Dad's. His unshaven jaw. Crazed eyes. Sour breath. And then we are no longer in the forest but back in my childhood house. I'm six years old. The lantern illuminates our kitchen after midnight. After Dad came home from the bar. After he hit me for having been sick at school that afternoon. "I had to leave in the middle of my shift to take you home! If it weren't for you, I wouldn't have lost my job today!" he yells, taking another swing at me—

I burst awake, up on my elbows. My blanket has been tossed from my body. But Renan's blanket has replaced my own, and it is toasty warm on my skin.

Hunched on his cot, Ren dangles his feet. "I heated mine for you in front of the stove," he says. "You were shivering."

No doubt, Renan witnessed my reaction to the nightmare, but I muster a smile anyway. "How long was I asleep?"

He shrugs. "Couple hours."

Better than before. Maybe I won't need Susa's pills.

He meanders to the closet door under the staircase and returns with arms full of old crème-coloured candles. After arranging ten on the floor beside my mattress, all shapes and sizes, he strikes a match to light one candle, then carefully uses that candle to light the rest.

The room brightens with their soft glow.

I settle back down, observing them.

Ren slides a chair beneath the hanging lantern and stands on it to blow out the flame. He then slumps on the floor beyond the sea of candles. "They'll help you sleep," he says.

My lips tug into a half smile as I remember all those nights back home when I'd light candles to help Renan fall asleep. Now he's the one burning them to chase away *my* nightmares.

The dancing flames engage him, yet his eyes fail to hide his inner turmoil.

I sit up and lean back against the side of his cot. He takes my hand and steps around the candles to sit beside me on my thin mattress. I cloak his blanket around us and pull him closer. Together, we watch the spits of fire eat away at the wicks.

The candles rouse memories of our old life. Of all we lost. Grief brims within me, and I hold my breath to contain it.

But then Renan looks up at me with those wide jade eyes. All I see is Mom.

I pull my hat from my head and press it over my mouth. The pain rattling me to my core, I take a sharp breath. My mental shield cracks. And I mourn the loss of Mom, the irreparable hole it has left in our family. It crushes me. I wish Renan didn't have to see me cry. As his anchor, I am supposed to protect him from this sorrow. Not drag him into it.

Ren lays his head against my shoulder, now crying silent tears. I scold myself for failing to contain my grief. But then I study him further. And over time, his look of longing seems to fade, replaced with a soothed serenity.

Was this all he needed? Was that craving for Mom's comfort really a longing for mine? For someone to share his grief and mourn with him?

The weight on my shoulders recedes as I realize he doesn't need me to prevent or suppress the pain. He just needs me to be with him through it. And I, him. In this moment, I feel closer to Ren than ever before. Perhaps I needed this as much as he did. Because the loss of Mom is agonizing, and nothing will ever change that. However, having him here makes me feel a little less alone.

Hours pass before he blows the candles out and curls up on his cot.

This time, I sleep straight through the night.

"COME ON, REE. Wake up." Renan shakes my shoulder.

I rub my eyes and squint up at his annoyed expression.

"Well, finally." He rolls his eyes and grabs my wrist, tugs me up to sit on his cot.

"What is it?" I stretch the kink from my neck, blinking my vision into focus.

He pulls a plate from the floor and sets it on my lap.

I stare down at the steaming mound of scrambled eggs and buttered bread on the side. "You made this for me?"

He nods and sits beside me with a plate of his own. He begins inhaling his eggs, then stops and meets my suspicious look with a smile—the first smile from him in over a week.

Astounded at the complete change in his demeanor, I return a grin. Our mourning together seems to have done more good than I thought possible. Freed him from his daze of yearning for comfort, at least for now.

Too hungry to figure it all out, I shovel scrambled eggs onto the bread and take a bite. Half of my breakfast is gone before I pause, mouth full. "Can you tell I've missed this?"

He offers a half grin, then looks down. "I was wondering if I could ask you a favour."

"Aha!" I dip my finger into a blob of butter on my bread. "So this whole thing you've done here—feeding me, keeping me warm and happy—was all just to *butter* me up." I dab the butter on the tip of his nose, and he giggles. I beam with satisfaction, only having made the lame joke to hear him laugh.

He wipes his nose on his sleeve and his laughter fades.

"Since I lost my dove back home…would you make me another one?"

Oh. I hadn't expected that. Hadn't even realized he didn't have it with him.

"I'd love to." A new task would be a great way to occupy my time. "And maybe if you find me something for a chain, this time I'll make it into a necklace so you can keep it close."

His eyes light up. "I'll start looking." He takes our empty plates and sprints upstairs.

DAD WATCHES ME through the window as I search the property for wood to carve Renan's dove. I didn't mean to wake him, but the door's hinge creaked on my way out. Now he's taken to his duty of ensuring I don't run off again.

Winding the black shoelace Ren found for a chain through my fingers, I locate a huge butternut tree—a species I've only ever seen pictures of, as they aren't native to Kinborough. I've heard their wood is stunning to carve.

I heard right. After chopping off a lower limb, I shred the bark away to reveal its beautiful, rich colour and distinct grain. Perfect for carving the dove's soft yet striking features. I collect a small block of the butternut wood, then decide to rinse my hair in the river before beginning the carving. I finger-brush my frozen hair and braid it down my back to keep it out of my face.

Meanwhile, Sinta and Bandit hunt for grass near the river. They can't go much longer without food.

I hadn't anticipated us settling here this long. It's been five days since we found the cabin. Dad says we'll only stay one more night. For our safety, I hope he keeps his word.

MY HAND CRAMPS, and I set the roughly shaped dove on the desk. Renan hasn't taken his eyes off the wooden block for over an hour, but when I stop to massage my palm, he returns upstairs to get a snack for lunch.

I eventually resume carving, but an unshakable restlessness builds within me. I can't help feeling trapped. Isolated. By both my mind and this cabin. Carving isn't transporting me from my thoughts as it typically does. The cabin is more suffocating than ever.

Anger grips me, regurgitating images of Mom's grave, of that rickety cross plunging into its soil.

I drop my chisel on the desk.

Unlike Susa's cottage, this cabin enhances my grief and anxieties. I can't take it any longer.

"BUT DAD SAID *he* would do that." Renan's tone wavers.

"Trust me,"—I sling the mesh sack over my shoulder—"he's not getting out of that bed anytime soon."

Dad's arm dangles over the mattress as he snores, a permanent scowl on his face.

"Stay here." I press a kiss to Ren's forehead. "I'll be back in an hour or two."

He wipes his forehead with his sleeve and crosses his arms. "That's what you said yesterday."

I pull my hat over my braided hair and zip up my coat, ignoring Ren's painful remark. "If Dad wakes up, tell him I'm downstairs carving. He won't care enough to check."

Ren nods slowly at the floor, biting his lip.

I attach Mr. Elscott's serrated knife to my belt and shut

the door quietly behind me.

Clouds sheet the sky in a murky mist. My breath fogs as I lead the horses down a tight trail in the direction Susa pointed me. I lift my crutch high with each step, careful to avoid another tree-root collision like yesterday.

The rope tautens as the horses halt behind me. The wind howls, and their ears twitch.

Unless the weather improves overnight, I doubt we'll be leaving the cabin tomorrow. I lift my collar over my nose and tug the rope, ordering the horses to follow.

Then the wind quiets enough to hear twigs snap behind us. And footsteps. Footsteps sprinting after us.

I turn my head, and the stitched incision on my neck stings—a painful reminder of what happened the last time I heard footsteps in the woods. My heart pounds as I fumble with my belt and retrieve my knife. I plant myself between the horses, wielding the weapon, confident from recent practice the damage I can cause with a flick of my wrist.

The footsteps draw closer.

I raise the knife over my shoulder.

And Renan comes trampling through sheets of vines and needles.

I freeze and my adrenaline wanes. "Renan, what the…?" I release a breath. "What are you doing out here? I could've killed you." I lower the knife to my side.

He treads toward me, apparently undaunted by the fact that I nearly impaled him. "Last time, I thought you were dead. This time, I'm making sure you come back."

"You didn't even ask to come with me."

He shrugs. "I knew you'd say no."

I roll my eyes. "You're right about that. You can't be out here, Ren." I steer the horses back down the path we came from and grab Renan's hand. "Come on, I'm taking you back."

"No." He pulls away. "Please let me come. I can't stay there anymore. I hate that cabin." He locks his eyes on mine.

I lower my gaze.

He hates it there as much as I do.

Finally, I look him over. His coat is much too thin for this biting wind. I open my bag attached to Sinta's saddle. "Here," I sigh, pulling out my blanket. "You'll need this if you want to last out here."

He beams, pulling the blanket around his shoulders.

I study him closely on our half-hour journey to the pasture. How has he changed so much since yesterday? I know there's more to it than I could've done in one night of grieving with him. There is such a peace to him now, and though he is clearly still struggling with his grief of losing Mom, I glimpse something else there too...

Hope.

I don't know where it came from, but I'm relieved he's found something to pull him through the storm. Because, as I've learned, I sure can't.

"So...what's this about?" I shuffle his hair. "Since last night, you're different."

He tilts his head to squint up at me. "Different?"

I duck under droopy pine branches. "For so long you were in a daze, not talking. But now you seem calm, happy even—which is good...just different. What changed?"

He steps in time with my slow hobble. "Last night...I remembered something."

"Remembered what?"

"That we're going to be okay."

I slow. "How do you know that?"

"Remember how, when we were in jail…we weren't together?"

I nod.

"I was alone in the dark. I couldn't see anything. I was scared, so I shut my eyes. But when I opened them again, I could see." His eyes gleam. "There were three candles on the floor around me, and a man sitting beside me. He didn't say anything, but I knew he was nice because he made the fear leave. He let me sit with him, and I fell asleep in his lap. He was gone when the soldier came to get me. But he made me safe—God did. So that's why I know we will be okay."

A shudder creeps across my shoulders as I envision that night in the jail cell. I had prayed to God that Renan wouldn't sleep alone in the dark. Now Renan is saying that God sent someone to…

How is that possible? God isn't real. If he were, he would've saved Mom. "That couldn't have happened." I bind the horses' rope around my wrist. "It's impossible."

He stiffens. "But I remember—"

"How did that man get in there? Did you see him open the door?"

"No, he was there when I opened my eyes."

I purse my lips, pitying his innocence. "I'm glad you weren't scared that night. But it had to be a dream. Things like that…they don't happen in reality. I'm sorry."

"You don't believe me?" He halts in his tracks. "I know it was real."

I stop at a field of long, wispy grass—just where Susa said it would be. "It's not that I don't believe you, Ren, I just… You probably fell asleep."

"It wasn't a dream!" His voice strains, then his face goes blank. "Wait…if you don't believe me, that means you don't believe Mom either." His eyes search mine, filled with dread. "Do you even believe in God?"

I hold his stare, scared to say no. Why does this matter to him? What is he getting at? Eventually, I shake my head.

His eyes narrow. "So when I asked if it was true that people could come back to life after they're dead, you said no just because you don't believe in God?"

I open my mouth.

"I thought you believed. You said nothing would happen if I prayed. But you didn't even know." Anger ripples through his small frame, so much like Dad, it's terrifying. He paces toward me. "This is all your fault. I could've tried! I could've prayed. Then maybe she would be here still."

I step back.

I know what he's saying isn't true, because God's not real. But to Renan, God *is* real, which is what makes his accusation such a slap to the face. "Ren, that's not true—"

"Stop!" His expression hardens, and he turns down the path through the forest.

"Where are you going?" I call after him.

"Back!" he yells, speeding up. The blanket flaps like a cape attached to his shoulders.

"Renan, wait!" I fasten the horses' rope to a low oak branch near the pond in the pasture, then chase after him with my uncooperative crutch.

He swerves right. Ducks under branches. Disappears down a trail of dense cedars.

"That's the wrong trail!" My crutch wobbles as I attempt to run. I stumble over brush. "Come back!"

He slips out of sight, and the screeching wind smothers any sound of him. Trees overrun the trail as I trek deeper. Roots and vines tangle around my crutch and trip me.

"Please, Ren! I'm sorry."

I push myself up, watching the trees ahead for signs of him. But the breeze sends every branch and bush thrashing, making it impossible to tell his movement apart from the wind's.

I wait, unable to move farther through the forest without snagging my crutch. My throat tightens, and my leg aches. "Renan?" I call repeatedly until my voice is but a croak amid the shrieking breeze.

Chapter 11

I burst through the cabin door.

Dad startles awake. "Rielle?"

I stumble over my crutch and catch myself on the counter. My whole body trembles, running solely on adrenaline. I scan the main level, and the terror sinks in.

He didn't make it back.

After descending the stairs, I search the basement. Under his cot, inside the closet. I bustle back upstairs, breathless. "No, this can't—"

"What were you doing outside?" Dad demands as he sits up in bed.

I grasp the doorpost for support. "Come! Please. Help me."

He jumps to his feet. "Where's Renan?"

"I'm sorry. I'm sorry." Tears blur my vision. "Ren—he's out there!"

"He's gone?" Alarm crosses his face, the first glimpse of emotion I've seen from him in days.

Bile rises in my throat, and I cover my mouth with my sleeve.

"Rielle." Dad clutches my wrists to make me look him in the eye. "What happened?"

I tense. "I took—I took the horses to the field. And he

followed." I take a gulp of air. "I didn't know. But then he ran the wrong way. I couldn't get to him."

"I told you to stay inside. I said I'd take care of the horses—"

"But you weren't!" I wrench my wrists free. "I knew you wouldn't. So I knew I had to. But I didn't know he'd follow me."

"Why didn't you bring him back?"

I strike the doorframe with the side of my fist. "Because he was as sick of this place as I was!"

"This *place*"—Dad points to the floor, fuming—"is the only thing keeping us alive."

"Well, I'd rather die now than rot here the rest of my life."

He storms out the front door, breaking off our argument. "First her, now him," he mutters to himself. He brings a hand to his mouth, and his fingers muffle his words. "Why couldn't you just let her...?" His hand falls to his side.

"What?" I limp out after him. "Just let her...what?" This isn't even about Renan anymore. "What are you talking about?" I plant myself in front of him. "Who's *her*?"

He glares at me, eyes narrowing.

I know that look of accusation all too well.

Chills trickle down my spine.

Her.

I bite my lip, taste blood. "You aren't just talking about Renan." I step back. "You mean Mom. You blame me for her too, don't you? You think it's my fault she died."

His jaw flexes. "Why must you always be so independent? So stubborn?" A vein bulges in his forehead. "You were injured. You knew you couldn't ride well. But you insisted. To prove...what? That you're tough?" He tightens his fists.

"Why couldn't you just let her ride? For once in your life, why couldn't you let someone help you? We could've *all* got away if it weren't for you."

I stare vacantly at the nearby rushing river, thoughts clouding my mind like my breath clouds the air. First Renan blames Mom's death on me for an illogical reason. That was hard but bearable. But now Dad is pinning her death on me for a completely logical reason.

My eyes burn. I steady the tremor in my tone long enough to say, "If it weren't for my independence, my stubbornness, we would all be dead. I've been slaving away, ignoring my own needs, while you do nothing but sleep. I've kept this family together. I have anchored us."

Dad's eyes flash with perception at my last few words.

My stomach knots. All I want is to get away from him. To find Renan.

Downstairs, I throw Ren's blanket and all my belongings into the mesh sack. When rolled up, my mattress has straps to wear over my shoulders like a backpack. I put on an extra pair of socks and slip back into my boots.

In the kitchen, I swipe a loaf of bread, half a brick of butter, six cans of soup, twelve apples, twelve potatoes, the can opener, the roll of tinfoil, the first-aid kit, two water canteens—one for me and one for Ren—and the carton of eggs from Susa. This leaves Dad with enough food for a week, maybe. He should be grateful I'm leaving him anything. I shove my braided hair inside my coat, pull the zipper over my chin, and storm out the door.

"Where are you going?" Dad grabs my shoulder.

"What do you care? You should be glad to see me go."

"I'm coming with you to find him. You can't survive on your own."

"Watch me." I shrug his hand off.

I hate the fact that when I look at him, I'm transported back in time, to before he met Mom. It's as if the last nine years of my life never happened. And it terrifies me.

I was wrong at Mom's burial. Renan doesn't need Dad in his life.

"You're not coming. When I find him, I'll be better off without having to take care of you too. Frankly, I'd be glad to never see you again." I hold my stare until he looks away.

Instead of angry, he seems hurt.

Like I care, after everything he just blamed me for. I turn away.

In his shock, he lets me leave.

FOR HOURS, I search the trails where Ren initially went missing. I follow every possible lead, imagining where I'd go if I were him. He has my blanket, thankfully, but it won't provide the warmth he needs to survive even a night out here. And though he knows how to build a fire, he doesn't have any matches to light it. Every faint boot print, every rustle of leaves gets my hopes up, only to slam me into a stupor of denial when the trail dies.

He is here, somewhere. I will find him.

Unfocused, I walk into a sharp branch. It slashes my cheek, but the icy air numbs my skin enough that the pain barely registers. The trees grow denser. Shrubs and vines fill any void the trees do not occupy.

By the time the sky begins to darken, I come across heaps of rocks and boulders that lead up the side of a small mountain, threatening to tumble down with every forceful shove of the wind. I hike around the mountain's base, observing every bit of every boulder.

Perhaps he found a small cavern to escape the cold.

"Renan?" I call into a cave that looks to be on the verge of collapsing. It echoes my voice back to me. Even if he's still mad at me, I know he'd respond if he were here. But there's no answer. Two other caves give the same result.

As daylight dwindles, I resign my search to collect my bearings. Conceal myself out of the wind's reach in a tight, vertical crevice of the eastern mountainside. Build a small fire to regain sensation in my fingers.

My limbs feel detached from my body, and my head throbs.

I slide down the rock wall, wrapping Ren's blanket around my body.

Since the day Mom married Dad, I've put myself through the torture of imagining what it would be like to lose her. I always knew that it could very well happen. But Renan? From the time he was born, he was someone safe. Someone I could love without fearing he might be taken from me.

Now I've lost them both.

And Dad blames me. Not only for losing Ren. For Mom too. How can he put this on me as if I wanted it to happen? Mom was the one person I truly trusted. I didn't want any of this.

It's not my fault.

But why did I refuse to let her ride? I should have been behind her on that horse. If I were, we'd probably all be together now because she wouldn't have slowed us down like I did. And even if we still weren't fast enough to outride the one who shot her, *I* would've been the one hit. If I rode pillion, I would've died in her place. Why couldn't I have let her ride?

It *is* my fault.

I untie my crutch and throw it into the stone wall. It crashes but remains intact.

The wind hollers beyond the crevice, and with it comes the first real snowfall of the season. White flecks whip by. Unlike a typically light first snowfall, these icy pellets could be blasted from a gun and survive to pierce their target. The temperature continues to plummet, sending an endless chill through my veins.

I can't give up on Renan, but I can't risk getting myself hurt or further lost by searching in the dark.

Unlike a cave, this crevice doesn't have a roof. Perhaps Ren will see the smoke from my fire and follow it here. Yes. That is my only hope now.

As hard as it is, I stay put. I unroll my mattress, lean back against the crevice's wall, and continue carving Renan's dove in the firelight.

Soon enough, an irrepressible shudder overtakes my body. I unweave my braided hair and tuck it around my neck for insulation. The cold numbs my fingers, making it difficult to carve more than two minutes at a time. I ultimately resign. Curl up on my mattress, feet warming by the fire.

The icy air subdues my thoughts and drives me to sleep within minutes.

I JERK AWAKE and scour the darkness. Above, drifting clouds blot out the moon. A thin layer of snow laces the ground beyond the crevice.

Renan hasn't come.

I revive the fire, then lay back down on my mattress and glare at the hazy moon. Unable to think or process the fact he hasn't found me, I retreat into myself. Uncaring. Incapable of feeling anything, physically or emotionally. Why should I want to? It's not like I have any reason to be alive anymore.

She's gone. He's gone. My home is gone. The man who was once my father is a stranger to me. I have nothing left.

I raise my injured leg and slam it back down, sending a blast of pain through the bone. I hate this useless leg. It's the reason I couldn't follow Renan.

I hate my father for blaming me for Mom's death…and for being right. I also hate him for making enemies.

I hate Mr. Peterson for selling us out.

I hate Foster for not informing me of his father's plans.

I hate Mom's misguided faith in God.

I hate King Ulric for creating the horrific law to kill her kind in the first place.

But most of all, I hate myself. For letting my stubbornness prevent Mom from riding.

I imagine myself back in that execution room, chained to the wall. The slave with sweaty hair and a crooked scar on his chin aims his gun at me. And inside, I beg him to shoot. Oh, that he'd pull the trigger on me. That way, all of this would have been over before it began.

I used to be afraid of dying. Now death is becoming more and more appealing.

I scrape the ground with frozen fingers. Over and over, until my fingernails seep with blood.

I don't belong here. I am not worthy of this life.

I deserve death.

My emotions are spent. I can't cry. Numbness devours me, both physically and mentally. And that is worse than being able to feel the pain. I wish the life would just leave my body. Then it would be over and—

I sit up.

The pills.

I dig through my bag, pull out the egg carton. Eight eggs remain inside, and in one of the empty cups is a paper bag containing ten sleeping pills.

Susa said they are all natural. But surely, ten taken at once would get the job done. I'd simply slip into a deep slumber and let the pills, combined with the cold weather, sweep me away.

I pour the pills into my palm and open my water canteen, staring at the thumbnail-sized capsules. Even considering such an action brings shame. It's one thing to wish past events would've ended differently, because when something or someone else kills you, it is out of your immediate control. But to purposely inflict death upon yourself…

It's entirely your choice.

The guilt grows. But I deserve this. Like Susa said, no one deserves a second chance.

Hand shaking, I bring the pills to my lips.

Just get it over with. My chin quivers, and I look away.

Just one more day. Just one more. Love made a way. The words make themselves prominent in my mind, though I can't pinpoint where they came from. But they somehow bring a shred of relief.

I drop my hand into my lap.

I can't do it.

Ren could still be alive. Still be waiting for me.

I slip the pills back into the paper bag, then stuff the bag inside the carton.

I won't do it.

And that's just it…I won't do anything.

I won't take my life, nor will I do anything to sustain it. I won't eat or drink. I won't keep warm. And if I happen to fall asleep and the fire happens to go out, and I happen to freeze and not wake up… Then I will accept my fate.

THE RISING SUN'S rays on my face drag me from sleep. Light floods the mountain crevice, its warmth trained on my body, making my nose and ears tingle.

I exhale and struggle to sit up. My vision warps, and I blink rapidly. Black spots dissolve the sunny sky, then fade as I regain awareness. My surroundings tilt and whirl.

The wind's howl pierces my ears. Then there's another sound, faint amid the violent breeze. But still there.

My ears tune out and back in. Crunching stones? The wind regresses, and I hear it again. My limbs itch, burn, and shiver all at once. My arms move as I want them to, but I can barely feel them.

The crunching again. Footsteps?

I grasp at a rut in the rock wall, pulling myself up. My legs support me, though I'm not even using my crutch to stand. Why can't I feel the pain? It's as if I'm watching my own body from the sidelines. I stagger forward and catch myself on a boulder to my right. My ears ring. A wave of nausea overwhelms me as I keep my head upright.

Why is everything spinning?

Crunch. The footsteps approach.

My purple-tipped fingers remove the hunting knife from my belt loop. The blade shakes as intensely as I do. Its metal reflects the sun in my eyes, and I stumble backward.

Crunch. Crunch. Who could it be? A soldier? Dad? …Ren?

Clinging to the rock wall, I turn the corner. The wind

knocks the breath from my lungs.

The crunching halts, and a masked soldier jerks backward.

I freeze. My eyes rest on his belt, a gun holstered on either side.

I should've taken the pills when I had the chance. Why'd I have to be such a coward? If he's going to kill me, he better get it over with quickly.

"Geez, you scared me!" the man snaps, mouth tense below his tinted eyepiece.

My adrenaline gives way to fatigue as black spots blur my vision. The ringing returns to my ears, and control of my movements slips away.

"Hey, I remember you—" His voice cuts out.

I watch the knife slip from my hand.

The soldier lurches forward as my legs give out. Catches me before I hit the ground. "What's happening?" Concern thickens his tone. He brushes his hand over my forehead, then pats my cheek. "Stay awake. Stay awake!"

Chapter 12

His black mask hovers inches from my face when I awake.

I try to scramble back, but my limbs give out on me.

"Easy." The soldier presses my shoulders back to the mattress beneath me and tucks my blanket around me.

A fire burns in the pit I made last night. Everything's blurry. Everything aches and burns and tingles. My heart races at having this soldier so close.

"Get…get away from me." I push at his arm, but he doesn't budge.

"No, don't move. You're hypothermic. Eighty-eight degrees Fahrenheit. Your temperature's improving, but still not good." He grabs my arms as I swing at him, and pulls off my knitted gloves. "Just stay still, don't waste energy. The fire's helping." He then slips my hands into his own thick, warm gloves.

What? He's helping me?

Though I shiver uncontrollably, my body is burning up. I pull off the gloves and fumble with my jacket's zipper.

"No, leave everything on." The soldier grabs my hands and slips his gloves back on them. Is this his chosen form of torture? Forcing me to wear heaps of clothing and blankets until I overheat—?

Wait. The scar. That crooked white scar on his chin…

He is no soldier.

"Take off—take off the mask."

"What? Oh." He lifts the helmet off his head. "Sorry, forgot I had it on." He brushes sweaty brown bangs from his forehead.

The slave. He's alive? How did he escape? I think back. What did he say his name was? "Ezra?"

His lips part slightly. "You remember. That's good, I guess. No brain damage." He retreats to add kindling to the fire, and I notice he's only wearing socks on his feet. Then I look down to see huge black boots on my own feet.

I sigh. Should've taken those pills. I wasn't supposed to live this long. And by the looks of it, Ezra's going to do everything in his power to make sure I return to full health.

Why'd it have to be him? He's ruined my plan. I was supposed to let the cold take me. By now, Renan's likely gone. Dead. Therefore, I have no reason to be alive.

My body thaws through the hours. I cringe as my limbs burn and throb, and the persistent headache eventually sends me to sleep.

"DINNER'S READY."

I wake to Ezra sitting beside me, his back against the wall. He sets a can of my soup between us.

"I never said you c-could go through my stuff." I glance at where my can opener, matchbox, and first-aid kit rest on the ground near my open bag. "I don't even know you."

He winces. "Maybe you *do* have some brain damage after all. I mean, to forget the guy who saved your life. Twice. That hypothermia must've done a real number on you." He smirks, then exchanges his playful look for one more serious. "It's been maybe eight hours since I first bundled you up. Your temperature's up to ninety-three. Honestly, it's a wonder you bounced back so fast, and without so much as losing a finger. You were so cold when you first passed out, I thought maybe your heart stopped. But now"—his lips curl into a side smile—"I think you'll live."

"When did you take my temperature?"

He huffs a laugh. "I learned from my first attempt to wait till you were fully asleep."

"First attempt?" I stare at him.

He lifts a brow. "You don't remember?"

I shake my head.

"Well, you *were* pretty out of it at the time, babbling nonsense. Still put up quite the fight though. Gave me this"—he tilts his head sideways to reveal a red bruise along his stubbly jawline. "Don't worry about it. I'm just the guy keeping you alive is all." He chuckles. "But I can't guarantee there'll be no retaliation if you're just as stubborn when fully conscious."

I stare into the fire, not appreciating his regular reminders that I'm indebted to him. Though I only caught a glimpse of his nature long ago in the execution room, he seems like a completely different person. His light, flippant side is so foreign to me. Not to mention annoying.

"Seriously though, you should eat something." He nods at the steaming soup can. "It'll help you warm up."

I swore to myself I wouldn't eat. I wanted the hunger, combined with dehydration and the cold, to end my life. But if I don't eat, he'll catch on as to why. And he wouldn't understand. He'd only ridicule me for wanting to end my life when he so clearly loves his own.

Looks like the choice has been made for me. I sit up, remove Ezra's oversized gloves from my hands, and take the dented can. It warms my palms but stings the scrapes on my fingertips. My lips curl around the metal rim, and the salty liquid floods my mouth.

Ezra looks relieved when I've downed half the can. He busies himself with searching my bag—again without my permission. "What's this?" He lifts out Ren's unfinished dove carving.

My stomach churns.

"Did you make this?" He leans closer to me, trying to catch my gaze.

I focus on sipping my soup.

"It looks like a bird, so far." He turns it over in his palm. "Amazing."

I glance back at it and my gaze falters.

Ezra goes quiet and carefully returns it to the sack.

Once I've consumed as much as my stomach can handle, I set the can down beside me.

"All done?" Ezra eyes the can longingly, like a hungry dog drooling over forbidden food.

"You can have the rest." I lie on my side.

Surprised, he lifts the can to his nose and takes a whiff. "Smells delicious."

"It's not."

He takes a sip and swallows. "I've had worse."

I shut my eyes, back turned to him.

He stops to burp. "So much better than the beans and rice," he says to himself before downing the remaining soup.

I shuffle farther from him, begging myself to fall asleep. I don't want Ezra here. I never wanted him to save me. It should be Renan sitting next to me, sharing my soup. Not this stranger.

I'm so sorry, Ren.

HE RAISES HIS voice, blaming me for Mom's death. He bolts back onto the trail and makes a wrong turn.

I chase after him, calling his name. Several seconds later, a shrill scream echoes in the distance.

Then the picture morphs, and he's thrown into a prison cell. "Ree!" he cries. "Help me!" He locks eyes with me as if I'm right there with him. Those wide jade eyes plead for relief, but there is something different about them. Their innocence, their light, begins to fade. Like glass, they appear cracked, splintering more and more, his vision becoming obstructed.

Then the cell door opens. A masked soldier enters. "Tell me where they are!" He holds a gun to Ren's head.

Renan sinks to his knees, trembling.

"Three," the soldier yells. "Two." He loads the gun. "One." He pulls the trigger—

"No!" I lurch upward, throwing off my blanket.

Ezra snatches it before it hits the flaming fire pit. "What's wrong?" He stoops beside me, eyes wide.

Renan. He's not dead. He was captured and taken to prison. I have to help him!

I stand up, but my injured leg gives me a painful reminder of its existence. I balance on my good leg, but pressure fills my head and the ground sways beneath me.

"Whoa, take it easy." Ezra lowers me back to the mattress. "You're fine. You're safe. Just breathe."

I have to get Ren out before it's too late! They will hurt him. They will kill him.

I pull away from Ezra's hold, slide my feet out of his large boots and into my own, slowly stand on one foot, and limp over to my crutch. Before I reach the opposite wall, my vision begins to blur. I lean back against the rock, pulse racing.

Ezra throws my arm over his shoulder. "You shouldn't be walking yet."

"I'm fine." I push past him and fasten the crutch to my leg. I roll up my mattress, shove all my scattered belongings into my bag, and hobble from the crevice.

He steps into his boots. "You can't be serious." Following me, he trips over his untied laces. "Don't you get it? You almost died yesterday. Your temperature still hasn't recovered fully. Just…give it some time."

"I don't have time." I take off his gloves and toss them at him, slipping my own back on.

"Why? Where do you need to get to so bad that it can't wait a few more hours?"

"None of your business." I turn away.

He steps in front of me. "Your family. Is that it?"

I lean on my crutch, shoving my hands in my pockets.

"Were you separated from them?"

Something like that.

"Because if you're trying to find them, I'll help you."

The wind shoves me, blowing curls across my face. "No." I regain my balance. "I don't need your help."

"Yeah, right. You nearly froze to death by yourself. If I hadn't—"

"What do you want me to say?" I stare at him. "Thank you? All right, thank you! Thank you for saving my life again."

"What? No." He groans. "I don't want your thanks. If anything, I owe *you* thanks. That soup was the first thing I'd eaten since my supply ran out two days ago." His tone bounces in attempts to lighten the mood. It doesn't work.

"So *that's* it. You want me to stick around so you can eat my food." I give him an accusing glare, one I'm sure my father would be proud of.

He scowls. "No, I don't want your food. That's not what this is about. I just... If I can't talk you out of leaving, at least let me come with you. I'll help you get wherever you need to go."

"Why?" I cross my arms. "What's in it for you?"

"Nothing. I just want to help." He bites his cheek and drops his gaze. "And honestly, I wouldn't mind the company. You're the first normal person I've talked to in...a long time."

"Clearly you haven't lost the ability."

"I'm just tired of being alone. Please, just until I find where I need to be?" His eyes meet mine again. But this time, I glimpse a hidden tenderness, a pool of sorrow beneath their surface.

I look away, unable to think up an excuse quickly enough.

"Thank you." He takes my silence as a yes.

"Just know I won't be slowing down for you." I shuffle around him.

He snorts, then motions to my crutched leg. "If anything, I think *I'd* be slowing down for *you*. No offence."

I ignore him and turn ahead.

"So..." He paces himself beside me. "Where are we headed?"

I halt. *Where am I going?* I was so flustered by the end of the night I lost Ren that I barely took direction into account.

I peer around, vaguely recognizing an overgrown path through the cedar trees. It's my best bet. I just have to get back to the deserted city. But if Renan was taken back to Kinborough, it will take weeks to walk the whole way—

My heart skips a beat. *The horses.* I left them tied in the pasture to chase after Renan. If I can find them, I can ride back to Kinborough.

"That way." I point to the cedar path, south from the mountain's base.

"Is that where your family went?" Ezra asks.

"I never said I was looking for my family."

"Then what's back there?"

I lift my crutch high over a fallen tree. "Horses."

Ezra holds out a hand to help me over, but I brush past it. "And why do you need horses?"

I lock my gaze ahead and clamp my jaw. What's with the interrogation?

He sighs. "All right, it's hard to tell where the landmines are with you, so I'll stop asking questions."

Finally.

He glances around impatiently as if unable to go five seconds without talking. "How about you ask me one?" He waits for a response I don't give. "Or-or I can ask less-personal questions. Like...well, you haven't even told me your name yet."

I roll my eyes. "How about we don't talk at all."

"Fine." He shrugs. "But whatever it is that happened to you out here...I just want you to know I'm here if you ever do want to talk."

The irritation increases. "How dare you? You don't know anything about me."

"Maybe not." His mouth forms a grim line. "But I do know something happened since you escaped the prison. I can see it in your eyes. You've changed a lot."

I curl my fists in my pockets, avoiding his penetrating gaze. "Thought you said we didn't have to talk."

"I'm done." He lowers his head. "And I'm sorry. For whatever it is." His sincere tone emanates. "I really am." His onyx irises blend with his pupils, so dark yet so warm.

I study him, stunned by the comfort his remark brings. "You're actually serious?"

He knits his brows. "Why wouldn't I be?"

Dumbfounded, I let the silence linger.

Ezra stays quiet for several minutes—to my delight—before snapping back to his chatty self. "Wait a minute." He eyes my leg. "Did you make that too?"

"The crutch?" I look down at my wooden contraption. "Yeah."

He puffs air from his mouth like a hushed whistle. "Incredible."

"It's just a few wooden beams and some nails."

"You have a gift. That and the bird… Do you carve anything else?"

My crutch slips beneath me, but I quickly reclaim my balance. "I used to." My arm shakes, weak from carrying my bag over my shoulder.

"Here, let me." He moves to grab the strap.

"No." I swing it out of his reach. "I'm fine."

He rubs the back of his neck. "You know, I don't mind. Really."

"I don't need your help."

His arms fall limply at his sides. "Okay then."

TWO HOURS GO by. He talks. I don't. The temperature plummets and the wind intensifies until we have no choice but to take shelter.

An uprooted Douglas fir, well over a century old at the

time of its fall, lies decomposing along the forest floor. Where its roots were once fixed in the ground now forms a large, three-foot-deep burrow. Twigs and needles entwine atop the suspended roots, creating a solid rooftop.

Ezra drops from level ground into the burrow. He crouches and pats the walls within. "It'll do, I guess."

I lower myself into the pit of darkness.

Ezra said he'd only stay with me until he finds where he needs to be. I'd gladly help him get wherever he wants if it meant I'd be rid of him sooner. But until the windstorm passes, I'm stuck with him in close quarters. I wrap myself in my blanket and lean against the dirt wall, keeping as far from him as possible.

He offers me his own blanket, which I decline. He then tosses it aside, not bothering to use it himself. His suit must be well insulated because his face glows with warmth.

I would ask how he acquired that suit. How he escaped the prison. But that would imply I am interested in his life, which I'm not, because he is not my friend. I have no reason to doubt his faithfulness to me after he's saved my life twice, but I can't afford to let him in. I don't need a friend—especially a noisy, obnoxious friend who makes it his mission to stick his nose where it doesn't belong. I can do this on my own.

All I need is Renan.

A small voice in the back of my mind counters that notion. *If the only thing sustaining you is your brother, you're going to fall short, no matter how much you love him.*

Susa. All she spoke to me in those few hours remain close to my heart. Though I don't understand it, that phrase lures me in. What could she have meant by it? I know there must be some truth to it, but why can't Renan be enough? Hasn't he always been?

Ezra pulls me from my thoughts as he taps his boot on the ground repeatedly. Sitting near the opening, he stares at a tree root dangling over my head.

"Do you mind?"

He clenches his jaw, eyes glazed over. His lips move as he mumbles quietly to himself. He taps his foot faster, taking heavy breaths.

"Ezra?" I lean over, invading his space.

His eyes look through me as if I'm not here. Just like in the execution room.

I wave in his face, then shake his shoulder. "What's wrong with you?"

He jerks away and breaks his stare. Wipes a hand over his face. His breathing slows, and he stops shaking his foot.

"What was that? You spaced out."

"I was thinking." His watery eyes avert my gaze.

"Thinking? That's it?" I spy a transition in his eyes, from a look of horror to one of detachment. "It was more than a daydream. You wouldn't snap out of it. How often does that happen?"

"Don't worry about it." He shifts his weight and plasters on a composed expression. "It's nothing."

"All right." I retreat to my side of the burrow. My foot catches on a protruding root in the ground, and I grimace. A wave of pain surges through the broken bone.

Ezra gets onto his knees and takes my elbow to help me back to my spot. "You okay?"

"Just perfect." I shift away from him, fixing the blanket around my shoulders. I stretch out my leg as the ache sets in.

The pulsing pain grows, and I already know from past experience nothing I try will soothe it. As Susa said, it may never fully heal.

I am done fighting the pain, anyway. Done yielding to it. I must live with it, push through it. To get to Renan. That's all that matters now. I can't waste time waiting out the pain or waiting out the storm.

After a few minutes, I crawl to the exit. Grasping the burrow's ledge, I pull myself up on it. The pain increases.

"What are you doing?" Ezra sits up and grabs my hand. "You're in pain."

"It's fine now." I yank my hand back. "We have to keep moving. Hand me my crutch."

"No." He kicks it behind him. "You can barely walk, the weather's only getting worse, and you still haven't recovered fully from yesterday." His breath fogs. "Just rest here until the storm passes."

"I don't need your permission." I hop down to get the crutch myself.

He swipes it first and hides it behind his back. "Sorry, but I'm not interested in letting you freeze to death."

I have to get to Renan. I can't lounge around while death threatens him further with every passing minute. I imagine him in that frigid cell. All alone. Without so much as the glow of a candle for comfort. I picture his eyes as they appeared in my dream. Dark. Broken. Blind. His voice rings in my head, calling my name. But I can't help him. Ezra won't let me go.

I grip the ledge as my chest swells with rage. Dirt gathers under my broken fingernails, and the wind whips my hair in my face.

He offers his hand to help me down.

I push past it, eyes stinging, not wanting him to see how close I am to tears. Thin roots dangle over my face as I curl up in the burrow.

"I'm sorry," he says. "I know you're worried about your family, but believe it or not, I'm doing this for your benefit. There wouldn't be any good in leaving now and freezing before you can reach them." He hunches on the ledge. "Get some rest. We'll move on when the wind lets up."

I turn my cheek into the dirt, pull my hat over my face. Secret tears of helplessness and defeat flow until I fall asleep.

Chapter 13

I pull the hat from my face when I wake. Alone. But Ezra tucked his own blanket around me while I was out. I toss it to his side of the burrow.

Though the sky is dark, an orange glow emits from beyond the burrow. The dangling roots overhead cast finger-like shadows across my face.

I've overslept. Now I will be stuck here with Ezra another night, and it will take that much longer to rescue Ren.

I drag myself to the ledge with my own blanket draped around me.

"At last, she wakes." Ezra beams, slumped on a flat rock behind a fire pit. Three logs form a teepee in the fire's centre and a can of my soup balances on top. "Hope you don't mind I took another can. I would've woken you to ask, but after waiting out the first few hours, I thought you might be out till morning. You snore, by the way."

I hoist myself out of the ditch.

"Saved you a seat." He pats a flat-topped log beside him.

I hobble to it, and he takes my arm, lowering me down.

The fire heats my face and thaws my outstretched legs. The air is crisp and cool, only a gentle breeze rustling through the trees. Above, the cratered half moon swims within a sea of stars. It's relaxing, for once, as an autumn night should be.

Ezra pokes at the fire with a stick. "So how'd you sleep, RJ?"

I raise a brow in response to my new nickname.

He sports a mischievous grin. "I may not know your name yet,"—he lifts my tool satchel to his lap—"but thanks to this, I know your initials." He traces a finger over the bottom right corner, where the letters *R. J. Rutherford* are engraved in the leather.

"Would you quit going through my stuff?" I snatch it from him and toss it out of his reach.

"I was bored, convinced I'd be growing grey hair by the time you woke up." He laughs.

I don't. Instead, I slouch, staring into the fire. My jaw tenses. I should not be here. I should be halfway home by now. Ezra thinks he's keeping me safe, but all he's doing is slowing me down.

By now, Renan may have already been killed.

Or…maybe he was never captured by soldiers in the first place. Maybe I'm just fooling myself, hoping he was taken back to the prison instead of freezing out here alone. After all, it was only a dream that led me to believe he was captured, and dreams are more often wrong than right. Perhaps believing that dream is just a stage of denial, not wanting to face the reality that he has most likely been dead for days.

A sudden surge of anguish crashes against the rocky reef of my mind, and I wish more than anything Mom could be sitting next to me. I want her peaceful presence to calm me. I want her lavender smell to engulf me. Want her gentle arms to hold me. I miss her so much.

I clench my fists, fighting the gut-wrenching emotions that make acid rise in my throat.

I wish I'd been brave enough to swallow those pills. This is all too much to bear.

The soup begins bubbling over the fire, and Ezra retrieves it with his thick gloves. He sets it on the ground between us to let it cool off.

"Isn't it a perfect night?" He lifts his face to the sky, eyes glistening. "I can't remember the last time I saw the stars."

I look to the ground, shuffling farther from Ezra.

"You know, I'm just trying to be nice." He sighs. "Why won't you talk to me?"

Elbows propped on my knees, I drop my chin in my palms.

"I know you don't know me well, but as far as I know, I haven't done anything to hurt you or betray your trust." Pain and confusion flood his face. "And I'm not the gloating type, but I just don't understand why you push me away. I saved your life—"

I meet his gaze, and my cheeks heat as I sense him infiltrate my mind. I glance down at my hands, feeling violated, afraid of what my eyes might have revealed to him.

"That's just it, isn't it?" His tone has dropped, and his expression settles as if everything is now clear to him. He pauses, eyes fixated on me. "I saved a life that didn't want to be saved."

I internally flinch. That was supposed to be my secret. Why do my eyes fail me? Why must I be so transparent? Here comes the lecture, I can tell.

He shifts uneasily. "I don't have all the facts, so I can't say I know exactly what you're going through. But believe me, I can relate." He takes a long moment, perhaps trying to convince himself to continue. "I've wanted to end my life many times. Tried, even." The fire's flame reflects in his glassy eyes.

I swallow the lump in my throat, recalling the time in the execution room when Ezra pressed his forehead to the barrel of the headsman's gun, silently begging him to pull the trigger. I was wrong about him loving his own life too much to understand why I'd want to end mine. He may understand even more than I do.

"I've been tortured more times than I can count, in more ways than I can remember, for resisting orders. Ulric took everything from me. I wanted to kill myself…so I wouldn't have to suffer anymore." He pauses, glancing at my neck.

I tense, raising my fingers to the stitched incision. I want to tell him it's not what he thinks, that I wasn't the one to inflict the wound—that in fact, a soldier was. But what difference does it make? The wound is merely a visual representation of what I've wanted to attempt since I lost Renan.

I lick my dry lips. "Okay, we unfortunately have that in common…but our reasons are completely different." I hug my blanket tighter to cover my neck. "You were innocent. Selfless. You were beaten for refusing to do evil for the king." My jaw firms. "I'm not innocent. I'm the reason for…" I trail off to avoid hearing Dad's gruff voice blame me all over again.

Ezra shakes his head slowly. "No one's innocent. I am *not* selfless. Never was. Sure, I'd refuse orders. But once they'd start the torture, I'd agree to anything to make it stop." A muscle in his jaw spasms. "You don't know what I did back there…all the people I hurt. The lives I took. Only after eight years did I decide to put another life before my own. I expected to die that night I helped your family escape. But even though by some miracle I got out too, I'm still a slave. I think I always will be."

"What do you mean?"

He lifts the cooling soup can from the ground and takes a bitter gulp. "So many lives, ended by my own hand. I still see them… I see their faces in my dreams." He glares into the fire. "All the children who became slaves. The ones who'd watch me as I was escorted past them in the hallways. They stared…because they would never forget the face of the man who murdered their parents." Blinking back the moisture in his eyes, he takes another sip of soup. "I'll always be a prisoner to my memories, my guilt, my actions. And I should be. It's what I deserve."

I strain to clear my throat clogged with horror and emotion.

I get it now. Though Ezra jokes around and bothers me endlessly, it is not for his own sake. It's for mine. He tries anything to distract me from my suffering because he knows the pain better than anyone.

"It wasn't your fault," I say. "They forced you to do it."

"I used to think the same thing. I told myself I didn't have a choice. That way, it would take the guilt off my shoulders." His voice quakes. "But there's always a choice, whether you acknowledge it or not. Even if you think you're being forced into something, you can choose not to do it. The harder choice is usually the right one. I've made a lot of wrong choices. I chose my life over countless others'. But…I can't do that any longer. I won't. From now on, I will choose right." He nods as if assuring himself of this claim.

His tense posture melts over the next few minutes of silence. Each breath decreases in volume and intensity until only exhaustion remains. He watches the hot coals dim as the fire dwindles.

He's revealed so much to me, I can barely absorb it all. I feel as though I should be scared to be so near him, an ex-slave who has tortured and executed countless people, and who could no doubt do the same to me if he wished. But truthfully, I've never felt safer around him—around anyone outside Mom and Renan, for that matter.

"I'm sorry, Ezra." I finally find my voice after the shock of his confession sinks in further. "I didn't know all that before…but I'm glad I know now. And I do trust you. But I've spent a lifetime pushing people away, so don't take it personally if I do it to you."

He swallows, clearing the tremor in his voice. "I've told you more about myself than I've told anyone before. So can I at least ask you one thing?"

"Sure. But whether I'll answer it depends on the question."

A grin pricks the corner of his mouth. "Your name?"

I roll my eyes, unable to fully stifle a smile. "Rielle."

"Rielle." He mulls it over, satisfied. "Thanks, but I think I'll stick with RJ."

IN THE MORNING, I squint up at Ezra's silhouette.

He sits cross-legged on the burrow's ledge, back toward me, tossing something circular from hand to hand. Then he brings the object to his mouth and takes a bite. It crunches between his teeth—an apple. *My* apple.

I yawn, stretching my stiff back. At this point, I'd do anything to spend just one night in my own bed. I reach into my bag, grab an apple, and bite into it.

Ezra snaps his head around at the sound, as if waking from one of his so-called "thinking" episodes. "Sleep well?"

I open my mouth, then pause, observing the dark circles under his eyes. "Did you?"

He takes another bite. "I was keeping watch."

"All night?"

He chews quietly.

I lower my apple. "Ezra, when was the last time you slept?"

His lip twitches and he crunches into the apple again. "Don't worry about it."

I recall our conversation last night. "The faces. You said you see them in your dreams..." I cross over to the ledge. "You haven't slept in days, have you?"

He clears his throat. "I've slept. Just...not much. Maybe a few minutes at a time before—"

"You have to sleep," I say. "You're clearly exhausted. You can't just not sleep—"

"It's not worth it," he snaps. "If all you dreamt about were the faces of every single person you ever..." He stops, lowering his voice. "Would you still want to sleep?" He chucks his apple core into the distant trees. "Just forget about it, all right? Focus on getting back to your family."

My stomach hardens, and I leave him to his thoughts.

I strap my crutch to my knee, roll up my mattress, and collect my belongings. After shaking the dirt from my blanket, I fold it and tuck it in my bag.

Puffy clouds block the sun. Pine branches drift in a weary breeze. Like last night, the air is cool and crisp.

I march away from the burrow in silence.

Ezra trails behind, his own blanket slung over his shoulder. His hands hang at his sides, and he sighs. "I'm sorry for snapping at you, I just..."

"I know." Because I do understand, and because if I can't

take even a small portion of what I've been dishing out over the past few days, I've got bigger problems to worry about—which I do, but still.

He eases and catches up. "So we're going to a pasture?"

"Yep." I focus on guiding my crutch through the brush.

"To find some horses?"

I nod.

His face scrunches. "Again, why do you need horses?"

I hesitate, fixing my gaze ahead to avoid his reaction. "To ride back to Kinborough."

"Wait...what?" He stops in his tracks. "Why? You just escaped it, and now you want to go back? They'll have an army of guards at the gate waiting for your head. What could be so important that you'd..." His eyes widen. "Your family. You weren't just separated from them... They were caught, weren't they?"

After everything Ezra shared last night, I should trust him with the truth. He deserves to know why I'm in such a hurry to get to Kinborough.

I slow down and lower my bag from my shoulder, then dig around until my fingers find Ren's dove. I pull it out and show him. "This is my brother's. I started carving it for him the day he ran off. We were bringing the horses to the pasture, and I said something that made him mad. He went running back to our cabin but turned down a wrong trail along the way. I looked everywhere for him, but he was just gone. And I think he was captured by soldiers."

Ezra blinks. "You think he's back in prison."

"I don't know for sure. But if he wasn't captured..." I swallow, returning the dove to my bag. "It was so cold that night. And I know it's horrible to hope he was taken, but I do."

"Because that's the better option," he says softly. "Because being taken by soldiers is the only way he'd be alive right now."

It pains me to hear those words aloud. "It's my *only* option. All I know is that he could be alone right now in a jail cell, or being tortured by Ulric's men. And he has no idea anyone's coming for him." My voice rasps. "I can't just sit and do nothing when there's a chance he's alive."

A grave line forms between Ezra's brows as if he's deciding something serious. He finally exhales. "I know how Ulric works... He doesn't care about the age of his victims, only that they're more impressionable the younger they are. He will use your brother. And if he finds out you're after him, he'll use him against you." Dread teems in his eyes. "I know the building well. I can get you in and out. But it won't be easy, and I can't say for sure it'll work."

I stare at him, mouth agape. He'd really risk his life going back there to help me rescue Renan? "Thank you, Ezra." I smile faintly, curiosity growing within. He could only know these things from experience. "Who was it, for you? Who did they use against you, to pressure you into obeying?"

"My mother." He bites his lip. "They threatened to have her executed every time I challenged orders. And it worked. They knew I wouldn't let them kill her."

A fuzzy memory springs into mind. The headsman throws Ezra to the centre of the execution room, saying, "Remember what will happen to *her* if you disobey." Ezra surrenders immediately, his eyes glazing over.

"They always told me that when I turned eighteen, they'd release me and I could go back to her. It gave me hope, but I still fought against their orders. By the time I turned eighteen last month, they revoked their promise. Apparently, I didn't learn to respect the authority as I should in all my time there. They wouldn't let me go, said I'd never leave. That broke me. I started living life in a constant haze. Stopped caring about what they'd do to me. Or my mother. For all I knew, they might've already killed her.

"I disobeyed big-time when I shot the king's men instead of your parents and helped your family escape. Soldiers are probably on their way to execute my mother right now. But I couldn't bear to continue following orders. I couldn't live with myself. If my mother knew how many people I hurt over the years just to keep her alive…"

"So when you helped us escape, it was sacrifice. You were trying to make up for all the pain you caused others, right?"

"No, not at all. I know I could never make up for what I did in the past."

"Then what was it?" I ask. "Regret?"

"No. It's just…in that moment, I remembered something my mother taught me, and it finally gave me peace to choose someone else over her. Over me. I wanted to save you, not to try and compensate for the people I hurt or to get something in return. But purely out of love. Because no one deserves a second chance, but that makes it all the more meaningful when you give one."

I halt, connecting his gaze.

Susa. She said something so similar after she returned me to my family. I had asked why she saved me if she knew I couldn't repay her. But she had only smiled, saying, "Doesn't that make it all the more meaningful?" She went on later to say, "I know no one is perfect, and no one deserves a second chance. Nonetheless, love made a way."

"What?" Ezra frowns.

"Nothing." I look down. "That's just…an interesting perspective."

Susa taught those words to Ezra. That's why he's out here. To find *her.* She's the one they used against him. She is his mother.

He is her son.

Chapter 14

I can't tell him. After everything he just told me, after he said he'd help me get into the prison…

I didn't know until now how much I need him to rescue Renan.

But Susa's his mother, the one Ulric stole him from, the one Ezra slaved away so long to protect. He thinks she might already be dead because of him.

Every part of me longs to tell him.

But he'd make me take him to her if he knew she was alive. And we are so close to the pasture, so close to riding away from this dreadful land. I need him. I can't risk Renan's life to reunite Ezra with his mother.

"Let's keep going." I turn away, twisting my fingers through my hair.

We walk a few short minutes in silence.

I eventually speak up. "You said you're eighteen, right?"

He nods.

"Last night, you said you were a slave for eight years. That means you were only ten when they took you from your mother…"

He looks ahead, numbness in his eyes. "It's been so long, I barely remember what she looks like."

The lump of guilt in my throat swells. "Think you'll ever

see her again?"

He glares around the forest. "I'm hoping. But like I said…she might already be gone."

What am I doing to him? He deserves to know she's alive.

But I can't abandon Renan. I've got to get him out. And Ezra is the key.

"I know you said you remembered your mother's words in the execution room…but there had to be something else that made you realize you couldn't kill my parents." I squint up at him. "Why them? What made them any different from the rest?"

He gives a surprised look, as if wondering how I don't know. "It wasn't them, RJ. It was you. Everything was a habitual blur until you spoke up that night. I always numbed myself to those situations to spare my guilt. But then you begged me to take your life instead of your parents'. You were willing to die to ensure your brother didn't grow up an orphan."

I blink hard. Despite all my efforts, an orphan is exactly what Ren has become. His mother is dead, father's gone. He is alone.

"You said, 'He's just a child. And a child needs his parents,'" Ezra continues. "Those words woke me up. I looked into your brother's eyes and saw myself. I saw the hopeless monster Ulric would twist him up to be. And I couldn't let another child fall prey to the king, end up like me. Your words reminded me of what my mother taught me as a boy. To put the needs of others above my own."

I swallow. I can't keep this knowledge from him. Before he saved me from dying of hypothermia, he was out here to find her. He gave up his search for Susa once he started taking care of me, and again when he vowed to help me find

Ren. He has put my needs and desires above his own since the moment he met me. He deserves to know she's okay.

And Susa. She also put my life above her own. She took me in, showed me such loving kindness. Although she remained strong and faced the pain with grace, there was an ever-present sorrow when she talked about her family's passing. She deserves to know her son is alive.

"Ezra?" I barely get the word out.

He stops, giving me his full attention.

The war rages in my mind. Telling him would be trading Renan's safety. Probably his life. No, I can't tell him. Without him, I stand no chance against Ulric's men. Ezra is the only one who knows the prison's layout and the guards' shifts. Only he can help me retrieve Renan.

"What's wrong?"

"I just need to say…" I clear my throat. "I'm really sorry. For everything. And thank you for helping me."

His brow flicks up skeptically, but he gives a meek nod. "Of course."

I amble onward, hating myself for my cowardice.

All I need is Renan, I remind myself. However, it's becoming harder and harder to find any truth in that claim.

I'm sorry for being so weak, Ezra. You deserve so much better than me.

WE REACH THE pasture's main trail by noon.

My insides simmer with eagerness. Each step closer lifts the weight of worry off my shoulders. I'll be reunited with Renan in just a few days now.

I hurry down the trail until the pasture's tall grass tickles my pants. I beam back at Ezra, incapable of containing my relief. We made it!

Through the grass I go, careful not to let it strangle my crutch. Ezra enters behind me, and I glance ahead at the giant oak. Stop stiff in my tracks. My smile vanishes.

The oak's bare branches trill, and the grass whips in the northern breeze. Gentle waves of water tease the nearby pond's shore.

But the horses are nowhere to be seen.

Ezra catches up and glares around. "Was this where you left the horses?"

My pulse races as I scan the secluded pasture. "They have to be here. I tied them up." I trudge to the lonely oak to find the lower branch I'd tied their rope to missing, snapped from the trunk. I rap my knuckles on the trunk's brittle bark. Hollow. The tree is dead, near ready to crash.

Just as I am in this moment.

My gut broils in distress. "I tied them up. But Ren was so angry, I—" Didn't pay attention to the tree I chose.

How could I be so foolish? Working with wood is my life! You'd think after all these years I could spot a decaying tree by as little as the smell, let alone the fractured trunk's condition.

The horses are gone. There's no way to reach Renan now.

The bag and rolled-up mattress slip from my shoulders into the yellow grass. I can't do this anymore. No matter what I try, what my intentions are—

"Hey." Ezra catches my eye. "We'll find another way."

"There is no other way." My voice slurs.

"There's always another way. We'll *walk* to Kinborough if we have to. I gave you my word that I'd help you save your brother. The circumstances may change, but my promise won't."

"It's too late. We won't get there in time." My eyes sting, and I can't seem to catch my breath. My face heats and my heart rate spikes as I struggle to restrain my terror. This wouldn't be my first anxiety attack, but as usual, it's impossible to stop the effects and think rationally. This is the last thing I want Ezra to see.

Ezra's eyes widen in concern as he watches me fight for breath.

Get a grip! I scold myself. *This is stupid. And embarrassing. Don't let yourself fall apart in front of him.*

The muscles in my limbs tense and spasm. I gasp for breath rapidly, but the fact that I can't fill my lungs only escalates the fear—thus, escalates the symptoms.

"Hey, just take a deep breath," Ezra says calmly, demonstrating one himself. "It's okay. I know what this feels like right now, but it goes away. It won't last long."

I attempt a deep breath, and he stretches out his hand, gently clasps it on my shoulder.

The physical contact hurts. I recoil, and he backs away.

He leans down before me until my eyes focus only on him. "You're getting there. Just breathe." His empathetic gaze hints at knowing this feeling all too well.

After I've taken several deep breaths and my muscles begin to relax, he rests his hand on my shoulder again. When I don't panic further, he draws me into his arms. "It'll be all right, RJ."

My chest locks. "No. He's going to kill Renan!" Pain surges through my lungs once again. "Ulric… He's gonna kill him." The fabric of Ezra's suit muffles my words.

"Listen." Ezra pulls back to ensure I look him in the eye. "Ulric will not kill your brother. He doesn't work that way. In fact, he needs Renan. So no matter how long it takes us to get there, Renan will be alive when we do."

My pulse begins to stabilize as his words settle inside. However, I study the sorrow in Ezra's eyes that makes me wonder if Ulric keeping Renan alive is a good thing.

He hugs me again. I stiffen, but his strong arms begin to soothe my trembling body.

Though I only hold onto him loosely, I can feel the prominent contour of his ribs through his suit. He seems to have turned every bit of meat on his body to muscle, but it can't hide the years of malnourishment that's left his figure sickly thin. This is Ulric's doing. Anger surges through me. I didn't think it possible, but my flame of hatred for the king burns stronger with every passing moment in Ezra's embrace.

Is this what will happen to Renan if our attempt to rescue him fails? Will Ulric starve him?

I try, but can't shake the image of Renan all skin and bones. His cheekbones prominent as hunger drains his face of its childlike roundness. His eyes glazed over, shattered, purged of their purity.

"Your brother will be okay." Ezra pulls me from my thoughts. My cheek against his chest, I feel the vibrations of his voice as he says, "I will do everything in my power to free your brother and bring him safely to you. You have my word."

I soak in the warmth of his embrace and match my breathing to his, slow and steady.

He gradually loosens his grip and waits to ensure I can hold my own weight. Then he digs through my bag, retrieves the canteens, and heads toward the pond to fill them with fresh water.

I lean back against the rotting oak, mentally drained and

physically exhausted. I feel I should be embarrassed for my inability to control the attack, but all I can think of is the comfort of his words and the warmth of his embrace.

He is serious. He really will help me no matter what stands in our way. He deserves so much more than my selfish silence. I cannot use him like this. I have to tell him, even if he leaves to go find Susa instead of helping me rescue Renan. He deserves the truth.

I lift my bag and meet him at the pond.

Crouching over the clear water, he gulps down a whole canteen, then refills it and twists on the cap. "Just filling up before we head on. There's a few rivers along the way, but it took me a week on foot, so we'll have to drink sparingly."

He's really going through with his promise. Putting my needs before finding his mother.

"Ezra…I know I should've said this sooner. But I think I know why you're out here."

"What do you mean?" He rinses out the second canteen.

"You came out here looking for your mother, didn't you?"

"Yes. How'd you know that?"

"Would her name…"—I bite my cheek—"happen to be Susa?"

He drops the canteen on the sandy shore and rises unsteadily. "You *know* her?" A flash of anxiety enters his expression, pleading for it to be true.

"Yes." I brush my fingers over the stitches on my neck. "She saved my life back when I had a run-in with some soldiers."

"She…she's alive?" His face pales. "She really saved your life?"

I force a smile. "The trait seems to run in your family."

"So she's okay? She's safe? She's healthy?" His dark eyes search mine, and only now do I realize the resemblance between him and Susa.

"She brought me back to her cottage to stitch me up and cast my leg." My smile fades. "But there's something else you should know."

"What is it?" His tone wavers.

I hesitate. "It's not just *her* living there. She took in three orphaned kids and has been caring for them for years… They're like her own now."

"She has a family." He drops his gaze. "So that's why she never came for me." His grieved tone tugs at my heart.

All these years, he's thought she just abandoned him?

"When I asked, she told me she lost her real family years ago." I tuck my hands in my pockets. "Ezra, I don't think she knows you're alive."

His face blanks, hiding any trace of sentiment. "She's moved on."

"I'm sorry." I purse my lips. "But I saw the way she treated those kids. She loves them. And if she treated you even half as well as she treats them, she loved you more than anything. If she knew you were alive, I'm sure she wouldn't rest until she had you back."

"Yeah, I know. I'm glad she was able to move on…and care for others who needed a home." He clears his throat. "How did you figure out she's my mother?"

"What you said this morning about second chances was similar to something she told me."

"That was hours ago." He paces away.

"I'm sorry. I wanted to tell you then, but…I couldn't. I thought you wouldn't help me anymore if I told you. I thought you'd make me bring you to her instead."

"I've been clueless for eight years, wondering if she's *alive*, let alone safe and happy. Every minute's worse than the last. You had the answer, but…" His jaw firms. "I may not deserve much, but this, Rielle, you should've told me earlier."

I flinch at his cold tone used in saying my first name. "I know—"

"Are you really that skeptical of me? Have I not proven my loyalty by now?" His eyes lock on mine, filled with pain and frustration. "I made you a promise to help you find your brother. And I won't go back on my word for anything. But apparently, my word isn't good enough. You still doubt me."

I have no words, and honestly, no desire to defend myself. I hate that I didn't tell him as much as he does. Why must I distrust everyone? He has proven himself loyal time and time again.

My face flushes in shame. I want to make it up to him. Put his needs first, for once. Even if it means rescuing Renan without him. "Ezra, I will bring you to her. It's the least I can do."

He stares at me.

Then my eyes widen in realization.

Susa has a horse—the horse that brought me to and from her home. If we can find her cottage, she might let me borrow her horse. *And* she will be reunited with Ezra.

"We can both get what we want," I say under my breath.

He rubs his eyes, and his posture slouches. "Huh?"

"You want to see your mother again, and I want to save my brother. I've been to Susa's home, which is where you want to be. And I know she has a horse, which is what I need to get back to Kinborough."

Though I expected him to be overjoyed, he merely gives a slow nod. "So which way?"

I curl my lip, taking into account the fact he can barely keep his eyes open. "First, we should stop by the cabin my family took shelter in." I point toward the trail leading out of the pasture. "It's a half hour back that way."

BY THE TIME we find the cabin, the setting sun casts long shadows through the trees. I reach the front porch and touch the dented doorknob, but pause.

What if Dad is still here? What if, in his grief, he never left? Or, more importantly, what if Renan is here? What if he found his way back after I left and he's been perfectly safe the entire time I've been searching for him?

Dreading the possibility of Dad, yet hoping for Renan, I turn the knob. The front door creaks open and a musty stench sails out from within.

Ezra enters warily, a hand on his holstered gun.

Memories come flooding back. Renan's look of longing. Dad forbidding me to leave. Renan following me to the pasture because he hated this place as much as I did. Dad blaming me for everything—

"So this is where you stayed?" Ezra peers around the dusty room.

I look ahead. The bed is empty, unmade, its wrinkled sheets wilting over the side.

Dad is not here.

I relax and drop my belongings beside the door.

But Renan's not here either.

I slump down on the wooden stool beside the counter to give my aching leg a rest.

Ezra descends the stairs to explore the basement, then returns upstairs without a word. Which means Ren isn't down there. "So you said we should stop here. What for?"

"To sleep." I motion to the bed.

"I thought you were in a hurry?"

"You can't go on like this. Once you get some rest, we'll move on."

"Me? Wait, you never said—"

"Trust me, I want nothing more than to be far away from this place. But you need to sleep." I cross my arms. "And we're not leaving until you do."

"It's not even that late. We can get to my mother's cottage sooner if we continue now."

"Don't start with excuses, Ezra. You won't win." I grab my pack of matches, shove some brush and twigs inside the wood-burning stove, and feed the fire until it burns steadily. I hold my hands above the flame to warm my icy fingers. "There's a clean set of sheets on the counter."

Ezra kicks his boots off resentfully, then remakes the bed with the sheets I cleaned and folded last week. He slumps onto the mattress and strips out of his soldier suit to reveal the same black t-shirt and beige slacks that he wore in the execution room.

"When was your last soldier sighting?" he asks.

"About a week ago. The day your mother saved me. Why?"

He grabs the compact guns from his belt, tucks one under his pillow, then hands me the other.

I shake my head, turning back to the stove.

"Just in case," he says sternly.

I drag myself to his bedside, and he places the cold metal mechanism in my hand.

Suddenly, I'm riding Sinta through a field, yelling and cursing, heart pounding. Chasing a distant shadow, shooting at it. And missing every time.

"RJ?" Ezra pulls me from my thoughts.

I blink and focus on him.

"You know how to use it?"

Unfortunately, I do. My hand shakes as I clasp the gun's handle. "Yes. Now try to sleep. I'll wake you when dinner's ready."

He eventually gives in and draws his bedsheet and blanket up to his shoulders. Hands crossed over his stomach, he closes his eyes.

I set the gun on the counter by the door, glad to be rid of it, and busy myself wrapping two potatoes in tinfoil. But my gaze often drifts back to Ezra, who grimaces in his sleep as if re-experiencing memories he wishes he could forget. My heart aches. And for the first time, I notice a longing inside myself to relieve his pain.

The fire in the stove cracks, breaking my daze.

I impale each tinfoil-wrapped potato lengthwise with wire prongs meant for roasting and set them in the coals.

Somehow, within these past hours, my entire perspective of the slave boy has changed. Protectiveness overthrows my aggravation for him. Compassion replaces indifference. Certainty substitutes skepticism.

How did this happen? Do I care for him out of pity for his past? Or out of guilt for the way I've been treating him? Perhaps both. But there is something else developing. A trust, unlike I've trusted anyone before. Somehow I'm growing more comfortable with him than with anyone else, other than Mom and Ren.

He seems to care about me in ways nobody ever has. Earlier today, during my anxiety attack, he didn't wave it off as trivial. Neither was he unsure what to do. Instead, he was patient and understanding, helping me overcome my distress one breath at a time. He grounded me with his calm words, then comforted me in his strong arms. Never once did he belittle or ridicule me in my time of vulnerability. And out of discretion, he hasn't brought up the matter since.

He truly does care for me.

I never thought I needed a friend, but the solidarity forming between us makes me feel as if I've known him for years. Maybe we would have even become friends long ago if it weren't for Ulric enslaving him...

I absentmindedly watch Ezra's chest rise and fall as I rotate the potatoes in the stove.

I think I do care for him too.

All at once, my stance changes. I make a decision. To defend Ezra and do whatever it takes to reunite him with Susa —a reunion long overdue, and frankly, one there should be no need for because Ezra should never have been taken from her in the first place. Nonetheless, it will happen. I will ensure he gets back to her, not because I feel I owe it to him, but purely because I want to help him.

"You have my word," I whisper.

Chapter 15

Ezra tosses and turns in Dad's bed, sweat forming on his brow and upper lip. I've waited it out, but this can't go on any longer. He breathes forcefully, clamping his jaw.

"Ezra?" I place a hand on his shoulder.

He bursts up, grabs his gun from beneath his pillow.

I jump back as he aims it square at my forehead.

Amid panting for breath, he sees me and lowers the gun. Shoves his blanket off, hunches over the bedside, and brushes dishevelled hair back from his eyes. He looks even more exhausted than before he fell asleep. As if sleep robbed him of strength instead of replenishing it. He avoids my gaze, wiping a trembling hand over his face.

I give him a flustered scowl. "Dinner's ready." I lower my outstretched arms and fetch his plate from the counter. "Tell me, did you put that gun under your pillow in case a soldier happened to find us? Or was it just to scare the crap out of me?"

He ignores me and takes the plate of steaming baked potato with butter. I also drop two of Susa's sleeping pills on his plate. "These should help with the nightmares. Your mother gave them to me. Take them now, and by the time you're done eating, they should start to kick in." I set a water canteen beside him.

He pops the pills in his mouth and washes them down with a gulp of water.

I drag the wooden stool to his bedside and untie my crutch. It slips from my hand and falls to the floor.

Ezra flinches at the crash.

I cringe. "Sorry."

He fumbles with his fork awkwardly, chopping the potato into quarters. Only now do I realize it's probably been eight years since he last used an eating utensil.

I devour my own potato, peel and all. But I can't help noticing his nauseated expression as he sifts through the mushy vegetable cubes.

"Was it the faces again?" I eventually ask.

He lets the silence linger, and I begin to think he's not going to answer. But then he stabs a potato cube with his fork and says, "Not this time." He chews it. "It's always either the faces…or my mother." He swallows and takes a sip of water. "This time, it was her."

I nod grimly, imagining what his nightmare had entailed. Susa likely being tortured in some way. Maybe executed. I don't question him further.

"When I wake up," he continues, to my surprise, "I can remember every detail of the dream, except for one thing. Her face. It's like, I know she's there—I can sense that it's her. But I never see her face." He waits until he's finished his meal before looking up at me, hesitant. "Would you…tell me what she's like?"

Memories come flooding back. The walls of cedar. The afternoon sunlight filling the little cottage with life. The mouth-watering aroma of peanut butter cookies. And Susa, living humbly, savouring every moment of life as much as the next. The feeling of being with her was similar to what I remember feeling when Mom came into my life. Immediate safety. Though I loved my old house, I don't think I quite understood the meaning of the word *home* until I visited Susa's.

Just the thought of her brings peace. "Of course." I smile. "She's let her hair grow in grey. It's long, twisted into loose...dreads, I guess you could call them. And her smile's the type that catches you off guard because of how bright and genuine it is." I pause, recalling how smiling made her cheeks lift and her eyes squint enough they were barely visible. "Her eyes...well, they actually look a lot like yours. Dark. Warm. Gentle." I study Ezra's eyes closely to get the details right, then catch myself staring and drop my gaze.

His tension physically decreases as he ponders the details I've shared, so I continue.

"I wish I could've stayed at her cottage forever. She has this presence that overflows with joy and simplicity. It's hard to put into words, but she's the kind of person who makes you feel loved no matter who you are or what you've done."

Ezra reflects on my words, a hint of a smile forming. "Unconditional."

Yes. I suppose that was the part about Susa that most reminded me of my own mother. Her unconditional love.

But Mom's unconditional love was taken from me the second she breathed her last.

I clear the lump in my throat, envisioning the moments after Susa shot the soldiers. How she knelt beside me, hugged me. "There was such a peace to her. It was contagious. It's like, from the moment she introduced herself, all my fears vanished..." I trail off as my words begin to feel vaguely familiar.

A man sat beside me. He didn't say anything, but I knew he was nice because he made the fear leave.

Renan. He spoke those words while describing his night in the jail cell. He believed with his entire being the man had been there. Could he have possibly been right?

"Thank you." Ezra draws me from my thoughts, eyes tired but content. "Wait—one more thing." He licks his lips. "I'm guessing she still…believes, after all these years?"

"Believes? You mean like…in God?" I pause. "She didn't directly mention God, but with all she did talk about, yeah— I'd assume she does."

His lips tighten.

"Why? Don't you believe?"

He clinks his fork on his plate. "I'm still deciding."

"Isn't it supposed to be one or the other? You believe or you don't?"

"It's not that simple for me. I've caused so much pain to so many people. In a way, I hope what my mother believes is real, because I want to think those people are in a much better place now. But I also don't want any of it to be real, because I'm responsible for hurting so many."

I think back to my interrogation in prison. I wasn't the only one who couldn't decide what I believe.

I replay how I argued with Mom in Mr. Elscott's barn, insisting she let me take the reins. Then I tell Renan his story in the jail cell is impossible and watch him run away in anger. And then I pour the ten sleeping pills in my palm the night I wanted to end it all.

"You don't want to believe…because if it's all real, there's no way you'd ever deserve heaven."

"Exactly." He sets his plate aside. "What about you? I mean—sorry. Of course you believe. Why else would you try to take your parents' death sentence?"

I shake my head. "It wasn't like that. I actually don't believe. It's just that…if it came down to me or my parents dying, I knew my brother needed them more than he needed me."

Ezra thinks over my explanation, then leans back into his pillow, eyes drooping.

I clear my head and take our empty dishes to the sink. "Told you the pills would kick in fast."

"Where will you sleep?" Ezra asks, placing his gun back under his pillow.

"I'll keep watch for the night."

"I know the exhaustion that follows an anxiety attack well. You need to sleep."

"No, my body just needs to rest. I'll spend some time working on the carving for my brother. Oh, and my dad left some of his clothes here if you want to change into them so I can wash yours for tomorrow."

"I don't think you even know what resting means." He chuckles.

"Another thing we've got in common."

I find Dad's oversized t-shirt, faded jeans, and belt for Ezra, then hobble downstairs to salvage a lantern while he changes.

In the corner of the chilly basement squats Renan's cot. And his ten candles of various sizes remain unlit on the ground in the same positions he had arranged them for me…the night before I lost him.

I grab the lantern from its hook and retreat to the main level before I can cry.

The bedsprings creak as Ezra rolls onto his side, having sprawled his dirty t-shirt and slacks over the end of the bed. "Wake me if you hear anything or if you want to switch lookout shifts. Remember where the gun is." His words slur as he closes his eyes.

I collect his clothes, and by the time I light the lantern and head outside, he's lightly snoring.

The trees create a thick canopy overhead, snuffing out the last enduring bit of daylight. Though the river water is ice cold, it flows fast enough to evade freezing over. I dunk my hands under to soak Ezra's clothes but must dry them off every few seconds to warm them with my breath.

After his clothes are washed and hung by the stove to dry, I grab Ren's dove and my tool satchel. Then I drag the stool to the counter and carve for the next few hours.

Ezra sleeps peacefully, never once stirring or grimacing from nightmares.

I imagine the ease he felt learning more about his mother, and I envision their future reunion, the joy it will bring. What an incredible mother Ezra has. To be living without her must be more torturous than any physical pain the king could have inflicted upon him.

I stop carving.

What an incredible mother *I* had. To be living without her *is* more torturous than anything the king could inflict upon me.

These past weeks have been truly agonizing. I wish I could talk about Ezra's mother without summoning the memories of my own. And how her death was my fault. I might as well have just grabbed a gun and shot her myself. It would have ended the same.

Craving Mom's comfort, I open my tool satchel and pull out the letter she wrote me the night before we were arrested.

Rielle,

I know this is frightening for you, as it is for all of us. I brought my faith into this family, and I am sorry for how hard it has been on you. But I want you to know that this isn't some choice I am making. I am not choosing my faith over this family, though it may seem so. My faith saved my life. It is the truth that gives me peace in knowing this world is not our real home. I know if it weren't for my faith in God, I would not have found my family in you. He has blessed me beyond measure—

I close the letter when Mom's voice begins to narrate the words in my head. I can't do this. Not now. I seal it back in the secret pocket and return to carving.

If only she knew how lost she was.

BY ROUGHLY TWO o'clock in the morning, I'm finished carving and sanding the dove as well as looping the shoelace through a hole whittled in its back. I then engrave my initials under the dove's rounded belly and apply a coat of rich stain over the entire carving. Lifting the shoelace, I wipe away the excess liquid and let the necklace dangle from my fingers as it dries. It may be one of my best pieces to date.

Bowed head. Closed eyes. Folded wings and detailed feathers. Its features are soft yet striking, just like Renan.

I struggle to keep my eyes open as I assess my work.

Just as I start to nod off, leaves rustle and crunch beyond the cabin's thin walls.

I set down the dove and peer out the window.

A shadowy figure approaches in the spotty moonlight.

My gut clenches. I blow out the lantern, then go to put out the stove's fire, but there's no time. "Ezra!" I whisper. Louder.

He doesn't wake.

The figure knocks on the front door.

I glide behind it, between the door and the counter, and pick up the gun I'd left on the countertop.

Another knock. Then the door creaks open, and an armed soldier steps inside.

They have found us.

The glow of the stove casts shadows over the space beside the counter, where I now squat. Frigid wind gusts into the room, and the soldier slams the door behind him.

Ezra still doesn't stir.

I pull my knees to my chest, sitting behind the stool in shadowy seclusion.

Like a moth to a lantern, the soldier draws toward the crackling stove across the room, unaware of my presence. Along the way, he bumps into the bed where Ezra rests. Then raises his gun on Ezra's defenceless body.

I train my gun on the soldier with trembling hands, ready to press the trigger.

The soldier studies Ezra, jostles his knee with the barrel of his gun. Once he sees that Ezra will not wake, he retreats toward the stove, peeling his coat off along the way. He kneels in front of the fire, holding shivering hands to the flame.

I lower my gun, baffled.

The soldier drops his helmet on the floor and runs a hand through his bristly black hair. Every few seconds, he looks back at Ezra. He's just a boy, no older than eighteen. This soldier, trained and ordered to kill, is desperately trying to warm his frozen body. I almost feel bad for him. Beneath the "soldier" title is merely a slave taken advantage of by the king, forced to do Ulric's dirty work for him.

I stop. How dare I think that? Soldiers like this boy were the ones who captured Renan. Tortured Ezra. Killed my mother. This boy, in fact, could have been the very soldier who shot Mom. Why am I defending him?

The soldier shudders, huddled in front of the fire. He doesn't want to kill. He put off shooting Ezra, chose first to warm himself.

But my heart skips when the boy rises, gun in hand. He collects his coat and helmet and heads for the door.

Will he leave the cabin, sparing Ezra's life?

He treads past the bed but then pauses, turns back to Ezra. He sighs and sets his coat and helmet back on the ground. Looming over the bedside, he aims his gun at Ezra's forehead.

My chest tightens. I lift my gun, fighting the flashbacks with all my might. But the image of Mom bleeding in that barren field interrupts my focus, and I set the gun on the floor. I grab the hunting knife from my belt loop instead.

The soldier plants his feet shoulder-width apart, looks back at the door, then returns his attention to Ezra.

No. He can't kill him! I have to reunite him with Susa.

The soldier places his finger on the trigger.

I can't let Ezra die.

I charge forward, grab the soldier around the neck, wrench him away from Ezra, and plunge my knife into his abdomen.

The soldier gasps and fires a bullet into the ceiling. The explosion resounds.

Ezra erupts from the mattress, smashing an arm on the headboard.

I exhale, releasing the soldier's body as my own goes limp. Pain flares through my injured leg and I drop to the floor beside the bleeding boy.

Ezra rubs his arm, then spots the soldier with the knife handle sticking out of his gut. He curses, gives me a stern look. "I told you to wake me if you heard anything!"

I swallow the saliva that floods my mouth. "There wasn't time."

"So you stabbed him?"

"I had to. He would've killed you." Acid bites the back of my tongue.

Ezra bends down, pressing two fingers to the soldier's neck. And pulls the knife out. He rushes to the counter, shoving all my food and possessions in my bag. "They're always sent in pairs. We have to go before the second one finds us." He packs his blanket and the clothes I hung by the fire, then pulls on his soldier suit and retrieves the gun I left on the floor.

I slide my leg into my crutch and tie Ren's dove around my neck. Then I douse the stove's fire with river water.

An icy gust devours the cabin's warmth as Ezra holds the door open for me.

I catch a glimpse of the dying soldier's face. Drained of colour. Stained with grief. Blood soaks his beige undershirt and pools on the floor beneath him.

I grab my belongings and leave the cabin behind as my dinner threatens to resurface.

Ezra snatches the lantern from the counter and shuts the door behind him.

With trees blotting out the moonlight, we head blindly into the forest.

I eye the lantern in Ezra's hand. "I'll get the matches." I begin to search through my bag.

Ezra reaches out and stills my arm. "Not yet. If others are

near, they'll see it."

My crutch hits something, and I blindly grope for a branch on my way down. Ezra clasps my arm and heaves me up.

I groan. "Well, we can't go far if we can't see where we're going."

"Just follow me. Step where I step." Ezra takes my hand in his and tests his foot on the ground in front of him.

I listen for the leafy crunch of his footsteps, then step roughly into the same spot as he moves on.

The river's rushing sound fades behind us as we continue on throughout the night, his hand warming mine.

BY THE TIME Ezra thinks we're far enough away to light the lantern, we no longer need it. The sky has lightened from its infinite black void to a fading tide of cobalt.

Ezra tugs me through bushes, around fallen trees, his grip constricting my fingers over time.

"Slow down, Ezra!" I eventually manage to yank my hand free. "We've been moving for hours. A five-minute rest won't hurt."

He stares ahead, eyes vacant.

I step in front of him and raise my brows.

He blinks hard, then readjusts his focus on me. "What?"

"Just five minutes to catch our breath." I lower myself to the ground, winded.

His breath fogs in his face. "Okay, sure."

I take a gulp of water from my canteen. "Want to tell me what that death grip you had on my hand was for?"

He sits down beside me, leaning back against a tree. "I don't know how to say it. But this is all just so…familiar."

"Familiar?" I pull off my gloves and warm my hands with my breath.

"The running. The hiding. The fear. It's all coming back." His posture remains rigid. "Before I was enslaved, that's all my mother and I did—run, hide, fear they might discover her beliefs. And then they did find out, and I was trapped in the fear for eight years. When I escaped, I thought I could go back to my mother, my home, my old life. I thought I'd finally be free." He shakes his head. "But now I'm out here. Still running. Still hiding. Still fearing. Nothing's changed." A crease forms between his brows. "Those soldiers are out here looking for me. And I don't think they'll ever stop until they have me. I killed their leaders. An eye for an eye, you know?"

I picture the soldier towering over Ezra, how hesitant he was to shoot. How he almost spared Ezra entirely. But in the end, loyalty to the king trumped mercy for the helpless. He knew he had to do it. Ezra is right. They won't stop until they have him.

I fist my hands in my lap. "If your mother can get away and start over, so can you."

"That's just it." His jaw loosens. "She only got away because he let her."

A sudden surge of protectiveness overwhelms me, and I clasp his forearm. "You will see her again, Ezra. I will see to it that you are reunited with her. For what it's worth, you have my word."

His glassy eyes meet mine, and I remove my hand, realizing what I just said.

My head spins. How can I guarantee safety to someone at the top of Ulric's kill list? Of course, I will defend Ezra. But other than my futile ability to wield a knife, I have no strength. He is twice as strong as me. How can I promise his protection when I can barely defend myself?

"RJ." He takes my hand in his. "*For what it's worth*,"—he mocks my tone—"you have mine too. After I see my mother again, I will go back with you and do all I can to rescue your brother."

So Ezra will finally get to see his mother after eight years, but will leave her behind right after? All just to help me? No. I can't let him throw his life away.

"It's settled," he says. "We'll find my mother, then ride her horse back to the prison, rescue your brother, and all come back here to live at her cottage."

I pull my hand away. "You make it sound so simple."

"My home can be your home. You can become part of my family."

His eyes captivate me, then warmth floods my cheeks, and I look away, shaking my head.

Deep down, though, my imagination takes over. What a joy it would be to live with Susa and her children. To spend my days with the ones I love and the ones who love me. To be able to call her cottage *home*.

However, that's only possible if we can find Susa.

I push myself up and ease into my crutch, scanning every direction. We ran through the forest blindly all night. Disorientation takes root in my bones, and I suddenly feel isolated from everywhere I know. The cabin. The region. The cottage.

Dread skirts down my spine. "Where are we?"

Chapter 16

Does any of this look familiar to you?"

My crutch squeaks as I walk in circles. I don't remember any of it.

What if we can't find our way to Susa's? What if we're lost for days and run out of food? I won't be able to get Ezra to his mother. I won't be able to save Renan.

"You don't recognize anything?" He clears his throat of its nervous hitch.

I chew the insides of my lips as I continue scoping the shadowy forest. "I'm sorry."

He rubs the back of his neck. "It's not your fault. We'll figure it out." He halts.

"What—?"

"Shhh… Do you hear that?" He inclines his ear toward a thick mass of fir trees, then takes off, following whatever is it he claims to hear. He returns seconds later. "I think it's the river! C' mon, maybe it'll lead us back."

After several long minutes trying to keep up, I lose sight of him.

When I find him again, he's hunched over the rocky riverbank, slurping handfuls of water. "Found it." He wipes his mouth. "Hand me the canteens and I'll fill them before we go."

I toss them to him. "You know, this river doesn't flow straight through the forest. If we follow it, we could end up more lost than we are now. And how can we be sure it's even the same one?"

Something catches my eye above the distant trees. A torn piece of red fabric flaps violently in the wind.

Ezra follows my gaze upward. "What the… Is that a flag?"

It certainly looks like one. "What could it be for?"

He caps the canteens and hands them to me with a combined look of curiosity and resolve. "Let's find out."

"No. I may not know how to get back, but I do know following that flag will take us farther from where we want to be."

"It'll only be an hour out of our way, at most. Come on, RJ. Aren't you even a little curious?" His eyes meet mine. In them I see the eagerness of a captive set free. For years he was locked away, denied the simple pleasures of the outside world that, on most days, kept me sane. Who am I to reject his hunger to explore?

I sigh. "Fine. But only an hour."

WE HEAD IN the direction of the red flag—if that's even what it is. I clench Renan's dove tied around my neck, its smooth exterior calming my nerves.

Ezra spots the carving in my hand. "You finished it?"

I open my fist to give him a glimpse. "While you were asleep—you know, just before I saved your life." I offer a sly grin and receive an eye roll in return.

"Now don't get smug on me. I'm still one up on you." He sneers, then studies the carving. "It's beautiful. But…why a dove?"

I shrug. "Renan lost the last one I made him, so he asked me to carve him another."

"No, I mean why a *dove*? Of all birds, of all animals."

I recall the memories of when Renan was born. The first time I held him in my arms, peace dethroned my every fear. And as I watched Dad lay eyes on his baby son, I could tell Ren had captured Dad's heart and changed him for the better. From that day on, Dad's overall presence was eased—something I never thought possible.

"I guess it became my brother's…symbol, of sorts. At least in my eyes. Because my father anchored us and provided for us. My mother brought love and safety. But from the time Renan was born, he was our peace."

Ezra muses over my words. "Wow."

"What?" My cheeks heat in discomfort.

"Just shocked is all. That's the most you've ever willingly told me about yourself." He gives a warm smile that expels my embarrassment. "So his symbol is a dove. What's yours?"

"My symbol?" I pause. "I don't have one. I've never really thought about it."

"Well, if you could choose your own symbol right now, what would it be?"

I knit my brows. "It would have to be something small, independent, not too significant. I don't know." I sigh, not caring for this question. "Maybe a rabbit—no, a cat…like one of those street mousers back home that fend for themselves."

He cringes. "Yikes."

"What *now*?" I huff, sensing the oncoming criticism.

"A cat and a bird…probably doesn't end well."

"You have something better in mind?"

He hesitates.

I wait another moment. "I knew it. You got nothing."

He gives a bored flash of his eyes. "Okay, then what would you say my symbol is?"

My smirk fades. I look away as an aching pressure builds inside. Suddenly, I am protective of Renan's symbol and feel that giving Ezra a symbol of his own would be betrayal. "I don't know." Hopefully my firm tone will make him drop the question.

He seems to understand and moves on. "Can I see it?" He holds out a hand.

I untie the shoelace and lower the dove into his palm.

He inspects every inch of it, lightly tracing a finger over each wing. When he flips it over to reveal my initials, he stops. "I meant to ask the other night. You told me your first name is Rielle, but what does the J stand for? Junior, or something?"

"I don't think they do that for girls." I snicker. "No, it's after my mother's name—Jaclyn."

"I thought your mother was Miriam."

I stiffen. "Yes, the one you met in the execution room was Miriam. But Jaclyn was my birth mother. She left me with my dad just after I was born and never returned. I was seven when Miriam came into the picture." I swallow. "She was my stepmother."

He blanches. "*Was?* You mean your parents are…"

"My dad's alive, as far as I know. I left him behind to find Renan. But my mom… She, uh, only made it an hour through the outskirts before a soldier caught up…" The words leave a vile taste in my mouth.

Grief and remorse flood Ezra's face. He stops in his tracks, and it takes him a while to speak again. "I'm such an idiot, going on about my own mother last night, asking you to tell me about her. You should've stopped me."

"It's okay. You didn't know."

"I've been wondering what happened to your parents. I thought maybe you got separated from them while looking for your brother. But I never thought…" His voice falters, and he wraps me in his arms. "I'm so sorry, Rielle."

Hearing him use my first name in that tearful tone hits me. I close my eyes and let him hold me, realizing what a relief it is to have this tragedy out in the open. As I've learned with Renan and now Ezra, it's easier for two people to bear this pain together than to battle it myself.

Unable to fake a smile this time, I sniff and take the dove back from him. "Stick with the nickname, Ez. RJ's growing on me."

WE TRUDGE FOR another hour as a ruthless breeze builds, spitting tiny snow pellets at us. I pull my coat collar up over my nose. My eyes water and sting as the wind reaps them of their moisture.

Soon we come to the right side of a thirty-foot-wide roadway, its cracked concrete raided by weeds, vines, and fallen trees. The torn red flag whips above the highest tier of a massive castle. At least half the structure's tiers have fallen to the ground in mountains of rubble at the top of the road-way. With no better place to escape the storm, we rush under an archway and toward the castle's shelter.

Ezra kicks in a wooden door and pulls me out of the wind's torment. He then fights against the wind to close the door behind us and doubles over, panting.

I lean into a wall, shivering and coughing for air.

Once I regain sensation in my fingers, I light the lantern Ezra brought along. The brick room we've entered is bigger than my entire house back in Kinborough. It's empty but for a fireplace built into the right-hand wall and charred bits of furniture scattered along the blackened floor. It looks as though a fire swept through and devoured everything in the room. Still, the walls and ceiling seem sturdy.

A dull, tinted glow illuminates a spiral staircase hidden in the left-hand wall.

The yellow and red colours captivate Ezra. "Let's see what's up there." He darts toward the staircase.

"Are you crazy?" I force a whisper. "We shouldn't be here." The eerie light makes my skin crawl.

"It's abandoned." He takes the lantern from my hand. "Did you see how many tiers were blasted to the ground? Trust me, no one's here."

I bite my bottom lip as uneasiness clouds my mind, then glance up at each steep step and down at my crutched leg. Taking a deep breath, I climb the first stair, bracing my hands on the narrow walls for support.

"Here." Ezra takes my hand in his free one, passing ahead to help me up.

Each step seems to be steeper than the last. We eventually reach a small landing on the twenty-fifth step and find the source of the coloured light to be a stained-glass window. Ezra sets the lantern down, and we stop to catch our breath and study the window's intricate design.

Black metal plates run through the entire piece, separating each glass segment yet also connecting them as a whole. Vibrant red wedges join to portray a queen sitting on her royal throne. The woman is clearly meant to be the beloved Queen Narah, Ulric's late wife. Above her, the clouds part as a giant golden hand reaches down, shining magnificent light over the queen. Her face expresses a serene smile in simple acknowledgment of the hand above.

A date in the bottom corner indicates this glass window was created over twenty-two years ago, just after King Ulric chose Narah to be his queen. She always was a stunning, strong woman, conveying such peace and compassion. To this day, I don't understand why she agreed to marry Ulric or how her warm nature never managed to rub off on him in all their years together.

I lower myself to rest on the landing step and massage my aching knees. "She was beautiful, wasn't she?"

Ezra studies the image intently. Silence ensues, and only after a long pause does he turn back to me. "Sorry, what?"

"The queen." I flick my gaze to the glass.

"Right." He clears his throat. "Yes, she's beautiful."

I discern that familiar haze in his eyes. "Why so distract-ed?"

He looks back at the window. "Just memories I haven't thought of in forever."

I catch his gaze for a brief moment. "What memories?"

A smile pricks the corner of his mouth. "The stories my mother used to read to me. One in particular, the story of Esther."

"Esther?"

"You know, the queen from the Bible."

"I've never heard that story before."

"Really? Your parents never read it to you?"

I shrug. "I never really had an interest in Bible stories. There were a few times I was curious as a kid and asked my mom to read some to me, but I didn't understand their sig-nificance. They were just a bunch of pointless fiction to me."

He rubs his jaw. "Well, I didn't see it till now, but I think you're a lot like her."

"Like Esther?" He's comparing me to a biblical queen? "In what way?"

"Your beauty, your courage, the risks you take and the sacrifices you make for your family."

I ponder his depiction, unsure how to respond.

He takes my hand and pulls me to my feet, motioning to the next set of stairs.

Knowing there may be as many as three more flights to go, and knowing the pain in my leg will only worsen, I decide to dig deeper into his comparison. "Ezra. Would you…tell me the story?"

AN INSOLENT KING. A queen selected for her beauty. A hidden agenda to execute all Jews. Ezra's vivid storytelling captured my attention from the start. He describes the ending with enthusiasm, a love for justice in his eyes. "Queen Esther risked her life to approach her king, but he showed favour to her, and her boldness ultimately saved her entire people."

I try to take in all he's told me. Though I cannot retain every detail, the main themes are clear. "She was willing to sacrifice her life for her people." That's one Bible story I wouldn't call a bunch of pointless fiction.

Ezra's eyes gleam with passion. "And it's not that she wasn't afraid but that she took courage in spite of the fear." He arches a brow. "Remind you of anyone? Maybe—oh, I don't know…a girl in an execution room who tried to trade her life for her parents'?"

We reach the top of the fourth and final stairwell. I take

this excuse to slip down the tight hallway, away from the conversation. Ezra drops it too as we open and explore each room along the corridor. Most are in disarray, wind wafting through shattered windows and littering the floors with old papers.

Near the end of the hall, I open the last door, and a violent gust of snow engulfs me. Ezra gasps and pulls me back from where the floor drops off.

The entire room rests fifty feet below us in the castle's inner courtyard.

I peer over the ledge at the mess of brick and board.

The bombings ruined lands and lives. Much of the castle's tiers crumbled, yet it still stands. At the end of the hall, another flight of stairs begins.

"We should go back down, Ez. The higher we go, the more we risk the tower collapsing."

He stomps up a few stairs, testing their endurance. "Seems fine to me."

My stomach knots.

Ezra reaches for my hand, but I pull back. "Oh, come on." He sulks. "After being locked up half my life, you're going to deny me the pleasure of exploring my newfound freedom a little longer?"

"Now that's just cruel. Using your poor-slave-boy bit to get your way." I subdue a smile and start up the steps after him.

"It worked, didn't it?" He takes my hand with a grin.

My muscles jitter as we climb the potentially unstable staircase. All I want is to be back on solid ground. Good thing there's only one door atop this flight. Ezra turns the rusted knob, and we enter a large room.

Stagnant dust clouds the air and covers the furniture.

Judging from the pale mattress on a metal bed frame, dressers overflowing with clothes, and the desk stacked with papers and personal family pictures in the corner, I'd guess this room to be the head's bedchamber.

I cower. How can something once full of light and life become so dull and desolate?

And why does this sadden me? These feelings should be integrated into my whole being by now. They are just as much my own reality as they are this barren land's. This is who I am now. My life is as bleak as this castle, tiers tumbling to dust one by one. Why can't I grasp that?

"Hey, RJ?" Ezra calls to me from a small window in the right-hand wall.

"Yeah?" It's a much-needed disruption.

He stares out a small window. "That wouldn't happen to be my mother's cottage, would it?"

I hurry to his side and peer through the glass.

He points to a small field in the distance, cleared of trees.

"That's it!" My breath fogs the glass. "That little brown house near the back of the field."

Relief floods his face, and he studies the cottage longingly.

"We should sketch a map of the land from up here." I rush toward the wooden desk across the room. Shuffling through papers, I search for a blank sheet and pen. Then I still, noticing an unusually large piece of yellowed paper with the king's royal seal and signature plastering the bottom. A pit forms in my stomach as I begin reading.

"What is it?"

I bring the paper into the window's light where we can both read it.

Ezra skims each word, and his mouth forms a grim line.

The letter reads:

Dear Mr. Tansen,

Based on previous and current circumstances, I regret to inform you that our country may be on the verge of civil war. Barely stable as it is, we both well understand this would bring utter devastation to Ulcadia. In an attempt to keep the peace, I hereby give ordinance to you, Head Tansen of Ardenburg, to declare a law alteration, effective immediately—one that will prevent catastrophic disaster among our beloved nation.

I understand you have allowed your region the liberty to be a Christian people for some time, and as head, you have the right to rule as you see fit. But as your king, I must voice my concerns and step in when need be. It is my duty to stand by what is right for my country as a whole. I have postponed this as long as possible, but I can no longer overlook the historic reality of what permitting this form of belief among your people will arouse. Your desired verdict of ruling has been a leading contributor to mass destruction and ultimate civilization failure in the past, including, but certainly not limited to, our former nation of Canada.

I formally apologize on behalf of my seemingly drastic decision, but I believe this is the only remaining option to ensure my country's endurance. I must urge you to publicly announce the alteration of your law regarding Christian beliefs, stating that all forms of Christianity be outlawed. Those suspected of holding Christian faith will be tried and, if found guilty, will be asked to renounce their faith to avoid further penalties. If the guilty party does not renounce their faith, their punishment shall be a region-wide broadcasted execution.

I must warn you, Head Tansen, that a senseless refusal on your part to publicly announce this law alteration will result in the bitter end of your people. This is not easy for me to say, as the residents of Ardenburg are the last people I would wish to harm. Nonetheless, I will do

what I must to protect my country.
Sincerely,
King Ulric

Beneath Ulric's seal is a straight black line demanding a signature of Head Tansen's consent to carry out this law alteration, and to then return the letter to the king.

But the line is blank. And the letter is still here.

"He didn't sign it." I'm not sure if I should be relieved or upset. I suppose both. Head Tansen stood by his people's freedom to the end. However, this resulted in the obliteration of his people and his land. "I should've known Ulric did this." I glare out the opposite window to beyond the vast expanse of trees where the city of rubble begins. "Your mother said some people got word and evacuated the region, but most weren't so fortunate. The kids she took in lost their parents in the bombings." My jaw clenches. "Ulric destroyed everything and everyone."

"And no one even knows." Ezra shuffles through files on the desk, uncovering a brown folder labelled *Ardenburg Destruction Level Updates*. He sifts through the sheets within and shows me photo after photo of black-and-white chaos. Collapsed buildings. Burnt houses. Capsized roads. Schools turned to rubble. "Kinborough will go on supporting Ulric unless this letter and this land are revealed to them. We've got the proof right here that Ulric shows no mercy. He wipes out entire regions because they won't conform to his demands, and deceives his people with smooth, scheming lies." He hands me the folder, a flash of defiance in his eyes.

I pack it and Ulric's letter in my bag. "We'll show them who their king really is."

Chapter 17

Ezra sketches out a map on a blank page from the window. Meanwhile, I rummage through a dresser for any salvageable clothing items, but they all seem too far gone to be used.

I lift a partially corroded hand-mirror from the dresser's edge and flinch, nearly dropping it on the ground. I can't remember the last time I saw my reflection, but I know I've never looked so dreadful in all my life. Scratched up, sickly pale, blotchy skin. Dirty, tangled hair. Cheekbones and jawline overly prominent from malnourishment. Eyes circled with dark rings. After just a couple of weeks out here, I appear to be more of a starved slave than Ezra.

These past weeks have drained so much of my strength. What was Ezra thinking, comparing me to Queen Esther? I am nothing like her. I'd be the last one defined as beautiful. Or brave.

Not that it matters. Every day spent dragging my broken leg through the woods is a day closer to giving up my hope of saving Ren. Sure, we know how to reach Susa's home now. And sure, we will probably make it back to Kinborough. But how can I trust Ezra to rescue Ren without getting caught? He himself was unable to escape for eight years. How can I be so naïve as to believe he can get in and out of prison undetected?

Ezra seems to sense my silent panic because he joins me at the dresser and rubs my shoulder soothingly. "Done with the map. Want to go down now?"

I take a breath of relief. "Yes. And we're *not* exploring any more tiers of this castle."

He snickers and follows me through the door. "As you wish."

ONCE OUT OF the castle's arched mouth, we stroll the stone pathway through the courtyard. The breeze has calmed since our arrival, and fluffy snowflakes drift to the ground like white confetti, coating everything in sight.

Ezra lifts his face to the sky and opens his mouth, lazy snowflakes melting on his tongue.

His delight in something so trivial eases my anxieties. I laugh at the weird faces he pulls while attempting to eat the flakes, then I copy his actions, catching a flake or two myself.

He accidentally inhales a flake and lurches into a coughing fit—which soon turns into a fit of laughter, face flushed and eyes watering.

I laugh along with him, unable to contain it. When I regain my breath, I lift my face to the sky. Eyes closed, I let the snow melt on my skin. "Ah, I've missed this."

"Me too." A hint of sadness laces his words, but he quickly collects himself and musters a genuine smile. His hair turns white, and he shakes the snow from his head.

With the pain in my leg easing, I drop my bag and turn in slow circles, arms outstretched. I smile and watch my breath cloud.

Ezra copies me, looking to the sky and spinning faster and faster until he topples over. Then he squints up at me, and as I circle closer to him, he sits up, grabs me around the waist, and pulls me down.

I squeal and fall on him.

Then he sees my crutched leg and his eyes widen. "I wasn't thinking. I didn't hurt you, did I?"

Collapsed in his lap, I shove a handful of snow in his face and melt into laughter.

He wipes the snow off with his sleeve. "I'll take that as a no."

I push myself up and run—as much as I'm able—from him. He throws a snowball and misses, then throws another that hits my arm. I swoop down to pack a snowball and launch it at him. It hits his leg, and the next one he throws hits my back.

After a few more rounds, he drops to the ground, winded. He folds his hands behind his head and closes his eyes. Pure bliss softens his rosy face.

I drop beside him and lay my head on his chest. The thin layer of snow packs beneath my body, moulding to my form. I study the old castle walls surrounding us, then close my eyes and inhale the fresh, wintry air.

For once, the subtle yet constant sense of dread unleashes its grip on me. Living in this strange tranquillity makes me wonder how I've never known it before. It's so new to me yet feels so right. When the unease begins to creep back in, I drive it away. Minute after minute, I breathe in this peace, loathing the thought of having to soon let it go and move on. Because for the first time in my life, I believe this is what true joy feels like.

He sighs, and I feel the vibrations of his words when he

says, "We should go if we want to reach my mother's before dark."

Though eagerness tingles through my limbs at the thought of Susa's warm cottage, I dare not open my eyes. "Just a few more minutes."

He doesn't argue. When he exhales slowly, I match my breathing to his.

Eventually, I prop myself up to sit in the snow. Then Ezra stands and pulls me to my feet.

I interlace my fingers with his, the wave of calm still saturating me, and look up into his serene eyes. "Thank you," I whisper. "This was the most fun I've had since…" My gaze falters.

"I know." His tone is empathetic and he tilts my chin up, studying me.

My face heats and my heart speeds at his attentive gaze. For a moment, I wonder if he might lean down and kiss me. But then I recall my horrid reflection in that mirror, how much I've changed, how repulsive I've become in these past weeks, and I lower my chin in shame.

Perhaps Ezra's just now realizing the same thing—how revolting my appearance is—because he drops my hands.

How foolish I am to think he would want me. How foolish I am to *want* him to want me.

But then he retrieves his gun from its holster, and I realize how wrong my assumption was. With a grave grimace, he aims to the right of the courtyard's entrance and fires twice.

A single soldier slumps to the ground at the arched gate.

I gasp, adrenaline and unwanted memories making me shudder. Though the deafening blasts elicit images of my mother lying dead in that field, I fight them back. I manage a shaky sigh out of relief for our safety.

But then the gun falls from Ezra's hand, and he staggers into me. Pulls off his gloves and clenches his lower abdomen. Grits his teeth, face flushing.

I freeze, my body numb and weak. Only when blood seeps between his fingers am I able to process this horror. He didn't fire twice. He and the soldier both shot once.

And both hit their target.

"No," I exhale, holding Ezra steady. "No, no, no!" I unzip his coat and pull it from his arms. The fabric of Dad's white t-shirt sticks to his body, stained red. "You're fine." I grab his wool blanket from my bag and wrap it around him. I throw his arm over my shoulder and steer him back toward the castle's front room. "We can fix this. You'll be okay."

He groans as I help carry his weight. But when his legs give out, I'm unable to hold him up myself.

I lower his head gently to the ground, take off my gloves and press my palms over his wound. But the snow beneath him turns crimson. I wriggle my fingers under his back, and when I pull them out, they're dripping blood.

The bullet went straight through. He's going to bleed out.

I draw back. My breath shallows and my head pounds, all hope dying along with him. I cover my mouth with the back of my hand as a wave of nausea overwhelms me.

Anxious eyes fixed on me, he reaches out. Squeezes my shaking hand. Then he swallows and coughs. His eyes shut in a painful grimace. He draws weak breaths, clasping my hand tighter.

How can I sit here, helplessly waiting as another person closest to me bleeds out?

I can't do this. I can't. Not again.

"I'm sorry, Ezra." The words are inaudible. I pull my hand from his cold, clammy grip. My limbs quake as I grab my belongings and escape the courtyard. I hobble from the roadway into the forest, to the river's edge. My bag falls from my shoulder, and I scrub my hands fiercely in the icy water. I dig under my fingernails to clean them of his blood.

This can't be happening. It's not real. He's not dying. He can't be.

I pace the forest madly, eventually stopping at an oak tree. Back against its bark, I sink to the ground, gripping my head in my hands. My body convulses as I fail to contain the rising sobs.

Oh God, he's gone. He really is. And I can't do anything to help him. How can he be gone?

My leg throbs and I grit my teeth. Rip the crutch from my knee. Anger swarms in my head, and I push myself up. I take my crutch and heave it against the tree. "How could you do this? How could you let this happen to him?" I cry out, smashing the crutch over and over until every beam is broken. By the time I'm finished, its former structure is no longer recognizable.

I huff for breath, exhausted. Every ounce of my being shivers from the cold. I build a fire by the tree and use my broken crutch as kindling.

I beg the tears to stop. Beg this all to just be a nightmare that I will soon wake from. But as much as I try to awaken, I can't. Because this is real. And he is gone.

My head feels as if it could burst. The wind freezes my wet face, and I bury myself in my blanket.

I promised I would reunite him with Susa. Told him I'd protect him. I swore to myself to put him first, as he always did for me. But I couldn't. And I didn't. And I knew at the time that I couldn't protect him, so why did I promise to? Why get his hopes up like that? How could I do that to him?

All he wanted was to see his mother again. But he sacrificed his own desires for me, put a complete stranger's needs before his own. And I couldn't even keep a simple promise. He died without getting the one thing he always wanted. He died without his family. Died, even without me.

I hit my forehead against my drawn knees.

I let him die alone. He looked so scared. All he wanted was someone to be with him. He gripped my hand, craving comfort. But I drew back. He was dying, and I ran off because *I* couldn't take it. I couldn't bear to see him through his final moments. What a coward I am.

He doesn't deserve this. He might have argued that no one is innocent, but his every intention was truly blameless in my eyes. This world took advantage of his humble heart. They enslaved him, intending to break him, but he came out the other side unbroken. Stronger because of the pain. Eager to help rather than hurt. During his times of vulnerability with me, I felt his internal guilt for sins of his past, and I know without a doubt he'd change them if he could. He was too gentle, too sweet, to deserve such a cruel ending.

I stop as an image materializes in my mind. Inspiration strikes. I rush to retrieve my tool satchel and hack into a thick oak branch. After chopping out a small wooden block, I sit down by the fire and carve away hours on end. Its shape takes form as the image solidifies in my head. I uncover one of Ren's extra shoelaces he'd collected for his own carving and whittle a hole through the back of the figure to loop the lace. Absorbed in every detail, my emotions numb and my tears subside.

The simple features, beautiful grain pattern, and curly texture all start to emerge from the wood. Head bowed. Eyes closed. Ears relaxed and outspread. Knees bent, lying down in submission. Gentle and precious and humble and sweet. The figure captures who he was and who he wanted to be.

Yes. I hold it between my stiff fingers.

The lamb. Ezra's symbol.

I lean back against the tree, inspecting the creature that so perfectly captures Ezra's essence. But as images of his death return, I clamp my jaw and look away. Though carving brought relief, that time is over now. And all I'm left with are my memories of him and this wooden figure.

I just want him back. Never have I felt so accepted, so free, around anyone other than my family. He didn't want the superficial stuff. He sought to know *me*. My passions. My past. My dreams and desires.

I think he might've even *liked* me… And I might've liked him too.

The loneliness gnaws in my chest.

How will I tell Susa? The eight years she believed her son was dead, he was really alive, being tortured and starved as Ulric's slave. And then within mere hours of reuniting with her, he was shot and killed. It will crush her.

And how will I save Renan? Ezra was my key in and out of prison. Now it's all up to me. Surely I won't make it without being caught. Then all will be as Ulric desires. Renan and I will be his slaves, doomed to a life of torment and misery.

I wish Mom's beliefs were true. I wish there were a God. Maybe then, she and Ezra would be alive. Renan wouldn't have been taken. Ulric wouldn't have changed that law. Or bombed this region. We wouldn't have been forced to flee our home. And Ezra wouldn't have been enslaved all those years ago. If God were real, and if he was who Mom said he was, things would be different.

I stretch my feet to the fire's dying flame.

This life is too hard. I wish I could give it up.

But Renan needs me. He's all I've got left. I know my odds at a successful rescue are slim without Ezra, but I need to try. I need to get to Susa's.

I twirl the lamb carving between my fingers. Tears blurring my vision, I look from the figure to the fire. It was a mistake making this. I can't bear to look at it. I could let it burn, along with its link to Ezra's memories.

I shuffle forward and hold it over the flame, taking in its features one last time. The fire licks at its feet. But before I drop it, something moves in the distance. I look up.

And there he is.

Mouth agape, I rise to my feet.

He stumbles from the courtyard's archway, bundled in the blanket I wrapped around him. When he spots me, he stops, then paces toward me.

My chest swarms and my body tremors. I blink hard. But he's still there when I open my eyes.

I shove the wooden lamb in my pocket and rush to him, heart pounding. In my arms his cold body trembles, and I hold him steady as he sways. Then he winces, and I loosen my grip, remembering his wound.

My lip quivers and I close my eyes, pressing my forehead to his chest. "I wish this was real," I whisper, though the splinter of hope in my heart only seems to grow. "Could it be, Ez?"

He shivers, and I gaze up at his pale face. His purple lips part and his voice croaks. "Guess it's your turn to save me again, RJ."

I smile and hold his freezing face in my hands, growing more confident this isn't an illusion.

I shouldn't believe it, but as much as I don't understand

what happened, I know this must be real. He's really here. He is alive. Barely, but alive nonetheless.

I gather my belongings and pull his arm over my shoulder. "Let's get you warm."

He observes my leg. "Doesn't it—doesn't it hurt you to walk without your crutch?"

I hide a wince as I hold half his weight. "Don't worry about it."

He gives a brisk laugh. "Who'd have th-thought it'd be you carrying me?"

I fake a smile, concerned only with getting him warm before he becomes too weak to walk. Through the courtyard and back into the castle's large room I help him. After lighting the lantern, I unroll my mattress on the ground beside the fireplace, then lower him onto it and tuck both of our blankets around him.

As much as I hate to leave him, I return to the forest to chop up a fallen birch and tear strips of its bark. Pain flares through my shin as I carry stacks of logs into the cold room. I use the bark to start a fire in the fireplace, then add twigs and logs over time. Soon a can of vegetable soup sits atop the teepee of steadily burning logs.

As the room heats, Ezra's eyes begin to close.

"No, don't sleep." I tap his cheek, and his eyelids flutter open. "Fight it, Ezra. If you fall asleep now, you might not wake up."

"The pain." He groans, clenching his jaw. "I can't—I can't…"

"Let me take a look at the wound." I bite my lip, anxious for what I might find. He may be alive, but that doesn't mean he's sure to make it through the night after a bout of bad blood loss. "Hey, stay awake." I shake his arm. "Find something to talk about."

Sweat beads on his ashen face. "Like—like what?"

I snort. "The one time you're short on words." He lifts his back as I carefully slide his blood-stained shirt off over his head. "Well, you could start with what happened, how you're still here."

I spot the entrance wound. Dried blood coats his lower abdomen and stains part of his jeans, but the wound itself has ceased bleeding and already begun clotting over. "How is this possible?" I stare at the clot.

"I'm still trying…to understand it myself." He grits his teeth, every breath hurting him. "All I can say is…he gave me a second chance."

I nod, wondering whether he's even conscious enough to know what he's talking about. I predict where the exit wound on his back should be, then help him roll onto his side. I spot the hole quickly. Slightly larger than the entrance wound, it has also begun clotting over. At least there's no bullet to extract—I wouldn't know where to begin. But I also know nothing about tending to any internal damage it might have caused.

Only after I've gone to the river to soak his shirt and returned do I detect the dozens of pale, rigid scars crossing his back. I remain quiet, using the damp shirt to dab away the blood and clean him up. Then I tape patches of gauze from my medical kit over both wounds, letting the silence draw on.

"Don't worry. The scars are from a long time ago. And I'm a fast healer," he murmurs, lying on his stomach in a position that least hurts him. His prominent ribs and spine display years of malnutrition.

His words stab my heart, producing pictures in my mind

of him hunched over, facing the wall in the execution room, chains clutching his wrists as the headsman draws a leather whip behind him. My head pounds. "How old were you?" I ask, thinking of Renan.

His shoulder blades sharpen and he hesitates. "All different ages."

I swallow the rising fear of Renan being tortured. "Ezra, I still don't fully believe you're here right now. Maybe I've gone crazy. You died, didn't you?"

"No… I'd say it was more"—he winces—"more of a near-death experience."

"It was a gunshot to your stomach. The bullet went straight through. You lost so much blood." I search his eyes. "How are you alive?"

"Like I said, he gave me a second chance." His eyes meet mine, a lightness in them I've never seen before.

The soup bubbles, and I retrieve it using one of Ezra's gloves. While waiting for it to cool, I unpack Ezra's clothes that I'd washed for him last night at the cabin. Only slightly damp, I help him slide his fresh tee on. Then I unfasten the belt of Dad's pants I'd given him to wear and slide them off his body, helping him into his own pair again. Under other circumstances, this would be awkward and uncomfortable—really, it still is—but he barely has the strength to lift his head, let alone change his clothes, so I must help him.

After throwing his dirtied clothes outside, I test the soup, then grab a slice of bread and dip it into the warm liquid. I prop Ezra's head up with my bag and feed him the soaked bread until he falls asleep, then finish off what little remains and rest beside the fire to monitor him.

By nightfall, his colouring begins to return and he stops shivering.

I wake every so often to check on him and add logs to the fire. With each passing hour, my hope for his recovery increases. I wish I could be content simply knowing he's growing healthier, but the question haunts me well into the night. *How is he alive?*

I fall asleep with the gnawing puzzle on my mind.

Maybe he'll start making more sense after some rest.

Tomorrow I will ask him again.

Chapter 18

I light the lantern in the morning to see Ezra. Cheeks flushed with warmth, he calmly gazes at the fireplace's fading coals.

I stretch my back from a stiff night's sleep on the concrete, then crawl over to him, place a hand on his forehead. Good—not too warm. By his rosy colouring, I feared he'd developed a fever within the past hours. I check his temperature with the thermometer in my medical kit to be safe, but it reads normal.

As I add kindling to the fire, he continues staring at it with that familiar, hazy look. I let him be this time because, unlike his typical trauma episodes, he seems content with whatever he's thinking about. His entire being holds a glowing peace that even calms me.

He eventually comes to and looks up at me.

"How are you?" I ask, rearranging his blankets.

"A little sore. But I guess that's to be expected."

I lift his shirt to check his wounds and change his bandages. Working quietly, I repress the question that's been running in my head for hours, but curiosity soon wins me over. "Last night, you gave a rather vague explanation for how you're alive. Care to elaborate?"

He frowns, slowly shakes his head. "I've been going over

it in my head. But it's so complex, so beyond words. All I can say is that…Jesus came to me. Saved my life."

So he's sticking with his story. "That's not possible, Ez. You were bleeding out, scared to die. Your mind probably just dreamt something up to help you cope."

"No," he whispers. "I'm telling the truth. It wasn't just some dream." His expression softens. "It was the realest thing I've ever experienced."

"Look." I tape a fresh gauze pad over his abdomen. "It's natural for the brain to create illusions to distract you from pain. They can look so real."

He wets his lips. "I get that it's hard to believe. But there's no way I could've conjured the vision myself… And it wasn't just about what I saw. It's about what I felt." He takes my hand, eyes gleaming. "I felt him, RJ. I felt his love. His forgiveness. His freedom. Still do."

Something hardens inside me. I pull my hand back and finish his bandages.

"I know it's confusing. But what other explanation can you give me? You've already said that I was dying, that I shouldn't be alive right now. Yet here I am. What's harder for you to believe—that I miraculously survived a bullet wound, or that God was the one to provide me with that miracle?"

Frustration surges through my veins. There's got to be some reason other than a miracle from God. But then I'm reminded of Renan, when he claimed a man brought candles into his cell and comforted him when he was scared and alone. I argued with him about his beliefs, and he linked my lack of faith to Mom's death. Then I lost him.

If I continue to argue Ezra's claim, he might leave me too. And as much as I hate his reasoning, what matters right now is I don't lose him again. After all, it's only a matter of time before he comes to his senses and forgets this miracle nonsense.

"You're right," I say. "It's confusing. And I don't understand. But I'm just glad you're alive."

Eyes smiling, he lays his head down and resumes gazing into the fire.

I KEEP HIM hydrated throughout the day, then feed him eggs for lunch and soup and baked potato for dinner. His strength builds incredibly fast, and despite my concern, he's up walking again by dusk, slowly but surely.

I work on staining his lamb carving while he sleeps through the night. Whether I'll give it to him, I haven't yet decided.

AT DAWN THE next morning, I quietly exit the castle to fill our canteens at the river.

The stiff snow crunches underfoot, and the sky is clear and calm. Only a gentle wind wafts over the courtyard walls.

I recover Ezra's bloody jacket on the ground and bring it along with me to wash.

A rotting smell by the castle's entrance nearly makes me gag. Averting my eyes, I pass the dead soldier slumped against the archway and make my way to the river. After washing the jacket and filling our canteens, I start back to Ezra.

A hissing noise breaks the silence, echoing through the courtyard. I turn around, tracing the sound back to the dead soldier. The fuzzy noise repeats. Holding my breath, I roll up the soldier's sleeve to find a communicator around his wrist. I unfasten it and listen for more static. On my way back to the castle, a computerized voice crackles through the microphone, though the words are unclear.

I pocket it and hurry back to the castle.

Ezra stirs as I let the door crash behind me. "Where were you?" he mumbles.

"At the river." I drop his wet coat and set down the canteens. "But I heard something on my way back and found *this* on the dead soldier." I hand him the device.

He pushes himself up on his elbows and studies it. "A transmitter."

"It was a loud, fuzzy voice. Like someone was trying to talk, but it was out of frequency."

He toys with its controls, and when the crackling voice roars through the speaker again, he turns a dial. The static subsides, replaced by an automated voice.

"Soldier, come in. Respond if you receive this alert." It waits, then repeats itself several times before saying, "No signs of geographical movement have been detected for over twenty-four hours. We must check in with your progress to ensure your safety. If no response is received, we will check for vitals. If no vitals are detected, we will alert a search party."

Ezra's thumb moves toward the button.

"What are you doing?" I grab it. "If you respond, they'll know you're not the real soldier."

"It's a machine. It won't know. But it *will* know the soldier is dead if no one answers. And then it'll locate our coordinates and send more soldiers to find us. I have to answer." He takes it back, holds down the button, and speaks clearly into the microphone. "Message received. No need to alert a party."

A flash of bright green glows below the screen. "Response sent. Vitals not required."

The worried look melts from his face.

Just before he sets it down, it beeps, and another voice resounds, this one deep and human. "This is your headsman speaking."

I still, staring at the device. "Malachi? Ulric's son? Didn't he die?"

Ezra shushes me, inclining an ear to the device.

"Here's what we've got so far on our execution escapees," the headsman continues, his voice strained and raspy. "The boy, eight, was recently retrieved from the southern forest area of the region of Ardenburg."

The boy, eight.

Renan. He really is alive.

"The girl, sixteen, was last spotted around the same area but got away. She could be anywhere by now. And though we doubt she's dangerous, several soldiers have been deemed dead. We have no indication so far as to the location of the father, but we do know from footage of the escape that he is armed and dangerous, the culprit of at least two guard's deaths. Whoever returns him will receive the reward previously announced. And as for the mother… She has recently been confirmed dead."

My tongue coils uncomfortably in my mouth. I look down, sensing Ezra's eyes on me.

"Though important, capturing this family is not our priority goal. A slave has escaped. Eighteen years old. Name's Ezra Henson. Many of you should be familiar with him."

Ezra rolls his eyes.

"The slave is now our number-one target, charged with

the first-degree murder of Head Damien, attempted murder of *yours truly*, and for assisting the escape of the wanted family. Though we are currently unsure of his whereabouts, we have good reason to assume he escaped to the same approximate area as the wanted family. He's expected to be armed and dangerous." The headsman begins wheezing, and the feed cuts out.

Ten seconds later it's back on, and he continues speaking. "Though we need every member of the escaped family, I advise you to keep the slave as your top priority. The king promises substantial rewards to whoever delivers him. Bring him back, dead or alive." The headsman's voice cuts out again, ending the message.

We both stare at the communicator.

"Renan's alive," I say. "I knew my dream was a sign."

Ezra tosses the device away and winces, pushing himself to a stand. "Let's go."

"No. You shouldn't be walking." I grab his arm to lower him back down.

"I'm fine. I can make it to my mother's. Too many soldiers have been killed."

I envision the soldier I stabbed. "We had to kill them. If we didn't, we'd be dead."

"I know. But the more we kill, the more they'll send. I've got to warn my mother. She's not safe where she is anymore."

I remember my discussion with Cree, the older girl Susa took in. She said they haven't dealt with soldiers in years, but now that I'm here, I've put Susa in danger of being discovered.

He takes small steps toward the door.

"Ezra, this is crazy. It'll take weeks for you to recover.

Walking will only make it worse."

"Trust me, I'll be fine. He said I'd be healed."

I groan. Why can't he just start making sense? "At least let me feed you breakfast first."

After hesitating, he nods and lowers himself back down onto the mattress. "Can't say no to that."

I fill an empty soup can with water and heat it over the fire until it simmers to boil the last three remaining eggs.

Ezra starts folding blankets and rolling my mattress. "We can eat as we walk."

Unable to talk him out of it, I douse the fire and collect our belongings once the eggs are boiled.

Ezra pulls out the map he drew from the castle, and we follow it. He eyes my leg as we leave the courtyard. "Are you okay walking like this?"

I nod, ignoring the slight ache each step brings. "If I said no, what would you do about it? Carry me?" I take in his pale face and weary posture.

"We make a good team, huh?" He nudges my shoulder.

I chuckle at the thought of our combined pathetic lives. As if it's come to that. The only way to ensure I don't cry about everything that's happened to us is to laugh about it.

I peel the eggs and make Ezra eat two of the three as we follow his map through the forest.

After an hour, his pace slows and he grows paler. He catches me staring at his hand held over his stomach. "What?"

"How are you doing this? How are you healing so fast? I know you're still in pain, but what gunshot victim is up walking this soon? Everything about the past three days confuses me."

He shrugs. "It's still hard for me to believe I'm alive. But it changed me. And I know this sounds weird, but it makes perfect sense."

I scoff. "It makes no sense."

"It makes sense that he would come to me in my time of greatest need and show me love," he explains. "It was a glimpse into my past, of how I felt around my mother. As a kid, I always thought the love and joy and peace she expressed was just who she was. But now I know it was really *him* showing through her. He was that constant feeling of love and safety I felt in her. Like, no matter what happened, I'd never lose her."

The same warmth I felt at Susa's cottage floods me. The heart-thawing, fear-ceasing kindness that radiated from her and the twins.

"Until I did lose her. After they took me away, I lost that feeling of safety for so long I forgot I ever felt it in the first place. But what I didn't realize was that I never stopped seeking it. That love. Only when God saved me the other day did I feel it again."

I process his words. So infuriating. So hard to grasp. "How can you expect me to believe in something…some*one* I can't see or hear or feel, who's never shown any evidence of his existence, and who the whole world has forgotten?"

"I'm not asking you to believe what I say is true. I'm just saying that, for me, when I felt him…that was the only time I've ever experienced a love that surpassed the love I felt from my mother. I just wish everyone could know him like I'm finally learning to."

"But there's a reason no one knows him," I argue. "Because he's not real."

"Okay, think of this." He wets his lips. "If he's not real, if there are no signs of him and only one in a thousand believe in him, why would there be such a cruel punishment brought upon the people who do believe? If the belief was false and those believers were living a lie, why would the king feel so threatened that he'd have those people executed? And why would those people keep their faith? I never understood it. But now I'm starting to. I'm starting to realize how people can risk their lives, their families, everything they love, for something they can't even prove."

"And why is that?"

"Because to them, it's the realest, truest thing they've ever felt. It makes the problems of this world vanish. It exceeds the joy that any earthly experience can offer. And if I could give up my life to live in that love forever, even if it meant I never reunited with my mother…I would."

"How can you say that?" My words come out louder than expected. "After everything that's happened to you. After all the king made you do? If God is real, why would he let an innocent child be treated like that? You say he loves you? That is *not* love. That is betrayal! That's a lie. He is not real. He is not here."

"But he *is* here," Ezra says. "He's always been here, even when we can't feel it. Even when I was living as a slave and the last thing I thought I could be was loved." He blinks. "He lives in me now. I can feel him healing me from the inside out."

"Well, that's great for you. Really. I'm glad you're alive," I say, suppressing the rising grief. "But I'm sure I've never felt him."

He sighs. "Look, I'm human. You know more than anyone I'm not perfect. I don't have all the answers. I don't know why he allows pain. But is it possible you've never felt him before…because you've never wanted to?"

"Believe me, I wish there were someone out there who could protect me and help me." I shake my head. "But faith is just too far a stretch. Too much of a bargain for me to try after all that's happened. I can't risk being let down again."

Ezra mulls over my words. "Before we heard the announcement on the transmitter about your brother being captured and brought to the prison, how did you know he was there?"

"I had a dream about it."

"So, if I understand this right, you didn't know for sure your brother was even at the prison, but you were willing to bet your life on returning to rescue him?"

I remain silent.

"Sounds to me like you put a great deal of faith in a dream that could've meant nothing."

"It wasn't about faith," I counter. "And definitely not about faith in God. It's just that…believing in the dream was my only hope."

He nods. "I can relate to that. As I was bleeding out, the guilt for all I'd done in the past was so overwhelming. It was then I knew God was real and I was going to hell. So I begged him to save me. To forgive me. He was my only hope. And it turns out, he was the only hope I needed."

I don't reply. And Ezra allows the silence.

EZRA SKIMS HIS hand across the snow-covered pine branches as we move deeper into the forest.

I rub my thumb over Renan's dove as our prior conversation evokes childhood memories of bedside conversations with my mother. The times when she'd stroke my hair and kiss my forehead as if I'd been her real child all along.

Whenever she spoke about her faith, a passion lit within her and her eyes sparkled with life. She made sure I knew that she would love me no matter what I chose to believe. But she'd also explain that the God she believed in made even her bad days worth living.

If Ezra happens to be telling the truth, and on the off chance he's right about God, could it be possible that what he said he felt with his mother was what I felt with mine? *Him through her?*

Distracted, I stumble over a root hidden beneath the snow. Pain pulses through my leg as I land on my hands and knees. An agonizing sting flares through the bone.

Ezra grunts as he pulls me up with all his might.

I balance on my uninjured foot and brush the snow from my hands.

"Here." He takes off his gloves and squeezes my hands in his, bringing warmth to them, then looks at my foot raised from the ground. "It really hurts, doesn't it?"

I take a step forward, and the pain bursts through my shin.

Just what we need now. More delay. Within minutes, the surging pain grows into a constant ache.

Ezra takes my bag from my shoulder to carry it himself. "Do you want to rest a while?"

I take another step. My leg bears my weight without buckling or giving out. "I'm okay."

Ezra steps in slow unison with me, ready to catch me if I fall. "What happened to your crutch, anyway?"

I cringe. "Well, this is just a hunch, but it may have somehow been smashed to pieces against a tree…and then those pieces may have somehow been burnt in a fire."

"Huh." He ponders that. "Pretty specific hunch."

I LIMP ALONG for another half hour before dropping to my knees on the side of the trail, unable to stand the pain any longer.

"We can rest here." Ezra sits down beside me.

"No. We're so close. Another hour or two and we'll be there, in her cottage. You'll get to see her again. I can make it." I grit my teeth, and Ezra helps me to my feet.

He kicks around under the snow and pulls up a thick pine branch. After snapping smaller branches off it, he tests its durability under his own weight. "It'll have to do." He gives it to me.

It takes some of the pressure from my leg as I lean on it. "Thank you."

We trek on slowly.

Each time my leg shoots with menacing pain, memories surface of that cell door slamming on it. Still, Renan's face remains constant in the back of my mind.

I bring my hand to my chest and clasp the dove. This time, it doesn't quench my longing for peace or for Renan. I suppose some problems are just too much for an inanimate object to bear. I just wish I knew he was okay, that they weren't starving him or abusing him.

Pressure builds behind my eyes, and I release the dove, putting all my effort into keeping up with Ezra. I push forward, but a sudden breeze slams me. It steals my breath, and I lose my footing. A cry makes its way from my lungs but gets stuck in my throat.

Ezra puts his arm around me and guides me through the forest toward a small cave within a rocky hill. I fall again as the wind bombards me. When Ezra pulls me up, black spots scatter through my vision and my hearing fades.

Not again.

"Stay with me." Though urgent, Ezra's voice is but a murmur to me. "RJ, stay awake!" He shakes me.

But I give in to the lure of sleep as the pain finally releases me from its prison.

Chapter 19

I wake with the metallic taste of blood in my mouth and open my eyes to see Ezra by my side, taping a fresh piece of gauze over his abdomen. He probably broke his wounds' clots to carry me here.

We are in a small cave, and the smoky smell of a fire built by the entrance consumes it.

My tongue stings, and I remove my top teeth from where they've cut into it. I close my eyes and swallow blood. Only when I push myself up from my mattress does the pain register in my leg. Dizziness consumes me, and I stumble back.

Ezra jumps up and lowers me down against the wall of the cave, then tucks my blanket around me. "Take it easy. You were out for half an hour." He presses the cold rim of my canteen to my lips, and I drink. The frigid water washes down any blood I hadn't already swallowed. "Speaking of passing out, is that a normal thing for you? Because I believe this would be the second time you've fallen for me—literally—and I'm curious to know if it's just me, or if you faint at the feet of every guy you hike abandoned forests with?"

"Nope, guess you're just lucky."

He grins, uncovering my casted leg. "I took your boot off. It was only adding to the pain, constricting your leg." He lifts my leg and rests my foot in his lap. "How long's it been since my mother casted it?"

"Almost two weeks."

"And how did you get the injury in the first place?"

I take another sip of water as the painful memory resurfaces. "When we were arrested, I fought back as I was brought to my cell. I heard my mom calling from down the hall and tried to get to her. I stuck my leg out the door to buy me some time, and Taima slammed the door on it."

"Man." Ezra grimaces. "Taima was always too tough for her own good."

"Her eyes were so cold, so cruel. She stared straight at me, slammed the door without so much as blinking." I lean back, glaring at my leg. "And now I've got a lifetime to pay for it."

"Don't say that. It'll heal. Might take a month or two, but it will heal."

I chew my lip. "It's not just the break. Even though I can feel pain, there's no external sensation from below my knee down to my toes. Your mother said if the nerves got damaged, there's a good chance the numbness will be permanent. I might never walk properly again."

Ezra stares at me, grief brimming in his eyes, and proceeds to prod my foot. "Can you feel this?" He pinches my toe through my sock, then moves my foot at the ankle. "How about this?"

"I'm sorry." My voice barely rises above a whisper.

He sets down my leg. "Why are you apologizing?"

"We'd already be at your mother's if I hadn't fought back in prison. You wouldn't be nearly killing yourself carrying me to shelter when I faint."

Not to mention, Mom would probably still be alive. That

thought comes out of nowhere.

"Hey." He clears his throat. "It's not your fault. We'll get there eventually. Stop beating yourself up about it. Taking care of yourself is the only thing you should worry about right now."

"I should be taking care of *you*. Not vice versa." How ironic is it that Ezra is caring for me two days after being shot himself? He seems too healthy. It's as if the bullet merely grazed him.

I lie down and pull my blanket to my chin.

"Try to sleep. I doubt you've had much the past few nights looking after me. I'll wake you for dinner."

BY THE TIME I awaken to the jabbing ache in my shin, the sun has set outside the cave.

Ezra hunches over the fire, lost in thought, turning two tinfoil-wrapped potatoes on their skewers. The flames flicker in his calm eyes. Usually, when he's unaware I'm watching him, he lets his true feelings of guilt and grief wear down his posture and expression. But lately I've sensed only peace within him.

I study him, intrigued by how such a guilt-ridden person can change so entirely. I didn't realize how much shame he'd carried with him daily until the weight of it was lifted from his shoulders. It was part of him for so long, he probably didn't realize it either. The shooting changed him. He seems so different now, so free. So much better for it.

If only I could grasp a bit of whatever he has, let some of my own guilt fall away.

"Hey, how's the leg?" He catches me staring and passes me a slice of buttered bread.

"It's the reason I woke up." I sit up and stretch. I have no appetite but eat the bread anyway.

Soon after, he sets a potato wrapped in tinfoil by my side to cool. When the other is done roasting, he sits down beside me, cuts the potatoes open, and drops a glob of butter in each.

I clench my jaw, breathing deeply in attempts to ease the pain.

"Talk to me," he says.

"About what?" I wince, curling my leg.

"Anything that'll take your mind off the pain. Tell me about yourself, your favourite things to do."

I take a bite of bread. "You already know everything about me and my hobbies. There's nothing left to tell."

"I know there's way more to you than that. I know you love carving, creating. I know you've got a soft side beneath the layers of ice and thorns, but I'm guessing not many people have ever dug deep enough to truly see it."

"If you think you've got me figured out, why are you asking more questions?"

"I never said that. Actually, I believe what I just described only scratches the surface of who you are. So I'm asking questions, not to figure you out but to know you deeper."

And what he's discovered so far hasn't scared him off? That's a first.

"Aha—I've got it!"

"Got what?"

"The perfect question. It's kind of like a game. I used to play it with my mom." He clears his throat. "If you could snap your fingers and have anything you wanted, what would you wish for?"

Does he know he's not the only one to have played this

game? It's a bit childish—in fact, I've played it with Renan many times. "I never understood this game. Why do people like to torture themselves? Wishing for things, knowing they'll never come true. What's the point?"

"The point is…to dream. You'll realize what's most important to you in life." He smiles, warmth in his eyes. "So what's your wish?"

"Right now, that this leg would stop torturing me."

"Okay, not a bad start, but try thinking beyond that. Beyond the pain, beyond current circumstances. What are your deepest desires?"

"Example?" I take a bite of my potato drenched in butter.

"Hmm. All right." He smirks. "I wish the girl I like would come to see just how special she is."

The girl he likes? Warmth rushes to my cheeks, and I'm too stunned to try and impede it.

With a goofy grin stretching up his face, he no doubt notices the flush of colour. "Your turn." He nudges me.

I remain silent, mind running full speed. How can he like me? I know I thought it a possibility after he was shot, and I know I thought maybe I liked him too, but that was when I didn't think I'd ever see him again. I was heartbroken and remorseful. Why would he want me? No boy ever has. And I've never liked anyone that way either. But Ezra…I have to admit, I'm starting to—

"RJ?" He cuts through my jumbled thoughts.

"Huh?" I meet his gaze.

A smile lights his eyes. "You're cute when you're startled."

My face heats even more, and I look down.

No. How can I be letting myself think about him that way? All that matters is saving Renan. I can't afford any distractions. This can't grow into anything more.

"Well, are you gonna go or not?" A slight dimple that I hadn't noticed before marks his cheek.

The smug look on his face forms a pit in my stomach. Numbness floods me, swipes any feelings of affection for him. It cripples my joy, makes me hate my life and my circumstances more than I already do.

"Freedom." I sigh. "If I could have anything with the snap of my fingers, I'd wish for freedom. Freedom from the king, his soldiers, his laws. Not just escape. I already have that. I'd need to know my family would be safe forever. We were discovered only weeks ago, but I feel like I've been fighting Ulric all my life. Always hiding, looking over my shoulder, mistrusting everyone I meet. I've felt like a prisoner, and not just to the king but to my parents' beliefs. I..." Realizing what I'm saying and, more importantly, whom I'm saying it to, I stop. "I'm sorry, I shouldn't be talking about this—with you of all people."

"Why not?" He tilts his head, eyes attentive.

"Well, because I-I'm complaining about feeling like a slave. Meanwhile, you actually lived as one for years."

"So?" His brows crease. "Just because I may have been physically enslaved doesn't make your own mental experiences invalid. You've felt like a prisoner your whole life, living in constant fear your family might be taken at any moment. That counts in my books. Fear is the worst slave master I know."

I smile, touched by his acceptance. "I've searched for freedom my whole life."

"And you haven't found it?"

"No. To be honest, I'm starting to doubt true freedom exists." The numbness fills any cracks in my tone.

Ezra eats the last bite of his potato, then rests his hand on mine, sending ripples of warmth up my arm. "Keep searching, RJ. If there's one thing I know, it's that true freedom isn't what you think. It's only when you come to the end of yourself that you're willing to see it."

Maybe that's just what I'm afraid of.

"So you never found the freedom you sought. What kept you going? How'd you find the will to keep fighting?"

I think back. "I must've been eleven or twelve when I started wood carving. It helped me relax, get out of my head. Still does." I hold Ren's dove to my chest. "The closest thing to freedom I ever found was when I'd go up the hill in the forest behind my house. There was an abandoned lumber yard where I built furniture and kept stock. But beyond that, there was a lookout. I called it the ledge. I'd sit on the cliff, dangling my legs and carving while looking out across the region. I'd go there to watch the sunset some nights. It was my escape."

"Maybe after all this is over, I could join you on your ledge some evening." He squeezes my hand. "Really, I get it. As a slave, once I found my relief, I couldn't believe I'd lived so long without it. My escape."

A dull pain gnaws my shin, and I tighten my fingers around his. "And what was your escape?"

"Writing." His posture loosens as he settles back. "A couple years after I was enslaved, I realized I wouldn't be leaving anytime soon. So one day, I asked a guard for a notebook and pen. To my surprise, he returned with both. I wrote in that book every day until I ran out of room. When that book was full and the pen was dry, the same guard brought me more. I wrote about anything and everything. Wrote all I could remember from my advanced English classes in school. Every verse and Bible story my mother taught me. It was my escape amid enslavement." He takes a gulp of water and lets the silence grow between us.

To think I once found his talking incessant and annoying. Now I long for him to talk more. To soothe me with that rich, raw tone. Just as he claims he longs to know me, I too want to know him deeper.

An hour after we finish eating, finish talking, the pain worsens into a surging current.

"Ezra, the pills. Your mother's sleeping pills—I need them."

He fishes through my bag and finds them in the empty egg carton, pours two into his palm.

I swallow them with water. Relief won't come soon enough.

Ezra sits beside me as I wait impatiently for the pain to ease up enough that I can sleep.

I squeeze his hand to ward off the agony, but he doesn't complain. I realize that as soon as he began talking, the pain faded, and when he stopped it returned. His distraction worked.

"Keep talking, Ezra." I lay my head on his shoulder.

You're my escape now.

HE STAYS UP with me through the night, as the pain continues.

Sweat beads on my forehead, and though the pills don't help me sleep, they do make me feel partially insane. I can barely hold my head up, drowning in fatigue, but my brain won't shut off. My heart races and my body shudders.

I grow mad, thinking of ways to stop the pain. "Take...

take it off."

"Huh?"

"The cast." I grab fistfuls of my blanket. "Please. Please just take off my cast."

"That's not a good idea. It needs to heal."

"I can't take it anymore!" I cry, flinching with each painful pulse. "I need it off."

"All right, I will. Just breathe." Ezra slides my pant leg over my knee. Using the scissors from my medical kit, he snips through the layers of my gauze cast. Long minutes of torment pass while he cuts through it all.

The pain remains, but I relax some when the compression eases. My leg can breathe.

"Oh, RJ." Ezra examines the bruises, the swelling, the scarred gashes on either side. "I'm so sorry she did this to you."

The sight nearly makes me sick. I lie back down, panicking. I wish it would all just end. If only I could fall into a deep sleep and never wake. Susa said the pills help ease pain. So far, they've only aided in amplifying mine.

God, just take the pain! Please take it from me! Either that or let me die. I can't do this anymore.

My head throbs, and I cry myself to sleep beside Ezra like a pathetic child with no dignity.

At times during the night when the pain swells and it feels like my leg is on fire, I wake to see Ezra, pen in hand, writing on a sheet of paper with a look of deep concentration.

The campfire keeps the cave warm, but with my climbing fever, it feels like a furnace.

I kick the blankets off, and my foggy brain dips back into sleep.

LIGHT BEAMS INTO the cave at dawn, and I groggily sit up. Exhaustion weighs down my body, but I know we must move on from here. In as little as an hour, we could be at Susa's.

Ezra presses his hand to my forehead. "Good. Fever's finally down. It got the best of you all night." A worried look plasters his face as I push myself to my feet. He holds out his arms as if expecting me to fall. "What are you doing?"

I follow his gaze to my leg, and the night's dreadful hours return to memory. However, the pain that accompanied them seems to be gone. I hadn't even noticed.

"It's gone," I whisper, then gape at Ezra. "The pain. It's gone!"

"Really?"

"I guess the numbness drove away the pain while I slept." I sit back down to examine my shin. As soon as my pant leg is rolled up, the air deserts my lungs.

The swelling has decreased drastically. The bruises have faded almost completely. My leg is no longer bent where the bone broke. And the scars from the door cutting my skin have healed all the more since Ezra took off my cast.

"Whoa." Ezra sits and lifts my foot.

I gasp.

He flinches, setting it back down. "Sorry, did I hurt you?"

I shake my head, struggling to find my voice. "I-I felt that."

His eyes widen. "You mean it's not numb?" He proceeds to touch each of my toes and bend my foot at the ankle. Then he gently presses on my shin.

"I can feel it all." My voice cuts out, and I laugh as tears cloud my vision. "It's not numb or painful." My lungs fill with energy that makes me want to walk and run and jump.

Ezra's face floods with awe. He takes my hand and helps me out of the cave.

I step carefully at first, but it doesn't hurt or go numb.

"You good?" he asks.

"I don't think I've ever felt such a strong desire to dance in all my life." I laugh.

He leads me away from the cave's mouth into dawn's orange light that glistens through the trees and over the snowy ground. I cling to him at first. But after a few more steps, I know the pain is gone for good.

When I try to let him go, he pulls me closer and swings me around. I find my balance and snicker. "I wasn't really serious about dancing."

"Course you weren't." He winks, slides his arm around me, and leads me about the clearing. He spins me away from him, arms outstretched, then pulls my hand. I twirl back into him. His warm breath floods my face as he weakly dips me toward the ground, and my hat falls off.

A breeze sends tiny flecks of snow down from the trees. They swirl around us, settling on the ground. But when Ezra starts stomping his feet and bobbing his head like a chicken, the snow whisks back into the air as if trying to escape his madness.

"This is embarrassing even to watch." I snigger.

"It's very freeing. You should try it." He thrusts his chin out and dances to his own beat with as much rhythm as a five-year-old.

I begin to walk away but pause and smile. "Oh, what the heck." I grab his hand and join him.

He bounces around and pulls me with him.

I hop lightly at first to ensure the pressure won't hurt my leg. It withstands my weight and movement, so I jump around higher. My heart races and I can't help but laugh watching Ezra give it his all even while his spent energy drains his face of colour.

"Don't overdo it," I say. "Remember, you're still the injured one."

As we both grow weary and slow down to catch our breath, we end up swaying together. I lay my cheek on his chest, and he holds me close, arms around my waist. I close my eyes, listening to the rhythm of his breath. Time slows, and the sounds of the world around us fade.

Then I lace my fingers behind his neck and gaze up into his eyes to see he's already looking down at mine. Our clouding breath collides between us.

My pulse pounds in my ears. His onyx eyes entrance me, sending a rush of warmth and weakness through my body. His eyes trace down my face to my lips, and mine to his. A deluge of tension emanates within me, and I waver, looking back into his eyes.

But then electricity surges under my skin as he grazes his hand over my cheek and leans down to kiss me. My breath hitches as his lips brush against mine. His eyes close, and he pulls back hesitantly as if worried he might've ruined whatever we had before this.

But stillness radiates between us, and the space draws me in. I push up on the tips of my toes, wrap my arms around his neck. And kiss him again.

He leans into me, tucking a lock of hair behind my ear.

Eyes shut, I savour every sensation, melting into the kiss. Eventually, I must pull away to catch my breath.

He steps back also, though I wish he wouldn't. By the

way he lingers in front of me, it seems he doesn't want to stop either. But after another minute or so, he reluctantly withdraws and returns to the cave to pack up.

And I'm left standing alone, trying to grasp whatever just happened.

WHEN WE ARRIVE at a wide trail on our way to Susa's, Ezra fumbles with something in his coat pocket. "Before we reach my mother's,"—he hides a hand behind his back—"I have something I want to give you."

I snap out of contemplating our kiss's meaning long enough to observe the nervous twitch of his lip. "What's the occasion?"

"Well, I know it's nowhere near Christmas yet… But growing up, my mother and I celebrated it a month early— you know, to throw off people's suspicions."

I furrow my brows. "Christmas?" The word feels so old, so foreign, yet evokes faint memories.

"You've never heard of it?" he asks. "Your family didn't celebrate it?"

"It's familiar," I say. "I think my mom tried to convince my dad to celebrate it one year, but he refused. Thought it was too much of a risk to our family."

Ezra looks downcast, then he clears his throat. "Well, I'm honoured to be the first to help you celebrate it. Now close your eyes and hold out your hand."

I give him a suspicious glare but follow his orders anyway.

He takes my outstretched hand in his and slides my sleeve up, exposing my arm to the chilly air. Then something cold folds snugly around my wrist. "Okay, open your eyes!"

A brown leather cuff encases my wrist. I raise my hand to

distinguish the elegant design of vines engraved along the leather's edges. A bold but beautiful cross symbol catches my eye down the centre of the thick cuff. The warmth of my skin thaws the leather, and it moulds comfortably around my wrist.

"What do you think?"

"It's beautiful," I stammer in awe. "Where did you get it?"

"Back at the castle. I slipped it in my pocket when you weren't looking."

I trace the vines and study it, then smile up at him, genuinely moved. "I love it. Thank you." I then recall the long hours spent carving and grieving after he'd been shot. "I have something for you too." From my pocket I take the lamb carving on its shoelace chain. I wasn't sure whether I wanted to give it to him since it was inspired and born in a time of my deepest grief. But after what he just gave me, how could I not?

His jaw slackens as I set it in his hand. He studies it intently and his eyes glisten.

"Well?" I wait for a response, grinning. This may be the first time I've ever truly made him speechless, and I plan to revel in it.

He swallows, then eyes me. "You made this…for me?"

My lip curls. "Remember when you asked what I thought your symbol would be?"

"You gave me—made me—a symbol…" His eyes gleam. "Oh, it's perfect!"

"I'm glad you like it."

"Like it?" He ties it around his neck. "I love it! RJ, this is the best gift anyone's ever given me." He hugs me.

"And yours is the best I've ever gotten."

He laughs. "Yeah, it's the only one you've ever gotten."

"I'm counting birthdays too."

He lifts it and rotates it between his fingers. "Thank you." He squeezes me again and leans down to kiss me.

But alarm rises inside me, and I pull away. As I follow a strong whiff of smoke to the trails ahead, my smile dies.

Ezra's breath snags. His wide eyes meet mine. Then he sprints ahead, pursuing the billowing cloud of black smoke in the distance.

My lungs lock tight with terror.

I chase after him on my newly healed leg, only one thing on my mind.

Susa.

Chapter 20

We tear down the trail, chasing the smoke that increases in depth by the second and cloaks the sky in darkness. My heart thumps to the pace of each sprinting step.

It could be anything. It could be nothing. A patch of trees. An abandoned cabin.

But the gnawing dread doesn't leave no matter what I tell myself. The sky grows murkier and grey ash litters the ground.

I beg the smoke to lead us away from Susa's home, but it only draws us closer.

My skin crawls as we twist through the narrow trails I rode with Susa to reach her secluded lot. And when I see the cottage on fire, my legs nearly give out.

Ezra speeds through the field toward the eruption of flames. He yells back at me over the blazing roar, "You sure this is her cottage?"

"Yes!"

He stops, staring into the fire. "You said she has children?"

Ice trickles down my spine, and I bound for him, predicting his next move.

His jaw locks and he charges up the porch steps, through the front door. The fire licks at him and he recoils. But then he buries his face in his sleeve and crawls under the swelling smoke.

"Ezra, no!" I tear up the steps after him. "You'll get yourself killed!" I yell over the crackling flames, inhaling a breathfull of smoke. My throat and lungs burn. Crawling behind him, I lunge for his leg, but he pulls it forward.

A piece of flaming wood drops from the doorframe and scorches the back of my hand. I gasp and shake off the coals.

Smoke engulfs Ezra and he wheezes.

I grab his arm, and he lets me guide him back out onto the ashen lawn.

I cough and gasp for breath. My hand spasms with searing pain. I dig beneath the layer of ash and cover my burn with snow. It stings, making me grit my teeth, but the snow brings some relief. I then stumble over to Ezra.

On hands and knees, he coughs and spits darkened mucus into the snow.

I direct my attention to the red patch of skin on his cheek. "You're burnt."

"I have to go back in," he says between fits of coughing.

I take a handful of snow and press it to his face.

He winces and wipes my hand away, stumbling up to go back to the house. "I have to get them out."

I follow and pull on his shoulder. "There's nothing you can do." Then I eye the snow to the left of the cottage. "Look!" I point out a trail of fresh footprints leading into the eastern forest. "They got away. They're not inside." I count at least five pairs of scattered prints, all different patterns and sizes.

He ignores me, fixing his eyes on the flaming doorway.

"Ezra." I drag him away from the cottage, forcing him to

look at the prints. "See? They got away. They're okay."

He stops fighting me. But then he slumps to his knees, hopelessness writhing through him. His jaw braces and his face reddens as he tries to fight back the tears but fails to.

I crouch in front of him. "What's wrong? They got away. Why are you so upset?"

His hands fall limply to his lap. "They didn't *get away*. They were taken. This place wasn't burnt down by chance. It was Ulric." His voice cracks. "He warned me this would happen. And I didn't listen."

"You think soldiers took them?"

"I know they did. That was always the headsman's threat—to send someone to kill her if I didn't obey."

He has a point. "Okay…maybe they did take her. But maybe they haven't killed her yet. Maybe they don't plan on killing her."

"They do. They will kill her." He coughs. "And—oh! Those poor kids."

"They won't kill them. Remember what you said about Renan? They need the kids alive."

"I know. That's the problem." He sniffs. "Serving as Ulric's slave is a fate worse than death."

I bite my cheek, eyes stinging. Though I always assumed that was the case, hearing him admit it makes me ache for Renan. "Well…" I steady my tone. "We'll just have to get back there and save them too."

He tunes me out and watches the cottage burn as his tears fall.

His silent agony pains me, but I take advantage of his distant state and apply snow to his burn. I brush the soot from his hair and convince him to move back to the perimeter of the field, away from the dangerous fumes and debris.

As he sits against a maple tree, I clean up his burn and tape a piece of gauze over it to prevent infection. He drinks water from his canteen to help soothe the throat irritation. I check for any other burns, and luckily there's just the one.

By the time I treat my own burn, it has blistered into white and red splotches, stinging with every movement of my fingers. I coat my hand with snow and wait till the pain numbs. Then I bandage it and lie against the tree beside Ezra, watching the cottage burn.

Soon its structure groans. Flames consume the roof, and it collapses. The rush of filthy air stings my eyes and sends Ezra into another coughing fit. Meanwhile, a burning tree behind the cottage is unable to endure the flames any longer. It plummets on top of the cottage and brings down what little remains of the structure.

Ezra watches with a look of helplessness.

I, too, must fight back an onslaught of emotion. I'd been inside her cottage. Felt the warmth within its walls. Spent time getting to know the lively beings it sheltered from the harsh world. I so desperately needed it to still be standing when we returned from rescuing Renan.

Ezra had painted such a lovely picture when he said we could come back to live here with his family. It would be our haven of peace. Our refuge from the storm. He said his home could be my home, and his family could become mine.

I wanted that so badly. I depended on that future for Renan and me.

But now it is no more.

After all of this is over, after we rescue my brother and Ezra's family, we have nowhere to go. Nowhere to hide. Nowhere to call home. And that in itself is scarier than the thought of trying to steal back our loved ones from prison.

"You all right?" Ezra asks hoarsely.

I shake my head. I can't even pretend anymore.

He doesn't try to make me feel better. Just draws me closer and lets the tears fall.

AN HOUR CREEPS by, and the cottage has burnt completely. Only small areas of the fire remain lit among the rubble. The roaring flames have hushed into stagnant silence.

My stomach churns at the strong stench of smoke staining our clothes and hair.

I observe Ezra, his bandaged cheek, the restless sleep he has succumbed to.

Just thinking it brings guilt, but perhaps this was just the reality check he needed to get the fantasy of an all-loving, protecting God out of his head. I hate to hope that his dreams would be crushed, but I do wish he'd come back to where he stood before he survived that gunshot.

I stretch my legs out and study them. Unease sprouts within me. How can something like this happen? A broken, bruised leg with little hope of ever feeling or functioning properly again… heals almost entirely in one night. Other than the subtle bruising and deep scars, it is perfect. I can walk and run and jump. I have full movement and sensation as if it never broke in the first place. Nothing in the natural could be responsible for restoring it so quickly and wholly.

In a way, it's similar to what happened with Ezra's gunshot wound. It should have ended very differently for us both. Yet we are here. Alive. Walking.

Healed.

I eye the cross symbol on the cuff Ezra gave me. It stirs a sense of pain and suffering, yet also evokes feelings of freedom and forgiveness. Memories of Mom reading from her sacred book about a man on a cross rise from the ashes of my mind. But I blow them back down to the dust to escape their discomfort.

Last night the pain intensified to the point I wished I was dead. I couldn't bear it any longer. I needed relief. I didn't know what else to do. So inside I cried out. Begged God to take the pain…

Rage boils within me.

Ezra can't be right. He can't be! God's not real. If he were, and if he truly loved us, he wouldn't let tragedies like this happen. There's got to be another explanation.

A sharp squeal echoes through the field, interrupting my thoughts.

I stiffen and wait.

A loud neigh resounds.

Susa's horse!

I scan the east side of the clearing and spot the small stable where Susa kept her horse.

In obvious distress, the horse squeals long and loud.

I leave Ezra asleep against the tree and race to the stable, heart teeming with relief. The soldiers mustn't have known about her. At least now we won't have to walk back to Kinborough.

The musty stench of hay combined with old wood and manure brings me back to all the mornings spent at Mr. Elscott's farm. Who knew such a smell could be missed?

I slip through the entrance and calmly approach the horse's stall. She lowers her head over the door to see me. Then she blows and tenses.

I reach up and pet her black muzzle. "I know, girl. I'm not who you expected. But maybe you remember me."

She sniffs the bandage over my burnt hand and stamps her hoofs.

I stroke her forehead.

Though she couldn't see the cottage from here, she could surely hear and smell it burning.

"I know you're scared. So am I." Etched across the top beam of her stall door is the word *Selah*, and I'm reminded of Susa calling her that. "You're all right, Selah. You're okay," I repeat softly until she settles.

As she probably hasn't been fed today, I fill her trough full of hay and grain, then wait while she eats eagerly. When she's finished, I saddle her up, fasten her bridle, pack loads of her food onto the saddle, and lead her out of the stable. The door slams behind her.

She jumps to the side and snorts.

I tighten the reins to ensure she won't bolt. "Shhh. You're all right, girl." I stroke her mane. "We'll be okay. But I need you to help me." I think of Susa and the children, captured by soldiers, headed to prison. "I need you to trust me." I gaze into her frightened eyes.

She lowers her head, and her breathing calms.

Weariness threatens to devour me, but I gather all my remaining strength for the days to come. I can't give in yet. The battle hasn't even begun. I slow my breathing and close my eyes, pressing my forehead against Selah's. "We're gonna be okay, right?" I whisper.

She nickers gently, and I feel a connection—or at least a budding understanding—between us. We're both afraid, both exhausted, both missing the people we love. But we're also both stubborn, so it seems. And though it's tedious and tiring, we must both take courage and forge forward to save our people.

"Come on now." I guide her into the field toward Ezra.

THE NIGHT COMES and goes. We've covered more distance than I'd anticipated in such a short amount of time. I keep at a smooth canter with walking intervals for the sake of Ezra's wound. We can't risk roaming the open city, so I follow hidden paths along the forest's border.

After several more hours of riding from morning until around midday, we hop off and I lead Selah to a small creek for a much-needed drink. "She's a good horse," I tell Ezra, patting her mane as she laps up the water. "We should rest a while, give her a break. She deserves it."

"Good—I mean, yes, she does," Ezra blurts, pale and queasy looking. He sits down on a snow-covered rock and pinches the bridge of his nose.

"Still haven't found any pleasure in riding, huh?"

"I've always been wary around horses, but riding them is a whole new level of terrifying." He sighs. "I never realized how high up it is, how much they rock side to side."

"She's a sweetheart. She wouldn't try anything to hurt you or make you fall. I guess I'll just have to teach you to ride, to face your fears." I grin.

"Only if you let me teach you to shoot." He pats the holstered gun on his hip.

I swallow. "I already know how to shoot."

"Then why'd you stab that soldier in the cabin with a knife instead of using the gun I gave you?"

I avert my gaze, focusing on Selah. "I'm just more comfortable using knives." The gunshots that took Mom's life boom in my ears, and I busy myself refilling our canteens in the creek. My pulse hastens and my fingers quake.

Selah flicks her tail and her ears perk up.

I blame my memories for the unease in my bones. But when Ezra pauses mid-sentence to scan the area, I know it's not just me.

Distant tire screeches in the city streets grab our attention.

I tug Selah's reins and follow Ezra out of the woods to the nearest house with a roof intact. Its brick walls, though singed, seem mostly stable, and its roof doesn't look ready to collapse today. I hope.

We coax Selah through the tight front entrance and hide away with her in a side room no bigger than her stall back at Susa's. Her hoofs clack on the brick floor strewn with ashes.

Patting her, I compel my lungs to breathe slow and even, in hopes she will sense my lack of fear and settle. She must instead sense my fake composure because she doesn't calm down. She snorts and stamps, eyes wide with panic.

"Make her stop!" Ezra forces a whisper.

I take off my coat and place it over her head to cover her eyes. This seems to calm her. She lowers her head and gives a final blow, then stills.

I clasp my bare arms around my abdomen and rub them for warmth. Ezra shawls me with my blanket, and I slide down the wall to sit on the cold floor. *We are safe. They won't find us here,* I tell myself. Then I lurch to my feet. "Ezra, the tracks! Our footprints in the snow—"

"I'm on it." He hastens out of the house with his blanket in hand and swipes it across our trail of boot prints and Selah's hoof prints to conceal them. He then shakes the snow from his blanket and hurries inside, closing both the front door and our small room's door behind him.

We huddle in the corner beside Selah and wait half an

hour in dark, fearful silence.

I think of Renan. Considering the time it takes to travel to Kinborough, he's probably been in a cell a few days now. Is he hungry? Cold? Hopefully they let him keep the blanket I gave him. Is he scared? Or hurting? I hope not, but what good does hoping bring, anyway?

At least he's alive.

The headsman's message on the dead soldier's transmitter springs to mind, and when I'm sure the vehicle isn't anywhere close to our area yet, I ask about it. "Ezra," I whisper, "when you shot the headsman and Head Damien to free us, I thought they both died."

"I thought so too. I did see medics rush down the hall after your family left, but I didn't think anything of it at the time. They must've been able to save Malachi."

"You sure it was him on that transmitter? They didn't just appoint a new headsman?"

"Yeah, I'd recognize that voice anywhere. He was the soldier assigned to train and torture the slaves, and I seemed to be his favourite throughout the years."

"You must wish the gunshot had killed him, then."

Ezra purses his lips, then relaxes and shakes his head.

Really? "Even after all he did to you?"

"At the time, I was aiming to kill them both. But looking back, I wish I'd gone for a limb or something just to disable them long enough."

I think back to the execution room. "Before Head Damien died, he struggled to say something… 'Forgive me.' Do you think he felt sorry for my family's situation? Or for how he served the king willingly all those years?"

Ezra gives a surprised half smile. "No, I think he was repenting."

"Repenting? To who?"

"God, most likely." His voice lightens. "Maybe he found his way."

"God?" I'd hoped yesterday's events would knock some sense into Ezra, but it seems he still trusts and believes in God even now. "All right then, say God is real. Say he heard Head Damien's repentance. How could he forgive him for all he did? How could God forgive someone like him?"

Ezra ponders my question. "Well, how could he forgive someone like me? For all I did?"

"That's different." I sigh. "You didn't want to hurt anyone."

"But I still did. Something I learned the day I nearly died is that not one person on earth deserves forgiveness. Yet God forgives." Tenderness shows in his eyes. "Everyone sins. But God will forgive them if they repent and are willing to follow him."

"That can't be right. How can he just forgive and forget and go on as if they never sinned? What about the ones—no offence—who've committed horrible things like murder? How can he just forgive anyone who repents?" My spine stiffens.

Instead of answering me right away, he lifts my hand and rolls up my sleeve to reveal the leather cuff he gave me. "One word." He points to the engraved cross symbol. "Jesus."

I pull my hand back.

He looks into my eyes, seems to sense my confusion. "God paid the greatest price imaginable to grant us our freedom. He sent his son to suffer in our world. Jesus was mocked, beaten, and nailed to a cross to pay for our sins. He laid down his life out of love for us, in hopes that we'd accept his gift and follow him."

Ezra's words stun me. I begin to grasp how people, such as Mom, are willing to risk their lives for their faith. I've never heard anything so pure, so compelling. But the concept still sits wrong in my heart. Though I long to live as carefree as Ezra, believing I will rest in eternal love someday, I cannot entrust my life to someone who would get us in this mess in the first place. Maybe God is real. And perhaps he does care, to an extent. But how much could he truly love me if he won't intervene when my life rips at the seam?

My heart hardens in resolve. God does not love me. God does not hear me.

God is not real.

Minutes stretch on as the vehicle creeps closer through the streets, crunching bricks under its tires. Then the brakes squeal and its engine cuts out nearby. Two pairs of boots clomp over uneven terrain, and muffled voices converse just beyond these brick walls.

Scared to even breathe, I bury my nose in my blanket and hope Selah stays quiet.

Ezra stands, plants his feet, and retrieves his gun, readying himself to shoot. Then he tenses and searches his belt, his pockets, my bag. "My last round of ammo. It's gone."

Chapter 21

 hat do you mean, it's gone?" I whisper, getting up to frantically check my bag and pockets. "You're telling me you have two guns and no bullets?"

"Actually, I left one gun back at the cabin. We were in a hurry and I forgot it. But this one I used to shoot the soldier at the castle and a few others after escaping prison."

I slide back down the wall as the urgency of our situation overtakes me.

No bullets. No defence. If they find us, we're at their mercy.

Ezra double and triple checks everything we own before dropping beside me in defeat. To our relief, Selah remains calm and quiet, without so much as flicking her tail.

The voices become quieter as the men keep walking, and all is silent for twenty stiff minutes. Then, every few minutes, doors of nearby houses creak open and slam shut.

I squeeze Ezra's hand in attempts to stifle the tremor in mine.

Please don't let them find us. We're dead if they do. At least Ezra is. He'll surely be put to death if he's captured. Such a substantial reward for his return, dead or alive, ensures he'll either be killed on sight out here or dragged back to the prison and slain by Ulric himself.

I can't let that happen. I can't let them hurt him. Not again. I don't just need him for the sake of rescuing Renan anymore. I want him. I want to be with him. I dream of spending the rest of my life with him. Of course, I know it's foolish to fantasize of such a pleasant future while our world is collapsing around us by the hour. But as I've learned out here with him, even the impossible is possible, so it seems. I know that goes both ways, good and bad. But for us, hopefully our impossible will comprise of more good than bad.

Ezra tightens his hand around mine as the front door of our borrowed house whips open. Rays of light poke through crevices in the splintered door dividing us from the main room.

I turn my face into the shadows. Blood slugs through my veins, weighing me down to accept the inevitable.

They have caught us. Ezra's as good as dead.

I stare at the door, awaiting the moment it will be kicked open, in turn spooking Selah and exposing us to the king's all-too-loyal soldiers.

Footsteps skid along the brick floor beyond the door.

I tighten my free hand around my hunting knife. But who am I kidding? A soldier would shoot us both in the time it takes to throw the knife.

Any second now.

I press my cheek into Ezra's shoulder, and he rests his chin on my head.

The soldier's shadow seeps through the gap under the door, flooding the room with darkness.

Selah flicks her tail and blows tersely.

The soldier's feet drag and stop at the door.

I shut my eyes, exhaling all hope of surviving the encounter to come.

But a loud, hissing voice resounds through the main room—an incoming transmission. "You'll want to come check this out, Conrad. House across the street with the half-caved roof, over."

"Copy that. Coming now, over." The soldier on the other side of the door rushes away, his footsteps fading into the snowy street.

The front door crashes closed, and we are left in stunned silence.

I drop the knife as my limbs go limp.

Ezra leans his head back against the wall, closing his eyes. "Thank you," he exhales shakily.

WITHIN THE NEXT half hour, the soldiers' vehicle fires up and deserts the area, travelling farther west into the city. Apparently, whatever finding had captured their interests was not enough to entice them to return to Ulric for assessment.

To be safe, we wait another hour before leaving the house.

I uncover Selah's eyes and pull my coat back on, then fish for her lead and lure her out of the house with one of our last three remaining apples. "Good girl." I feed her the fruit whole, brushing my fingers through her mane. "I've never seen a horse stay still and quiet so long. Although you did nearly give us away at the end."

Her ears perk up once out in the open space of the street.

Ezra scans the area and points out a trail of tire tracks leading into the far city. "They're gone. But they likely won't be the only soldiers we encounter on our way back."

"Will we be safe along the treeline with others out here?"

"Without ammo, we're not safe anywhere. But riding the

treeline behind the hills is still safer than travelling the open city."

We mount Selah and head into the forest, remaining concealed among the coniferous hills. Ezra clutches my waist, flinching with every sway of Selah's body. We continue on for several hours with short intervals to let Selah drink and rest.

When the sun dips behind the trees and the temperature drops, we have no choice but to return to the outer city and take shelter for the night in one of the sturdier-looking houses with a roof. Much like the last house, the floor is burnt, strewn with debris and shattered glass. I unearth an old broom in the closet and sweep it all into a pile while Ezra unrolls my mattress on one side of the room and spreads his blanket for himself on the other. A doorway in the left-hand wall leads to an empty bedroom, which I also sweep out, planning for Selah to spend the night inside it to ensure she won't freeze or give away our location.

I go to retrieve her but pause before leading her through the entrance. "Ezra, come outside," I call. "Time to face your fear."

"Now?" He appears in the doorway. "It's getting dark. I've got to get a fire going."

"It'll be brief. The fire can wait a few minutes. Besides, you've already collected the kindling, and that's half the work." I wave him out.

He hesitates, then follows. "Fine, let's do it. But you're getting off your part of the bargain easy, with there being no bullets to learn to shoot with and whatnot."

"Maybe there *is* a God after all." I smirk, guiding Selah toward the open street. "Okay, first off, you have to show her she can trust you. To do that, she has to sense that you're comfortable and in charge. If she feels you're afraid and nervous, she won't be as willing to follow your orders."

He exhales, petting her side.

"Since you've already ridden her with me, she knows you a little. So she should be okay with you taking the reins. First step is to ensure the saddle is secure so it won't slide or fall off when you mount." I jiggle the saddle. "You want to adjust the stirrups to fit you comfortably." I lower each several notches for him. "And you always mount from the left side." Sliding my left foot into the stirrup, I hold the reins and push off the ground. My right leg swings over her and into the other stirrup, then I dismount swiftly and motion to the saddle. "Your turn."

He begins carefully as to avoid hurting his healing wound, then looks back at me for approval.

"Other foot. Good. Now shove off the ground with your right foot and swing it over."

He follows my instruction, stumbling back on the first try, but mounts correctly on his second attempt. Once safely mounted, he takes a few deep breaths.

"You got it!" I take hold of the reins and lead him slowly through the boulevard. Over the next hour, he grows more confident, and I finally talk him into taking the reins himself. He learns proper posture and how to walk, trot, and steer, though he's nowhere near ready to ride unaccompanied.

When the moon begins to rise and both our hands are frozen, he dismounts and returns inside to start the fire.

"You were great!" I crouch beside him after getting Selah settled and fed in the side room.

"You're a bad liar." He snorts, forming a teepee out of logs by the front door.

"No, really. I admit it was a little rocky at first, but that went better than I thought it'd go."

"Well, I had a good teacher. And I admit it wasn't as terrifying as I thought it'd be." He strikes a match and lights the kindling. We share my last two slices of bread.

When finished, I hold my hands to the fire, a wave of fatigue hitting me hard. "I wouldn't normally ask this, but would you mind taking the first lookout shift tonight?"

"Course not. Go on, get some sleep."

"Thank you. Wake me for my shift." I kiss him on the cheek, almost wishing he'd pull me in for a real kiss, but then my window of weariness would slip away and I'd never get to sleep.

Chilled to the bone, I pull my blanket over my chin as the day's tension fades into a dreamless night.

I WAKE EZRA at dawn after my shift and feed Selah before we pack up our belongings and head into the forest. By midmorning, the temperature has risen to the warmest it's been all week. The snow on the ground becomes heavy and wet, and the trees drip with sleet.

Around lunchtime we stop at the base of a small waterfall to refill our canteens and let Selah drink. Our stomachs growl, as we've not eaten since last night, but considering our food supply now consists of two apples and four potatoes, we decide to ration the last of it in hopes we won't starve before reaching Kinborough.

I fill my canteen and swish the water around my dry mouth.

Ezra takes a swig from his, then swipes the slush off a flat rock and sits down. He lowers his head, knits his brows, and whispers under his breath as if in a one-way conversation.

A one-way conversation. Just like Mom used to do. *Prayer* was what she called it.

Eventually lifting his head, he meets my steely gaze. "What?" He shrugs.

I choke back the emotion and shake my head. "I'm sorry. I can't bear to watch this anymore. I can't stay silent while you fall deeper into this trap of lies and delusion."

"Ah…" He nods calmly. "This trap. You mean my beliefs. Tell me, what part of my faith is a lie?"

"All of it." I look down on him with pity and guilt for how big I let this problem become before confronting it. "Ezra, this isn't you. You never believed this before. You're letting it consume your life. And I'm truly scared for you." I crouch before him.

Now his eyes meet mine. "There's no reason to be scared for me. My faith is not some disease to be rid of. It won't tear me down. It will only build me up."

"I can't believe we're actually having this conversation." I sigh and rub my forehead. "What about your mother? Have you forgotten the pain of finding her gone, her house burnt to ashes?"

"Yes, thank you for the reminder." His stubbly jaw hardens.

"See? How can you still believe so strongly in a loving God when he would let your mother be taken minutes before your reunion? How can your faith not waver after all the pain you've been through these past eight years?"

"Of course my faith wavers!" Agony shines in his eyes, and I'm taken aback. He pushes himself up from the rock and paces. "You think it's easy believing in something I can't see? Someone the world has forgotten? Keeping my faith is the hardest thing I've done in my life! It would be so easy to just give it all up—"

"Then why don't you? It would save you so much misery." I stand and take his hand, internally pleading he'd just forget this and return to reality.

"Because I believe what I felt with him was real." He pauses, and his voice returns to normal volume. "When we discovered my mother's cottage burnt down, I nearly gave up. I prayed God would just let me die so the nightmare would be over. But he didn't. Instead, he comforted me. He never abandoned me. During my grief was actually when I felt him the most." He straightens. "I can't give up my faith. Because living with it is hard, but living without it is harder."

"And how is that?" I ask. "I'm living without it, but it seems you're having a harder time."

Ezra stops, eyeing me in suspicion. "Are you really so blind? Is your pride and stubbornness actually preventing you from seeing what's right under your nose?" He unzips his coat, slowly lifts his shirt to reveal his bandaged gunshot wound. Then he drops his shirt and gestures to my leg. "You've been given more proof than most. If all this doesn't confirm to you what the truth is, nothing will."

I hold his gaze, then look away when my inner alarm of vulnerability alerts me.

"No." His eyes narrow with chilling discernment. "I think it's safe to say you do believe. I can see it." He steps forward. "Can't you?"

I scowl. "So what if I believe? Maybe I do. But maybe I just don't want God in my life."

"That may be true, for now. But he will never stop pursuing you. I know you're hurting and you're afraid that putting your trust in him is just another opportunity for someone to let you down. But he won't. If you give him a chance, I promise he won't fail you."

I glare at Ezra, furious with the lies coming from his tongue. I step toward him, inches from his face. "He already has." The words are cold and clipped.

He looks down at his boots and weighs my answer. "I understand how you can think that. I used to believe the same about my situation. But just because you can't see or feel him working for your good doesn't mean he's not. He hasn't forgotten you, RJ. Now you've got to get out of your own way. You've got to let him in."

I turn away as the rage builds in my chest.

"I know you're angry with him. But in order to start sorting out this mess, you're gonna have to talk—not even to me if you don't want. You just need to talk to him, let him sort through things with you. Don't hold anything back. Let the buried rage and heartbreak rise to the top. You'll never have peace until you release it."

Wrath bites like a snake at the back of my tongue. I can't endure swallowing the poison any longer. I stare at Ezra, fisting my hands at my sides as the root of my reproach for God blazes.

"It pains me to see you this way. What is it? What has you so bound in bitterness toward God?"

My throat tightens and I grit my teeth. "He didn't save her." Aggravation writhes through me. But there's no taking the words back. My face heats. "Why would he save you and not her?"

Ezra's expression cools with understanding. "Your mother."

"If God is who you say he is—if he's loving and forgiving and powerful, why would he let one of his own followers die?" I throw my bag to the ground. "She gave him everything! She sacrificed herself for his sake. She trusted him with her life. But as she bled out in that field, he abandoned her, refused to even acknowledge her. He could've saved her like he did you. But he didn't! Why wouldn't he save her?" My eyes burn, hot with tears of rage and hatred.

"I don't know." Ezra's voice breaks on the last word. "I wish I had all the answers. But I don't. I'm new at this. I don't know why he allows one to die yet saves another." He draws me into his arms, cloaking me in consolation. "I wish I could take your pain. But I can't be God for you, RJ. If you really want to get answers for your questions, you're gonna have to ask him yourself."

"No." I throw his arms off me. "I'm done with God."

A HALF HOUR later, many unlucky branches and twigs have become victims of my vengeful knife. I sit on a wet rock at the edge of the waterfall, peeling their bark and carving their tips into spears.

Ezra has given me space to cool off, but now he approaches while I'm at work and sets a hand on my shoulder.

I jolt and clutch my knife tight.

His palms come up. "You won't spear me with any of your sticks if I sit down, will you?"

I exert unneeded force into slicing the stick in hand. "I'm not making any promises."

He lowers himself beside me, dangling his feet over the river. For a while, he just watches the water drift downstream, breathing quietly. Then he eyes me and says, "I'm sorry for bringing all that up. It had to come out eventually, but I could've been easier on you about it."

No kidding.

"You need to know that even though there was pain and suffering in her last moments…God was with her. He was comforting her. Silencing her fears, pouring his love on her like never before. And he can do the same for you if you let him." He picks up one of my sticks, taps a finger on its pointed tip. "I don't know why he didn't save her, but I do know he can use the grief for good. Her death wasn't the end. It was only the beginning. Though her time on earth has passed, she's more alive than ever before. She's no longer in pain. She will never feel pain again. She's in her real home now."

I stop my knife from carving, familiar with those words. *Her real home.*

I open my tool satchel. My fingers eagerly unzip the secret pocket and pull out the folded slip of paper. I trace over each of her elegant, handwritten words until I find the part I'm looking for:

My faith saved my life. It is the truth that gives me peace in knowing this world is not our real home.

"That's what she meant," I mumble to myself. "Her real home." Dazed, I hand Ezra the letter.

He reads it through. "She knew the risk, but also the reward."

Tears blurring my vision, I take the letter back and focus on Ezra, desperate to understand. "You really think she's in heaven? Free of pain?"

"I know she is."

I wipe my eyes. "I saw her in death. I'd never seen such pain in a person's eyes."

"Yes, there was pain. But only for a little while. And it

can't compare to the joy and peace and love she gets to experience now and forever. She is free."

I don't know if I'll ever understand it. But for now, I know all I need to know. The grief is still raw, still unbearable. Ezra's explanation is still rather senseless. But I can't ignore the clarity his words bring, the prodding in my heart that says she's okay. Nothing's ever felt so right, so real, so comforting.

She is safe. She is free.

I release a slow breath.

She is home.

Chapter 22

We walk alongside Selah for the next hour to give her a break from carrying us. I keep a firm grip on her reins as two red squirrels chatter and chase each other through the trees.

I study Ezra the whole time, torn on what to feel about our prior dispute. Hands in his pockets, he soaks up the warmth of the sun. His placid expression turns into an amused beam as the red squirrels chirp at us for trespassing.

I don't know what to think. His insistence on the topic of God shook the foundation of my hatred for the all-powerful, ignorant deity. Though I wish he hadn't, he uncovered my foolish spark of belief in said deity. I'm still angry at him for that. But I can't ignore the simple sincerity in how he answered my questions. It seemed he argued with me not for his benefit but for mine. Because he cares for me and believes his God does too. Can I blame him for trying to help heal my wounds in the only way he knows how? I suppose not.

I also can't say his beliefs entirely make no sense. Though I don't like admitting it, divine healing from God seems to be the only explanation for how Ezra survived that gunshot wound and how my leg healed overnight. I might even be able to get on board with his beliefs…if not for the fact he claims God is loving and caring. That seems impossible with the way he seemed to blatantly disregarded Mom's life despite her devotion to him.

No. I cannot put my faith in a God who abandons his own, even if it's all true—that she's safe in heaven now. Because it's not just about her death. It's about the lives she left behind.

Renan needed her. I needed her. Even Dad did.

But as for Ezra… He is trusting what he deems true to him, no matter the cost. Choosing to believe in what gives his life meaning. For that I must commend him, either in his courage or stupidity. Nonetheless, I look to Ezra and see a leader. A wounded yet unyielding warrior.

The carving around his neck says it all. It expresses every quality I originally carved it to symbolize, conveys the same virtues in him I initially fell for. Humble. Kind. Gentle. Brave. Selfless. He hasn't lost or forsaken any of those qualities since. If anything, he's only grown stronger in each of them.

I can't blame him for wanting to impart in me the peace he so firmly believes to have eased his own guilt and grief. I know he means well. So even if I wish this God of his were different, I can't remain angry with Ezra. Who knows? Maybe his God really is the reason he's alive today.

We continue leading Selah through the forest, more for our sake than hers now. We've not eaten for over a day, and the effects are slowly but surely setting in. I'd likely drop off the side of the saddle if I tried to mount, lacking any strength for safe, basic riding whatsoever. Ezra, though still wary of horses, drapes an arm over Selah's saddle in efforts to hold himself upright.

Minutes slug by as we trudge forth.

Then my head snaps up at the blasting echo of a gunshot. Blackbirds erupt from distant trees and soar in our direction. Tapping into a reserve of energy I didn't know I had, my adrenaline pulses to life. I hasten through the brush, tugging Selah along.

Ezra charges ahead to lead us out of the treeline and toward an outer block of houses.

I stumble through the rubble, yanking Selah's reins. Then slow to a stop as Ezra's old words spring to mind. *I don't think they'll ever stop until they have me.*

Ezra waves me toward the door of a rickety house. "What are you waiting for? Come on!"

Slush seeping through the toe of my boot and numbing my foot, I look around the abandoned block. Burnt and crumbling. Dead. This is what the king does to people like us. Like Ezra. I've known that since the execution room. But it doesn't get any easier to digest over time. It seems Ulric's always gotten his way.

Until us. Until my family. We got away because of Ezra's sacrifice.

I observe him, the lines of concern in his forehead as he waits for me. The cool breeze tugs at my hair and sneaks down the back of my coat. Chills caress my shoulders in light of this dreadful insight. *They're never going to stop.*

"No." My stomach hardens.

"No? What do you mean, *no?*" Ezra treks forth until he's right before me. "We have to hide."

I shake my head. "*You* have to hide. I…have to leave."

He blinks, snorting a laugh. "And where, might I ask, are you going?"

"Ulric wants you." I roll back my shoulders. "He'll have to settle for me."

His playful smile dies. "You're serious? You're giving up?"

"No. I'm saving us. If those soldiers catch me, they'll end their search to take me to Ulric. It'll throw them off your trail. Then you'll follow two days behind and break me out of prison."

"That's crazy! I won't let you risk your life like this. Let's go inside. We'll think up another plan." He takes Selah's reins as I grip them and pulls me forward.

But I let go. "Ezra,"—I swallow—"please let me do this. I need to do this. I need you to live. I know there's probably a better way, but we don't have time. They're coming. And you're dead if they find you."

"You think Ulric only wants me? He wants you too. The soldiers could kill you on sight!"

"I won't provoke them. I'll fight at first, but then I'll let them take me peacefully. I'll hike up over the hills and wait for them to find me along the main trail. That way they can't trace my tracks back to you." I stroke Selah's snout. "You know how to ride a little. Once you reach the field, ride fast. You'll be out in the open with no protection." I lower my bag from my shoulder and retrieve my canteen, then hold out the bag. "Take this. The food, the medical kit—use what you need. Selah's food is packed on her saddle. And remember Ulric's letter, the pictures…they're all in my bag. If for some reason you can't save me, do whatever you can to expose him."

He takes my bag in stunned silence. "You're leaving because of our argument, aren't you?"

"Actually, I'm leaving despite our argument. I know you just want what's best for me. But so do I. For you. I'm leaving for your good. So that maybe we'll both come out of this alive."

His brows sink. "I can't believe you're going through with this."

Neither can I. In my mind the masked soldier pins me to that tree, slicing my throat. I stifle the tremor in my lip.

"This is the stupidest…bravest thing I've ever heard of. Is there nothing I can say to get through that thick head of yours and convince you to stay?"

I muster a weak smile. "From the moment I left you to what I thought was your death in that courtyard, I regretted it. But I have to leave you again. I'm sorry." I shut my eyes as another gunshot echoes through the forest.

Ezra draws me into his arms, and I soak in his warmth. "Two days in *prison*, RJ," he stresses.

"Only two days." I gather every bit of courage in my starving body to walk away. Looking up into his anxious eyes, I think about kissing him but refrain. That would make this parting mean something more than it is. Something such as a last goodbye—which it is not.

Everything in me longs to stay with him and face whatever challenges arise. But if I get this right, we will make it. Rescue our loved ones and escape the region to live somewhere under the radar. We can have a good life. A safe life.

Another shot rings, maybe a mile beyond the forest's border. So just like that, I turn away.

And head straight for the gunfire.

HEART SLAMMING IN my chest, I crouch behind a wet boulder. Waiting. I can't turn back now. I'm close enough to the soldiers that they'd track my prints and follow me straight to Ezra.

My stomach pangs from hunger. I take a sip of water from my canteen and close my eyes, preparing my mind and body for a fight. I know I won't win against soldiers, but I have to at least show them I'm no coward for trying.

The crunches grow louder. Every step brings them closer to their awaiting plunder.

Me.

I touch my scarred throat, thinking of my first soldier encounter out here. I can't let them kill me. I can't leave Renan alone to suffer in this cruel world. My story has to be believable—I was separated from my family and recently ran out of food. That should be easy to lie about, considering I *was* separated from my family and I really *haven't* eaten in over a day. Hopefully my captors will have food to spare.

Who am I kidding? They'll probably starve me to death deliberately by the time we reach the prison. I should have eaten before leaving Ezra and yielding myself to the will of Ulric's minions.

I press back against the boulder. After such a long, hard trek over those hills, my head swirls with fatigue. Then a branch snaps close by, and I shake the dizziness away.

A low voice echoes from beyond the boulder. I steal one even breath before ditching my hiding place and darting down the trail across the soldier's path. I sprint fast, though not fast enough to miss hearing a startled gasp erupt from the man as he slips and falls in the slush.

I look back as the black blur of a second soldier tears after me. I gain quite a distance on my newly healed leg. But as my lungs burn and my vision blurs, the soldier charges full speed, grabs me around the waist and tackles me to the ground.

Facedown in the slush, I thrash. Then the soldier kneels

on my back and presses a gun to my temple. I let my body go limp and drop my cheek back to the muck. My adrenaline gives way to weariness. At this point, I doubt I could move even if I weren't pinned down.

The soldier seems to sense my lethargy and steps back, holstering the gun, then hoists me to my feet and calls to the other soldier. "You can quit having a coronary back there, Jerod. She's harmless." A higher, more feminine voice than I expected. However, as my ears ring and my vision blurs, it's safe to say my senses aren't entirely trustworthy at the moment.

I look the masked soldier over. Only two inches taller than me. Much leaner than the other one jogging toward us. Then I catch a glimpse of braided orange hair beneath the unzipped coat and determine it is a woman who chased and caught me. Who now holds me up like a prized stag or some other game animal—which is precisely what I am to them, to Ulric. A mere pest to be rid of.

"Hey." The other soldier catches up, lifts his eyepiece to reveal a crooked nose and rust-coloured eyes. "She's the daughter, that girl we've been looking for." He crosses his arms and ogles me smugly.

"You sure?" The woman lifts her eyepiece. "She barely looks anything like her picture." She rifles through my jacket and pats me down, removing the hunting knife I'd forgotten was attached to my belt loop.

"You ain't cut out for the fugitive life, kid," he says, though he can't be more than five years older than me. And the woman, maybe three.

I examine her delicate blue-grey eyes and buttercream complexion and wonder how she got sucked into the line of soldier duty. I'd say it doesn't suit her, but judging by her athletic physique and the solid force she used to knock me to the ground, I wouldn't be surprised to see her beat this soldier Jerod in a wrestling match.

"At least we got one of 'em in all our time out here." She sighs.

He looks me over once more, then sneers. "Nah, she's nothing compared to the prize awaiting us if we snatch the slave." He takes deliberate strides toward me until he's glaring down into my eyes. "Maybe she knows something. Maybe she's had the misfortune of running into him out here." He studies my eyes as if they display my thoughts like words on a screen. Perhaps they do. But even if he could read my thoughts, all he would learn is how much I despise haughty soldiers like him. Almost as much as I hate Ulric himself. Almost. It is because of callous, compliant soldiers like this man that Mom was killed and Renan was kidnapped.

"Talk, girl." He leans in closer, and I nearly taste the stale stench of his breath. "Where is the boy?"

"If you're looking for my brother, you're two steps behind," I say. "Your people already took him."

"You think I'm stupid? I heard about your brother days ago. I'm talking about the slave."

"Slave?" I mock. "Does Ulric have nothing better to do than send his soldiers off to freeze in search of runaway slaves?"

He scoffs and tightens his grip on my arm. "How are you alive out here, anyway? How long have you been alone?"

"You should know," I spit. "I've been alone since your people kidnapped and enslaved my eight-year-old brother." My only point in saying this is to test the existence of any empathy left in these soldiers' frozen hearts.

It doesn't faze him. But the girl... She stiffens and drops

her gaze at my words. Yes. She *cares.* Though not enough to push her to help me, possibly enough to convince her to help Ren. She is my weak link. My ticket in and out of the prison.

"Where are your belongings? Your food source?" Jerod continues pressing, and when I hesitate, he jerks me back and slams me against a tree. "Answer me!"

My quickening pulse threatens to cut off my voice. I grit my jaw and glance to the girl, hoping she'll interfere. But Jerod jolts me and crushes my arm. So I talk. "I had enough food for a c-couple weeks. Food that I…stole before escaping the region." Though Mr. Elscott has likely already been detained or worse for helping us, I can't betray his loyalty. "But my stock ran out two nights ago." Just the thought of food incites a cramp in my belly.

The woman remains motionless through his interrogation. But when he refuses to let up on me, she eventually moans. "All right, quit torturing her. The poor girl's been freezing out here alone for weeks and hasn't had a decent meal in days." She tears him away from me. "We caught her. You've already won. Now just let her be."

"Fine." He grabs some rope from his backpack and shoves my sleeves up.

Crap! My leather cuff from Ezra. I left it on. He'll see the cross symbol—

"What's this?" He halts and rips it from my wrist.

"No, please! It was a gift."

"One you'll have to live without." He tosses it behind him, paying little attention to its design. He then clutches my wrists and binds them tightly with the coarse rope.

THE SOLDIERS WALK me an hour through the forest's overgrown trail.

Jerod, scrutinizing me minutes on end, gives one of his arrogant smirks that grow more infuriating each time. "Soldier Taima told us she did quite a number on your leg. Said she almost felt sorry for you, which is rare."

I think back to her cold glare as she slammed the door. She certainly wasn't sorry.

He frowns. "Shouldn't you be limping?"

"I'm a quick healer," I snap, fearing he will press me for details. I wouldn't know where to begin. He'd probably kill me for lying—which I wouldn't be doing—but I couldn't blame him for not believing me. Even I'd shoot me if I heard such a story.

To my relief, he doesn't pry.

The woman remains stone silent as she tugs me along with little force. I notice a rectangular patch stitched over her chest that reads *Maven Pierce*. My vision fogs, and in a fleeting tick of lunacy, I blurt, "What's with the nametag? I've only ever seen them on guards. Not soldiers."

"That's because she's still just a guard," Jerod teases.

Maven rolls her eyes and turns her focus to me. "Don't listen to him. I *was* a guard, but Ulric promoted me to soldier early to send me out here—"

"Had nothin' to do with skill though. She's just expendable to him." Jerod shrugs. "King's getting sick of sending his best soldiers—like me—out here with the chance they'll die."

"Would you let me finish?" Maven shoves him hard and continues to explain as he topples over. "Ulric promoted me but had to send me out before my new suit was ready. I'm still using my guard suit, which sucks because it's got next to no insulation, and it's been freezing out here the past week—all except today. But anyway, that's why I still got the nametag."

"Oh." The fogginess in my brain prevents me from grasping much.

Jerod, clearly cross with Maven, yanks my rope from her grasp and hauls me ahead of her. I strain to keep pace with him on my buckling knees. Whenever I fall a step behind, he tugs the rope and my wrists pay the price.

Over the next half hour, my head spins and my starving body yearns for nourishment. Several times when Jerod jerks me forward, I stagger into him, which throws him into a fit of rage that ends with him clutching my upper arm tight enough it goes numb. Maven forces him to let me sip from my canteen every few minutes, but it's not enough to quench the ache in my stomach. Another ten minutes or so of dizziness continues before my legs give out. I fall to my knees. But instead of fainting, I lurch forward into the snow and throw up all my recently downed water.

Even dizzier now, I slump back against a tree stump, sprawled in the wet snow.

"What's wrong with her?" Jerod jerks the rope and curses my defiance, but I can hardly lift my head, let alone stand up and continue walking.

"We've got to build a fire." Maven kicks through the snow, collecting wet twigs.

"What for?"

"What do you think? To *feed* her, Jerod. She's starving to death."

"We were sent out here to capture prisoners. We're not in charge of keeping them healthy."

"That depends," she counters. "Do you want her to *walk*

back with us, or would you rather *carry* her the whole way in a body bag?"

"Fine, go ahead. Feed her," he mutters. "But if she dies anyway, that's one less meal we could've eaten."

I lift my head enough to see Maven riddled with aggravation. Then she looks back at me with…*concern?* She's probably just worried she'll be the one carrying me to Kinborough if I die. Why else would a soldier care about a hostage's health?

I slip in and out of consciousness as they squabble over building a fire and argue about what food to feed me. After what feels like a lifetime of Jerod pelting Maven with criticisms for accidentally smothering the fire, she sets half a can of noodle soup beside me to cool in the snow.

I take a few shaky sips at first, longing to down the whole can but knowing that would only make me sick again. Five minutes later, I sip a bit more. Maven then hands me a plain piece of bread, which I dip in the soup. Slowly but surely, I consume it all within an hour. I'm still hungry when finished, but at least the dizziness has eased and I've regained some strength.

Oh, that Ezra was here… Or better yet, that I was there. I should've stayed. Even if we were sharing our last meal before starving to death, at least we'd be together through it. With Jerod as my captor, I'll be lucky to make it back to the prison alive, anyway.

He hacks off a bite of bread while holding a hand on his holstered gun.

I can't let him kill me. I must survive this, not just for Renan but for Ezra now. Hopefully Maven will continue to keep her partner in check for the remainder of the trip.

Jerod catches my stare and sips his soup, a sly spark in his eye.

I tense and avert my gaze, then lift my canteen to take a gulp of water.

"Liar." The word is but a whisper, and very likely to have come from my imagination. But chills traipse the nape of my neck. And when I lower my canteen, he's crouched in front of me.

I jolt and chuck my empty soup can at his chest.

"There's no use lying now." He pulls me to my feet. "Tell me where the slave is hiding."

Maven's brows snap together. "You *know?*"

My head swirls as Jerod shoves me back against the stump. "No, I—"

He slides out his gun. "Your life is worthless to me, girl." He forces my head back, driving the icy barrel to the underside of my jaw. "Sure, King Ulric wants you back. But he wants the slave more. And I intend to give him the best."

"Is this really necessary?" Maven pulls at his shoulder.

He blinks once, then backs off. "You're right." He lifts his fingers to his mouth and lets me drop back down. "We don't have to kill her." He crouches before me, cold precision in his eyes. "We just have to inflict pain worse than death. Hurt her where wounds haven't yet healed." He lifts my pant leg and rips off my boot.

I freeze and release a shaky breath, concentrating on keeping my dinner down.

His eyes widen at the sight of my leg. No swelling. No bruising. Scars long and deep but faded nonetheless. Baffled at first, he quickly collects himself and clears his throat. "Whatever hurried your leg's healing process won't matter after I'm done with you. You'll be worse off than how Taima left you." He kicks my shin. "Where is the slave?"

"I don't know who you're talking about." I can't betray Ezra. He wouldn't survive an unarmed hour with this vicious soldier.

"Interesting." Jerod shares a smirk with Maven, though receives nothing but a scowl in return. "The only reason I can think of why she would lie about knowing the slave or his whereabouts would be because…she doesn't just *know* him. She *cares* for him."

Maven sighs. "Sure. Or she could be, you know, telling the *truth* about not knowing him."

"Call me crazy, but you'll thank me when King Ulric gives us our reward for finding him." He steps down on my leg.

The pain surges, and I grimace. Perhaps it would've been best if the feeling had never returned.

"That's enough." Maven pries him away. "We've at least got one of them to bring back."

"Not. Good. Enough." He grits his jaw, turns, and stomps on my leg.

"All right!" I cry. "I'll talk."

Chapter 23

He removes his boot from my leg, and I cringe. It flares with pain but thankfully doesn't look broken again. I curl it in toward me, and Jerod nudges my arm with his gun. "Get on with it, then."

I swallow the pain and think up credible lies to weave with the truth. Enough lies to protect Ezra. Yet enough truth to get by without Jerod sensing my fraudulence.

"I met the slave out here over a week ago," I begin. "He saved my life when I nearly froze to death while searching for my brother. We got to know each other well. But one day, we came across an abandoned castle. We explored it. Then on our way out of the courtyard, a soldier found us. He and Ezra both fired…and both died." I let the tears slip out for effect, but they're also somewhat genuine as I relive the agony of that time, believing he was dead. And for the honest likeliness that I'll never see him again.

"Right." Jerod snorts. "Now tell me what really happened."

"What?" Maven says before I can get the word out.

"She's obviously lying. Who'd risk their life to protect a dead man?"

"I may be a criminal, but I do have some decency," I say. "I'd rather let the body of the one who saved my life lie in peace than be handed over to the enemy."

"Where is he?"

I glare at him, hoping my eyes don't betray me like they so often do. "I told you. He's dead."

"His body!" He swears at me. "Where's the body? Did you bury him?"

"No, I…I couldn't. The ground was too frozen. I had to leave him."

"Where?"

"The castle courtyard."

He sets his jaw, then lifts me and throws me into Maven.

She stumbles back but swiftly recovers her footing and grasps my arm. Harder this time.

"Take her back with you," Jerod says, a flash of malice in his eyes. "I'm gonna find him." He snatches up his backpack and plods down the trail in the direction we just travelled.

Maven throws me aside and storms after him. "So that's it? You're just leaving me alone with this girl to find him? What if she's telling the truth? What if he really is dead?"

"Dead. Or. Alive. That was the order. You heard him say it. I'll drag his body all the way back if I have to." Jerod jogs ahead, yelling back over his shoulder, "I'm gettin' me that reward!"

"Fine! But Ulric's gonna kill you when he learns you left me to handle the prisoner alone. Oh, and I'll be taking the truck back, so good luck getting home!"

"Whatever. I'll just hotwire one of the others."

"And leave your fellow soldiers stranded out here?" Maven's shoulders raise, and she shouts louder, "That's low, even for you!"

Jerod echoes something back, but he's already too far over the next hill to understand.

"Well, good riddance. See you at your funeral!" Cursing under her breath, Maven returns. Face flushed. Eyes raging. For the first time, I view her as a real soldier. One of Ulric's followers. Overwhelmed in her anger, she turns her back on me. I could probably escape, find my way back to Ezra before she'd notice. But her wrath is a fate I'd rather not face.

So I stay here, slumped against the old maple stump. Waiting for my hands to quit shaking.

Over the next few minutes, the coarseness in her body deflates. Finally, she turns back to me. Her cheeks return to their natural buttercream hue. Then her shoulders droop and she rubs her forehead, looking about ready to cry. "Ulric's gonna kill me. Oh God, he's gonna kill me."

I watch her pace as she tries to collect herself. Her body may grow calm, but the fear refuses to cease thrashing through those delicate blue-grey eyes. And I realize this soldier—this should-be enemy of mine—is just as scared of Ulric as any criminal I've come across.

Even more so, it seems.

AN HOUR AFTER dark, we arrive at a small, sturdy house apparently pre-selected for tonight's stay, considering Maven followed a GPS to get us here. She unravels the rope around my wrists once inside, replacing it with metal cuffs and chaining me to a solid wooden post that seems crucial in supporting the structure of the house.

She then unbolts a closet door and retrieves a large duffel bag. Unpacking it, she says, "Since Jerod's gone, I guess these are yours," and heaves a rolled-up sleeping bag at me, followed by a massive downy duvet.

I get to work setting up my sleeping quarters, though the

shackles put up a challenging fight. I've never touched such luxurious material in all my life, let alone been allowed to use it. The duvet, dense and unbelievably soft, begins to warm my body on contact.

"That bracelet of yours, the one he took…" Maven makes direct eye contact with me for the first time. "It was from *him*, wasn't it? Ezra."

I look down at my wrist, the metal cuff in place of the supple leather, and try not to think of how much I miss it. How much I miss him.

"Jerod's a jerk. He shouldn't have done that." She tosses me an apple, and I catch it midair.

I stare at the bright red fruit, then at her. Why is she treating me this way? Talking to me like I'm…human?

Whatever the reason, I don't care at the moment. Because this apple calls out to me. And I answer by taking a bite. Crisp. Juicy. Sweet. I melt back against the wooden post. Delicious.

Maven watches me eat, the liquid running over my lips. "What all did you eat out here before you ran out of food?"

"Mostly soup. Potatoes. Apples." I close my eyes, savouring each bite of the sugary fruit.

"Hmm…well, how'd you like to try something else for a change?"

When I finally swallow and open my eyes, she's sitting cross-legged in front of me with a jar of something creamy brown. Swirling and sticky looking. Peanut butter, I think.

She hands me a spoon, and I hesitate, but can't resist the nutty, salty aroma. I stick my spoon in and scoop out a large dollop, then eat half of it all at once. The sticky, buttery mixture pastes to my tongue and melts in my mouth. Ah, peanut butter. The delectable stuff I've only had the pleasure tasting twice before—once on a special outing with Mom as a child, and once just weeks ago in the cookies the twins baked at Susa's cottage.

Maven grins and scoops a spoonful herself. "Better yet, try it and the apple together."

I bite into my apple, then stick the rest of the peanut butter in my mouth. Oh, how the mouth-watering flavours merge. Better than anything I've ever tasted.

I shoot her a glance, attempting to communicate gratitude through my gaze, but she looks down. I know she can't be trusted. No follower of Ulric's will ever earn my trust. But that doesn't mean I don't feel safer with her than Jerod. Or any other soldier, for that matter.

Just when I thought the king couldn't throw me any more surprises, he goes and sends this girl my way. An angel of a soldier compared to the rest.

CLUMSY SHUFFLING NOISES wake me from a peaceful sleep.

Odd. This must be the first night in weeks I haven't woken to stiff joints or an aching back. I haven't felt so cozy in all my time out here, thanks to Jerod's duvet and sleeping bag.

I jerk my arms down from resting above my head. The chains clank and the cuffs grind into my wrists.

Oh, right. I'm a hostage. How could I forget?

The open room, shadowed with pre-dawn's dreary light, becomes chillingly quiet. Then again, the silence is broken as Maven's boots hit the ground. I crane my neck to get a better look.

She stalks over to where I lie chained to the wooden post,

a hazy glare coating her eyes.

My chest tightens. Something is off, though I can't pinpoint what exactly. Just that her eyes no longer display a delicate ease. Instead, they are hollow. Yet they also pierce the shadows.

The insulating warmth holds captive my body, tempting me to remain in its restful embrace. Nonetheless, I push myself up on my elbows.

And freeze at the glimpse of my hunting knife in her hand.

She slowly kneels down beside me. Inhales stiffly. Her gaze bores into me—through me—and she grits her jaw. Then lunges for me.

I dive sideways. The cuffs wrench my wrists.

Her face seeps with sweat. Loose strands of her braid dangle in my face as she pins me down.

Now I get it. The friendly manner. The standing up for me. The peanut butter. It was all a hoax. A scam. Meant to lure me in. To create a false sense of security in her, then trap me in it.

I thrash and kick, but with my arms ensnared, it's useless to fight.

She brings the knife to my throat, stammering, "You can't…can't have her!" She breathes raggedly through clenched teeth. "Via's mine!" Tears collect in her foggy eyes. And I realize it's not really her. Nor is it really about me. It's merely a night terror she's acting out.

Sleepwalking.

She pulls the knife away and straightens. Enough to land a hard blow to my jaw. Then another.

I wince as my left ear rings and my eyes water. A moment of fogginess passes before I detect her tactful movement.

She straddles my body and raises my hunting knife over my chest.

My pulse races as I fail to shove her off. I scan her belt for a key to my cuffs—nothing. I twist my body under her weight, but she holds me down. And readies herself for the kill.

The jagged edge glints, preparing to swiftly plunge through my heart.

Impaled by my own knife? *No.* That's not how I go. Not that I believe I'll have a real say in how I die when my time comes, but I will not be brought down by my own weapon. That much is certain. Nor will I die at the hands of some disturbed, sleepwalking soldier.

I shove my hands out as far as the chains will allow. "Maven, s-stop. Wake up!"

Perhaps it's in hearing her name. Or rather, due to the intensity in how it is said. Either way, she halts, studies my face. And loosens her grip on the knife.

I take advantage of her hesitance. Lunging upward, twisting. Throwing her off me. She staggers but comes back for me, and I kick her square in the ribs, launching her backward.

She lands flat on the concrete. And gasps. She writhes and winces, releasing a pained whimper. After another minute of measured breathing, she pushes herself to stand with a grimace, blinks hard at me, and her eyes return to normal. She sways and staggers back into the wall. Her breath catches as she eyes the dagger in her hand.

I sit up, back against the post, keeping a wary eye on her while rubbing my raw wrists and tending to the burn on my hand, the healing scabs now ruptured from the cuffs.

She studies me uneasily. "Y-your jaw. Did I...?" She eyes

her bruised knuckles. The knife slips from her hand, crashes to the ground. She shoots one last guilty glance my way before shuffling back to her sleeping bag.

AROUND MIDMORNING, SHE finally rises. Though with all that tossing and turning through the hours following the incident, I doubt she ever fully reclaimed sleep.

I sure didn't. Instead, I spent the ages rotating Ren's dove carving between my fingers and wondering about him. If we all come out of this alive and escape the region, what will become of him? He's a slave like Ezra now. Ulric decided to claim him as his own property. And if my and Ezra's situations have taught me anything, it's that the king doesn't take kindly to escapees.

If we rescue Renan, will he become like Ezra? A fugitive with soldiers breathing down his neck, mercilessly hunting him? Will he have to hide out his whole life in fear of being spotted? Will it be the same for Ren? Will they never stop until they have him?

The questions loop in my head for hours on end with no answers. I get so fed up I even attempt throwing them at Ezra's God. They are met only with silence. Predictable, yes. But also disappointing. Ezra said if I want answers for my questions, I have to ask God myself.

What a joke. Even if God were real and he could hear my questions, who am I that he would care enough to answer them? Is an answer to my question even what I want anymore? I've been out here, fighting for my life for so long. I do want answers, but I think what I most want and need is just to have someone who truly understands, who will comfort me. But Mom is gone.

I'm sorry, God. Forgive me for whatever I've done to deserve your silence.

THROUGHOUT THE MORNING, while we eat a breakfast of bread with peanut butter and afterward as she packs everything up to head out, Maven remains silent. Veiling any thought or emotion about the sleepwalking incident with a perfect, blank expression. As we begin our last hours of hiking before reaching the outskirts—I'd guess three more hours remain in total—never once does she make eye contact.

A straight half hour of silence passes before I gain the nerve to ask, "Who…who's Via?"

She sends me a startled glance, as if I interrupted thoughts so weighty she'd forgotten she was holding my chains. "Oh," she sighs. "The night terror. What did I—did I say?"

"Just something about Via and that you didn't want someone to take her." When she says nothing more, I probe further. "How often do you get them? The night terrors?"

The corner of her mouth twitches. "Once a week. Maybe twice. It depends." She looks down, then grins. "It's not all bad though. Gave Jerod the scare of a lifetime the other night."

I snort a laugh. "I wish I could've seen that." Wish I could've seen him struggle, seen the fear in his eyes. Although I can't really blame him. She can be terrifying when she's about to slit your throat.

Her smile fades and she grows quiet. "Via—Vianna… She's my daughter."

I study her. "Your daughter?"

She bites her cheek and nods. "She's two and a half now. Had her when I was seventeen."

"Where is she now?"

"Back home with the nanny."

"And the father, is he…?" I stop in my tracks, eyes widening. "Wait, it's not—"

"Don't even finish that sentence. Jerod is *not* the father. And I hope he's never careless enough to become one. Think of the poor kid that gets stuck with him for a dad." She clears her throat. "No, Via's dad is long gone. Wanted nothing to do with her. Or me."

"Oh." I can't help thinking of my own birth mother, whoever she is. How she took off one day and never cared enough to return. "Is that why you're out here? To take care of her?"

"Yeah. I didn't choose the life of stalking deserted regions with no indoor plumbing for the fun of it. The only reason I took this job two years ago was that I was homeless with a four-month-old, and they were threatening to take her away from me if I didn't shape up. Ulric promised to provide for us if I'd work for him. I'm only out here now because I'll get four weeks off with full pay if I bring back one of his escapees. Four weeks, no work intrusions. Just spending time with my kid, getting to raise her myself instead of the nanny for a change." I catch a glint of longing in her eyes before she shifts her gaze ahead.

"Makes sense now."

"What makes sense?" She frowns.

"That you're a mother."

Her grip tightens on my chains. "Why? You sayin' I'm soft?"

"The opposite, actually," I clarify to avoid a third punch

to the face. "The other soldiers out here… Sure, they're all fighting for something. The reward, revenge, themselves. But from the beginning, I could tell you're different. You have something more valuable to fight for."

A few moments pass as we head on before she says, "I knew him, you know. Ezra."

I halt. "You did?"

She swallows. "Before I was a soldier or even a guard, I was a janitor in the prison. In charge of cleaning out cells. I hated the job. The smell alone was enough to make anyone gag. The slaves were always taken away while I cleaned their cells, so I never saw them or knew their names. Except for one. I'd never even seen him face-to-face, but out of them all, I knew Ezra."

"How?" My gut clenches.

"His writings. He was the only one to own notebooks and a pen. He always hid them under his mattress or in a crack in the wall so I wouldn't find them. I always did find them. But I never took them away. After I flipped through his books the first time, I didn't have the heart to take the only thing the boy had. His words were everything to him, but they were so hopeless. I can't blame him. After so many years of living as a slave, he thought he'd never leave." She swings the chains attached to my cuffs. "Now here we are. Ordered to search every inch of this place until we find and return him to his eternal doom. And none of us even know why, what he did to deserve such a life in the first place."

"Nothing." I blink back moisture. "He did absolutely nothing to deserve it."

"Anyway…" she says after a long moment, then eyes me. "How's your jaw?"

The throbbing set into a dull ache hours ago. I just shrug

and observe the way she holds her arm tenderly over her abdomen. "How are your ribs?"

She shrugs stiffly. "Eh, I've dealt with worse than a bruised rib or two in my time." But she can't mask the wince as she shuffles along.

I've been able to excuse her of the sleepwalking episode, considering how guilty she looked after waking from it. But I can't indulge her in any more conversation, ordinary or otherwise. She might still be trying to lure me into a trap, coax me into sharing more about Ezra.

She is not my friend. Never will be. She's working for the king. Whether or not she agrees with everything he's doing is beside the point. She may say she's only in it for her daughter's sake, but she is still a soldier working for Ulric.

That makes her the enemy. No matter how nice, how different from the others she appears.

She is not to be trusted. I'd be wise to remember that if I want to see Ren and Ezra again.

Chapter 24

I don't remember any of it. The downed, rotting trees that mush underfoot even in the cold. The tattered kite snagged in the maple's bare branches. Deflated wheels of toppled vehicles submerged under heaps of debris.

We walk along the last strip of the brick-laden street before reaching the outskirts. Whirling a keychain around her finger, Maven points out a spot near the forest's border where a mini black box truck, caked in snow, awaits us.

I've been here before, but I hadn't noticed much about the place. I must've been a bit preoccupied, what with having just lost my mother and all. With having just…

Oh.

Something catches my eye beyond the edge of the vast field. Poking through the snow.

Marking the place where Mom was buried.

I root my feet and stare out at that pathetic little cross I built.

That wood is not worthy to bear her engraved name. Those warped planks have no right to mark the resting place of the most beautiful, selfless being to ever exist. That patch of earth has no business concealing her body.

The chains jolt my wrists as Maven trudges onward. Then she stops and turns. "What's wrong?" She follows my gaze to the field but doesn't seem to spot the object of my sorrow.

Everything hurts.

Too many memories come flooding back at once. Days spent baking with her in the kitchen when she'd tie one of her blue aprons around my waist. That December day she took me to the hair salon and allowed me to colour a strip of my hair red. The night she let me snuggle up beside her in the hospital bed and hold the little pink thing that was my brother, for the first time. All the days my heart fluttered at the sight of a crisp letter folded on my pillow.

And then the day I watched Dad lower her body into the ground. The day my world shattered, when her love and safety fled my life forever.

I look away, swallow the lump in my throat. "Paper… I need paper."

DANGLING MY LEGS out the trunk of the truck, I stare at the blank notepad in my lap. The pen in my hand hovers over it as I'm, for once, unable to convert my thoughts to written word.

How could I? After all she did for me. After how she changed my life, took me in as her own daughter. How she loved me unconditionally. She cannot be defined by words. And no amount of words could begin to convey how grateful I am for her. Or how much I miss her.

I think back to the first time she ever wrote to me—the first night Dad invited her for dinner at our house. I hadn't met her yet, so it was more of an introduction dinner for her and me than a date for her and Dad. He had spoken of her plenty throughout the weeks prior and I'd noted how his tone softened in saying her name. Still, I loathed the thought of this woman becoming my stepmother. One parent was enough trouble.

But as much as I opposed, Dad insisted on having her over. He helped me prepare for our introduction, setting out my best clothes, even trying his hand at brushing my unruly hair and braiding it down my back. "Behave yourself," he urged me, "and she will love you."

Behave isn't exactly the word I'd use to describe my actions that night. From the time she arrived until the time dinner was ready, I didn't say a word. Didn't answer any of her questions about school or my hobbies or my friends. Mostly because my seven-year-old-self hated school, had no clue what having a hobby meant, and didn't care much for any of my so-called "friends." Then, in the middle of dinner, she tried to ask me if she could take me out shopping sometime so we could get to know each other. At that, I dropped my fork on the table, shoved my chair back, and headed for my bedroom.

Dad stood and started after me. "Rielle! Come back to the table. Now."

But before I could close my door, Miriam stopped him, saying, "Let her go, Evan. I know this is hard for her. Don't expect her to warm up to me in a day. I didn't expect that when I asked to meet her."

I stood with an ear inclined out the doorway, wondering why she would say that. Didn't she just want to worm her way into our family and take over in any way she could? She couldn't really care for my feelings, could she? It must've been an act to deceive Dad into marrying her.

I spent the rest of the night hunched on my bed, arms crossed, with a scowl on my face in case Dad—or better yet, she—would get fed up with my absence and come busting down my door. Nothing of the sort happened. In fact, quite the opposite. They ate and talked, my door muffling their voices enough I couldn't eavesdrop. But no way was I desperate enough to give in and open the door to overhear their conversation.

They'd spent hours talking and laughing, which made me hate her even more. But then a time of silence passed, and before she left, an envelope slipped under my door. I spent another hour debating whether to give in to curiosity and retrieve it. When I did open it and unfold the letter within, I found her writing easy enough to read. Just plain, penned letters. Not the fancy cursive stuff I had yet to learn in school.

It read something like:

Dear Rielle,

I'm sorry if my visit tonight has been uncomfortable for you. I can imagine what it feels like, having some strange woman over for dinner when you know where her intentions lie with your dad. But I don't want to pressure you in any way to like me or want to know me. And I promise that I will keep my distance until you are comfortable. I would never deliberately try to intrude on your personal life. I only ask questions about you because I can tell you are a very bright girl, and I think we could have a lot of fun together. Maybe even become friends.

But I assure you, I will not try to force my way into your life or your family. Yes, I do like your dad very much, but I don't want to disrupt things between you two. Before your dad and I decide on any sort of future together, I want to get to know everything about him and about you, Rielle. Because you are as much a part of this equation as your dad and me. So I won't try to force anything on you before you are ready. And if you're ever uncomfortable, you can tell me.

I want you to know that I don't expect anything from you. You shouldn't feel you must act any way other than yourself. We don't have to go shopping together if you don't want to. For now, I only hope you might write me back so we can start getting to know each other, and then we'll go from there. If you don't want to talk about school or friends or hobbies, maybe you'd like to tell me your favourite food and what place you've always wanted to visit?

It was lovely meeting you tonight, Rielle.

Sincerely,

Miriam

Long story short, I ended up writing back to her that week, telling her my favourite food was pasta and admitting I'd always wanted to visit a farm and ride a horse.

She made it happen. Talked to Dad about Mr. Elscott's farm and set up a riding lesson for the week after. First, we picnicked in his forest by a small lake, eating pasta and chicken sandwiches. Then we saddled up and had our first riding lesson together.

That was how the years of letter-writing started between us. And how she joined our family.

"Well? Are you just gonna stare at it forever?" Maven jars me from the memory.

I come to, but don't answer.

"Who's the note for, anyway?"

"My mother." I don't bother glimpsing her reaction. I force my eyes shut to concentrate, but no words come to mind.

What's the point of writing to Mom without any chance of receiving a response? She's gone. Never again will I receive a beautifully handwritten letter from her.

No. I can't write her another letter. The last one was buried with her. It was a response to her final note to me. It was an apology and a promise. I can't write her anything I haven't already said. It'd just get repetitive and pointless.

But I can't just write nothing to no one. I must take advantage of this writing privilege before Maven whisks me off to prison. It's wise to assume no guard will be as kind to me as the one who gave Ezra his pens and notebooks. This might be my last chance to ever write again. Now, the question is…who to write to?

Renan? Maybe. But anything I write to him will be useless, so long as I cannot help him escape. Besides, it would say more to simply give him his new dove carving.

Ezra? I wish. Whatever I write, Maven will see. So if I write to him, she'll know that he's alive, that I lied, and that Jerod's on a dead-end mission to find him. She'll alert Jerod, in turn prompting his return. In every scenario I can imagine, writing to Ezra always ends with my own death. No thanks.

Next.

An image of Susa sweeps through my mind. The way her smile overtook her face, pinching her eyes and sending a contagious wave of peace through me as well. But then I note her smile wilting. The light deserting her eyes as the inability to hold back her grief weakens her.

Susa, now imprisoned. Alone. Only able to think of her impending death. And the children she raised…gone. She doesn't even know her own son, taken away eight years ago, is still alive.

That's it. She is the one I will write to.

First, I work out the wording as to throw Maven off my plan. Make it seem so natural that she assumes I'm writing to my mother when in fact I'm coding a message to Susa.

I bite my lip, tracing pen to paper. Then I evaluate it carefully for any obvious tells.

Maven eyes it over my shoulder, and I brace myself for confrontation. But none comes.

I read it over in my head again.

Your son is alive. He is healthy. And he misses you, longing for the day he will finally see you again. We both miss you.
—Rielle

Not perfectly natural. But it'll have to do. I tear the sheet from the pad and fold it twice over. "Done." I slip it in my pocket and hop down from the trunk.

Maven shuts and bolts the trunk doors, then rounds the truck to start the vehicle.

"Before we leave…could I have a moment alone… there?" I flick my gaze to the rugged cross.

This time, when she skims over the snowy field, her eyes stop on the cross. She stills and her lips form a grim line. Now she understands. Of course, she would've already been informed of my mother's death. But now she knows she was killed during our escape and buried out here by us—not returned to Ulric. She swallows and sets her jaw, then nods. "Get in."

When we come to the cross, she pulls up close, trunk to the front of the grave. She idles a while before shutting off the engine. "Take as long as you need. But I gotta keep my eye on you. And to ensure you don't run off," —she retrieves her pistol— "this thing's loaded."

I swallow dryly, eyeing the cross in the rear-view mirror.

"Whenever you're ready," she adds, avoiding my gaze.

How could I ever be ready? How could anyone prepare

themselves for this? I stall, fidgeting with my hat and my coat zipper. But staying here with Maven—the stiffness of her shoulders, her forced blank expression—is just as daunting as the thought of confronting that grave.

So I swallow the lump in my throat and push the heavy door open against the wind. Once around the back of the truck, I stare at the cross, unsure what to think or feel.

No, I know exactly what I feel.

I feel that Mom was cheated. Robbed of her beautiful, humble existence. Ulric thinks he's ridding people like Mom for the greater good of the country? All he's doing is fast-tracking the country's collapse by killing off the only ones worthy of living in it. Mom doesn't deserve to be buried in the ground where she will be stepped over and forgotten.

Heaviness weighs on my heart. I crouch down before the cross and clear the snow off the horizontal beam to see the letters carved beneath. *Miriam Rutherford.*

I wish I could talk to her. But whether in my head or aloud, I can't seem to conjure anything but silence. No amount of communication would satisfy so long as she's gone.

My eyes blur. I stand up and turn my back to the cross.

Maven eyes me through the side mirror, but I couldn't care less what she sees at the moment.

How could this be Mom's fate? Is there no hope for even the kindest, gentlest of souls? Was her faith all just a fallacy? Because if there's any truth in it at all, I'm not seeing it. I'm not seeing any hope for life beyond the grave.

I think back to my argument with Ezra, how he told me I had to release what's holding me back and making me bitter. I thought that's what I did when I let my reproach for God blaze. But that wasn't even scratching the surface.

How can I release what makes me bitter when the pent-up rage is what I'm made of entirely?

Wrath has been my motivation, my ally, for so long. And I hate myself for it. Hate being angry. Mom was never fuelled by anger. Even when I'd argue or pick a fight with her, she would fight back if only to knock some sense into me. Not out of rage or hatred.

I always wanted to turn out to be like her, but I've become the complete opposite. And she's the one who had to pay the price. I am the one that deserves to be buried in the ground, but I'm the one left standing over it.

I turn to face the cross again and sink to my knees.

How could you let this happen, God? I don't understand.

"Why wouldn't you save her?" The wind steals my whispered words and carries them away. I close my eyes, dropping my chained fists to my lap.

The question echoes in my head, repeating minutes on end. Receiving no response. Same as this morning, when I got so fed up searching for my own answers that I threw the questions at God. It seems my hope for a response from God is just as dead as my desire for a responding letter from Mom. However, whereas she would no doubt respond if she could, God *can* respond.

But he won't.

I can't do this anymore. God, how can I believe in you? Believe in love and freedom and second chances when you won't even answer my cry? If you won't help me, who will? I have no one left.

The biting wind batters me. My back aches, and I hang my head, crouched in the snow.

Emptiness takes hold of me. Numbness washes over me. And the hopelessness sets in.

I sit in it. The nothingness. The burden that is my life.

For many moments, the grief plagues me, riddling through my veins and crushing my chest with its claws of agony.

Then, as I force myself to inhale a sharp breath, the coldness of the wind retreats. Its raging pressure continues to flog my face. But the biting needles of ice it pelts me with...they become soft. Warm, even. Like an onslaught of silky feathers.

I dare not open my eyes for fear this strange sensation might depart. As the mighty yet tender wind caresses me, a peace enters my lungs and spreads through my body. Warmth. Light.

Life.

Then my limbs grow weak and tingly as an overwhelming sense of security binds me and bears me. Just holds me. For a long minute or an hour—I really can't say—but it is there. I feel it. Though there are no words spoken directly to me, the understanding through it all stands firm. It's a sense of awe that imbeds hope in my heart and says I am not alone.

It says I will be okay.

Then chills ripple over me and through me and beyond me. Not from the cold, but from the intensity of comfort. Relief from my pain. From understanding that I'm not fighting this fight alone. That no matter how hopeless it looks from my viewpoint, it will all be okay.

Surely that understanding didn't come from me. I would've instantly objected to such a blatant notion—that I will be okay. From my eyes, nothing, no part of me or my situation is okay. But that calming warmth urges me to accept the idea that I know nothing of what the future holds, and that it is okay. I want to receive it. If it feels this freeing to accept such a notion, I really do.

When I finally open my eyes, the wind once again nips

my face with its needles of ice. The physical warmth recedes. But the peace continues dwelling within me.

It is real. The consuming sensation of the divine was real, and not anything I could've expected or conceived myself. The warmth wasn't just warmth as in entering a house that's had the furnace running all day. It was a warmth that breathed life into the dead crevices of my being. A heat that pricked me with an incredible sense of something greater. Something beyond myself.

Great. I'm starting to sound like Ezra.

He was right though. I do believe in God. I think I always have. I held too hard a grudge against God to consider it. But I knew. I knew my parents weren't reckless. There was a valid reason they chose to risk their lives for a belief.

God was the reason Dad changed. When he stopped abusing me, I thought it was because he met Mom, but it was really because he met God *through* her.

I clamp a shaky hand around the horizontal stick and look to the base of the cross, knowing Mom's body lies below. Knowing she is gone. Knowing when she died, the letters died with her. But also knowing death is not her end.

One by one, snowflakes bury the letters of her name.

I return to the passenger seat of the truck, an odd fullness in my heart that smothers any fear.

That is, until a fuzzy voice blasts from Maven's transmitter, reading, "Mandatory report from Headsman Malachi. Urgent update on the wanted escapees. Listen in, all soldiers."

Every lasting ounce of warmth in my core turns to ice.

Chapter 25

By now the nation knows of my near-fatal injury result-ing in hospitalization, immediate surgery, and weeks of bedrest." Malachi clears his throat, though I can't tell if his weak voice and irregular breathing are due to his health con-dition or nerves. "Nevertheless, this will not hinder me from assuming my job as your headsman."

I think back to Head Damien's final speech. How his typ-ically crisp, confident tongue was tainted with stuttering and riddled with nerves. Similar to how Malachi sounds now.

"And as your headsman, but also as your future king, it is my responsibility to stand by the horrific murder of our faithful and beloved Head Damien. His death will be neither forgotten nor unpunished." He clears his throat once more, then his speech begins to drone as if reciting from a script—which is likely the case. "Unfortunately, Head Damien was not the only victim in this incident. Eight of our highly trained guards and soldiers sent to find the escaped criminals have been deemed dead also."

He pauses for a moment, then continues, "Our past as-sumptions were pitted against the runaway slave, Ezra Henson, and the wanted father, Evan Rutherford, to have been the sole culprits of the murders. Yes, both are danger-ous and have surely contributed to most of the murders, but we now have reason to believe the daughter, Rielle Rutherford, is responsible for the murder of at least one of the fallen men. Therefore, whoever returns the slave, the father, or the daughter will be rewarded in equal wage as previously announced for the slave's return. I ask that each of you work your hardest and bring them all back, dead or alive."

Several seconds of fuzzy silence emanate from the transmitter before he speaks again. "There are two soldiers' bodies still to be found and returned home for proper burial." He recites both soldiers' names, ranks, and approximate whereabouts. "Within the week, there will be a region-wide memorial ceremony for the citizens of Kinborough to show their gratitude, pay respects to Head Damien, and honour the guards' and soldiers' noble sacrifices and service to our country. Thank you all for listening. Headsman Malachi, signing off." The crackling noise stops abruptly, ending the broadcast.

My heart wallops in my chest as I try to wrap my mind around the message. Only one word comes to mind.

Valuable.

Never in my life have I used that word in reference to myself. Naturally, I've always wished to be of some value. But not like this. To know I am this kind of valuable…it leaves a sickening ache in my gut. This is not the type of value I ever longed to achieve. Worth only as much as they can trade me in for, only what my crimes have made me.

I'm now just as valuable to them as Ezra. Maven will receive the same sum of money for my return as if she'd returned him. That can only mean I'm to be slain too. If they have reason to believe I murdered one of their own—which they're not wrong about—they will ensure I pay the price.

They are going to execute me.

Maven sucks in a breath, then lets it out slowly. "Man." She shakes her head with a revelling smirk. "I'd like to see the look on Jerod's face right now. To learn he didn't have to go raiding the whole forest to find someone worth something. It's a good thing though—that he left to look for the slave. Good for us both. He'd really have it in for you if he were here. Probably kill you before you ever reached the prison. Maybe even kill me off to claim the full reward himself."

Noise fills my head, and I barely register her words.

This was supposed to work! I was supposed to hand myself over so they'd be thrown off Ezra's trail. Then he'd follow behind and break me out of prison, and we'd rescue our family and escape to another region. But now I'm worth just as much as him. They'll probably kill me upon arrival.

Restlessness floods my veins as I relive plunging my knife into that young soldier's abdomen. Why did I kill him? I didn't have to go so far as to kill him to ensure he didn't kill Ezra. If anything, killing him only brought us more trouble. They probably located his whereabouts and sent more soldiers after us. That's likely why Maven and Jerod were sent out here in the first place.

I lean back against my headrest.

If only I could convince Maven to help me. She doesn't want me to die. I know she doesn't. She's my only hope. I don't care if they execute me, but I do care about staying alive long enough to ensure Renan escapes. I can't let Ulric do to Ren what he did to Ezra. Force him to kill. Torture him for resisting. Starve him. Turn him into a weapon. That can't happen. I can't let that happen.

"Maven, I know you're my captor, so this will sound ridiculous and naïve, and I don't expect you will actually help me…" I pause as she fixates on me. "But my brother was captured. He's a slave now. Probably will be for the rest of his life. And I can't do a thing for him. So…" I stop mid-request, as her refusal already shows through her sharpening shoulder blades.

"I hate this." She sighs. "I really do. I don't want to be the cause of you or your brother getting hurt."

"*Killed.*" I tighten my grip on the chains in response to her making light of my situation.

Her eyes flash with frustration. "If you did kill a soldier, would I be right to assume it was an act of self-defence?"

I maintain firm eye contact, though admit to nothing.

"You seem like someone who doesn't deserve any bit of this." She bites her lip. "But I can't help you."

"Won't," I correct.

Her posture tenses. "Look. This is my first job as a soldier. I hate it, but I need it. If I help you, I'm dead. And if I'm dead, that means my daughter belongs to Ulric." That same look of fear thrashes through her eyes as when Jerod ran off and she nearly broke down, saying that Ulric was going to kill her. "Who knows what he'd do with her or why he wants her."

"How do you know he wants your daughter? Why would he?"

She presses her lips as if restraining the desire to spill everything she knows. "I…I think he sent me out here on a futile mission." She keeps her gaze alert while driving. "A test. I think he expects me to die. When I signed the contract to work for him, he promised my daughter and me a good life. But he warned me, if I were to fail him or defy his orders, he would take everything he gave me away. And since he practically saved our lives when he hired me…that means he will take *her* away."

"Does he have a reason to? Did you do something wrong?"

"It was unintentional…" She cringes. "I stuck my nose where it didn't belong last year, tried to prove a guilty man innocent of his crimes and undeserving of his sentence. It was an amateur mistake. But to Ulric, even that small breach of trust means he believes my loyalties lie elsewhere. He wants me to prove my allegiance remains with him. If I can't, then I've failed him. And he'll be rid of me."

I draw my brows as clarity strikes. "Then come with us. Come with me and my brother, away from Ulric. If you help me rescue my brother, you and your daughter can escape the region with us. You can start over. Have a new job. A new life."

"That would only bring more risk to Via's life. I can't just run from my problems. I'm out here and I'm doing my job because I'm determined to prove Ulric wrong. Prove my loyalties lie with him, that I deserve to be here. Then he will realize my potential and use me for my strengths instead of trying to oust me to get to my daughter. That's the only way I can win."

"You think that's winning? Showing him your potential only makes you more of a slave to him than you already are." The words are spoken by the time I realize I've gone too far.

Her eyes narrow and she slams her foot on the brake. "Let's get one thing straight." She grips the steering wheel so tight her knuckles turn white. "I am a slave to *no one*."

Her sudden brashness stuns me. "Whatever you say." I fake a smile.

"And one more thing." She twists toward me, furious. "We are not friends. Just because I don't press a gun to your head and threaten to kill you every five seconds doesn't mean I'm on your side." Her eyes pierce mine like shards of ice. "Understood?"

A lump forms in my throat. I nod.

She finally breaks her stare and clamps her hands back on the wheel.

I must be losing it. To think my captor, my enemy, would want to help me. How could I be so stupid? So vulnerable as to let the idea consume me—that she could become my friend?

I don't make friends. Even Ezra I tried to shake off for days. The only reason he's my friend now is that he stayed when I'd wished he wouldn't. He braved my anger.

But Maven. She is nothing like Ezra. She doesn't care to know me. She might not be torturous or manipulative like other soldiers. She might step in to prevent me from suffering unwarranted cruelty. But she only cares about the reward she will collect for handing my life over to the king.

Like I told myself before. She is not to be trusted.

But…that first time I spoke of Renan's enslavement, she stiffened and looked away. She might not be on my side, but does that mean she'd turn a blind eye while an innocent child suffered?

"All I ask…"—I wet my cracked lips—"is that, if you find any opportunity at all, you will help my brother, Renan. I don't care that you won't help me. But I beg you, please help him. Help him have a different future from the one you read about in Ezra's journal. Help him escape."

She clenches her jaw and fastens her eyes on the field ahead. "I can't."

Every ounce of hope sinks to the pit of my stomach like a ball of lead. Pressure builds behind my eyes, and I can't help but voice my revulsion. "You are a coward, Maven Pierce. A coward and a hypocrite. You aren't strong enough to stay loyal to your king, so you run off and befriend his enemies behind his back, tricking them into thinking you have some empathy for their circumstances. And then you stab them in the back."

"It's for my daughter—"

"No! That's just what you say to make yourself feel better. If you were really doing all this for her, you would understand why you should help my brother. You'd want to help him in any way you can. Because he's an innocent, just like your daughter, probably being tortured and turned into a weapon for the king as we speak. And you won't do a thing—"

"Neither would you! If you were in my shoes, which you practically are. I've only got my daughter left, you've only got your brother. Now go on, tell me you would risk his life to save a stranger. Tell me you'd trade his safety to help the enemy. Tell me!"

My shoulders stiffen. I avert my eyes as they blur, hot with rage. Because she bested me.

I can't. I can't tell her I'd risk Renan's life to help someone I'm supposed to hate. I wouldn't.

She waits through the silence, then cajoles the vehicle forward again. "That's what I thought."

SHE GRUDGINGLY HANDS me a platter of grapes and a peanut butter sandwich for dinner.

I resentfully take the meal and scarf it down.

One hand on the wheel and one holding her sandwich, she squints through the oncoming flurry and steers cautiously through the field.

A sharp beep cuts through the heavy silence. Maven straightens and swallows her mouthful of food, then lifts her wrist and presses a button. "Soldier Maven Pierce. Come in."

An all-too-familiar snort blasts through the speaker. "Stop answering with that. You know you're not a real soldier. At least not until the commencement next month."

"Shut up, Jerod." Her tone loses its professional edge. "I'm already more of a soldier in a week than you've been in three years."

The snob on the other end scoffs and grumbles. "Whatever. I only called to check in. Make sure you're not dead."

"Oh, how sweet," she says with more than a hint of disdain. "But that's not why you're checking in. I admit I'm shocked how long it took you to call after hearing of the reward for the girl. I was nearly convinced you'd died out there."

"You do still have her, right?"

She rolls her eyes. "Yes, Jerod. I have her."

"Good, because she's all we got now."

Maven gives a bored exhalation. "All right, spill."

"Halfway to the castle, I found an abandoned truck and drove it the rest of the way. Made good time, even found one of the dead soldiers the headsman ordered to be returned for burial. Loaded him onto the truck, then started my search for the slave."

"And?"

"He's not here. I just finished searching the whole castle, in and out. The girl lied to us."

Maven glares at me, then her tone bounces. "And you don't seem even a bit fazed by the fact. Rather unlike you, considering her lie cost you a two-day journey for nothing."

"It's a bit of a let-down, but at least I've got the dead guy. And I keep reminding myself that in less than a week, I'll be attending the girl's execution. That'll make it all worthwhile—that and the reward coming for finding her. So wait up for me before turning her in."

"And why would I do that?" She arches a brow. "So you can claim half the reward for the girl *I* caught and held captive? The girl you left me alone with while you went off on your own little quest?" She barks a laugh. "Yeah, that sounds fair. I do the work and you get the credit."

"That's what newbies are for, right? Higher-ranking soldiers like me get to give 'em crap and take advantage of their achievements. But hey, half-and-half ain't bad. After all, it'll give you the recognition you need to rank higher. Then no one'll mess with you. Including me—as long as you wait for me to get there before handing her over."

"Gotta go. I'm driving in this squall, and I won't be risking a wreck just to argue with you."

"Fine." He groans. "Meet me at the prison in two days. You better not screw this up, Pierce."

"Bye, Jerod." She ends the call and returns her full attention to driving.

I stare ahead at the blank field and rolling hills turning dark with dusk.

Two days? Jerod's already on his way back. Driving. Not walking. That'll shred the time in half at least.

Ezra will likely begin his venture for me tomorrow morning. Which means it's highly possible he will encounter Jerod along the way. And though Ezra's got Selah, he's a novice rider. I doubt even a practiced one could outride Jerod and his onslaught of bullets.

That sense of peace and comfort I felt at Mom's graveside now seems like a distant dream. An illusion. It seemed so real, so clear at the time. But how could it be true?

How am I supposed to trust everything will be okay when both Ezra and I are being led like lambs to the slaughter?

Chapter 26

I don't remember dozing off, but when I jerk awake, numbness devours the right side of my face. Neck stiff, I shift away from the side window. If only our seats were reversed. That way my jaw, still sore from Maven's unconscious spell, would've been soothed by the cold glass instead.

It seems she's driven straight through all night, slow but steady through the squall. Reason tells me it's to ensure she receives the full credit for my capture.

Nausea prevents me from reclaiming sleep, conjured from both the thought of reaching the prison and the vehicle's harsh motion. Though I've ridden in a truck only once before, I believe even *I* hold the right to declare Maven a bad driver. Well, perhaps not as in being un*safe*. Rather, in being un*smooth*—at least according to my stomach.

The ride's not all bad though. Heat blasts through every vent in the vehicle. A heat that helps me realize just how numb and rigid my body has been these past few weeks. It seeps into my fingertips and loosens the kinks in my spine.

Even so, this heat is nothing in comparison to the kind that consumed me at Mom's graveside. If only I hadn't opened my eyes so soon, I might've experienced that divine warmth long enough to put into words what it was. *Why* it was. It made no sense yet felt so right. If it really was God…why? Why would he choose to answer me, and not just answer me, but flood me with that…that sensation? That peace, comfort.

The assurance that I am not alone and I will be okay.

I didn't hear a voice or see a source, but those words came to me, dwelled in me, sent my insides leaping at having encountered something essential. Something I hadn't even known was missing from me until I felt it. Someone I didn't realize I craved and sought after constantly until I found him—

Him?

Was it really him? Is God who I was seeking after?

How could it be? I didn't even know *what* I was seeking, or that I was seeking anything to begin with.

Seek. The single word evokes a phrase of Mom's last letter to me. Though I left it and the rest of my belongings with Ezra, the sentence emerges clearly in my mind. *You will understand someday; you just have to seek.*

Is that what she meant? That I must seek after God to understand him?

It still doesn't make sense. If I am meant to understand God and his ways by seeking him, why do I know nothing more now than I had before experiencing him at the gravesite? Sure, I felt something wonderful, but I learned nothing new about him—unless learning he really does make himself known to those who seek and cry out to him counts.

It could've only been him. But here I am, still just as clueless about why he wouldn't save Mom as before.

My thoughts break off as we round a sharp hill and a large, familiar gate comes into view. Shudders traipse over my shoulders. The towering black rods puncture the clouds.

Yet the more unnerving part of the picture lies within that small square room built into the gate's base.

Where the guards await.

It's not nearly as daunting now as the last time I came across the giant grating doors, but nausea still tightens its grip enough that I must close my eyes to fight it off.

"Good idea," Maven says. "Pretend you're asleep while they search the vehicle."

I moan as the wave of vertigo refuses to let up. "What for?"

"Hopefully they'll let us through faster. And with fewer questions." She stops the vehicle where the gate doors join together. "Oh, please let these guys be decent," she says under her breath.

I eye the twinge in her jaw. "You're scared of them. Why?"

"If they know of your worth, and if they put two and two together—that I've defied orders by separating from my assigned partner—they'll detain us both here and now. Have me arrested."

"And why should I care? How is that scenario bad for anyone but you?"

"Would you rather spend the rest of the drive back with me? Or with them?" She nods toward two grim-faced guards approaching, one man and one woman, both aiming guns at the truck.

"Point taken." I let the dizziness engulf me and lie back, eyes closed.

"Thankfully most guards are left out of the soldier loop. Let's hope they haven't heard of your reward." Maven shuts off the vehicle and opens her door. I peek as she shuffles out and holds up a badge of some sort. "Soldier Maven Pierce, on assignment by King Ulric. Came through here last week. I've received orders to return to the Kinborough prison straightaway, so if you've got questions, get on with them."

"Why the urgency?" the woman asks, sounding none too pleased with Maven's directives.

"I got a delivery to be made." Maven's tone sharpens with a convincing pitch of authority.

"Adhering to protocol, we'll sweep the vehicle, scan your badge, and check your weapons. Then you'll be on your way." The woman takes Maven's backpack and rifles through it. She holds up my hunting knife. "What do you need this for when you're cleared to carry a gun?"

A pause, then Maven says calmly, "See that girl in the truck? Escaped the prison three weeks ago. She's wanted for murdering a soldier. I found the knife on her, so I'm bringing it in for testing—to prove she's responsible. I've already called in her capture. The king's waiting for my arrival. And I think we all know he's not one for patience."

The queasiness suddenly retreats and leaves my stomach a rock-hard pit.

Footsteps approach the vehicle and my door opens. I close my eyes completely and slow my breathing, even as the guard checks my pockets. Then he searches the trunk, gives an "All clear," and slams the doors shut.

"Ah—not so fast," the female guard cuts in. "Where's your assigned partner?"

I open my eyes just enough to see what they're doing.

Maven crosses her arms. "He ditched me days ago to hunt down a missing slave. I tried to stop him, but he went anyway. He should be passing through here tomorrow."

The guards share a suspicious glance. "Sorry, but we'll have to impound the vehicle and call this offence in, wait for an answer from Ulric himself whether to let you go. In the meantime, give me your partner's name and I'll put it on the list for questioning when he arrives."

Maven stiffens. "His name's Jerod—Jerod Nelson."

The large man frowns. "*Jerod's* your partner? Now it all makes sense. This being his third offence in a month, that jerk deserves what's coming to him. Tell me he at least found the slave?"

Maven remains silent.

The man curses Jerod's foolishness. "I'm sorry, Soldier. Dealing with him's enough trouble for one week. I'll ensure Jerod pays for his actions upon arrival. You're free to go. Sorry for the delay."

Maven nods. "No hard feelings."

The woman looks about ready to snap in half at the man's breach of regulation. But he retreats to the square room and she follows.

The gate squeals open as Maven returns to the truck. She starts the engine, then sags back into the seat, releasing a breath. "For once, bearing with Jerod's horrible personality has actually done me some good." She presses the gas as the gate widens for her.

The bulky guard raises a friendly hand on the other side of the tinted window, sending us on our way.

EACH HOUR WE drive, the closer I come to Renan. I can feel it, my heart drawing nearer to his. It's what I've longed for since I lost him. But my heart also teems with grief at the gaining distance between Ezra and me.

Why, as I'm approaching the place of my impending death, can I only think of my many-yet-too-few days with

Ezra? They weren't particularly good days. Most of them were spent freezing or arguing, suffering broken legs and gunshot wounds, or hiding from bloodthirsty soldiers. But each of those days, however unpleasant, was worth it. Worth all the anguish and anxiety. Because those days weren't spent alone. They were spent with him. Getting to know him. Getting to understand and appreciate him. Getting to feel the beginnings of a love unlike any other toward the boy I once loathed for saving my life.

The thing is, I think I'd rather not have experienced those days at all than have experienced them without him. No person outside my family has ever made me care for them so much I'd admit to not wanting to live life without them. I should tell him that—give him something to gloat about—when I see him again. *If* I see him again…

We arrive at the parking garage beneath the Phalanx Centre by midafternoon. Maven lowers her window and swipes her wrist through a glowing red scanner. The light flashes green and the gate opens.

She rolls up in one of the parking spots closest to the prison entrance. And idles. Minute after minute. If it weren't for the alertness in her puffy eyes, I'd say she's lethargic from the overnight drive. But her forced blank expression is back. Whether that means she's warding off feelings of guilt for turning me in or she's just plain afraid of how the king will handle her separation from Jerod, I can't tell.

A tap on the window shakes her up. She groans, then rolls it down.

"Hey, Pierce. You're back!" the soldier greets her. When she doesn't respond, he glances past her and eyes me up and down. "Is that…? You found one of them?"

She gives a brisk smile and opens her door to climb out.

"Well, look at that. And on your first assignment!" He claps her on the shoulder. "Why aren't you happy?"

She shakes her head. "Just exhausted. Hiking abandoned forests and driving a day straight can really take it outta you. Trust me, I'm partying on the inside." Her jaw clamps, stifling a yawn.

"Let me help you, then. A lifetime of wealth and fame among the ranks awaits you." He rounds the truck.

She presses a button on her keychain, locking my door from the inside before he reaches it. "Thanks, but I got it from here."

"Oh, come on. I want to see the king's face when he realizes a newbie finished what soldiers with years of experience failed to." He lifts his eyepiece to observe me through the windshield.

I fasten onto his glare, unblinking.

He sneers. "By the looks of her, you could use a hand."

"No offence, but I've held her hostage for days—alone, I might add. I know what I'm doing."

He raises his palms. "Say no more. I'll leave you to it. Just thought I'd offer my congrats." He grins, then turns and weaves his way through the parking lot to start up his own vehicle.

Once he exits the garage, Maven sinks back to her seat and resumes her stony silence.

After a few minutes, I work up the nerve to say, "Can I ask one last thing of you before you hand me over?"

Her eyes droop and she locks them on mine. "You want me to take you to see your brother."

"Ye—actually, no. A different prisoner. Her name is Susa. Susa Henson, I think."

Her expression turns cold, and I prepare to argue her refusal. But then she nods. "Okay."

I release a breath. "Thank you."

She pockets her car keys and rounds the truck to retrieve me.

Her hand tugging my arm, we wind down the halls of the building I never thought in a million years I'd want to return to. If only there weren't a reason for returning.

If only I hadn't let Renan go.

"Prisoner Susa Henson—know where I can find her?" Maven asks a passing guard.

"The holding cells, last I checked. Rumour has it her execution's scheduled for this evening."

Bile rises in my throat.

Susa. Executed. Today.

Ezra will arrive in two days at the earliest! She'll be gone by then.

"Thanks." Maven changes direction, and the chains jolt me from my daze.

I follow her through the maze of hallways until she stops at a steel door. She swipes her wrist through a scanner and it buzzes, then the door opens automatically. Shoulders rolled back, she lowers her eyepiece and surveys the room of cells.

The cold lights flicker every few seconds.

Unlike the secluded cell I once spent a night in, these have only thin, vertical bars for doors. I can easily see through each of them. Empty. At least all but one…

A straggly strand of grey hair catches my eye.

I charge for the cell ahead on the right. "Susa!" The chains jerk my wrists, but this time Maven releases them.

Susa rises from her tattered mattress. "Rielle?" She grasps my hand through the bars, pulling it to her chest.

Remorse overwhelms me as I take in her appearance.

Eyes red and swollen. Hands trembling, as cold as the river's icy water. Purple bruising marks the side of her face. And black soot stains her clothes. Some locks of her hair are singed from the cottage's fire.

I take her hand through the bars and lift it to my face.

She cradles my aching jaw in her palm. I wince, and she retracts her hand, saying, "I'm so sorry you're here." Anguish fills her broken tone.

I take off my hat and wrap it snugly around her icy hands. Guilt clogs my throat. Pressing my forehead to the cool bars, I close my eyes.

Then I remember the letter in my pocket. I glance over my shoulder to ensure Maven's not watching. To be safe, I press closer to Susa, slip a hand in my coat, and feed it back through the bars. She once again takes my hand in hers. Her brows crease as I open my hand and fold the paper into her palm, then give her a cautioning glare.

She nods and tightens her fist around the paper. Though she smiles, the light I once saw in her eyes seems to have faded. Given way to despair, to brokenness. Or perhaps her pool of grief always ran this deep and she just did a better job of hiding it before.

It sends a painful reminder that I failed. I failed her, Ezra…everyone.

I promised Ezra he'd be reunited with his mother. Now it'll be too late. If he ever does see her again, it will be after her execution. When only her lifeless body remains.

I shake away the image and take a ragged breath. "I'm so sorry, Susa."

"Don't blame yourself, dear."

But after I leave and she reads the letter…she'll understand the true meaning of my apology. The depth to it, in knowing she won't live long enough to see her son again.

My vision clouds.

This was a mistake. I shouldn't have given her the letter. She lost Ezra a lifetime ago. She's come to terms with it. If she reads the letter, everything long settled will resurface. She doesn't need another thing to regret, to blame herself for. Not now, mere hours before her execution.

I reach for her hand to take back the letter.

But the steel door buzzes and skims open. A single guard enters.

Maven jumps into action, mouthing the word *sorry* before charging at me. She grabs my arm and drives me into the bars next to Susa's cell.

My cheek hits the metal and I lose my footing. An alarmed cry comes from Susa.

Next thing I know, I'm staring up at the swirling, flickering lights. A pulsing pain slithers into the back of my skull. My vision warps, and I can't quite discern what the voices around me say.

Warm liquid seeps through my hair. I lift my pounding head to see Maven and the masked guard stooped over me. I shut my eyes in an attempt to stop the dizziness.

A sharp grit enters Maven's tone as she yells, "That's what happens when you try to escape!" She lifts me from the concrete floor.

The guard's forehead wrinkles. "What are you doing here with her?"

"Taking her to Ulric. Seems she got a little burst of courage along the way." She shoots me a scowl and grips my arm tighter.

The room begins to cease spinning by the time the guard plods toward Susa's cell with a food tray. He repeatedly glares back at Maven, so she tugs me out the steel door.

Two soldiers approach from down the hall.

She hands me my hat, which I didn't realize she took back from Susa. "We have to go." Down several long hallways she drags me. The dizziness wanes. Then we board an elevator, and she presses the button for the top floor. Once the doors close and we begin our ascent, she lifts her eyepiece and releases my arm. "I'm sorry. I didn't mean to make you fall like that."

The upward motion muddles my vision. I slump against the corner walls to keep steady until we glide to a stop and the doors open.

We pass through a long, sunlit hallway with many closed doors along either side. The interior walls match the outside of the building, mottled off-white marble. Maven stops short of the double doors at the end of the hall, where two masked guards stand motionless, one on each side. Plush leather chairs line the walls alongside the guards, all empty. Maven motions me toward the first chair, and I sink onto its cushion.

A skeletal man in a plain suit and red tie sits behind a desk off to the left. Maven approaches him, and he glances up from the file under his nose. "Name?"

"Soldier Maven Pierce, here to deliver a fugitive."

The man eyes me over her shoulder. "Have a seat. The king will see you shortly." Hands folded behind his back, he steps away from his desk and enters the room as the guards open the doors and close them behind him.

Maven takes the chair beside me. With poised posture, she waits. Her only tell of nervousness lies in how she hastens to run her fingers through her hair and re-braid it messily over her shoulder.

Soon the guards pull the doors open again and the skeletal secretary returns to his desk. An old woman hobbles out behind him. Based on her worn clothing and the poorly crafted cane she clings to, she's an ordinary citizen—might even live around my old neighbourhood. Another man, sharply dressed, exits last. A golden tie glimmers beneath his stark black suit, much like the one Head Damien wore. Perhaps this man is Damien's replacement.

He clears his throat. "Soldier Pierce, the king will see you now."

Chapter 27

The king's office is not at all what I expected. A taupe rug leads from the entrance up to the front of a rich-stained desk that matches the dark marble floor. Immaculate tiered bookshelves run the length of the back wall. Several rectangular skylights flood the room with natural light. Plain yet elegant. Nothing about the place suggests it belongs to Ulric.

Nonetheless, there he waits. Reclined in the beige leather chair behind his desk. A twinge in his jaw and a vain smile in his eyes.

Once the doors close behind us, he rises leisurely and rounds the desk, gripping me with his gaze. He clasps his hands behind his back as Maven shunts me forward.

I fall before him, and he towers over me as I gain my balance and rise.

Here I am, at the foot of the king, face-to-face with the one who wreaked havoc on my life and destroyed my family. Yet all I can think about is how small and dirty and pitiful I am in contrast to him.

He gives an amused, slightly humbled smirk as his eyes settle on Maven. "Yes." His crisp voice resounds. "You have done well, Soldier Pierce. Better than any other thus far. I offer my sincere apologies for doubting your motives, along with my gratitude for returning the prisoner."

Maven drops her gaze. "Thank you, Your Majesty."

"This is the daughter." His eyes skim over me again, and I back up beside Maven. "Do you happen to have any fresh news on the whereabouts of the father or the slave?"

She sighs. "I'm afraid not, Your Majesty."

"What about the murder weapon? My guards posted at the border gate informed me it was in your possession."

Maven pauses, then slides off her backpack and digs through it. She hands over my hunting knife wrapped in a strip of fabric.

After unravelling it, Ulric lifts the blade to the light for inspection. "Excellent. Just the type of weapon Forensics predicted. To be certain, however, I'll have it sent to the lab for analysis."

As if telepathically summoned, a guard appears in the doorway and collects the knife.

Then Ulric grows still. Too still. His brows crumple and, as the door opens again for the guard to depart, he calls, "Potters! Come in here a minute."

The Damien-clone with the golden tie rushes forth. "Yes, Your Majesty?"

"Change of plans. The memorial service arranged for the fallen soldiers—when is it?"

"The eighteenth. Two days' time, midday, Your Majesty," the man says.

Ulric nods as something hard sets in his eyes. "The execution of prisoner Susa Henson set for this evening will be postponed until then. Following the service, my soldiers will carry out the execution of Henson and Rutherford publicly."

The man glances at me. "Rutherford…the *father*, Your Majesty?"

"The *daughter*. Ensure two stakes are constructed in the

stadium's centre for the live executions—three if the father is returned before the service." He looks Maven over. "Also ensure Soldier Pierce here receives her new uniform before the service."

"Understood, Your Majesty." He bows and backs out of the room.

My head pounds harder and the vertigo returns full force.

My execution. Susa's execution. Public. Two days from now.

"Pierce,"—Ulric flashes a grin her way—"it is my great honour to bestow upon you the reward for Miss Rutherford's return. It will be deposited to your account within the week. I also hereby grant your promotion and four weeks off duty, full pay, beginning now. Your loyalty to the crown is invaluable."

"Thank you, Your Majesty. I truly am honoured by your generosity." She gives a pained look in my direction. "But...I can't accept the reward for her capture."

I halt and stare at her.

"And why not?" Ulric's smile fades. His eyes drill into her.

"Because I am not worthy of it. Yes, I brought her here, but it was my partner who deserves the credit for her capture. Jerod Nelson earned that reward for his courage, not me."

"Ah, Nelson. Tell me, what has become of your partner?" He arches a brow. "As I'm sure you're aware, intentional separation during an assignment is punishable by suspension."

"We were...separated accidentally, shortly after capturing the girl. He should arrive back here by tomorrow night. In the meantime, it would please me if you'd grant the full reward to him instead of me. He's earned it."

"How modest of you… All right. It will be done as you wish. Nelson will receive the full financial reward. Though I insist you accept the promotion and the full-pay month vacation."

"Of course. Thank you again, Your Majesty."

"One last thing. A useful pointer to avoid future penalty." He motions at me. "Prisoners must be blindfolded during transport, as to inhibit visuals of the building's layout. That's precisely what enabled the slave who murdered Head Damien and shot my son to escape."

Maven lowers her chin. "I'm sorry, Your Majesty. It won't happen again."

He steeples his fingers together. "Because you are my only soldier to return with one of the escapees, I'll let you slide with a warning. Anyway, if I remember correctly from the day her parents were sentenced, this one's mouth is more of a concern than what she sees around here." He strides closer and towers over me. "Doesn't know when to shut it, even for her own good." He returns his focus to Maven. "Enjoy your time off with your little one." Then he calls to the assistant head again, and the man comes rushing in. "Potters, fetch a guard. Have them escort Miss Rutherford to a private cell."

"No—" Maven blurts. Then her cheeks flush and her eyes widen.

"*No?*" Ulric coarsens.

"I mean…" She clears her throat. "If it's all right with His Majesty, I'd like to escort the prisoner myself. I've brought her this far. I think it's only right to see her through till the end."

Ulric's stony glare remains glued on her. "Very well." He

dips his head, then lifts a hand. "That will be all."

Maven bows rigidly, then retrieves a blindfold from her bag and ties it around my head. She takes my arm and tugs me out of the room.

I follow her blindly around the corner and back into the elevator. My stomach spasms as we descend. Her hand around my upper arm tremors, barely keeping its grip.

"You gave up the money." I turn toward her, though I can't see a thing through the blindfold. "Why?"

She remains silent, then pulls me forward as the elevator lurches to a stop and the doors skim open. The harsh fluorescent lights of the prison penetrate my blindfold, though not enough to distinguish anything but hazy shapes.

Eventually a scanner beeps and we enter a room. The mixed stench of metal, mould, and stale urine greets us.

The smell seems to be the least of Maven's concerns. She walks me through the long, dim-lit room. Then keys rattle and a door unlocks. It scrapes open, and a long minute passes before she leads me inside.

She unlocks the shackles around my wrists, and I rub the raw bruises beneath.

A heavy air sets around her. The chains clank in her hands, then hit the ground.

My head throbs and spins. I outstretch my hands to avoid falling. Maven grasps my arm and lowers me onto a hard mattress, but she doesn't let go once I'm settled. Instead, she pulls my hand in toward her.

"Maven, what—?" I stop as something cool and smooth folds snugly around my wrist.

Then she unties my blindfold.

My breath snags. I trace a finger over the vines and cross symbol engraved in the leather. "How did you…?" My skin thawing the soft material, I close my eyes. She must've re-covered it after Jerod threw it away, snuck it in her bag when neither of us was looking. "Thank you."

She swallows and forces a smile that doesn't quite reach her eyes. She sniffs, clamps her jaw. For once, her impassive expression cracks. It's painful to watch. She presses a hand to her mouth and stifles a sob, then crumbles to the floor before me. "This is not how it was supposed to go," she stammers. "I'm so sorry, Rielle. You were right about every-thing… I am a coward and a hypocrite. I didn't even try."

Her words tear at the foundation of my dream for a good future—or any future, really. The false hope I'd grasped at since the moment I left Ezra behind collapses under the real-ity of the situation. I was never going to make it. I couldn't bear that fact, so I created a stupid fantasy that Ezra would come and we'd all escape with our loved ones. Utter lunacy. The truth sinks in and exposes the major flaws in my plan.

Ezra might very well be dead by now. If Jerod found him, he's bound to be. And even if he's still alive, if he dodged Jerod and is already on his way back here, he'd never get through the building without being spotted. He's unarmed. Alone. He can't rescue me. He can't rescue Susa. Or her children—wherever they're being held. Or even Renan. Of course, he'll try till his dying breath. After all, he promised to do everything he can to rescue him, and never have I met someone as serious about keeping promises. But anything he tries will ultimately end in his own demise.

"I know I can never make it up to you," Maven contin-ues. "I'm not looking for your forgiveness because I know what I've done to you is unforgivable. I…just needed to tell you I'm sorry."

I stare at her for a long time, letting her words slam me

back into reality like fists to my jaw.

This is it. The end. I'll live out my last two days in this filthy cell, then die alongside Susa at the memorial/execution ceremony. I can't do a thing more for Renan.

Except maybe…

Overwhelmed with urgency, I grasp for her hand. "That's not important right now. What *is* important is my brother's somewhere in this place, scared and alone. He needs me. But I can't help him. So I'm begging you, please do one last thing for me." I untie the shoelace around my neck and set the dove in her palm. "Please find a way to get this to him. If nothing else, I ask you at least do this for me. For him."

She stares at it in the dull light, eyes welling. Then carefully curls her fingers around it and locks my gaze. "I'll try. And I will try to help your brother in any way I can. I promise."

"Thank you." I hold her shadowy gaze, unable to cry, unable to feel anything. Knowing I should feel relieved Renan will finally receive his dove. But only feeling empty knowing I won't be the one to give it to him. Knowing that I'll never see him again.

Knowing I'll never weave my fingers through his wavy hair. Never see another smile light up his eyes in the way that so clearly captures Mom's essence within him. Never light another candle at his bedside to chase away the nightmares.

He will remain here, alone, those nightmares becoming his daily reality. And I will be gone.

Maven wipes her eyes, squeezes my hand once more before rising and backing out of the cell. Renan's dove in hand, she shuts the door and slowly twists the key in the lock.

THE HOURS PASS as I lie sprawled on the clumpy mattress.

Staring up at the ceiling, I try to make out cracks in the concrete by the muted hall light. When night comes and someone kills the lights, I spend the empty hours tracing my fingers along the vines of my leather cuff.

My head stings, and I prod the swollen gash. Dried blood coats the clotting wound and part of my hat. At the time I hadn't noticed, but it seems Maven left a blanket behind for me. I wrap it around myself and bury my nose in its soft material to drown the stench of urine and rodent droppings.

I think of Susa. The letter I wish I hadn't given her. Was she confused when she read it? Relieved that her son is alive? Grieved that she won't see him again before the execution?

And Ezra. Is he on his way here or still in hiding? Has Jerod tracked him down? Killed him? I should know within the next day whether he's still alive. If he fails to free me by the time of the execution, I will know he's either captured or dead.

I wait out the endless solitude, all hope draining from my heart, my head. I sleep most of the first night and second day away as the exhaustion from the past month catches up with me.

My stomach cramps, groans for nourishment, but even the tray of beans and rice brought to me by a guard in the early morning does nothing to fill the void. I have nothing to live for. I've failed in every way I most needed to succeed. Everyone I love is gone. I will never see them again.

The pounding from the trauma to my head slowly recedes over the next day. But nothing can convince the subtle tick of my inner clock to quit beating. It slowly conquers more and more space in my mind until it's captured my entire focus, reminding me how little time I have left.

The emptiness overtakes my body, as numb as my leg

once was. I glare at the rusty bars in the door's high window. A sudden surge of anger overpowers me. A hunger for justice. A harsh hatred for my current state of helplessness.

The wrath broils, and I shout within myself, *God, you told me everything would be okay! Look around! None of this is okay. Why would you lie to me?*

I envision Mom sitting beside me on this mattress. Feel her warmth as she wraps an arm around me and draws me close. As she lays my head on her lap and strokes my hair. Gently kisses my wet cheek.

And then I open my eyes, her warmth gone.

I rise, back against the wall, draw my legs up, and hug my knees.

God, I'm tired. And angry. And I know you don't care. Why should you? It's not like I've done anything right in my life. I know I deserve this ending. But…why did Mom?

I hate the question. I hate how it steals my time and consumes my mind without ever receiving a straight answer. But I have to know.

"Why wouldn't you save her? I don't understand." I lower my forehead against my knees. And wait.

The isolation berates me. The darkness caresses me. The coldness seeps into my brittle bones. Never have I felt so alone as in this very moment, as God decides to ignore my cry for comfort.

Then my mouth runs dry and a bold awareness settles in my mind. Every thought, every feeling scatters. Only one remains. A voice, yet not an audible one—more of a sudden burst of clarity—asserts itself within my chest, saying, "Daughter, I have not called you to understand my ways; I have called you to know my heart."

The words paralyze me. They become so prominent that

I don't think I could forget them if I tried. They encase me with consolation, revive my vacant soul. As at Mom's graveside, a living warmth consumes me.

I feel Him. I do. He's here. He is with me.

Always was.

I am not alone. I will be okay.

I lean my head against the wall and bask in him. Even in this isolated pit of darkness, his loving presence and radiant light immerse me.

This is it. This is what I was always seeking. Even if I didn't know it.

AFTER ANOTHER NIGHT of sleep and another brunch of beans and rice, the soldiers come for me. One man and one woman. I check the woman's hair beneath her helmet, but it is dark, curly, and chopped off at chin length.

Of course it's not Maven. Why would I expect her to escort me? After all, she got what she wanted—a month off to spend with her daughter. That's how much my life was worth to her. And even though she refused the money for my capture and gave me back my leather cuff, those must've just been ways for her to clear her own conscience. She told Ulric that since she brought me back, it was only right to see me through till the end. I guess she didn't mean till the *very* end.

The soldiers cuff my wrists, cover my head with a dark mesh bag, and escort me through the hallways. But stop sooner than expected. We haven't even entered the underground garage yet, when the woman clears her throat and says, "I'll handle this. You go get the truck started."

The man clomps away with a soft grunt.

A door buzzes open and she drags me inside. "All right. There's soap, shampoo, a towel, and clean clothes on the bench. You are required to wear the clothes provided and leave yours behind, but you can wear your own boots, hat, and coat to the execution." She unlocks my cuffs and uncovers my head. "You've got ten minutes." She then backs out of the room, closes the door, and slides the small panel window shut from the outside.

The large tile-floored shower room echoes my footsteps. Three shower nozzles stretch out from each of the four walls, no curtains or stalls to divide them. The floors gradually slope down into the centre, where a grated drain accumulates rust.

I still sense the soldier's presence beyond the door, but at least it's *her* keeping watch and not the man. And thankfully there's no one else to share the room with.

I collect the towel and soap bottles from a steel bench and select the shower spout farthest from the door's view. It spews warm water with a twist of the knob, luring me in. I drape the towel on a peg in the wall close by, in case of any sudden intrusions.

But the water. So fresh, so warm, so enticing. I've not had a real shower since escaping Kinborough. So although I'll be escorted to my execution in less than ten minutes, I lather the soap over my body, taking advantage of such luxury one last time. It stings the cuts around my wrists, but the pain is worth suffering for this refreshing pleasure. I rub my face under the steaming stream as all the dirt, blood, sweat, and tears from the past three weeks wash away. Finally, my skin can breathe.

I wait for the water to soak through my filthy, matted curls, then massage a handful of shampoo through my scalp.

Tenderly over the bump on my head, the stuff rinses all the blood from my hair. I scrape away as much dirt from under my fractured fingernails as I can manage.

When changing into the fresh garments set out for me, all plain black, I idle a minute, studying my leg. The bruising and swelling, gone. The bone aligned, sensation returned, healed perfectly, all but for the rigid scars along either side of my shin. Even they've faded faster than expected.

Marvelling at it, I wonder why the healing happened in the first place. Why heal me when I'd ultimately wind up executed? What's the point? Wouldn't it have been easier, better, if God had just let me die out there? Why help someone who is destined to be undone?

A single word resonates within me. *Daughter.*

Immediately I recognize its significance. I am nothing. No one. The lowest of the low. And yet he still claims me as his daughter. If he says I am called to know his heart, that must mean he already fully knows mine. He knows all my sins and mistakes. And still he calls me *Daughter.*

It's a relation unlike mine to my earthly father. It's without fault, without accusation. Perfect.

The divine, healing heat cloaks me with a claim. *Mine,* it says.

I am his. He wants me, claims me, calls me as his own. Loves me.

He is my Father. I am his daughter.

And Mom is too, I realize.

How did I not see it before? He is her Father. And if he loved her how he loves me, that is enough. She is with him now.

He didn't forsake her. He saved her.

And if he has called Mom and me as daughters, then he

has called Renan as a son.

God, I know you love my brother. I know life as a slave is not what you want for him. I can't do a thing more for him. I'm done. I failed to save him. But if you love Renan like you love me, I know you are with him. I put his life in your hands. I can't trust myself or Ezra or anyone to save him. Only you. So please, God…take care of him when I'm gone.

He's yours now.

THE BRISK WIND assaults me when they open the trunk doors and tow me out. It freezes my still-wet hair, and I shiver from the cold even while wearing my own hat and coat.

They uncover my head for a second to tie a strip of fabric around my mouth, and I spy a massive stadium up ahead. I've never been here or even seen this place before, but I'd wager there's enough room inside to fit every citizen of Kinborough. And by the crowd's muffled commotion, I'd say every citizen *is* here. To pay their respects to the king's fallen men. To watch me die.

The soldiers secure the mesh bag back over my head, and all is dark. The walk from the parking lot to the stadium doors takes several minutes.

The crowd's chatter tapers to silent anticipation before we enter. Then a rich, crisp voice travels through speakers around the room. Deafening in volume, threatening in tone—at least to me. My mouth dries as the gag strips the moisture from my tongue.

"Again, thank you all for gathering and paying your respects to our fallen guards and soldiers, who sacrificed their lives to ensure Ulcadia remains a haven of hope and security for years to come. Now, before we conclude this service, we have a very important act to perform. A chance to respect the fallen warriors of Ulcadia." Ulric pauses. "Courageous soldiers like the fallen, sent out after the escaped prisoners, have been successful in capturing two of the four murderers responsible for these deaths so far. Therefore, it is only right to serve justice where justice is due. And you, my friends, are invited to stay and behold this glorious feat." After waiting several seconds to simply revel in his announcement, he says, "Bring them in."

The soldiers drag me from snow to solid ground. A long walk. Then the roar of chatter surrounds me equally on all sides. They shove me back against a wooden post and chain my arms above my head.

The crowd's clamour grows denser.

Chains clatter to my left, and I take it Susa is here.

Once we are secured to the stakes, Ulric continues, "Miss Rielle Rutherford, on the left, sentenced to death for stabbing a soldier and leaving him to die. The murder weapon was found on her upon detainment. And Miss Susa Henson, on the right, sentenced to death for killing two partnering soldiers with a shotgun. The weapon was retrieved from her living quarters, and the bullets were traced back to a purchase under her name. These women have both been proven guilty of their offences. But…they have something in common other than their murderous crimes. Something interesting, yet not at all surprising."

I can't see a thing through the mesh, but I close my eyes anyway.

"Both Rutherford and Henson have been accustomed to, and/or raised under, the same ideals of the illegal Christian faith. In fact, Miss Rutherford's father, after refusing to renounce his beliefs, escaped prison with his family and is now guilty of murdering multiple guards and soldiers. The only reason he is not here to be executed alongside his daughter is that he fled the region and has not yet been located."

Ulric continues after the crowd settles again, "One lesson to be learned from this… Faith in God creates monstrous murderers. People such as these are the reason for our world's chaos. And they must be eliminated if we ever hope to achieve peace within our nation. It will take time and effort. But it will happen. Starting with them. Now,"—a sharp grit enters his tone— "let's meet the executioner."

The crowd hushes entirely within seconds. An air of shock and confusion sweeps through the room, though with my being blindfolded, I cannot see why.

After another minute of anxiety rapping at my heart, the mesh bag lifts off my head.

And there, standing twenty feet ahead with a pistol in hand…is my brother.

Chapter 28

Our newest and youngest recruit. Turns out, he's gifted with impeccable aim." Ulric stands on a large platform ahead, near the border of the stadium, microphone in hand. A camera films him while he speaks. Mechanized cameras also focus on Susa, Renan, and me. A massive four-sided screen hovers high above our heads for the audience to watch.

Renan eyes me with bleak exhaustion, then cowers and glances at the gun in his small hands. What have they done to him? His face, thinned of its childlike roundness. His hair, flat and lifeless. His posture, shrunken and timid. How have they managed to break him so badly in such little time? How did Ezra ever survive eight years living like this? It's already sucked the life from Renan in two short weeks.

Ten feet to my left, Susa is gagged as well, arms chained above her head. She remains still, staring blankly ahead.

The stadium has to be at least triple the size of the Phalanx Centre. Where the dirt ground stops, the safety walls begin. Rows of bleachers climb beyond, packed with citizens.

Of course, there cannot be a live replay four times over of our deaths, such as with the biannual Gathering speeches. So the king selected a place big enough to seat the entire population. Every citizen of Kinborough. Every guard and soldier.

My knees weaken, and the cuffs grind into my wrists.

I crane my neck behind me to glimpse a line of closed caskets, each scattered with flowers and framed photographs. One of those holds the body of the soldier I killed.

I shudder as a breeze creeps through my frozen hair.

"Young warrior, you have your pick." Ulric motions a hand toward me, then Susa. "Who will you choose first?"

Renan looks between us and back at the king standing on his platform. He surveys the audience, then turns to Susa, planting his feet and squaring his shoulders.

"Very well." Ulric beams. "This boy is proof that even the youngest, smallest of our generation can conquer the oldest, most-deceitful offenders. First Henson, then Rutherford."

As he continues, an uproar overpowers his voice. Most of the crowd applauds Ulric, yet others shake their fists at him and holler jumbled insults. Bits and pieces reach my ear clear enough, like "sentence a minor to death?" and "serve her time in prison!" But the rest assault me like white noise, a tide of violent waves thrashing into a rocky coast.

Renan scours the audience. He looks to the exits on either side of the stadium, then eyes the guards positioned near them and stays put. He can't escape and he knows it.

"Settle down." Ulric raises a hand to silence the crowd. Then he frowns to conceal his look of alarm. "I now see this event to have brought up some controversy among my people. And since I am a reasonable man...I have chosen to reassess the situation. I understand some might think it unfair of me to sentence an underage citizen to death for her crimes. Because I am most dedicated to keeping the peace between my people, I will propose an alternative."

He pauses, then raises a palm level with his shoulder. "I pledge to postpone the execution of Rielle Rutherford until her eighteenth year. She will serve her time in prison until then. However, this applies only if my young recruit follows through with the execution of Susa Henson. If he fails to do so, Rutherford will be executed alongside Henson today."

The fabric around my mouth slices at my cheeks and presses into my tongue.

The people murmur among themselves, and when no new disputes arise, Ulric smiles, satisfied, and takes a watchful seat on his royal throne set behind him.

Renan lowers his head as the people analyze him. If only they knew he's my brother. He locks his jaw, then lifts his gun with both hands toward Susa.

I struggle against the gag covering my mouth. His hollow eyes lock on mine. I shake my head, all hope draining from me just as the feeling drains from my arms.

Don't shoot, Ren. You can't save me.

His shoulders droop, and he looks to where his gun is aimed. Then takes his finger off the trigger. He glances down and unzips the top of his red vest. Reaching inside, he pulls out something hanging from his neck. *The dove.*

I slacken and drag in a breath.

Maven did it. She got the carving to him.

His nimble fingers fasten around the wood. He looks to me, tears of guilt and grief clouding his eyes. Fear. Pain. And everything in between. He exhales, and for a second, a chilling look of defiance enters his gaze, imitating Mom in the same way as when she refused to renounce her beliefs in the execution room. And it scares me. Because that was just hours before we lost her...

He loosens his stance. Then drops the gun to the dirt beside him and slumps to his knees.

But for a baby's cry, not a sound emerges from the surrounding crowd.

I smile through tears. He chose Susa. He could've spared my life by killing her. After all, she's a stranger to him. But he found the strength to choose peace. To choose life.

I was wrong. They didn't break him. Couldn't, even if they tried.

Shivers prick my palms like wooden shards as I watch the king rise. Jaw braced and eyes pinched, he stands stiff for a long moment. Then nods to the soldier closest to Renan.

Crouched in the dirt, Renan hangs his head. The soldier pulls him to his feet and escorts him through the stadium's side exit. Renan follows along, reluctant but unresisting. He peers back at me over his shoulder, sorrow gripping him in a way it should never be able to.

The tenseness in Ulric's body reveals his wrath. My brother will pay for his public defiance. No one humiliates the king in front of the whole nation and gets away with it. Not even a child.

I thrust my feet into the ground and strain against the chains to see him depart through the open doors. But once the audience returns their focus to Ulric, a large man scoops Renan up. I stretch as far as the chains allow, fear coursing through me. Until I realize the man is not hurting Renan. He's hugging him. It is the tender, tearful embrace of a long-awaited reunion.

Dad. He sinks to the ground, holding his son, weeping over him as Renan clings to him.

I knit my brows in awe, unable to convince myself what I'm seeing is real. But all my confusion fades when I glimpse a flicker of orange beneath the soldier's helmet.

Maven. She lifts her eyepiece, and her anxious gaze fastens onto mine through the doors. But then she nods firmly at me and turns back to my family, guiding them away from the stadium.

Toward their freedom.

A fullness in my chest, I let the chains relax as Maven disappears with them.

He's going to be okay.

Because of Maven. She met my last request to give Renan his dove. And not only that. She exceeded my hope entirely in finding a way to free him *and* reunite him with Dad. How?

Peace washes over me, comforting me. Renan will be safe with Dad. Sure, he and I had a falling out, but Dad truly does love Renan. He will take good care of him. Of that I am certain.

However you did it, God…thank you.

Another soldier fills Maven's place along the wall.

The audience rumbles, every eye glued to Ulric in anticipation. The cameras also zoom in on him.

He fixes his microphone in its stand, then joins his hands behind his back. "It seems I was mistaken. Nerves must've got the best of the boy today." He motions at a soldier who joins him on stage. Not just any soldier—the headsman. "Moving on." He rests a hand on the headsman's shoulder. "My son, Headsman Malachi, will carry out the executions."

Malachi descends the stairs, gun in hand.

Ulric speaks as Malachi approaches the place Renan dropped his gun. "Several weeks back, the night Miss Rutherford and her family escaped the prison, the night Head Damien died at the hands of a rogue slave, my son was shot as well. I presume most are aware of that news by now, but what might come as a shock to you is that…he was dead on arrival to the hospital. His heart had stopped. But the doctors didn't give up. They revived him, and without them, my son wouldn't be here today." A proud smile overthrows any aggravation the king had against my brother.

"After surgery to remove the bullet lodged in his chest, blood transfusions, weeks of bedrest, and physical therapy, my son is alive and healthy. He will now have the honour of executing the very kind of people who nearly cost him his own precious life." Pure love for his son now gleams in Ulric's eyes in a depth I've never seen him expose before. "Good luck, my son."

The cameras focus on Malachi as he rolls his shoulders and readies himself. With natural ease that suggests years of experience, he lifts the gun to his first target. Susa.

She glances over at me with heavy despair. Tears drip from her quaking jaw, and she leans her head back against the post. She takes a breath and closes her eyes, waiting for the ear-piercing clash of death. But it doesn't come.

I watch Malachi's hands shake. He lifts his eyepiece, then takes off his helmet and drops it on the ground. Wiping sweat from his forehead, he blinks hard. Resolve hardens in his eyes. He steadies himself and sets his finger on the trigger. But then he flicks the safety switch and the gun slips from his hands. His face flushes and he drops to his knees, a hand clamped to his chest.

"His heart!" Fear swells in the king's tone and on his face—yet another new expression. "Soldiers, help him! Get him to the hospital!"

The twelve soldiers lining the stadium wall sprint toward Malachi. But the soldier who took Maven's spot reaches him first. He clasps a hand around Malachi's arm and helps him to his feet. Two others throw Malachi's arms over their shoulders to carry him. But Maven's replacement pulls out his gun and presses it to Malachi's head.

The king, descending the stairs to help his son, halts. Panic sears through his eyes. But he keeps himself composed and slowly returns to the stage, grips the microphone stand. Every other soldier draws their own weapon and aims at Malachi's captor. With a wave of the king's hand, the soldiers lower their collective aim. Ulric leans into the microphone and forces a clear tone. "What is the meaning of this, that one of my own soldiers would so publicly threaten the headsman's life?"

The soldier removes one hand but keeps the gun set on Malachi's temple. He unbuckles his helmet and throws it to the ground.

The sight stuns me like a slap to the face.

"The slave!"

The other soldiers raise their guns again.

Ezra! It's really him. He's alive. He made it back… And he's doing possibly the most idiotic thing imaginable— aiming a gun at the king's son while surrounded by armed soldiers.

He tightens his grip on the headsman and drags him around in a circle for all to see. He eyes me as he turns, and I shake my head, fighting to scream at him for his stupidity.

He can't save me. Shouldn't he realize that by now?

But then his gaze drifts to my left and lands on Susa, who falls back against the post. The cuffs draw blood from her wrists as her knees falter. She doesn't seem to notice.

Ezra wipes his face free of emotion, turning back to the king.

Malachi coughs and grimaces, veins bulging in his neck.

Ulric pales. He again waves a hand at the soldiers, and they stand down. Clearing his throat, he leans into the microphone. "How dare you interrupt in such a manner, slave? I demand you release the headsman this instant, or you too will be executed here today beside these convicts."

Ezra's shoulders tense, and he presses the gun harder against Malachi's temple.

"No—stop!" Ulric stretches out a hand. "Just tell me what it is you want."

Ezra eyes Susa again, then grits his teeth. "I will release him only when you release both of the convicts. Rielle…and my mother. You will free them and clear all charges against them both. You let them leave. And I let him live."

"Are you mad? He needs a doctor now!"

"All the more reason for you to hurry your decision." Ezra jabs an elbow into Malachi's back.

Ulric hesitates, but worry plagues him as he watches his son writhe in pain.

"You know I'm not playing games here! I've already shot him once before. I'll do it again."

Ulric's face reddens, but he loosens his fists and nods at his soldiers.

Several of them approach Susa and me. They unfasten Susa's chains first, and when she drops to the ground, Ezra throws Malachi aside. He drops his aim and races toward her as Malachi doubles over in the dirt.

Ulric's mouth twists, and he lifts a hand toward the soldiers releasing me. They stop and leave me with my arms chained above my head. "Now get my son to the hospital for medical attention."

Three soldiers crowd around the headsman and lift him to his feet.

Ulric watches them take him away, looking near ready to jump off the stage and follow. Never have I seen the king so rattled. Ezra knew his one true weakness was his love for his son.

But it seems the king predicted Ezra's weakness as well. His mother. So eager to finally see her again, so foolish, so blind to Ulric's scheme.

Susa holds his face in her hands and studies him. Then she grins through tears. Sobs wrench her body as they embrace, huddled on the ground. Ezra buries his face in Susa's jacket.

My chest sinks, not because he's thrown away his leverage to save me, but for the distress guaranteed to flash on his face and tear at my heart when he comes to realize his mistake.

Still, their loving embrace saturates me with peace. A peace I can live with, and die with, knowing his reunion with Susa to have been a success. Knowing my promise to have been fulfilled. They will leave and live in peace, away from Ulric. They will be free.

"Wait." Ezra turns my way and rises to his feet. "What about her? You said you'd release them both."

"I agreed to no such thing."

Ezra's thinly veiled concern cripples me. "What kind of game are you playing?"

"This is no game, slave. But even if it were, I assure you I am playing quite fair. More so than you." Ulric glares at him. "A life for a life. If you think me a fool, to grant two their freedom in exchange for only one, you are mistaken. Rutherford will die. But at least you have the one you came for. Your mother is free. Now I suggest you take advantage of my thinning patience while you can. Take her, leave the region, and let the execution ceremony continue."

Ezra pales. He looks at me as hard, cold reality sets in his eyes. He frowns and says something under his breath. Then his expression softens. "Take me in her place."

My blood runs cold. *He wouldn't…*

"This is no time for trickery," Ulric says, though the tic of his lip reveals an interest.

"Come on. Head Damien and three of the soldiers in those caskets are dead because of me. If it weren't for the doctors, your son would be too. I helped the prisoners escape. Face it—if not for me, we wouldn't even be gathered here for a memorial in the first place. You want me. You know you do. I've done a lot for you these past eight years. I know too much. You've wanted me dead for a long time. So what do you say?" Ezra's glare flickers with intensity. "Let her go, free from all her past crimes. And I will surrender myself to you."

Ulric glances around, then fastens his eyes on Ezra, a hunger for blood blazing in them. Ezra keeps a steady grip on his gun, prepared to shoot any soldier who tries something.

I hold my gaze on Ezra as the weight of the crowd's stare settles on me.

"You have a deal." Ulric nods.

I kick at the wooden post and shout against the gag, my throat turning raw.

But Ezra drops his gun and kicks it out of reach.

Soldiers march toward me, and soon my wrists fall free from their shackles. Numbness spreads through me, but Ezra catches me as my legs give way. He lifts me to my feet and removes the gag from my mouth.

"How could you do this?" I shove him away. "Take it

back. Get your mother and get out of here. Please, Ezra. Go!"

He catches my fists despite my best effort in shoving at him. "No. It's already done."

"Why? Why would you do this?" My voice breaks. With such weakness in my arms, I give in to his persistence and let him hold me. "Why me?" The words muffle in his soldier suit.

He doesn't answer. Just wraps his arms around me, holding me tighter than ever before. Trembling.

My stomach churns as it all sinks in.

There's no turning back. He's dead. This is goodbye.

I press my face to his chest, and he rests his chin on my head.

The world around us fades as I shut my eyes and the tears soak his suit. Time stills as he holds me. Eventually, he draws back enough for me to look down and see the lamb I carved for him, now tied around my neck instead of his. I clasp it in my shaking hand. He also slips a black bag from his back and drapes the strap over my shoulder.

"It's okay. You're free now, RJ," he says into my hair. An arm secured around me, he presses his lips to my forehead. Their warmth lingers on my skin long after he pulls away.

As I look up, two soldiers drag him back, forcing his arms behind him and cuffing his wrists. "No!" I grasp for him and pound on the soldiers. "I need more time!"

Two more soldiers seize me from behind and slog me to the side wall.

Ezra's eyes widen and he fights against his captors. "We made a deal. Let her go!"

Microphone in hand, Ulric makes his way down from the stage. "It's merely a precaution. We wouldn't want her getting in the way of any bullets meant for you, would we?" Ulric treads toward him. "She will be freed when it is finished. You have my word." He makes a point of gazing around at the audience as if they'd ensure their king remains loyal to his deal. I suppose it's true though. If Ulric does anything other than he promised, his citizens will witness his fraudulence. They'd see their king for who he truly is. And Ulric can't have that.

Ezra calms and surrenders to the soldiers. They force him to his knees before Ulric. He glances at me, tears trailing down his grimy face, over the fading burn wound on his cheek and the pale scar on his chin. Then he looks up at Ulric, stares him straight in the eye.

"My apologies for the delay," Ulric addresses the audience. "But it looks like I get to do the honours of ridding the land of one of its deadliest inhabitants today." His eyes smile through the attempt to hold a front of indifference. He then turns and shoots Ezra in the shoulder.

He lets out an agonizing cry, unable to fight the pain with his arms bound.

I struggle against the soldiers holding me and kick off the back wall, but they lunge forth and reclaim their grip. The last time Ezra was shot, I fled like a coward. This time, all I long for is to run toward him. To console him. Take his place, even. But I can't.

Ezra forces a few deep breaths, then straightens, grimaces, and stares the king straight in the eye again. But this time it's not a spiteful stare. Just a gentle one.

Ulric circles Ezra leisurely. Presses the gun to the side of his head.

And fires again.

Chapter 29

Ulric hurries off after his son as soon as Ezra hits the ground. Drops his microphone at his feet, leaving the remaining soldiers and guards to dismiss the citizens themselves.

The soldiers restraining me release their grip, and I fall to a heap on the ground.

Susa is gone. I don't know where. Don't know whether she left before or after, whether the soldiers dragged her out or she departed voluntarily. But once the soldiers clear the field to usher the crowd out into the streets, it's just me left within it.

Me. And him.

I don't know if the audience applauded his death or observed in silence. I don't think my ears were working. They're still rather muffled. My eyes are working fine. I wish they weren't. At this point, I wish I was blind because I can't seem to tear my gaze from him.

I can't stop myself from approaching him, when I finally find my bearings and stand. Shaky steps. Both legs as numb as the right one used to be. Numb yet painful. I stumble over my feet at the sight of the blood-drenched dirt.

So revolting. So familiar. I crawl the rest of the way, the scene unfolding, becoming clearer. Clearer in a way I know will haunt my dreams. But I can't remove myself. My body takes over and brings me to what it wants. And what it wants is him.

The bullet's impact drove him sideways. I gather my strength and roll him onto his back. Vision blurring, I sweep the hair back from his closed eyes and brush the dirt from his ashen skin. I crouch down, laying my face on his chest. It doesn't feel like him.

A chain of choked sobs reaches my ears. I don't realize they're my own until tears have drenched his suit. Many minutes pass as I lie in weak, worthless expectancy. Waiting to feel his chest rise, his body warm, even a single heartbeat. Anything but this hard, frozen shell.

But this time is different from the last. It's certain. A wind washes through my heart, my soul, layering me with a dense sheet, a consoling blanket. It says he's gone.

I drag in my first full breath since arriving at the stadium. And look up, expecting every citizen to have left by now. But there they are. At least a third of the crowd remains seated sporadically on the bleachers. Men and women. Old and young. All eyes glued on me. How long have they been watching? Ten minutes? An hour?

I clutch the lamb carving around my neck. And recall him sliding a backpack on my shoulder before the soldiers hauled him away.

I wish the people would leave, let me grieve in peace. They probably only stayed to enjoy the sight of my unrestrained sorrow. To revel in it.

I wipe my eyes to see them better. But doing so only adds to my confusion. They seem to be…upset. Sympathizing with my grief. Not one face looks satisfied in the slightest. Some watch me numbly, eyes glazed. Some blink back tears or draw their brows in concern. Others clamp their jaws or flash their eyes in anger. Not anger toward me, it seems, but *for* me. Why?

Why should they care about me? About him? We're criminals. Killers. Still, the remaining audience waits. For what? I don't know. And I don't intend to find out and fulfill their desires. I don't care what they want or why they're here.

The mechanized camera closest to me buzzes, adjusting its lens to focus on me.

I turn away, pressing my face to my drawn knees. I don't want this. "Stop filming me!" I'd scream at the robotic device if my throat weren't so swollen. Maybe I should charge toward it instead, tear it from its stand, shred its wires. See how *it* likes the attention.

I stay put. The soldiers are gone. So are the guards. Which means I can stay here as long as I want, *do* whatever I want. I can mourn and shout and curse Ulric. All I really want to do is sleep…submerge myself in darkness until the artificial lights stop burning my eyes.

My chest tightens with the awareness of thousands of eyes still on me.

I spot the microphone on the ground. A low humming sound travels through the stadium, meaning it's likely still linked to the speakers. I also spy the black bag Ezra left me with, and I can guess what it holds.

I don't owe these people a thing. But I feel the urge to explain. They look eager enough to soak up anything I have to say.

Ulric would hate it. That's a bonus. But on top of that, I think informing them is something I need to do. It was, after all, a big part of our plan—to show the document, the photos. To expose our king. Reveal his secrets to his citizens.

They deserve to know who he really is.

And by the way they watch me, I can tell they're already questioning Ulric's means of ruling on some level. Or else they wouldn't still be here.

I retrieve the black bag and unzip it. The old document and photos are inside, along with my tool satchel. I round his body to where the microphone lies. And pick it up.

A breath loosens my throat and I find my voice. "I…I'm not supposed to be talking to you," I start, appalled by the broken tenor of my tongue. "I think the king ensured my mouth was tied for exactly this reason. He's afraid what might come out of it. Smart man…" I blink away tears and start reading.

By the end of the letter, an air of shock hangs in the stadium.

I hold the page up for the camera to see. "This letter was found in our neighbouring western region of Ardenburg, addressed to their head. The message is clear. Ulric threatened that he banish Christianity throughout his land or be destroyed. But at the bottom of the page,"—I point to the blank line—"there is no signature. Their head didn't agree to change the rule. He didn't return the letter in consent. He stood by his people's freedom of belief. And the result…"

I withdraw the stack of photos. "Our king remains true to his word—I'll give him that." Disgust shreds my throat. "The entire land was demolished, and it remains deserted to this day." I flip through the photos, pausing a good amount of time for the camera's lens to adjust to each one. "Ulric did this. Destroyed thousands of his own people because they wouldn't conform. But that's not the only secret he's hidden."

I turn back to the body in the middle of the field. "This

boy, Ezra, was taken from his mother, Susa Henson, at age ten. He was enslaved by Ulric, forced to torture and execute criminals and Christians for eight years. Ulric threatened to kill his mother when he refused orders, and tortured him for any form of disobedience. All because his mother believed in God."

I wait for the people to quiet down. "That other boy you saw earlier—the executioner, the new recruit… Ulric gave him the chance to spare my life, if only he killed Susa." I clear my tone of its tremor. "But what he didn't mention was…that little boy is my brother. Yet he still refused to shoot. And I couldn't be prouder of his courage. He's only eight, and it seems he has a better sense of morality than our king or any of the ones meant to serve and protect us.

"Three weeks ago, my family was detained, my mother and father sentenced to death for refusing to renounce their beliefs. My brother and I were to become the king's slaves, and we were going to be forced to watch our parents die. But the executioner decided he couldn't continue killing for Ulric. Instead of shooting my parents, he shot Head Damien and Headsman Malachi, who were there to oversee the executions. That executioner who showed us mercy and helped my family escape was, in fact, Ezra Henson, who to-day…sacrificed himself for me."

I bite my quivering lip. "Though we were able to escape the prison, we were followed, and my mother was shot and killed soon after. We fled to a region we'd only heard of before, hoping for a new life. A safe life. But we were met with that desolate land, destroyed by Ulric years earlier. While there, my brother was captured by soldiers, returned to the king, and enslaved as an executioner."

The weight on my chest gives way to weariness. But I

continue. "The king is right about my crimes, and Ezra's. We both killed soldiers. As much as the guilt and memories plague me, I won't try to deny that fact or justify my actions."

The people listen intently. As I speak, a cluster of guards gathers in the doorways. They don't try to stop me. They seem somewhat interested in what I have to say. So I keep talking.

"Ezra…was my friend. I met him in the forest of Ardenburg. He saved my life when he didn't owe me a thing. He was the most selfless, loyal person I've ever known. His memories brought him so much pain. The years of torture and lives taken by his own hand burdened him more than I can ever understand."

I swallow hard. "I almost lost him out there to a gunshot. He really shouldn't have survived that day. But he did. He told me he was saved by God. I wouldn't believe him. But I also couldn't explain his miraculous healing. He changed completely overnight. Not only was he healed, but it was like the guilt and shame weighing him down for years just…floated away. I still don't understand it, but since I took the risk to ask God for help, he hasn't let me down." Closing my eyes, I sigh, unable to hold back the tears any longer. "I guess what I'm trying to say is…no one should have the power to choose which people will live and which won't based on their beliefs."

The camera suddenly powers off and the lens lowers toward the floor.

The air deserts my lungs.

At my last words, the guards charge toward me from both entrances, fear and anger flashing in their faces.

What have I done? Ezra's sacrifice only erased my past

crimes, not my future ones. Definitely not this—telling my experience with God to the entire nation.

I drop the microphone, and a loud squeal rings through the speakers.

I am trapped. They will arrest me and take me to Ulric to be executed. Ezra's sacrifice will be for nothing—

No. Not nothing. What I just did, just said… He would be overjoyed. To know I've not only accepted Jesus into my life but risked everything to share my story—our story. It's all worth it.

The guards encircle me. But before they lay a hand on me, about a thousand people from the remaining crowd bustle into the centre stadium toward me.

I slacken and will myself to accept the crowd's imminent attack.

But to my shock, they surround the guards and attack *them.* They lunge at them and force them down while other men and women surround me, forming a human barrier. Hundreds of them gather, protecting me and holding me steady.

More guards and soldiers arrive, some with weapons. Chaos ensues. Shouts and gunfire. Several citizens fall to the ground. But one by one, they bring down all of Ulric's men.

They separate around me and create a narrow clearing between them, from me all the way to the back exit. "Go, go!" I grab my tool satchel as they hurry me along through the channel. Meanwhile, new soldiers tackle the citizens on the outside. The people push me gently yet urgently through the stadium. Out the doors.

Once outside, I look back as citizens flood the clearing. More shots ring, and I flinch.

People are dying in there. For me. I didn't mean to start

this. I should be the one getting shot at. Not them. What have I done?

And Ezra. What will they do to his body? It's in there, probably getting trampled in the mess.

But it's not him. The deluge of fear and loneliness crashes through me as I realize the one person I could count on to protect me is gone. He gave his life to protect me, but I couldn't feel more exposed at the moment.

I inch backward, clutching my satchel, unable to take my eyes off the cluster of citizens fighting my fight. I try to breathe, but the air comes in sharp bursts until I grow faint. I back up into something—someone—and jump, expecting a cold hand to clamp around my arm and tow me off to prison.

"Whoa, easy." The voice is gruff but soothingly familiar.

I turn to face the man. "Mr. Elscott?" I blink hard and stare at him. "You're—"

"Alive." His leathery face wrinkles as he gives a sad smile and draws me in for a hug.

I cling to him and bury my face in his shoulder. His calmness radiates through me. I didn't realize how much I've missed him until now. The tension releases me, and I tremble in his arms. I cry as he rubs my back and holds me upright. Embarrassment wrenches me, but I can't control myself. It doesn't matter anyhow. Surely he saw everything in there. "I don't...I don't understand. You helped us. I thought they'd kill you."

"I know." When I draw back, he has tears in his tired eyes. "But there's no time to explain right now." He wraps an arm around me and leads me to the side of the building.

I stop. "Is that...?" My heart fills at the sight of the golden-coated mare.

He smiles. "She and Bandit found their way back to the farm the second week. I feared the worst. I'm just glad you're all right."

I rush to her and lay my head against her mane. "Sinta. You made it."

She nickers.

"Your dad and brother left on Bandit after Renan was escorted from the stadium. And that soldier friend of yours— she took Susa to save some kids from prison." He hands me a folded map. "Once Susa's got her kids, she's leaving. East. To another region called Hagenborough. The soldier's heading there too after she picks up her daughter—said the king will eventually find out she helped your brother escape, so she can't risk staying here anymore."

"What about you?"

He hesitates. "I've got some stuff to take care of. Eventually, I might end up there. But for now, my place is here."

I swallow. "Thank you for helping them. And me. If it weren't for you…"

"I know." He pulls me in for another hug. "I'm sorry for how it all happened. Your mom…and that boy in the stadium."

I close my eyes as my chest constricts. Another bout of gunshots rings within the stadium.

"You better get going." He hurries me onto the saddle.

"Goodbye, Mr. Elscott," I manage to squeak out.

His lips thin and his eyes glint. "Goodbye, dear."

Chapter 30

I am free.

I could run. I could ride to that distant land where my friends and family are headed. There, I could start over. And I will. Eventually.

Renan is safe with Dad. Surely Susa is heartbroken over Ezra, but at least she has her children back. And Maven... She might have to leave her life behind for helping Ren, but she still has her daughter.

I am free, I assure myself, *just like I always longed to be.*

But Ezra. And Mom... If their lives are the cost of my freedom, I take it back. I always longed for freedom. But I didn't know there'd be such a grave price to pay for it.

True freedom is what Ezra found when he nearly died in that castle courtyard. That was free, wasn't it? He said Jesus saved him, freed him, even though he deserved nothing but death. He said Jesus paid the price of life so we don't have to. So we could live in freedom forever. All we have to do is accept it. But if Jesus paid the price of life, why did Mom and Ezra have to?

If I'm free, why do I feel more trapped, more confined within my own mind than I ever did in that awful prison cell? The chains of guilt tighten around my wrists, my ankles, my neck.

Guilt that they are gone. And I am not.

Am I free?

I pull the reins and scan the area. I rode so far, so fast, I forgot to select a destination.

But the street is familiar. It is my street. *Was.* Where every shabby little house is identical in structure to the next. Except for one…

I try to avert my eyes to spare the pain. But it's so blatant, so broken.

My house. Scorched inside and out. The windows smashed. Its contents dumped on the front lawn, burnt to a crisp. All that remains partially intact is the structure, and even it threatens to collapse in the breeze.

It never was a beautiful home. But it was a good one.

I dismount before the heap of ashes on the lawn that was our furniture, our clothing, our belongings. Shattered glass glints within the rubble. I spot cabinet doorknobs here and there, shreds of burnt fabric and springs from our worn sofa.

I could walk straight through the side wall, but that seems too informal. I enter under the cracked beam of the front doorway. Ash clouds the air with every step.

It's gone. Everything. Unrecognizable. The memories distort, and I can't recall how it used to look. Was that left room the kitchen or my bedroom? Where did the front hall stop and the sitting room begin? There's no cinnamon scent wafting from the kitchen, no vase of blue flowers on the windowsill.

I've never felt so out of place in my own home. Probably because it's no longer mine. I've been homeless for weeks. I should be familiar with the feeling of belonging nowhere. But it never fully hit me until now.

I pass through a wall, to the back right of the house.

Mom and Dad's bedroom, I think. The structure groans, and bits of rubble from the roof cover me.

I jerk up my sleeve to expose my leather cuff.

Why'd he have to do it? It wasn't supposed to go this way. I rip the cuff from my wrist and chuck it across the floor. My eyes burn, and I sink to my knees. "You should've just let me die!"

Wooden splinters and glass shards crush into my shins.

I don't move.

God, why'd you let him save me? I am nothing compared to him. I have nothing to give.

My chest swells with sorrow, and I look across the floor. Something white sticks out of the leather cuff—inside it, between the layers. Paper?

I crawl to it, inspect it. The paper slides out the length of the leather, folded multiple times. Ezra must've hidden it inside before giving me the cuff. I vaguely remember falling in and out of sleep the night my leg healed, and at one point I saw him writing something by the firelight.

I unfold the note, and my hands shake at seeing his penned letters.

RJ,

The other day you told me the symbolic meaning behind the dove you carved for your brother. I then asked what you would symbolize yourself as if you could choose, and you said you'd probably be a rabbit or a street cat—something small that fends for itself. I couldn't believe it. I wanted to say something then but didn't know how. So I'll say it now.

You think so little of yourself. You think your past mistakes define you. But you have strengths, gifts, and value in God, who created you for a reason. You are priceless to him. To me.

Don't you see, RJ? You are a lioness!

You are a bold leader with great purpose. I've seen in it you since the execution room.

Ulric might have this nation fooled, disguising himself as a gentle lamb, but you see through his deception. You see the snarling wolf behind the mask. He thinks the size of his pack means he can slaughter and oppress anyone different from him and justify it as a noble obligation. But he doesn't know what I know.

I didn't tell you this, but when I nearly died from that bullet and God saved my life, he told me something about you. He said that with him you are going to achieve big things. Things that will shake the nation and cause his people to awaken and rise up.

If I can be even a small part of that, to help you on your way, it will be worth it to me.

You are worth it to me.

Love,

Ezra

I clasp the wooden lamb to my chest and trace the cross carved into the cuff. Then look up to see a corner of leather peeking from beneath the floor's ashes.

I fold up the letter, slip it back inside the cuff, and crawl toward the singed leather.

The piece is bigger than expected. Thicker. Heavier. I dig my fingers under the ash and remove the whole thing.

A book. I dust off its cover to read the inscription, but I already have an idea what the title will be. *Yes.* Mom's Holy Bible I'd hidden beneath the floorboards ages ago.

Its edges and the tip of its spine are singed. But as I open the cover and carefully flip through the thin pages, I find not a single word to have been touched by the flame. This frail old book should've been the easiest thing to burn. Yet it winds up virtually unscathed while the floorboards and beams around it are scorched to ash.

I inspect the pages while flipping through, having never truly attempted to read anything from the book in all my years. Certain words and phrases have been carefully underlined in dark ink, and I picture Mom at the kitchen table, pen in hand, memorizing each sentence as she highlights them. I scan the titles of the chapters as I go—Joshua, Ruth, 1 Kings, and so on. But one name snags my attention. I never knew *his* name was in this book.

I gently turn Ezra's pages, searching for underlines like the other chapters have. But no phrases are underlined until near the end.

"Rise up; this matter is in your hands. We will support you, so take courage and do it."

I soak up the words, repeating them inside until Ezra's voice begins to narrate them. The verse reflects and adds depth to his letter.

Rise up. Take courage. And do it.

But how? How can I achieve big things, or do anything of benefit, while the loneliness and guilt corrode my mind?

I close the book, hugging it to my abdomen as the pressure stresses my inadequacy.

"God, I'm sorry. I can't take it! Forgive me, but I'm too broken to do anything for you. Right now, please just help me... I've been through hell losing Mom. And losing Ezra is going to be just as hard, I already know. But if I'm going to walk through hell again, I'd rather not do it alone. Jesus, I need you. I need you to hold me and keep me on my feet. And when I can't stand, I need you to carry me. Because I feel so weak, so empty. I think it will destroy me if I try this on my own again."

I suck in a ragged breath as my insides constrict. "I'm sorry for killing that soldier. I'm sorry for doubting you and hating you. I don't hate you. I'm sorry for causing so much pain, for all I've done wrong. I'm sorry to let you down now…but I can't do anything. I'm done. Please take it all from me—the guilt, the shame, the fear, the pressure, the loneliness. I don't know what you'll do with it, but I need you to take it. I give up. I have nothing left in me, but I surrender myself anyway. I am yours now… Please take me."

Bible clung to my chest, I sit and wait.

His weighty presence falls over me. My tears hit the ashes, and I breathe him in. Here I am, at the foot of the King, face-to-face with my creator, the one who saved my life and reunited my family…yet all I can think of is how small and dirty and pitiful I am in contrast to him.

Then he settles my heart, and again calls me *Daughter*. He meets me here, right where I am. In all my brokenness. Not where I wish I were or where I'll be in the future. But here, now.

The unseen shackles and invisible chains retract. They shatter and fall away.

Finally, I can breathe. Eyes closed, I surrender to his comfort and remember I'm not alone. The fear is gone, replaced entirely by his love.

Fire fills my lungs. It pours over me and through me. Not a scalding, destructive fire that wreaks havoc through homes and destroys lives. It is a healing fire—a cleansing, refining fire.

It's not filled with condemnation or ridicule or pressure to perform. Just to *be*. Be in this moment with him. The rest can wait. Right now, he wants to heal me. Help me. Comfort me in my time of grief. He doesn't rush me into action or burden me with demands. *It is already done*, he says. In this moment, all he wants is me. All I want is him.

I think I finally understand. Why they did it—risked their lives. This book, the hope within its pages, and the God that created them… This feeling of intimacy with him, my helper, my healer, my Father…

I believe it could be worth dying for.

Through tears, I smile.

I am truly free.

Acknowledgements

It all started with a thought. *Maybe I should write a book.* At the time, I didn't know where that idea came from or why it made itself prominent in my mind. Who was I—a teen girl who didn't even enjoy English class—to think I could do such a thing? Now I know that prodding thought came directly from God because I never could've made it here without him. Looking back at those years, I can see He knew just what he was doing when he planted that hope in my heart. He used it to bring me closer to Him through the hardest time of my life.

So first and foremost, thank you God for Your undying faithfulness. Even when I was at my worst, even when I couldn't see it, You were always with me. Thank you for rescuing me and inspiring me daily. I wouldn't be alive let alone a published author if not for You.

Next, I'd like to say a huge thanks to my amazing parents who stood by me and supported my dreams even when they went against the grain. You helped me realize my gifts, press on when I wanted to give up, and unwind when I needed a break from the madness of writing.

Thanks to my crazy, comical siblings, Ben, Rachel, and Ethan, for taking the weight of the words off my shoulders and making room for fun just when I need it.

I want to thank all my friends and family for bearing my random spells of intense (sometimes incoherent) "writer-talk" and cheering me on through this long journey.

Britney, you've been like a sister since we were kids, and I know our childhood games of make-believe were the foundation of my fascination with creating stories. Thank you for supporting me all these years!

Sarah, you are one of the most fearless people I've ever met, and your friendship means more than I can say. I believe your passion for Jesus can truly change this world because it has already changed mine.

Thanks to my awesome pastors who guide me and help solidify my faith when times are tough. Greg, your Sunday messages motivate me every week, move me when I feel stuck, and help me connect with Jesus on an intimate level. Sheila, you excitedly read the later draft of my manuscript, enduring the expanse of time between receiving each chapter (even the ones ending with cliff hangers). Your eagerness, encouragement, and insight helped in so many ways!

To my incredible editor and proofreader, Christy Distler—your editing was such a blessing! You were able to clearly and concisely bring out the best in my work.

Thanks to my fantastic cover designer, Cherie Chapman. You knew what I wanted to see even when I didn't. Your ideas and creations are truly breathtaking!

I'd also like to thank Dennis Colley for shooting my author photo. You're a creative genius and your snaps are stunning!

About the Author

As a debut novelist, Jessica is passionate about helping people grow closer to their Creator through the lives of her characters. She believes that some of the deepest truths in life are found woven into works of fiction, and she loves to create authentically flawed characters who aren't afraid to ask the big questions about God, his plans, and the purpose behind his actions. Jessica lives in a small town in Ontario, Canada with her family, dog, and two cats.